THE GILDED SHROUD

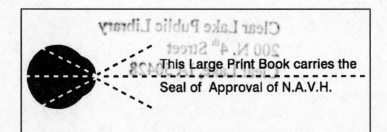

THE GILDED SHROUD

ELIZABETH BAILEY

THORNDIKE PRESS
A part of Gale, Cengage Learning

GALE
CENGAGE Learning®

Detroit • New York • San Francisco • New Haven, Conn • Waterville, Maine • London

GALE
CENGAGE Learning®

Copyright © 2011 by Elizabeth Bailey.
Thorndike Press, a part of Gale, Cengage Learning.

Thorndike Press® Large Print Clean Reads.
The text of this Large Print edition is unabridged.
Other aspects of the book may vary from the original edition.
Set in 16 pt. Plantin.

LIBRARY OF CONGRESS CATALOGING-IN-PUBLICATION DATA

Bailey, Elizabeth.
   The gilded shroud / by Elizabeth Bailey. — Large print ed.
      p. cm. — (Thorndike Press large print clean reads)
   ISBN-13: 978-1-4104-4666-4 (hardcover)
   ISBN-10: 1-4104-4666-2 (hardcover)
      1. Large type books. 2. Nobility—England—Fiction. 3. Family
secrets—Fiction. 4. Murder—Investigation—Fiction. I. Title.
PR6052.A31857G55 2012
823'.914—dc23   2012000816

Published in 2012 by arrangement with The Berkley Publishing Group, a member of Penguin Group (USA), Inc.

Printed in the United States of America
1 2 3 4 5 6 7 16 15 14 13 12

For my father, Eric Bailey,
who would have been delighted.

CHAPTER 1

The chambermaid, creeping into my lady's room to light the fire, noticed nothing amiss. Prey to all the discomforts of a cold in the head, with her hearing muffled, Sukey was unaware of the unusual silence. Nor could any unpleasant odour penetrate beyond the thickness of a stuffed-up nose. Indeed, her concentration was intent upon trying not to sniff too loudly, for fear of disturbing her mistress's rest.

With deft and practised movements, she went about her accustomed task with the minimum of noise, scraping out last night's ashes and setting fresh coals and faggots in their place. When it came to blowing up the embers to encourage a fitful flame, however, the shortness of breath induced by Sukey's condition made her cough involuntarily.

Catching a hand to her throat, the chambermaid paused in her work, her fearful head automatically turning towards the great four-poster behind her, poised for the slightest sign of wakening within.

At this juncture a faint sense came over her of something out of true. Unformed and eerie, the feeling momentarily froze Sukey's spine as she stared at the dark shape of the curtained bed, only half-visible in the grey tint slipping round the edges of the shutters at the windows.

A shiver shook her, and she jerked round towards the fire again, watching the struggling flame without seeing it or remembering for a moment what she must do to make it flare brighter.

A drip at her nose recalled Sukey's attention to the task in hand. Wiping her sleeve across the offending moisture, she resumed her work, tucking flinders into the flame with unconscious haste and blowing now with a will, her ills pushed to one side in a bid to be done as quickly as she might and be gone from my lady's chamber.

A little more than an hour later, her ladyship's personal maid, stepping quietly into the dressing room next door, was less fortunate. Burdened with nothing worse than the morning cup of hot chocolate destined for the delectation of her mistress, Mary Huntshaw yawned the remnants of sleep out of her eyes and paused as they took in the condition of the room. What she had left in meticulous order upon retiring to her bed the night before had become a shambles.

The silken bodice, the overskirt, and its embroidered petticoat had been carefully laid up in the larger press by the lady's maid herself, but her ladyship's under-petticoats lay in an untidy heap on the floor, together with a crumpled shift and her discarded stays, the laces half-ripped from their moorings. The drawer in the dressing commode had been left open, and a dusting of colour overlay the disarranged pots within, indicating a hasty application of paint and powder. The maid's disapproving glance next caught upon an object thrown carelessly into the mess, and a betraying twinkle in the gloom forced from her lips a shocked gasp.

The fan, my lady's precious fan, relic of a bygone age, a prized family heirloom, had been flung down as if it were of no account. It was an exquisite object, its guards encrusted with gemstones, its painted leaf of finest kid decorated with a scattering of tiny diamonds. Now it lay carelessly discarded, half unfurled, its delicate sticks spread across the open pots, exposed to disfiguring smears and breakage.

As she stood there, dismay and consternation gathering in her breast, Huntshaw grew aware of an acrid odour emanating from the bedchamber. Her instant thought was of the chamber pot and the unpleasant duty which must fall to her lot, of emptying its contents and washing it out. An immediate reflection followed: How unlike her ladyship to leave it under the bed rather than stowing it in the bedside cupboard where the smell would be somewhat contained.

Like Sukey before her, Huntshaw fell prey to an inner prescience that slid a ripple of apprehension through her bosom. Moving without realising that she did so, the maid went to the connecting door and seized the knob. For a moment she hesitated, a tingle in her fingers. The little silver tray she held in her other hand trembled slightly and Huntshaw was obliged to tighten her grip for fear of dropping it. Her mouth felt dry and her heartbeat quickened.

Come, she told herself, this was fanciful. She had only to open the door and step into the room to find that all was well.

Gently, she turned the knob and pushed the door slowly open. Shadows, thrown by slivers of light escaping through the shutters, played eerily across the curtains of the big bed. It was a sight to which Huntshaw was well accustomed, but now it seemed portentous. The silence yawned at her as she strained her ears for the muffled sound of the sighing breath that should have signalled my lady's rest. Instead she became conscious only of the faint regular tick of the gold-mounted clock on the mantel.

The smell of ordure was stronger as Huntshaw's feet shifted her closer to the bed. She was hardly aware of her own motion, impelled by the growing sensation of wrongness that thumped at her brain in rhythm with the pounding of her heart.

The tray became leaden and she needed both hands to steady it, but they trembled as she set it down on the bedside table. This close the stench was overpowering, but the maid scarcely noticed, her senses strung like a bow taut for scraping.

Her timorous fingers crept towards the break in the curtains. She grasped an edge and wrenched it back.

Shards of light raced across the dark mound within, one arrowing up to the face, illuminating a bulging eye, fixed and staring.

The screams, delivered at a pitch of terror that jangled nerves all over the household, drove into the dreams of Lord Francis Fanshawe and jerked him awake. For a

11

space of several seconds, he blinked uncomprehendingly into the gloom of his curtained bed, half-fogged in the remnants of sleep. Then, with a speed ingrained through years of soldiering, he flung aside bedclothes and curtains, launched himself out of bed, thrust his feet into a pair of embroidered slippers, and gathered up his dressing gown on his way to the door.

The anguished wails were coming from the other side of the house in relation to where his chamber was situated, but Francis made short work of the lobby and came out into the vestibule in time to witness several flying figures racing downstairs and up, heading for the commotion. By the time he reached the scene, fastening the belt of the gown he had dragged on over his nightshirt as he sped, a veritable crowd was gathered in the hallway between the principal bedchambers. The screams had subsided into a violence of sobbing, joined by a riot of comment and question.

Francis's mind raced, the intense urgency of the clamour lacing query with foreboding. His brother Randal? Or was it outside Emily's room that the knot was gathering? What disaster could have occurred to merit this level of panic?

Arriving at the edge of the hubbub, Francis halted perforce. He adopted the voice of penetrating command.

"What the devil is amiss? Who was it screaming?"

A swift hush fell, even the intensity of sobs reducing a fraction. Several faces turned in his direction, written over variously in shock, horror, and bewilderment.

Then he saw the butler standing just inside the aperture of the bedchamber doorway, his customary urbanity severely shaken. His wide jowls trembled, his eyes looked bleak, his complexion ashen.

"Cattawade?"

The butler passed an agitated hand across his bald pate. He had been caught in his shirt-sleeves and looked discomfited — for being discovered by one of the family incompletely dressed, Francis wondered?

"I hardly know how to express it, my lord," he managed, casting a shaken glance over his shoulder into the room behind. "It was Huntshaw who found —"

He broke off, casting a hesitant glance at the distraught female nestling on Mrs. Thriplow's ample bosom. The housekeeper was still attired in her bedgown with a voluminous dressing gown half-falling from her shoulders and her nightcap awry, revealing a couple of rag curls in her hair.

"Well?" Francis prompted sharply. "What did Huntshaw find?"

A wail, renewed in strength, burst from the lips of the lady's maid, but the house-keeper clasped her more tightly, hushing urgently. The surge of lamentation had the effect of urging the butler into speech.

"It's her ladyship, my lord. She's dead."

The blow hit like a douche of cold water. Francis went momentarily numb. Automatic refutation rose to his lips, but he curbed the words. He did not trouble to enquire who, if any, had verified the fact. Long habit of command took over and he began to push through the bodies thronging the door.

"Make way! Stand aside!"

He was aware peripherally of the scramble to get out of his way, but his intent carried him through the open doorway before his imagination could supply him with what he might find. The stench struck him at once, and he realised he had been partially aware of it earlier. It was an odour he recognised: the stink of death. He'd known it again and again, for the most part dissipated in the open air. Here the enclosed space contained it, forcing it crudely upon his notice. Francis put up a hand to shield his nose.

Someone had opened the shutters and raised the blinds, flooding the chamber with light, but the bed-curtains remained closed on this side. He strode below the four-poster and turned the corner. Here the curtains were wide open, revealing a sight that brought him up short.

His sister-in-law was sprawled on the bed, her blotched face stained dark red, her eyes open and bulging, her tongue protruding. The single glance sent Francis searching down her neck where the blue bruising finger marks told their own tale.

Emily had been strangled.

All his experience of violent battlefield deaths did not prevent nausea from rising up in Francis's stomach. The horror of it gripped him, not least the hideous realisation that the deed must be laid at someone's door. And that perpetrator must inhabit this house.

The thought galvanised him into action. Turning from the horrible contents of the bed, he walked quickly around to the doorway where Cattawade's bulk was now stationed, preventing the intrusion of prying eyes.

Vaguely recognising that the maid's understandable griefs were now muted, Francis rapped out a question, jerking his head towards the closed door opposite.

"Has my brother been awakened?"

An uneasy silence greeted this. The bevy of servants eyed one another, glance flying to glance in a shifty manner that roused a demon of suspicion. Francis fixed upon the butler.

"Well?"

Cattawade coughed, a sign of discomfort which showed equally that the man's shattered poise was returning.

"His lordship is not in the house, my lord."

Which was obvious, had one time to think of it, Francis reflected. A heavy sleeper, doubtless due to a habit of heavy drinking, even Randal could not have remained oblivious, considering the close proximity of his room. The thought gave place to another, one so unpalatable that Francis could hardly bear to put the next question.

"Does anyone know where the marquis has gone?"

Again the shifting feet, heads going down to avoid his gaze. Cattawade went so far as to fetch a sigh. Francis lost patience.

"It is of no use to keep it from me. Where is his lordship?"

The housekeeper cleared her throat, a worried frown increasing the lines across her forehead. Francis caught her gaze over the top of the maid's head still resting on the woman's shoulder.

"Yes, Mrs. Thriplow?"

"It ain't as it means anything, Master Francis, sir," she said in a flurry of words, forgetting in her agitation that she was no longer addressing the stripling she'd known from his childhood. "The case is, sir, that his lordship left the place in the early hours. Abel here was sent for to go to the stables."

The footman so indicated, one of the few servants fully dressed, nodded in fervent corroboration. "Foscot came for me, my lord. His lordship was wishful to have his travelling chariot brought round."

Francis's stomach dropped. Randal had bolted. He fought to keep his voice steady. "At what time was this?"

"I'm not rightly sure, my lord," said the footman, "but it must have been four or thereabouts, for it took me a while to rouse Turville, and it was near five by the time the carriage left and not worth going back to bed."

"I take it both Foscot and Stibbs accompanied him?"

"Yes, my lord. Stibbs was driving, my lord."

A measure of relief dissipated the ugly fear gnawing at Francis's stomach. Would it befit a guilty man to take along his valet and his groom? Francis made a mental note to question Abel further, but for the moment he was beset by more urgent matters. His sister-in-law was murdered. His brother had fled the house — and the country, for all Francis knew. It fell to him to deal with the aftermath.

Thrusting all his misgivings to the back of his mind, he turned to the butler. "Cattawade, I am going to lock this room. None is to enter, do you understand?"

"Yes, my lord."

The man's tone indicated that he had regained his equilibrium. Relieved, Francis bent his mind to priorities.

"Pellew must be sent for. See to it, Cattawade."

At this, the lady's maid flung up her head. "Of what use to send for the doctor? What can he do for my poor mistress now? He cannot bring her back."

A fresh outbreak of sobs ended this outburst, and Francis was obliged to raise his voice to make himself heard over the top of the housekeeper's clucking and the mutterings of the rest of the company.

"The doctor is needed to certify the death, that is all."

"Certify? Certify?" cried Huntshaw, her tone becoming frantic. "When anyone can see my poor lady has been throttled in her own bed!"

"That is enough." The sharp tone had its effect. Francis looked from one to another, taking in the varied degrees of stupefaction and alarm. He would swear that until this moment the full story had not been understood by most. He could wish it had remained unsaid, but there was nothing to be done about it now.

In a kinder tone, he said, "Mrs. Thriplow, take Huntshaw away and look after her, if you please. I will keep Cattawade only a moment, but I rely on the two of you to keep everyone as calm as possible."

The housekeeper, already hustling the weeping lady's maid to the vestibule, paused, turning her head. "You know I'll do my best, Master Francis, but this is a terrible business, and no mistake."

"Which is why we must try to get through it with as little noise as possible. Now go, if you please. I need only Cattawade, Diplock, and Abel here. About your business, the rest of you. The house must still run."

He was gratified to see the knot of persons begin to disperse almost before he had finished speaking.

"And, for the love of heaven," he called after the retreating forms, "keep this affair within these walls, I beg of you all!"

A murmur started up at this, and several heads turned, startled faces glancing back at him. Francis trusted that one or two nods were to be relied upon, though it could only be a matter of time before the news escaped. The imminent threat of an appalling scandal pushed him into further action. There was but one friend he might trust in a predicament such as this.

"Cattawade, send someone at once to fetch Colonel Tretower to this house. Nothing is to be said about this affair. Tell him only that I will be grateful for his immediate aid in a matter of extreme urgency."

He saw the butler's glance flick towards the footman, and swiftly intervened.

"Not Abel. I need him to guard this door, at least until the colonel gets here. Take note of anyone who attempts to enter, Abel."

The footman thrust out his jaw. "No one won't get past me, my lord."

"Excellent. Cattawade, why are you standing there? Get going, man! And don't forget the doctor."

The butler hurried away and Francis turned to the last of the remaining servants.

"Diplock, I must dress directly. Make all ready in my chamber, will you?"

The valet, a man who had seen military

service with Francis and was consequently to be relied upon to recover readily from even such a cataclysm at this, gave a small bow. "As you wish, my lord."

In a blinding flash, a new duty presented itself to Francis's mind. Much stirred, he seized the valet's arm as the fellow began to walk away.

"One moment, Diplock. I have just had a perfectly ghastly thought."

The valet registered concern. "Indeed, my lord?"

"It falls to me, I must suppose, to inform my mother."

And how the Dowager Marchioness of Polbrook would react when she heard that her daughter-in-law had been slaughtered in her bed and her elder son had done his best to ensure suspicion centred upon him was a question Francis could not contemplate with any degree of equanimity.

From Diplock's expression, it was evident he shared his master's dismay. "It is early, my lord, but in the circumstances, perhaps a tot of brandy would not go amiss?"

Francis gave a short, if mirthless, laugh. "You must have read my mind."

The valet permitted himself a slight smile. "I shall attend to it immediately, my lord."

With real gratitude, Francis thanked him.

Then he braced himself and went back into the bedchamber. Distasteful as the task was, it behoved him to take a more thorough examination of the bed and its unhappy occupant.

Breaking her fast in company with her new employer, Mrs. Ottilia Draycott reflected uneasily on the wisdom of her decision to abandon the familiarity of her brother's household to take up a post as companion to a lady of advancing years. One could naturally expect little in the way of entertainment, but she had dared to hope the change of scene might dissipate the tedium of her days now that she no longer had the care of her two enlivening nephews. She had not thought a lady of some sixty summers was likely to replace the amusement supplied by Tom and Ben, but the tone adopted by the Dowager Marchioness of Polbrook and the acerbic nature of her remarks was promising.

"You have realised, I hope, Mrs. Draycott, that the position is merely temporary?"

Ottilia nodded. "It was made quite clear to me, ma'am, by Mr. Jardine, when he offered me the appointment."

"If only Teresa had not so foolishly broken a limb, I need not have set Jardine to find me a replacement," grumbled the dowager, as she had already done several times since Ottilia's late arrival the night before.

To her surprise, she had found the elderly dame still up, though attired in her night-gown, covered with a handsome, embroidered silk dressing robe and what appeared a quantity of shawls draped over her shoulders. Her personal maid in attendance, she had waited, despite the advanced hour, ensconced in a cosy parlour with the fire burning and all the candles alight, fortified by a glass of port and the third volume of a work of fiction by the noted authoress Fanny Burney.

"Why in the world should I not sit up?" the dowager had demanded in response to Ottilia's mild protest. "I might as well be reading here as in my bed."

"I am truly sorry to have kept you from it," Ottilia had said. "We were severely delayed by the state of the roads after so much rain. I would have put up at an inn, but we were so very close to the metropolis by nightfall, I had supposed it would be only a couple of hours to reach you."

"Well, it makes no matter. Now you are here — which you need not have been if that silly creature had been more careful — I may go to bed with a quiet mind. You look sensible enough, if a trifle pasty. But I daresay that may be due to fatigue. Good night."

With which the dowager had departed, leaving Ottilia prey to lurking merriment and reliant upon the lady's maid to direct her to her quarters. Defying expectation, the Dowager Lady Polbrook had appeared at the breakfast table betimes, none the worse for her late night and clearly determined to extract the last ounce of discontent from the situation.

"Teresa is your usual companion?" Ottilia asked.

"Teresa Mellis. *Miss* Teresa Mellis. Never caught a husband, the ninny, though she might have married the curate if she hadn't been so nice. She's a relative of sorts. Been with the family for years and years. My late husband took her in, and when he died, she came with me to the Dower House."

"How did she come to break a limb? Was it her arm?"

"Her leg, more's the pity. It may be weeks before she is able to get about again."

Conscious of her kinship with the unfortunate Miss Mellis, who was clearly condemned to a life of dependence upon the charity of her relatives, Ottilia ventured to turn the dowager's mind on the subject.

"She is the more to be pitied, surely? Is

she laid up in this house? May I perhaps be of service to her?"

The dowager gave a snort. "Of service to Teresa? I hardly think so when you are here for my benefit. But you need not fret. I am sure she is well served by her sister, to whom I had released the wretch for a spell." She looked down her Roman nose at Ottilia. "And there you have Teresa Mellis in a nutshell. She goes, if you please, to care for her widowed sister in her recent bereavement, and she can think of nothing better to do than to fall while alighting from the coach and break her leg. If I'd thought about it, I might have predicted some such contingency. It is perfectly in accord with her nature."

The indignation in her tone severely tried Ottilia's control. Suppressing the bubbling mirth, she again tried to look for the bright side.

"It is most unfortunate, but perhaps one may look upon it as a blessing in disguise?"

A pair of delicate brows was raised at her. "How, pray?"

"Will it not give her widowed sister's thoughts a different direction in being obliged to care for Miss Mellis? There is nothing like engaging in bustling activity for the purpose of dissipating melancholy, or so

I have always found."

The dowager looked struck. "You're more intelligent than you look."

Ottilia burst into laughter. "I thank you, ma'am. A most acceptable encomium."

"Is it? How so?"

"We females strive for beauty, do we not, rather than brains? If I do not look intelligent, ma'am, it is safe to assume I am not wholly devoid of countenance."

Then she rather regretted having spoken, for the dowager's keen black eyes appraised her, running over her features one by one. Ottilia bore the scrutiny without comment, but was chagrined to feel warmth rising in her cheeks. It was a long time since anyone had troubled about her appearance.

"Well, you're no beauty," pronounced her employer at last, "but you've got good bone structure and bone structure is everything. Can't abide the pudding-faced creatures with pug noses and mouths like a bow that pass for beauties these days. Cheekbones are most necessary if a face is to have any character at all. That and eyes. You can discover a great deal from eyes."

Ottilia inclined her head. "Then I am flattered you do not find me deficient in these particulars."

"No, and you're not deficient in brass,

young woman!"

Ottilia was obliged to laugh. "Oh, pardon me, Lady Polbrook, but not 'young.' At close on thirty, I am entitled to a modicum of maturity, surely?"

"Thirty is young to me, Mrs. Draycott. And as for maturity, age has nothing to do with it. Teresa is close on five and fifty, but she had as well be nineteen for all the common sense she displays. Break a leg, indeed."

At this point they suffered an interruption, for which Ottilia could only be thankful. The door to the breakfast parlour opened and a gentleman hastily entered the room unannounced.

"Forgive my bursting in on you at the breakfast table, ma'am, but —" He broke off, his eyes falling on Ottilia. "Ah. You are not alone."

The fact appeared to Ottilia to afford him no little dissatisfaction. In light of the current trend of her conversation with the dowager, she was led to take note of the gentleman's personable appearance. A lean figure looked to advantage in the prevailing mode of well-fitting cloth coat and breeches. He was not precisely handsome, but there was a lively mobility in the strong-featured face, framed by hair of rich brown tied at

the nape. Although he bore a slight resemblance to her employer, his nose was more
aquiline than Roman, his lips more full, but
he had the same delicate brows over deep
dark eyes and the same stubborn tilt at his
chin. Ottilia's gaze swept his cheeks, noting
at once the high cheekbones that caused the
planes to appear lean — taut even, at this
moment, when she judged his whole appearance to be overlaid with anxiety. And
distress?

"It's only my new companion," said the
dowager, with a gesture Ottilia could not
but find dismissive.

The gentleman came fully into the room
and shut the door, his frowning gaze shifting from Ottilia's face to the dowager's.
"Where is Teresa?"

The dowager's brows shot up. "Great
heavens, Francis, can you have forgot that I
gave her leave to visit her sister?"

"But I thought she was to return within a
week or two."

Ottilia inwardly groaned as the dowager
once more launched into a recital of her
perceived wrongs.

"I was obliged to direct Jardine to find me
someone else," finished her ladyship, "and
this is she."

The gentleman struck a hand to his forehead. "Jardine! I should have sent for him at once. Confound it, there is no end to the business!"

Ottilia gazed at him with growing concern. That some misfortune had occurred could not be doubted. She saw that the dowager was looking astonished, having at last taken in the condition of the gentleman, whom she must guess to be her ladyship's son. Impulsively, Ottilia stood up.

"Pardon me, sir, but I think you are come to convey news of some import to her ladyship. Would you prefer me to withdraw?"

Taken aback, Francis looked at the woman properly for the first time since his entry into the room. She was a good deal younger than Teresa, although her style of dress suggested otherwise. She looked the part, dowdy and dull in a plain gown of some dark stuff, relieved only by a lace ruffle at the neck. But her features, framed by a cap that showed a mere glimpse of neatly banded hair, were pleasing, if unremarkable. Except for the eyes, which caught his gaze, a look in them of such clear understanding that Francis was startled.

"You read me aright, ma'am," he said, summoning the ghost of a smile. "But it makes no matter. The news will undoubtedly be all over town by nightfall, so there is little point in keeping it from you. Besides, you may be of use to my mother."

He was interrupted. "What in the world is to do, boy? You look as if all the devils of hell were after you."

Francis gave a dry laugh. "They are, ma'am."

"Out with it, then. Don't keep me in suspense."

He drew a tight breath. Of all the tasks that had held his attention this morning, this was the one he dreaded most. He was aware of having put it off for as long as possible, but his friend Tretower had more or less taken charge, leaving him free to accomplish it. This companion of his soldiering years had sold out to take up his inheritance but, finding civilian life sadly flat, had raised a local platoon of militia, which made him just the man to be brought in under the present eventuality. Tretower had authority, and Francis trusted him absolutely to do all in his power to hold off officialdom until Randal could be found. Although he could not prevent the coroner's being called in, particularly since Doctor Pellew had stated his inability to sign the death certificate without this necessity. In a word, the complications were mounting already, but they were as nothing to the awful necessity of apprising his mother of the circumstances.

Wishing he had fortified himself with another dose of the brandy with which Diplock had thoughtfully provided him, Francis crossed to the table and lifted his mother's hand, holding it between both his own.

"I am more distressed than I can say, Mama, to be the bearer of such dreadful tidings."

To his dismay, the dowager's face blanched, and he read the instant fright in her eyes. His grip tightened.

"Oh, what is it?" Her voice had hoarsened. "Tell me at once. I can bear anything but the horrid thoughts now teeming in my head."

There was nothing for it. Francis brought it out flat.

"Emily is dead."

He heard the sharp intake of breath, saw the quiver cross her face.

"No. Oh, poor children. Poor Randal."

This was the least of it, and Francis felt acutely the horrid necessity to elaborate on his story. His eyes were fixed on his mother, but in the periphery of his vision he saw the new companion rise and shift around to stand close beside the dowager's chair. One slim hand went down to his mother's shoulder. Francis glanced up.

"Pray prepare yourself, for I am afraid the rest may utterly discompose her."

The woman nodded gravely, her gaze moving from his to the dowager again. His mother's black eyes bored into his.

"The rest?"

He drew breath again, steeling himself. "There is no easy way to say this, so I will not attempt to varnish the dreadful truth. Emily was murdered, Mama. Strangled to death. And Randal —"

Here he was obliged to pause, a restriction in his throat making it hard to breathe, let alone speak.

"What about Randal?" A harsh whisper. "Tell me, Fanfan, quickly."

Francis cleared his throat, keeping his tone as even as he could. "Randal left the house in the early hours of this morning. He called for his travelling chariot. No one knows where he has gone."

For the space of several seconds, the black eyes stared fixedly into his, their expression unreadable. Then his mother withdrew her hand from his protective ones, set her fingers on the tablecloth, and looked blindly at the coffee pot.

"I don't believe it." The harshness was still there, but her voice had strengthened. "I don't believe it for one moment."

CHAPTER 2

There was a silence. Francis knew not what to say. He was perfectly aware his mother was referring to the possibility of his brother having murdered his wife. He wished he might share her conviction, but his own faith was severely shaken. The second, more prolonged examination he had made before locking the fatal room and going to his chamber to dress had served to cast doubt in his mind. Emily's wounds were such as to suggest the application of brute force. Someone, and a man without doubt, for a woman's fingers could not have inflicted such damage, had gripped her around the neck and held the grip until the life was forced out of her. There had been intent behind the act, that much was certain.

Francis could not be blind to the tension of his brother's marriage. There had been disputes for years, more so lately. He had remarked it particularly since the family's return to Town for the October sessions. And now Randal was gone without a trace. Was one expected to take his departure as merely coincident with the murder of his wife? God knew he did not want to believe his brother capable of such an act! But the facts could not but point in that direction.

Movement behind his mother's chair drew his eyes. The companion took up the coffee pot and shook it. Absently, as if her motions offered some distraction from the painful realities of the day, Francis watched her cross to the bellpull and tug upon it. When she turned, she caught his gaze, and smiled.

"I think we shall all be the better for a fresh pot of coffee." Ottilia held out her hand as she returned toward the table. "We might as well observe the civilities, do you not think? I am Mrs. Draycott, Ottilia Draycott."

The gentleman looked bemused, but he took her hand. "Yes, forgive me. I should have presented myself long since."

"My dear sir, pray don't disturb yourself on my account. You have far too much on your plate to be thinking of inconsequential things. But do let me know how I should address you. I cannot be calling you Francis."

A faint smile briefly lightened the worry in his face. "It would not trouble me if you did." He gave a little bow. "Lord Francis Fanshawe, ma'am, entirely at your service."

"Thank you, my lord, but I am sure you are fully occupied elsewhere, and I shall do very well without any service."

He laughed at that, and Ottilia was pleasantly surprised to see the change in him engendered by even this tiny lift of spirits. His whole countenance lit, and a smile in the dark brown eyes struck a chord in her she had long believed had ceased to exist. The realisation made her look quickly away, and seeing the dowager still sitting in an attitude of silent distress, she recalled her duty with a twinge of conscience.

The door opened to admit the housemaid, and Ottilia put in her request for fresh coffee. When the girl had departed with the pot, she resumed her seat and gestured to Lord Francis to take the one next to his mother on the other side of the table. He did so, and Ottilia saw his attention had returned to the dowager.

"Forgive me, Mama. I had no choice but to tell you."

Lady Polbrook made a faint motion of her head. "You did right."

There was a tremor in her tone and Ottilia

noted her fingers tighten, the knuckles going white. She reached over and laid a hand on the dowager's nearest one.

"The first shock is always numbing," she said gently. "You will find you can think clearly again presently."

A pair of wan black eyes shifted to find Ottilia's. "I can think clearly now, and I don't like anything I am thinking."

"I don't blame you," Ottilia agreed. She glanced across at Lord Francis. "Painful though it may be, I daresay it may help to tell your mother everything you know. One's imagination is apt to supply far worse than the truth, don't you find?"

From his expression, the suggestion appeared to horrify Lord Francis. "I should think the bare facts are quite sufficient at this juncture."

The tone was decidedly acid, and Ottilia eyed him with interest. "Dear me, sir, am I to take that for a reproof?"

He flushed darkly, a frown appearing between his brows. "I beg your pardon, but if you are suggesting I should distress my mother further with a description of —"

"Tell me it all."

The dowager's voice had strengthened and her countenance showed determination as she turned to face her son. The look he flashed Ottilia must have crushed her, had she been of a less hardy disposition. She met it with as bland an expression as she could contrive, merely raising her brows in mute question. His jaw tightened, and Ottilia guessed he was keeping his temper with an effort. She ventured a tiny sympathetic smile.

"You are having a trying day, are you not?"

Something very like a snort escaped Lord Francis. "An understatement, ma'am."

"You will feel a great deal better for getting it off your chest."

At that, he gave vent to a muttered oath. "How old do you take me for?"

Ottilia laughed. "Did I sound like a governess? You must pardon me, sir, for I have only lately begun to learn how to address myself to adults. But the principle holds nevertheless. It never does to keep one's feelings bottled up."

At this point, the dowager entered the lists. "I wish to hear no more of this. If we are to talk of age, let me remind you, boy, I have lived far more years than either of you and I can stand a knock or two. Do you suppose me to be made of sugar?"

Lord Francis sighed out a defeated breath. "I am outnumbered. Since you will have it so, I will relate all there is to tell. Lord knows it is little enough!"

"Before you begin, sir," Ottilia cut in, "let me be quite clear, if I may. Have I understood correctly that Emily is — or rather was — the current Marchioness of Polbrook?"

" 'Was,' " he repeated dully. "What a hideous word that is."

"Only in that particular connection. One must strive not to place significance upon such things." His eyes narrowed, as if he did not relish her comment, but he refrained from responding to it. "And Randal, I take it," she pursued, "is the marquis?"

"Yes."

"Thank you," she said, ignoring the clipped tone. "Pray begin your narrative."

"With your permission, ma'am."

The ironic inflexion was not lost on Ottilia. She merely smiled at him in a friendly spirit. He gave a faint laugh and capitulated.

The tale that unfolded was brief and to the point, and Ottilia suspected he was guarding his tongue as to detail, fearing to sully feminine ears with unpalatable facts. If only the male sex would realise how much less squeamish was the distaff side. She yearned to point out that few men bar doctors had the stomach to attend a birthing, than which little could be more bloody and agonising. On the other hand, she must allow for his and the dowager's personal involvement, which naturally exaggerated the loathsome nature of this situation.

"I obliged myself to examine Emily's body further and to take a good look around the bedchamber," Lord Francis concluded, "and then I locked the door and left a footman to guard it."

Ottilia gave voice to her instant thought. "Did you lock the dressing room door?" His frowning glance met hers, and she added quickly, "I must suppose there is a dressing room in such a house?"

"Of course there is," said the dowager. "But why should he lock it?"

"Because there will be a connecting door to the bedchamber and anyone might go in and tamper with the scene."

Lord Francis was staring. "As it happens, I forgot to begin with. I recalled it after I had dressed and went to remedy the omission. But Abel would have seen anyone going in." Puzzlement entered his features. "What made you think of it so swiftly?"

Ottilia could not help laughing. "My dear sir, if you had ever been called upon to incarcerate a pair of enterprising little boys, your mind would jump in much the same vein."

"You have been a governess, then?"

"Oh no. But I have managed my nephews for a number of years. My sister-in-law is sickly and so the care of them fell to me. They have gone away to school now, however."

"Which is presumably why you have taken up this post as my mother's companion?"

Ottilia spread her hands. "I had to do something. What would you? I should have died of boredom else."

The stiffness and preoccupation that had hitherto held Lord Francis relaxed a trifle. "I don't think I have ever heard a less convincing argument for entering upon a life of drudgery."

Warming to him, Ottilia would have answered in kind but that the dowager intervened, in some little heat.

"When the two of you have quite finished, perhaps we may confine the conversation to more pressing matters."

"Pardon me, ma'am," said Ottilia, contrite. "You are perfectly in the right. Lord Francis had reached the point of locking the door."

He shrugged. "There is little more to tell. I waited for Pellew, but he says he cannot sign the death certificate in such a case and must defer to the coroner."

"You've sent for the man?" demanded the dowager.

"My friend Tretower did so, and I have left him in charge while I came here. I believe you are acquainted with him, ma'am."

"George Tretower? Of course I'm acquainted with him. Charming fellow. But what can he do?"

"I am in hopes he may keep the officials at bay while I discover Randal's whereabouts."

Ottilia saw the dowager's hand clench. "He did not do it, on that I will stake my life."

"Unfortunately, ma'am, the matter does not rest upon your testimony."

The curt tone brought about a depressed silence and Ottilia was relieved that the maid chose this moment to reenter the room, equipped with a pot of fresh coffee and clean cups and saucers. She thanked the girl and busied herself with supplying the dowager and his lordship with the much-needed restorative before dealing with her own requirements.

Downing a gulp of the welcome coffee, Francis was moved to wish it might have been laced with brandy. With the worst task

over, he was conscious of a feeling of deflation, like the drop after the tension of battle.
Buoyed by the necessity to set things in motion, he had been carried to this point
without allowing himself to dwell on the
darker implications. They loomed up now
like a thick fog, wreathing him in impen-
etrable difficulties.

"I wonder, Lord Francis, did you find
time to enquire at the stables?"

The question flicked into his abstraction,
and he looked up. "The stables?"

"Is it perhaps possible," said the new
companion, "that your brother let fall some
chance remark which might give you a clue
as to his destination?"

Francis felt instantly culpable. "Lord
above, I never thought of that!"

Her smile was warm. "That does not
surprise me, for you have had a severe jolt,
besides being obliged to take all in hand."

His discomfort did not alleviate. "It's no
excuse."

"Does it matter? You may go round to the
mews presently and question the grooms."

The snap in his mother's tone was an ir-
ritant, but Francis curbed a sharp retort,
reminding himself that she was as deeply
distressed as he.

"I will do so, but I am vexed to think I

may have wasted valuable time. If I knew where Randal had gone, I could have sent a messenger after him."

"Of what use to send a messenger?" argued the dowager. "You will have to go yourself. If Randal did indeed kill Emily — God help us all, if that is so! — he will not return at the behest of a servant."

"If he did," rejoined Francis, "he is unlikely to return at the behest of anyone less than a Bow Street Runner." His mother visibly blanched, and Francis instantly regretted allowing his tongue to run away with him. He put out a hand to hers. "Have no fear. Tretower will take care it does not come to that."

A faint cough from the other side of the table drew his attention. Mrs. Draycott was wearing a look of slight reproach. Torn between indignation and a sneaking feeling of guilt, Francis knew not how to respond, but she spoke before he could open his mouth.

"Should we not bend our minds to discovering who in fact did the deed?"

Francis was taken aback. "We?"

He was startled to observe a twinkle appear in her eyes. "Why yes, my lord. As Lady Polbrook's companion, it is surely my bounden duty to see to her comfort, and as it is very uncomfortable for her to be thus anxious, I must do all in my power to alleviate her distress."

Despite everything, Francis could not but be amused. But he was not deceived. "I begin to believe, Mrs. Draycott, that in fact you have an insatiable curiosity."

She threw up a hand. "Guilty as charged, sir." But as he laughed, a more serious expression crept across her countenance. "Although I would not have you believe I do not appreciate the true horror under which you both labour."

He knew not how to reply to this, but his mother had no such qualms. She set down her cup with a snap.

"She is perfectly correct. We must find out the real culprit. But how we are to set about it, I have no notion."

Somehow it did not much surprise Francis that she turned to her companion as she spoke, as in a tacit expectation that Mrs. Draycott might supply the answer. Indeed, he was much inclined to do likewise, though he could not imagine how in the world the woman had so readily insinuated herself into such a position.

"It is much easier for me to look at the situation objectively," she said, as if she had read his mind, "since I am not intimately connected with the parties involved. A stranger is often better placed to perceive what might be less obvious to those in the family circle, do you not think?"

Francis took up his cup again. "I am fast coming to that conclusion. Pray tell us what you may have perceived."

Mrs. Draycott's clear gaze met his. "Would you object to describing what you saw when you examined your sister-in-law's remains?"

The image of Emily's mutilated body leapt into his mind, and he cast a glance at his mother's set face. She waved an impatient hand.

"Do not withhold yourself for my sake, Francis. I am made of sterner stuff than you suppose."

Suppressing his doubts, he complied, confining his remarks to the bare minimum. "As I told you, Emily had been strangled. And if you would ask me how I know it, I could not mistake. Her face was deeply reddened, her eyes were bulged out, and her tongue was protruding. She had blue stains on her neck, finger marks, not to put too fine a point on it. And there were stains of blood and froth around her nose and mouth."

His mother's lips were tightly compressed, as if to stop the onrush of nausea, and her black eyes snapped dangerously, almost daring Francis to comment. Instead, he looked to the companion and found only a faint frown between her brows. It struck him that her earlier pronunciation was sound. She had no picture of Emily alive with which to compare this sickening portrait. That she was undisturbed seemed to be borne out by the meditative tone when she spoke.

"Did you note what she was wearing?"

Francis looked at the picture in his mind. "A nightgown, I think."

"Was she between the sheets?"

He noted his mother's puzzlement that mirrored his own. He could not prevent a slight disgust at the turn of these questions, but there was no reason not to answer. Again he consulted the image of his remembrance and found it wanting.

"I cannot be sure."

"Well, did it seem to you that she had been asleep prior to the — the event?"

He shrugged, perplexity deepening. "I cannot tell you that, either."

Mrs. Draycott took a sip of her coffee, as if she sought to fortify herself. Then she looked at him again. "The nightgown. Had it been — pardon me — disturbed?"

Francis was struck dumb. He was recalled by his mother's voice.

"Don't sit there with your mouth at half-cock like the namby-pamby nincompoop I know you are not. Answer the question!"

Exasperated, he let fly. "I don't know the answer! I did not think to look for such a thing. Besides, what in the world can it signify?"

Mrs. Draycott's gaze did not waver. "It may mean the difference between your brother's guilt or innocence, if — pardon my candour — your sister-in-law had been dispensing her favours elsewhere."

Shock ripped through him. "You are trying to find out if there was a lover involved?"

"It is possible."

"Not merely possible," stated his mother in a voice of triumph, "but certain. We all know Emily has been dispensing her favours elsewhere."

Sympathy for the dead woman made Francis jib. "If she has, she can scarcely be blamed. My brother's conduct has been far from blameless on that score."

His mother summarily dismissed this caveat. "That is different. He is a man."

"Why?"

Francis glanced curiously at Mrs. Draycott as she chimed in, showing hackle for the first time.

"Pardon me, ma'am, but why? Why should

48

the male side be less faithful to their marriage vows than the distaff? I know there is the precious question of inheritance, but a promise is a promise."

Her vehemence impressed and intrigued Francis. So Mrs. Draycott believed in a certain equality between the sexes. It was a novel view. He began to be interested in the evident complexity of this female's mind. Intelligence she obviously had in abundance, but this was the first intimation she had given of underlying passion.

His mother looked to be inclined to argue the point, but Francis intervened before she could have an opportunity.

"Be that as it may, do I understand you to suppose, Mrs. Draycott, that some other man could have been in the house during the night?"

She was still frowning, and her tone was tart. "I am supposing nothing at this present, sir. I am merely inspecting the possibilities. By the by, did you get an opportunity to look in the dressing room? There may be some little thing to show whether — or no, wait! Did you not say her ladyship's maid found her mistress in this sorry condition? It might be politic to question her. And any other who entered the room before she did."

"I can't think of anyone who might have done that."

"A chambermaid? Someone must have made up the fire."

"Devil take it, how right you are! It never occurred to me."

"And if your brother left in the early hours, there will be servants who were stirring. Someone may have heard or seen something. They may not have thought it significant, perhaps, but —"

"Enough!"

The cry came from his mother. She was holding up a hand. Francis felt his sympathy stirred as Mrs. Draycott, halting mid-sentence, looked suddenly dashed. She sank a little in her seat, setting her hands in her lap.

"Your pardon, ma'am. I have no right to interfere."

"Don't beg my pardon," snapped the dowager. "I am only too happy for you to be interfering, but it's of no use to do so here. We will repair to Hanover Square so that you may see for yourself."

Francis was moved to rise from his seat. "Have you run mad, Mama? You cannot mean to go to the house. I will not allow it."

"Oh, indeed?" His mother stood up.

"Since when do you tell me what to do? I am certainly going. What is more, I will see Emily for myself."

He threw a fulminating glance at the companion. "Now see what you've done!"

To his chagrin, the wretched woman looked utterly composed. "I have known Lady Polbrook but a few short hours, but I am ready to believe her constitution is strong enough to support the experience, my lord."

"Of course it is," his mother corroborated. "Set your mind at rest, Fanfan. Mrs. Draycott will ensure that I will not faint or collapse with shock."

This was so absurd, Francis could not but smile. "Perhaps not, but it will be extremely unpleasant, and so I warn you."

"I am prepared for that."

He turned to Mrs. Draycott, who had also risen. "And you, ma'am? This is hardly what you expected in taking up this post."

She smiled. "Hardly, but I daresay, I may brush through the ordeal — without fainting or collapsing with shock."

Laughing, Francis threw up his hands. "I am outgeneralled and cannot do other than capitulate."

"Excellent," said his mother. "Ring the bell, Francis. I will have Venner fetch a pelisse. You had best put on something warm, Mrs. Draycott. I daresay it is cold out. Francis, did you walk round?"

"I did, but we will call up a chair," he replied, tugging on the bellpull. "Things are bad enough without finding myself obliged to carry you."

"And then," said the dowager, disregarding this, "we must turn our attention to the children. Thank the Lord neither of them is home."

Mrs. Draycott paused in her way to the door. "Are they of an age to be told the truth?"

"I doubt it can be kept from them," Francis said, "but it will be some time before my nephew can be reached."

"Giles is on an extended tour abroad," put in the dowager. "His last letter came to me from Italy. Francis, you will have to fetch Candia from Bath."

He nodded, having already foreseen the necessity. "I had best bring her to you, Mama."

"She is at school there?" asked the companion.

"In her last year," said his mother. "Poor child. Her coming-out will have to be postponed."

"That, Mama, is the least of the troubles

heaping around Candia's head. If we don't look sharp, she may lose her father as well as her mother."

The first thing that struck Ottilia about the Hanover Square mansion was its atmosphere of suspended gloom. The butler who opened the door had a countenance grey and drawn. They entered upon a long marbled hall with landscapes on the walls that led into a wider vestibule affording access to a grand staircase of carved and polished wood. Ottilia became immediately prey to a sense of hushed expectancy, which did not, she was convinced, originate within herself. It was as if the whole house were waiting for the skies to fall down.

Even the dowager, following Lord Francis as he headed for the stairs, seemed part of it, her silence fraught with tension. Ottilia wondered if they had made a mistake to come.

She trailed behind, her darting gaze taking in dark panelled doors, an alabaster bust on a stand, the sumptuous patterned curtains at the landing window, and the row of silent watching portraits lining the walls above the stairs. She got a glimpse of a black skirt swishing swiftly back into the shadows, and her ears caught the sound of a door closing softly below. The place was alive with peeking servants, doubtless thrown into a curious agitation of horror mingled with awed excitement and expectancy. Ottilia at once wondered how useful they might prove. In her experience, servants, party to all that occurred in a household, were a fount of information, often knowing far more than they themselves realised.

The party slowed at the top of the second flight and halted in the carpeted vestibule. Ottilia caught sight of three men up ahead, standing in close conversation in a small lobby. One, red-coated in the attire of an officer of the army, stepped out of the group to greet them.

"Ah, Fan, dear boy. Just in time. Mr. Satterleigh is about to make his examination." His expression changed as his eyes fell upon the dowager. "Lady Polbrook! Good God, ma'am, is this wise?"

"Good day to you, Colonel Tretower," returned her employer with a calm Ottilia could not but respect. "I am come to see for myself, and I do not require any argument to the contrary."

The colonel, whom Ottilia judged to be much of an age with Lord Francis, broke into a grin, considerably lightening both the atmosphere and the suitably grave expression he had worn hitherto.

"I should not dare argue with you, ma'am. I have it from Fan here that you are in the habit of doing precisely what you wish upon every occasion."

A thin little smile hovered on the dowager's mouth. "I am glad he understands me so well."

"If I did not, ma'am, you would not be here now," retorted her son. His glance went to the other two men. "I'm not sure we are opportune, however. I take it this gentleman is the coroner?"

In defiance of protocol, the colonel hastened to perform the necessary introductions, by which Ottilia understood the third gentleman to be the doctor. Then the colonel's questioning gaze fell upon her.

"My mother's companion, Mrs. Draycott," announced Lord Francis, forestalling any attempt she might have made to explain her presence.

Mr. Satterleigh, a spare little man with a businesslike manner, coughed. "Shall we proceed? Or would her ladyship prefer to go in before me?"

The dowager waved a dismissive hand. "You have your duty, sir. I shall follow."

Ottilia observed her closely, noting the tightness at her lip and the rapid blink of her eyes. She moved closer.

"Will you take my arm, ma'am?"

The dowager cast her a sharp glance. "I am perfectly all right." She added in a murmur, "Besides, you have work to do." She raised her voice and held out a hand. "Colonel Tretower, will you oblige me?"

"With the greatest of pleasure, ma'am," he said at once, offering his arm.

Ottilia held back as the party made its way into the room, only now noticing the footman standing away from the chamber door but with his back against a door in the centre. The dressing room? Yes, it must be so, for the third door, opposite the marchioness's chamber, was likely the master's room.

Ottilia turned her attention to the footman. He was a handsome fellow, with a head of burnished hair and a fine physique flattered by his livery. Ottilia smiled at him in a friendly way.

"Ah, the guardian at the gates. A sombre task for you, I'm afraid."

The servant looked at her oddly, as if surprised at her singling him out. He bobbed his head in a bow. "Yes, madam."

"What is your name?"

"Abel, madam."

"No one has tried to enter while you were

56

here, Abel?"

"Only the gentlemen here present, madam."

Ottilia eyed him, running over in her mind such details as she could recall of the story Lord Francis had related.

"Was it you, Abel, who was sent to the stables in the early hours?"

His astonishment was plain, either at her knowledge or at being questioned on the matter. She kept her gaze steady and remained silent, knowing he must answer.

"Well, yes, madam."

Ottilia leaned confidentially towards him. "There is no time now, but would you object very much to talking of the matter a little later? Lady Polbrook has requested that I find out as much as I can on her behalf."

His face cleared. "In that case, madam, I've no objection, of course."

"Thank you."

She smiled at him again, and passed through into the bedchamber. The word, she believed, would pass rapidly from tongue to tongue, opening the way for a barrage of questioning. It might even cause minds to think, going over what they knew in preparation. She resolved to be selective at first, thus ensuring that those she missed would be eager to be included.

An unpleasant aroma pervaded the bed-chamber. Ottilia, moving silently past the closed curtains of the four-poster, saw as she reached its end that the windows were open and the room consequently cold. Undoubtedly the smell must be a good deal reduced from what it had originally been. Had Lord Francis been within hearing, she would have been tempted to chide him for leaving such an obvious mode of access available to any marauder. Although it was less of a danger in the metropolis, she conceded, than it would be in a country house. At least there were no nearby trees to afford an easy climb. But a determined man could readily negotiate a brick wall or a drainpipe, should one happen to be within grasp of a window. Lord Francis, however, was out of reach, standing with the doctor on the other side of the curtained bed, while the rest of the party had disappeared from sight.

Ottilia glanced around the chamber, taking in the opulent paper on the walls, the customary chest at the foot of the bed, the long mirror in one corner, and the chaise longue just ahead of her, positioned to catch the heat from the fire.

There was a discarded garment upon it,

and she moved closer to see what it might be. A sumptuous silken dressing robe lay there, open in a manner to suggest the wearer had slipped it off in situ. In which case, Ottilia reasoned, noting its angle, its occupant had been sitting sideways at the time. Could another person, a man, have been sitting beside her? Could it have been his hands that slipped the garment from her shoulders during a moment preparatory to lovemaking?

A feeling of being under scrutiny came over her, and she looked round to find Lord Francis watching her. Was his frown curious or admonitory? In a bid to explain without drawing the notice of anyone else, she gestured briefly towards the dressing robe. His eye fell upon it and then returned to her, this time with clear question in his face. Ottilia gave a tiny shake of her head and unobtrusively put a finger to her lips. The frown disappeared and he gave an infinitesimal nod.

His attention was at this moment diverted, for the dowager came into view, a handkerchief held to her mouth. Despite her courageous intent, she was leaning heavily on Colonel Tretower's arm and her face was ashen. Under her cloak, Ottilia dived a hand through the slit in her petticoats to find her pocket and brought out a little silver box. She crossed to intercept Lord Francis as he followed his mother to the door.

"Sal volatile," she said quietly, handing him the box.

He nodded, called to the doctor, and the two of them passed out of the room.

Ottilia took a breath and walked purposefully around the bed to confront the sight that had wrought such poignant dismay.

CHAPTER 3

By the time Ottilia came out of the bedchamber, her mind was churning as thoroughly as her stomach. Holding herself well
in hand, she followed hard upon the heels
of the coroner, who had taken notes with a
pencil in a little book he took from his
pocket. She discovered only Lord Francis
awaiting them in the lobby. The footman
had presumably at last been dismissed from
his post at the dressing room door.

"You may wish to call in the undertakers,
my lord," said Mr. Satterleigh. "I have seen
all that is necessary."

"Thank you. My friend Tretower will see
to the matter."

"There will have to be an inquest, of
course."

"So I understand."

An embarrassed cough proceeded from
the coroner's throat, and Lord Francis
raised his brows.

61

"Well?"

"It is not within my province, my lord, but if you will take my advice, you will make all speed to locate your brother the marquis and discover his movements last night."

Ottilia was unsurprised to see quick anger flare in Lord Francis's eyes. "What do you know of my brother's absence?"

Another cough escaped Satterleigh as he reddened. "He is not here, my lord, which is, in the circumstances, a trifle unexpected. When I mentioned this to Colonel Tretower, he told me his lordship's whereabouts are not known at present."

"And from this you deduced what precisely?"

The little man pursed his lips and his tone became clipped. "I deduce nothing, my lord. I merely observe the evidence and make a judgement as to the cause of death. Other matters are, as I say, outside my province." When Lord Francis would have spoken, he held up a hand. "All I am endeavouring to convey to you, my lord, is that there are other parties whose business it will be to discover the perpetrator. I am obliged, you understand, to inform them of what I have found here."

"You mean the justices at Bow Street."

The coroner inclined his head. "I mean

just that, sir."

Lord Francis eyed him with ill-concealed resentment, and Ottilia wished she might intervene. Mr. Satterleigh was but performing his office, and it did not behove him to give even the mild warning he had done. His lordship ought to be grateful.

"I suppose I must thank you," said Lord Francis, echoing her thought as if he had read her mind.

"That will not be necessary, my lord. I will take my leave of you now. Pray convey my respects and commiserations to the Dowager Lady Polbrook."

With which he bowed and departed. Lord Francis watched him hurry away and then turned to address Ottilia in a tone savage with resentment.

"I hope to God you have found something that will dig us out of this mess!"

Ottilia gave him a sympathetic smile. "If not that, at the least there is enough to cast doubt upon the spectre of your brother's guilt."

So eager a look sprang into his face that Ottilia was touched. Until this moment she had not fully recognised the strain under which he was labouring. He was clearly far less assured than he appeared. Impulsively, she put out a hand and grasped his fingers.

"Don't feel so worn, my lord. There is hope, I promise you."

For an instant, his fingers returned the pressure of hers. A sensation not unlike the shriek of ice water slithered between Ottilia's ribs. Then he let go and she unconsciously took her own fingers into the protection of her other hand.

"How you came to take your place with my mother at precisely the right moment is a mystery," he said, speaking rapidly and low, "but believe me, I am glad of it."

Ottilia was aware of a flutter in her bosom, but she did her best to ignore it. "If I can be of service in any way, I will be glad of it, too."

His face broke into a smile, startling and sudden, making the dark eyes glow. "Then we are of one mind." He drew a breath. "Speaking of my mother, let us go in search of her. She will be as eager as I to hear what you have found out."

He led the way to the stairs and Ottilia followed, beset by a swift lowering of spirits. Perhaps too much was expected of her. She had little enough to report, after all. What there was led to mere speculation on her part, and not proof.

The dowager was found in a downstairs parlour, divested of her pelisse and sipping a restorative provided by the hovering butler, with Colonel Tretower and Doctor Pellew in attendance. The colonel looked towards the door as Lord Francis opened it and held it for Ottilia to enter.

"Has Satterleigh gone, then?"

Lord Francis nodded, crossing to where his friend was propping up the mantelpiece. "He says we may call in the undertakers. Would you — ?"

"My dear fellow, it is all in hand," interrupted the colonel. "I set the business in motion while you were attending Lady Polbrook. The men will be here presently."

Lord Francis clapped a hand to his friend's shoulder. "I cannot thank you enough, George."

"Then don't try. Instead, allow our friend Cattawade here to supply you with some of this excellent Madeira. I can thoroughly recommend it."

"I don't doubt it," said Lord Francis, a laugh in his voice. But he looked first to Ottilia. "Can we tempt you, ma'am?"

The suggestion was welcome. She might not have known Emily, Lady Polbrook, but the ordeal had nevertheless been testing.

"Indeed, yes."

After removing her cloak, of which Colonel Tretower relieved her, Ottilia was supplied with a glass and a chair by the fire opposite the dowager, to whom Lord Francis, having dismissed the butler, now turned. But his address was to the doctor who was standing beside her.

"Is my mother recovered?"

"Why not ask me directly?" cut in her ladyship, very much in her usual tone.

Lord Francis's lip tightened, but he bowed with a dutiful air. "I beg your pardon, ma'am. Are you recovered?"

"You can see I am, can't you? But since you ask, I am perfectly well again."

Doctor Pellew's gaze was upon his lordship. "I have recommended that her ladyship should take to her bed with a soothing draught. I will make one up before —"

"I want none of your draughts, I thank you, Pellew. Do you take me for an invalid? And I am not going to bed."

"I have no doubt your ladyship enjoys the best of health," said the doctor primly. "And though you may not feel in need of it at this juncture, it is my duty to warn you that the effects of shock can be delayed for some hours and the draught I am proposing —"

"Will probably send me to sleep just when I need my wits about me. Don't fuss, man. Madeira is all the draught I require."

Doctor Pellew was inclined to argue the

point, and Ottilia began to think of intervening when Lord Francis forestalled her.

"Make up the draught, Pellew, if you will. Let Mrs. Draycott have it, and she may put it to use if the need arises."

The dowager's black eyes turned balefully upon Ottilia. "She had better try!"

Ottilia smiled. "I should not dare, ma'am." A grim laugh escaped the elder lady, and Ottilia added, "Unless you should request it of me."

"Well, I won't," snapped the other. "And I don't need this."

She opened her free hand and Ottilia saw her little silver box reposing there.

"My vinaigrette? Then I shall relieve you of it."

She made to rise, but Colonel Tretower was quicker. Deftly moving in, he took the box and handed it over. Ottilia thanked him with a smile and caught a grudging look from the dowager.

"I must thank you, child. It was of help to me."

An unaccustomed note of underlying distress struck the company to silence, and Ottilia could not think how to break it. To her relief, Lord Francis turned the subject.

"Doctor Pellew, I shall be glad if there is anything you can tell us from your examination that may help to establish when the deed was done."

Alarm sprang into the doctor's features, and he threw a meaningful glance at the dowager, as if to deprecate such discussion in her presence. Lady Polbrook saw it, for she at once took it up.

"You may safely speak before me, Pellew. Do you suppose I should have subjected myself to the horrid sight we have all just witnessed if it were not of vital importance to me? I need not give you the reason, for it must be obvious."

Doctor Pellew bowed slightly. "As your ladyship pleases." He turned back to Lord Francis. "By the time I saw the late Lady Polbrook, a degree of rigor had set in, which must put the time of decease more than four hours earlier."

"What time was it when you arrived here, eight or nine?"

"Past nine," put in Colonel Tretower, "for it must have been near nine by the time I answered your summons and Pellew came after me."

"I can tell you precisely, my lord," said the doctor, removing from an inner recess in his costume a small notebook, which he consulted through a pair of spectacles acquired from the same place.

Ottilia noted, with some amusement, the impatience in both mother and son as they waited, the dowager going so far as to click her tongue.

"It was seventeen minutes past the hour, my lord. I set it down along with my findings to pass to the coroner."

"Around five in the morning, then," said Tretower.

"More than four hours, George."

"Four o'clock?"

"It is impossible to be exact," said the doctor firmly. "One might put it as early as three or a little after, for there are many factors to be taken into consideration. It is an inexact science with a large margin for error."

"Then we may safely say at least that it was no later than five, may we not?" suggested the colonel.

The doctor pursed his lips. "I would say four and thirty at the outside, and I believe that is conservative."

Which, as far as could presently be judged, placed the absent Marquis of Polbrook on the premises at the time. Ottilia, glancing at the dowager, saw dismay in her eyes. Looking to Lord Francis, who was markedly silent, she found him heavily frowning. Which was hardly a surprise when one considered how much blacker was the case against his brother under this supposition.

The doctor, having delivered himself of this unwelcome deduction, then made a move to take his leave. No one attempted to detain him, and with a punctilious bow to the dowager, he departed.

Ottilia found Lord Francis's eyes upon her, their expression serious but eager.

"It appears we are even more in need of that ray of hope you proffered, Mrs. Draycott. Will you tell us what you found, if you please?"

It was not a recital to which Ottilia was looking forward. All eyes were now fixed upon her. She looked towards each in turn. "I shall be perfectly frank, I warn you."

The dowager emitted a derisive noise. "We are already becoming accustomed to your tendency to be outspoken, although it is scarcely the proper obsequious manner to be expected from your calling."

"Thank God for it," came from Lord Francis, moving to bring forward a straight-backed chair and set it near his mother. "It comes as a welcome relief, ma'am. Your poor Teresa is positively cringing in her manner."

Colonel Tretower cocked an amused eye

at Ottilia. "You do not cringe, Mrs. Dray-cott?"

"I am not known for it, I confess."

"You appear to be an odd sort of companion."

Ottilia laughed. "I am a novice."

"She is also intelligent and astute," put in Lord Francis, taking his seat. "We are relying on her ingenuity to extricate us in this extremity."

Tretower looked intrigued. "Indeed? A tall order, ma'am."

"Yes, and I have little expectation of fulfilling it," said Ottilia, a touch of acid in her tone. "But as I told Lord Francis, I think we may at the very least cast doubt on his brother's being responsible for the unfortunate Lady Polbrook's demise."

The dowager's black eyes showed painful anxiety. "After what Pellew said, I am eager for any scrap of hope, however slim. Waste no more time, I pray you. Tell us everything."

Thus adjured, Ottilia took a sip from her glass and marshalled her thoughts. "I think there can be no question but that the marchioness entertained a lover in her chamber last night."

"I knew it!" burst from the dowager.

"How can you tell that?" asked Lord

Francis. "Has it to do with what you were looking at on the daybed in there?"

"In part." Ottilia explained about the position of the dressing robe and the construction that might be placed upon it.

The dowager looked disappointed. "Well, it is possible, I suppose. But hardly convincing."

"In itself, no," Ottilia agreed. "But that is not the full sum of it."

Lord Francis's eyes were fixed on her face in an intent look she found a trifle uncomfortable. "Go on."

Ottilia took another fortifying sip of Madeira. "I took time to look around the dressing room, which was in considerable disorder. Lady Polbrook seems to have divested herself of — pardon me — her undergarments, in something of a hurry. We know she had donned her nightgown and dressing robe. She had also applied paint and powder to her face."

There was a silence while her audience digested these facts. The dowager looked rather disgusted, while Lord Francis was frowning in thought. The colonel was the first to enter a caveat.

"Forgive my plain speaking, but with the condition of Lady Polbrook's features, it is surely impossible to say whether or not she had applied aids to beauty."

The other two looked struck, but Ottilia firmly shook her head. "Oh no, sir, there are quite visible traces."

"Indeed?"

"Enlighten us, pray," cut in Lord Francis.

Ottilia glanced at the dowager. "You found the inspection more difficult than you had supposed, ma'am. Are you sure you want to hear this?"

The dowager waved an impatient hand. "It will be long before I forget. Nothing you say could make it any worse."

"Very well." Ottilia sighed a little. "It is very sad to see it, but if you look closely, you may observe the red colour clinging to her lip over the unnatural blue. It is quite distinctive, and readily compares against the bloodstains near her mouth and nose. Furthermore, where the countenance is of a dark red from her sufferings, nothing else may be remarked. But if you look where the skin is merely blue, or upon the forehead where there is less evidence of congestion, you will note the white pallor that accompanies the use of powder. Indeed, in places you may observe very clearly how the powder was sketchily and hastily applied. Oh, and she had darkened her eyebrows, too."

Lord Francis was looking stunned, and the dowager stared with her mouth at half-cock. Only the colonel, less intimately involved, appeared to take these observations with equanimity. It was he once again who demurred.

"Forgive me if I play devil's advocate."

Ottilia turned to him with interest. "Pray do. It is always helpful to look at matters from another point of view."

"Then allow me to say this: Granted, you have made out a case to suggest Lady Polbrook may have been entertaining a lover. But how can you know this man was not her husband?"

The dowager gave vent to a snort, and Lord Francis threw up his eyes. "You will not have my mother's support in that, my friend. And I am bound to state there is little likelihood of this phantom lover having been Randal himself."

"But would a jury of his peers accept that?"

"Unlikely," said Ottilia flatly. "At least without considerable evidence to support such a claim."

"Which we can't supply without dragging Emily's name through the mud," said Lord Francis with a groan.

"That is past praying for," snapped the

dowager. "Not that it will matter when this scandal breaks."

"I don't think it will be necessary to introduce any sordid details," Ottilia said, cutting firmly into these comments.

"Why not?" asked Tretower with interest.

Ottilia sighed. "This is a crime of passion, sir. There was a fight."

"How can you know that?"

"By the wounds on Lady Polbrook's palms, and on her arms, too. She fought back. She struggled with her attacker."

The dowager was looking quite sick, but she spoke with scarcely a tremor. "Would not anyone do so if someone tried to strangle them?"

"Not if they were asleep when the attack was made. She would have been too dazed, too full of the mists of sleep to make so forceful a rebuttal. It does not take very long to throttle someone. Unconsciousness occurs within a few seconds. Unless the victim is able to struggle, driving the murderer to use more force than is strictly necessary to kill. And you will have seen how severe was the damage. This was a brutal attack. It cannot have been done by one who could choose his moment and perform it at his leisure."

All three were gazing at Ottilia in the

blank fashion that signifies stupor or disbelief. After a moment, a frown entered the colonel's features.

"I beg your pardon, Mrs. Draycott, but how in the world do you come to know these things? I should have thought only a medical man could make such judgements."

Amusement flickered in Ottilia's breast and she had to smile. "Justly spoken, sir. I have learned from my brother, who is indeed a medical man."

Lord Francis's dark eyes widened. "Your brother is a doctor? That explains a great deal."

"Indeed it does." Colonel Tretower spread his hands. "In that case, I am dumb. I can think of nothing at present to offer in refutation."

Lord Francis tossed off his wine and stood up. "Then don't try. I, for one, am ready to accept all you have said, Mrs. Draycott."

"And I," chimed in the dowager.

"But you are both interested parties," objected the colonel. "You are bound to accept it."

"It is not only that," said Lord Francis. "I know, none better, how quarrelsome Randal and Emily had become." He shifted restlessly away and back again as he spoke. "Indeed, I had settled it in my mind that if

76

Randal had done the deed, he had done so in a fit of rage. But what I cannot believe for one moment is that Emily would trouble to prepare herself to welcome a lover if only Randal was expected."

"Well thought of, Fanfan," uttered the dowager, clapping her hands.

Colonel Tretower shook his head. "What if Randal came upon her after this supposed lover had left her?"

"No."

He turned back to Ottilia. "You sound very certain."

"I am. Recollect that Lady Polbrook was discovered in her nightgown. Pardon me, but I did look further. The nightgown had ridden high and there are indicative marks upon her thighs. There is no possibility but that the quarrel erupted during or after she had indulged in — pardon me but there is no point in mincing words — an act of sexual congress."

Three pairs of eyes were focused upon her in varying degrees of revulsion. Ottilia heard the echo of her words in her own head and felt her face go warm. She took refuge in her glass, supping a gulp of wine that burned in her throat. Defiant, she glared at them all.

"I told you I was going to be frank."

A quiver disturbed the severity of Lord Francis's lip and his eyes crinkled at the corners. "Yes, you did. We have only ourselves to blame if we failed to heed your warning."

Then Colonel Tretower was laughing outright. "You must forgive us. It is rare to encounter a female with the courage to speak with such refreshing candour."

Ottilia smiled. "Well, in the normal way of things, I would not. But you will admit the circumstances are decidedly out of the ordinary."

"For my part, I am perfectly satisfied," said the dowager. "You are a woman after my own heart, Mrs. Draycott. I can't bear this fashion for mealymouthed talk. In my day, we called a spade a spade."

"And in the cause of proving Randal an innocent man," said Lord Francis, "I am ready to endure any amount of a like candour." He came to Ottilia's chair and reached down to lift her hand to his lips. "I thank you, Mrs. Draycott. You have relieved my mind of a great weight."

Retrieving her hand, Ottilia fought against an unexpected breathlessness. But she felt compelled to curb his enthusiasm. "It is only supposition and speculation."

"Precisely." Colonel Tretower was frowning again. "Fan, you are too previous. I now think I can attempt to counter Mrs. Draycott's suppositions."

Lord Francis groaned. "Oh, Lord, must you?"

"Better it should come from me than from Bow Street." He looked to the dowager. "Forgive me, ma'am, but there is nothing to be gained by shying away from inescapable questions."

Lady Polbrook flapped a hand. "Go on."

"Very well. Let us grant the marquis was not the lover in the case. Who is to say he did not come upon the act of adultery and there and then take his revenge?"

"Where is your lover then?" Lord Francis threw in swiftly. "The natural act of any man would be to attack the rival, not the erring wife. What, did the man run off and my brother then exact his revenge on Emily? No, no, it won't fadge, George."

"Then let us say the lover had already departed. Polbrook enters the chamber to discover his wife —" He broke off, frowning. "No, that won't fit. How would he know there had been any wrongdoing?"

"Exactly so," said Lord Francis.

Ottilia regarded the colonel's dissatisfied expression without comment. She hoped he would think of another tack, for the more theories presented and exploded, the better pleased she would be. She was by no means convinced by her own arguments. Having no acquaintance with the individuals concerned, she could not be certain that the marchioness would not receive her husband's advances.

"What if," suggested Tretower slowly, "Polbrook had caught the fellow as he was leaving the chamber?"

Lord Francis demolished this without hesitation. "He would have chased after him."

"Yes, I daresay you are right. But he could have returned and quarrelled with his wife."

"Having caught the fellow, or the man having got clean away?"

Colonel Tretower suddenly struck his hands together. "There! I knew there was something that did not fit, but I could not put my finger upon it."

Ottilia felt the stirrings of alarm, for there was a species of triumph in the man's tone. "What is it, sir, that does not fit?"

He turned to survey her, a regretful look in his face. "I am sorry to be obliged to put a spoke in your admirable wheel, Mrs. Draycott, but that is the matter in a nutshell. If there was a lover, how did he get into the house? For the matter of that, how did he get out of it?"

She stared at him, aware of the sudden tension emanating from both the dowager and Lord Francis. "That is a considerable flaw, I agree."

"Fudge," burst from Lord Francis. "There must be any number of ways he could get in and out."

"Not without the participation of one of the servants," Ottilia pointed out. "How many entrances are there besides the front door?"

"Dear Lord, at least three! There is the door to the garden, the scullery, and the area below the front. There may be other entrances, of which we know nothing. This is a mansion, after all."

"Come, Fan, it is a town house," objected the colonel, shifting out into the room to join his friend. "In the country, you may readily assume anyone could get in unobserved, but not here."

"And even if he could do so, he would need to know his way around," said Ottilia. She observed that the dowager's black glance was travelling from one to the other, although she had not so far entered the debate. "What do you say, ma'am?"

The elder dame's gaze settled upon her. "It is not beyond the bounds of possibility that a favoured paramour might be given a key." She shifted in her chair, a sign of discomfort. "The wiles of women are ingenious."

"That is true," Ottilia conceded, "but I submit, much against my will I hasten to add, that a lady of the standing of your daughter-in-law, ma'am, is unlikely to be in the way of locating such a key without assistance."

"Perhaps she had assistance," said Lord Francis. "We have questioned none of the servants so far."

"Agreed. But Colonel Tretower raises an important consideration, and we can readily see how a skilled advocate may work upon such speculation to turn it against the marquis. It cannot end here. If we are to clear your brother of any breath of suspicion, we must find indisputable facts to prove his innocence."

"You have carte blanche, ma'am," said Lord Francis with vehemence. "Question whomsoever you wish. The household is at your disposal."

Ottilia met his gaze. "It is not only for me to do, sir. You must play your part, for there may be people you can better question or places I may not go."

"Not in this house, there are not," stated

the dowager flatly.

"That is all very well, ma'am, but if we are to succeed we must go further afield."

Lord Francis was once again regarding her with one of his intent looks. "Why so? To what purpose?"

Ottilia looked from one to the other of them. "Do you not see? Is it not obvious? There is only one sure way to clear your brother's name. It is all very well trying to prove him innocent, but that isn't enough. We must discover another suspect — in a word, the real murderer."

CHAPTER 4

Taking the short walk round to the mews where the Polbrook stables were situated, Francis took opportunity to probe something of the background of the extraordinary female who had landed on his mother's doorstep in so timely a fashion.

"I take it you are a widow?"

The companion, swathed in a thick travelling cloak against the October chill, nodded beneath her hood.

"I have been so from the year of my marriage. My husband was ordered to the Americas within a few months of our wedding. Jack was killed at the Battle of Monmouth."

Francis was dismayed. "How shattering for you. I lost my wife young, but at least we had a few years of happiness."

Her clear gaze came around to meet his. "How did she die?"

He winced, the memory ever sharp though

it had been more than seven years. "A carriage accident."

"Were you driving?"

Her tone was hushed, and he was struck by her instant comprehension of the worst possible scenario. The actuality was hardly less blameworthy.

"I thank God, no, I was not. Judith was in the habit of driving herself. It had come on to rain and the roads were slippery. A misjudgement only. She went over the side of a bridge."

Disconcertingly, Mrs. Draycott's eyes did not waver from his face. "Yet you can find it in you to wish you had done something to prevent it? Curbed her desire to handle the ribbons? Forbidden her to go out that day?"

A laugh escaped him, despite the familiar gnaw of guilt. "How well you understand the human mind, ma'am."

She smiled. She had a smile of great warmth, he reflected, friendly and intimate.

"It is merely a trick of taking notice, sir. I assure you I am no better informed than another. It is natural, is it not, for those left behind on these occasions to look for ways in which the worst should not have happened? I daresay you have caught yourself thinking even today that there might have been some fashion in which you could have

85

prevented your sister-in-law's death."

It was precisely what Francis had been thinking. Had he only accompanied his brother to the Endicott ball last night. Or if he had not taken a second glass of port before going to his bed, perhaps he might have slept less soundly and woken at some betraying noise.

"You are uncannily accurate, Mrs. Draycott. How do you do it?"

"Merely experience, my lord. There was no possible way I could have changed Jack's orders, but I promise you, I thought of a dozen impossible means by which I might have done so. I think it is in part due to one's desire for the event not to have happened at all."

"In particular when one is confronted by all the attendant difficulties," agreed Francis feelingly. "But here we are."

The massive wooden doors of the stables stood open, and two grooms were sweeping debris from between the stalls where the whiffle and shift of horses could be heard. Francis called for the head groom.

"Turville!"

An elderly individual emerged from the shadows within. Francis noted the heavy frown and inwardly cursed. "You've heard the news, then?"

"Aye, my lord. A bad business."

He threw a curious glance at Mrs. Draycott, but Francis did not trouble to explain her presence. "Then you will understand my anxiety to ascertain some vital information. At what hour did his lordship leave?"

The man scratched his chin. "I don't rightly know, my lord. It were dark still, I know that, for we had to light the lanterns. Must have been four or five, by my reckoning."

"The devil! I'd hoped you could be more precise."

"Sorry, my lord, but all I know is I woke to find Abel shaking me, saying as how his lordship were wishful for his travelling chariot to be brought round immediate like. So I woke the lads and set to, my lord."

Disappointment rode Francis, but from beside him, he heard Mrs. Draycott speak.

"Pardon me, but was it you, Turville, who drove the carriage round to the house?"

The man's gaze went frowningly from Mrs. Draycott back to Francis, as if he sought instruction.

"Answer the lady," Francis said impatiently.

Turville grunted. "Aye, miss."

Mrs. Draycott smiled, and Francis noted the instant lessening of the head groom's surly look. She had a way about her, this companion of his mother's.

"Thank you. Do you recall just what your master said to you?"

Turville screwed up his face in an effort of concentration. "He complained of the time we'd taken, I remember that. Not that we could've done it any quicker, and so I told him."

"Did he say where he was going?" asked Francis, disregarding this terse aside.

Turville shook his head. "As to that, his lordship ain't in the habit of confiding in me."

"But you might take a guess, man. Have you no notion at all?"

The fellow lifted his shoulders and blew out his cheeks. "I might've paid mind, my lord, if'n he'd gone by daylight. I can't say as how I was more'n half awake."

"Confound the fellow!" Francis burst out. "Why could he not have said something?"

He felt a touch on his arm and looked round, but Mrs. Draycott still had her eyes fixed on Turville. It occurred to him that she was adept at signalling her wishes. He was to keep silent, was he? They would see about that. But he nevertheless held his tongue as she spoke again.

"Turville, should you object to closing

your eyes and allowing your mind to dwell on the moments when you handed the reins to the coachman? I presume you sent a coachman along?"

"Stibbs, miss, his lordship's personal groom. He rides postilion, miss, for the chariot only takes a pair."

"Very good, then. Close your eyes."

The man blinked for a moment, but rather to Francis's surprise, he did as he was bid.

"Now, you are handing over to Stibbs. Can you hear anything said?"

For a moment there was no response, and then Turville's frown cleared and his eyes flew open. "Aye, miss. His lordship said as he hoped to catch the early tide. He must have been heading for the coast."

The surprise that the companion's ruse had worked was overborne in Francis by the jar of realisation. "France, by heaven! He must be heading for Calais."

He found Mrs. Draycott's eyes upon him. "France? Surely not? At a time when there is so much unrest and danger?"

It was a valid objection. News from the continent had been riddled with panic. Since the April riots, the troubles in Paris had escalated, with the change of government in May, the forming of the National Assembly in June, and then the fall of the

Bastille in July when the ensuing riots had spread to the country. Only now did it strike Francis to remember how Randal had appeared inordinately exercised for the possible fate of those born into the upper echelons of French society, raising his voice in the House of Lords and calling for action to be taken. Already there was a trickle of refugees crossing the Channel. English Society was sweeping them up into their ranks, calling them émigrés and condemning the uprisings of the French populace. Only last week, the terrible news had reached them of the storming of Versailles, leaving the Bourbon King a prisoner in his own palace.

"Nevertheless, it is entirely possible that Randal is heading for Paris," Francis said slowly. "He is a frequent visitor. Or had been before the French began upon their internal squabbling."

"Begging your pardon, my lord," cut in Turville, "but the word among the stage coachmen is that it's still safe for English travellers. No Frenchie wouldn't touch 'em, for fear of reprisals. Them Frogs don't want no war with England, my lord."

"There is something in that, I suppose."

"Did you not say, Lord Francis, that your nephew is on the continent? Is it possible your brother might be trying to reach him, fearful perhaps of these happenings across the Channel?"

Francis shook his head. "Unlikely, I think. Giles can be in no danger in Italy, and word will no doubt have reached him of what is happening in France. His tutor at least would have the sense to bring him back via a longer route, avoiding France altogether. No, if Randal had wanted him home, he would have sent a messenger. As I must do without delay," he added, recalling this duty. "Turville, send one of the grooms on horseback to Mr. Jardine, if you please. He must speak to him in private, explain what has occurred, and ask him to wait upon me at Hanover Square as swiftly as he may."

"I'll send Jem directly, my lord."

"Come, Mrs. Draycott. There is nothing more for us to do here. Unless you have any other questions?"

"Only this," said the companion, turning once again to Turville. "If your master has indeed left the country, where will his horses and the chariot be stabled during his absence?"

"There's a stables he uses at Portsmouth, miss."

"Have you the address?"

"Aye, miss, I know it well."

"Why did you wish to know that?" asked Francis as they retraced their steps towards the house.

"Because you must send a man down to bring the carriage and horses back."

Francis stared down at her, befogged. "Why in the world should I do so? And how is Randal to get back here when he returns?"

"If he returns," she corrected soberly. "I assume you have the intention to instruct your lawyer to find him? Then the person who does so will see to hiring transport. Meanwhile, if you do not wish your brother's whereabouts to be discovered by the authorities, it will be politic to remove any possibility of their finding his carriage and horses and putting two and two together."

On returning to the mansion, Ottilia found the dowager haranguing a quivering and tearful woman who turned out to be the late Lady Polbrook's personal maid. The woman, Huntshaw, was being championed, with a good deal of belligerence, by a stout dame whose black serge gown, adorned at the belt with an enormous bunch of keys, proclaimed her calling.

"Mrs. Draycott, thank heavens," the dowager called out the moment Ottilia walked through the door. "I will be glad if you can get some sense out of this creature here, for I have done."

"And so you might, my lady," came angrily from the woman Ottilia took to be the housekeeper. "As nasty a shock as a body could stand has this poor girl had today, and she ain't nowise in any state to be ranted at. I'll not have it, my lady, if you shoot me out the door for saying so."

"It is not in my power to 'shoot you out the door,' as you put it," snapped the dowager. "I am no longer mistress here, as you well know."

"No, and it wouldn't make no difference if you was, my lady, for I'd say it just the same."

"You always were a tartar, Thriplow. I don't know how I bore with you all those years."

"It takes one to know one, my lady," returned the housekeeper with brutal candour. "And with the house in this terrible upset, it's my part to keep my girls calm. Master Francis asked me and Cattawade in particular to see to it."

"Very well, very well." The dowager waved an airy hand at the lady's maid. "I'll say nothing more, Huntshaw, but you'll oblige me by answering any questions Mrs. Draycott may put to you."

Ottilia found two pairs of astonished eyes trained upon her and made haste to make herself known. "I am her ladyship's companion. Temporarily, I hasten to add, while Miss Mellis is laid up. Lady Polbrook has entrusted me with the task of discovering just what occurred last night."

The housekeeper nodded. "I'd heard as much. Not that I can tell you anything. It was poor Huntshaw here who took the worst of it."

"Yes, indeed," agreed Ottilia, infusing sympathy into her tone as she went to the maid, taking her hand in an impulsive fashion and enclosing it warmly. "It must have been horrid for you. I should think you must wish to lie down upon your bed with a soothing draught."

For the first time, the woman spoke up, a quiver in her voice. "I couldn't sleep, ma'am. And I couldn't bear to be alone, not for a minute I couldn't."

"I am not surprised," Ottilia said, pressing her hand. "You are to be commended for your bravery. I daresay any other might have swooned on the spot."

Huntshaw looked gratified, and her tone became stronger. "Well, I'll admit I did scream."

"So would anyone have done."

"To see her lying there like that! My poor mistress."

"Do not think of it, I pray you. We need not dwell upon that picture."

Ottilia led her gently to the sofa situated against the wall behind the dowager's chair and obliged her to sit, herself taking a position such that the elderly dame would not be immediately visible to the lady's maid.

"Now," she began, "I wonder if you would be able to cast your mind back to last night."

Huntshaw nodded, but her eyes showed she was still apprehensive.

"Had your mistress been out for the evening?"

"She had, miss. She attended the ball at Endicott House."

"Did you wait up for her?"

The woman's features were calming now, as she concentrated on the questions. "My lady told me not to, but I did, for I knew she'd need help to take off her gown and her jewels."

"Do you know what time it was?"

Huntshaw shook her head. "It must have been one or after, for the house was quiet and I'd dropped off in the chair."

"But you did not prepare her ladyship for bed?"

A look of discontent crossed Huntshaw's

face. "I was going to, but his lordship went in."

Ottilia heard the faint intake of breath from the dowager and quickly put out a hand to prevent her from breaking into speech. She did not look away from Huntshaw's face.

"He went into her bedchamber?"

"Yes, and my lady went in to him."

Ottilia lowered her voice to a confidential murmur. "Can you tell me what happened? Did you hear anything that was said?"

At this, the maid's eyes became wild and she hunted frantically about until her gaze settled on the housekeeper. The woman waddled over.

"No need to be afraid, Mary. No one ain't going to blame you for listening, not at a time like this."

"How could you help but do so?" put in Ottilia gently. "You were waiting to put your mistress to bed. You cannot be accused of eavesdropping."

Huntshaw's fingers fiddled with the folds of her gown. "I don't like to say, miss."

"Of course you don't. But you, of all people, know what it is we fear. The least light you can throw upon the matter may be of use."

"Well, that's just it, miss," uttered the

96

woman in a burst of candour. "I wouldn't want to be the means of putting a rope round his lordship's neck."

"No indeed, and it is that very apprehension that prompts us all to find out the truth. What was it, Miss Huntshaw? Did they quarrel?"

The woman put her fists together and thrust them against her mouth, muffling her words. "Terrible it was. I've never heard his lordship so wild, and I've heard them at it hammer and tongs often and often."

"What was he wild about?"

The maid leaned out to cast a fearful glance back towards where the dowager was seated, but to Ottilia's relief, the housekeeper's bulk was in the way.

"Come now, Mary," she said in a friendly tone, deliberately using the woman's given name, "you must have heard enough to deduce what the quarrel was about."

Nodding unhappily, Mary twisted her fingers into her ill-used skirts and sighed. "It was always the same. His lordship accused my lady of being unfaithful. My lady countered with asking him what he did in France. He said it was none of her affair, and she threw back at him that what she did in England was none of his." Here the lady's maid sighed again. "Then my lady slammed the door to the dressing room and I could hear no more."

Ottilia noted a certain shifting in the woman's eyes as she said this, and resolved to pursue the matter further. "Then what did you do?"

"I put my lady's gown away and laid up her jewels."

"Did you leave after that?"

"No, for I heard the other door slam and I thought his lordship had gone."

"And then?"

"The door opened and my lady came in. She must have forgot she had not dismissed me, for she says, 'What, Huntshaw, are you still here? Go to bed at once,' she says. 'I will manage on my own.' Then she goes back into the chamber and I can hear her pacing back and forth, back and forth. Talking to herself, she was. Whispering. If it hadn't been as I once heard her laughing, I'd have thought she were praying. And then I heard his lordship's voice again, and realised he must have come back in. So I — so I left."

Ottilia reached out and set a hand over the unquiet fingers in the woman's lap, holding her gaze. "But you did not go to bed, did you? You were worried about your mistress, I think, and so you listened at the keyhole." Dismay was in the woman's eyes, but dumbly she nodded. Ottilia smiled at her. "And what did you hear, Mary?"

Once again, the woman looked to the housekeeper for guidance. Mrs. Thriplow, who was looking grim, gave her a tight nod. "Go on, Mary."

Huntshaw drew a breath and capitulated. "His lordship was asking for the fan."

"The fan?"

For the first time since the recital began, the dowager spoke. "It's an heirloom. It is passed down through the Polbrook brides."

"Thank you, ma'am," Ottilia said calmly, and turned back to Mary, who was once more looking scared. "Go on, Mary. He asked for the fan, you say."

"He was accusing my lady of losing it. He wanted it back, he said. My mistress said he couldn't have it back for it belonged to her. He said it didn't, for it was hers on loan. And my mistress said —" Here Huntshaw's voice quavered on the edge of hysteria. "She said — *'For my lifetime.'* And now she's dead!"

"Softly, Mary," urged Ottilia. "These are mere words."

"I'll never forget them, miss, never."

"Do you recall what the master said to that?"

"He said she was entitled to the fan only as long as she was his wife. And if he had his way, that wouldn't be so long, neither."

There was a muttered expletive from the dowager, but Ottilia ignored it and pressed on. "And then?"

Huntshaw's distressed features had taken on a frown. "I can't think what he meant by saying such a thing. My lady said nothing to it, but when his lordship demanded to see the fan, she refused to show it to him. She said she had it safe. Then his lordship shouted at her. 'You had it not this night, madam,' he shouted. Then he said she had given it away, to one of her lovers, for he'd seen it in the fellow's hands."

"And what did your mistress say to that? Did she deny it?"

"She screamed at the master to get out. Then I heard his footsteps and I ran to hide. I watched him come out and he went off down the stairs in a bang, miss, shouting for Foscot."

"His lordship's valet that is, ma'am," put in the housekeeper.

"Thank you," said Ottilia. "You went to bed then, Mary?"

"Yes, but the mistress did have the fan."

Mrs. Thriplow cut in before Ottilia could respond. "How do you know?"

"I found it in the morning when I — when she —"

She faltered, and Ottilia once again caught her hands. "Where did you find it?"

"It was thrown down, all among the pots in the dressing commode. So careless of her, as I thought, for it could easily have been broken or been marked."

A dark thought was revolving in Ottilia's head. She had no choice but to put the question. "Did you put the fan away?"

To her secret dismay, Mary shook her head. "I had no time to think of that, for it was then I smelled . . . and I went into the chamber and . . ."

Quickly, Ottilia held up a hand. "There is no need to go into that, my dear Mary. We understand." She got up. "I must thank you. What you have told us is extremely helpful."

Huntshaw rose, glancing towards the dowager who, Ottilia noted, was looking white and strained. And no wonder.

The housekeeper claimed her attention. "Will that be all, miss?"

"Oh yes, thank you, Mrs. Thriplow. It is Mrs. Thriplow, is it not?"

The woman nodded. "Yes, ma'am."

"Then, if you do not object, perhaps we may have a little talk at another time."

"But I don't know anything," protested the housekeeper.

"Perhaps not, but you are best placed to help me understand your late mistress's household. I rely on you absolutely."

Mrs. Thriplow visibly swelled, preening a little. "Well, it's true enough I know what's what. I've been housekeeper here nigh on twenty-five years, and I came up the ranks through fifteen before that. I've seen them all in and out. Except Cattawade, of course."

"Then we are agreed."

Ottilia held out her hand. The housekeeper looked at it and back at Ottilia's face, and gratification spread over her features. She took the hand and shook it vigorously.

"I'll look forward to it, ma'am."

Ottilia watched the two pass from the room and turned to see that the dowager had let her head drop into one hand as she rested an elbow on the arm of her chair.

"Do not distress yourself, ma'am," said Ottilia, going quickly towards her.

The dowager looked up again, a haggard look in her face. "The fool! The wretched, addlepated fool! Who will believe him innocent after this?"

Ottilia went to her, kneeling by her chair and grasping her trembling hand.

"Do not despair. It is a setback, but the

facts I outlined earlier remain."

"What use are they against that girl's testimony? And why in the world did you not ask her about a door key?"

"My dear ma'am, the woman is in no condition to be revealing secrets of that nature."

"If indeed such secrets exist." The dowager groaned aloud. "Where is Francis when there is this fresh disaster falling upon our heads?"

"He will be here presently," Ottilia soothed, patting her hand. "He meant to set about writing letters, for he says there are several persons who must be informed at once."

"Too many."

"I believe Lord Francis means to despatch a number of messengers about the country. And he sent for your Mr. Jardine."

"Not merely mine. Jardine is the family's man of business." The dowager groaned deeply, and Ottilia grasped her hand tighter. "The thing becomes worse and worse. All we need is for the world and his wife to be apprised of what we have just been told, and the fat will be in the fire."

"Fear not, ma'am. There is more to this than meets the eye. Did you remark what Mary Huntshaw said about the fan?"

The dowager snatched her hand away. "Of course I remarked it! Do you think I am in my dotage? That thing is worth thousands. And Emily treats it like a twopenny fairing!"

Ottilia stood up and confronted her, setting one hand upon the mantel.

"Be that as it may, ma'am, the fan is of significant interest."

This caught the dowager's attention. "How so?"

"Mary Huntshaw said that when she went in this morning, she saw it had been thrown down among the pots, and she did not touch it. When I went into the dressing room, I saw no fan in that place. If it was there this morning, it is now missing."

By the time Francis had finished penning a number of urgent letters and was applying his brother's seal, the housemaid came into the library to inform him that a repast was to be served in the dining parlour.

"Is it so late?"

Even as he asked, his stomach reminded him he'd had no time even to take breakfast.

The girl bobbed a curtsy. "It's nigh on two, my lord. My lady —" She faltered, flushed, and hurriedly added, "I mean, your lordship's mother, my lord, she give order for tea and something light, and Cook done what she could."

"Excellent. I will come at once."

"And Mr. Jardine is waiting, my lord," added the maid conscientiously.

Hearing which, Francis took up the sealed papers. "In good time. You had best invite him to join us in the dining parlour."

"I'll tell Mr. Cattawade, my lord."

The girl curtsied again and had reached the door before Francis thought to take advantage of her presence.

"One moment."

Pausing, she turned. "My lord?"

"I don't suppose you heard anything last night, did you? Or saw anything?"

A fearful look came into the girl's eyes, but she shook her head fiercely. "I were asleep throughout, my lord, for which I'm that thankful. I didn't know nothing until I come into the kitchen first thing."

Francis crossed to where she stood at the door. "Who told you, then?"

The girl looked frightened. "I don't rightly know, my lord, there were so much talk. There weren't a body there but hadn't summat to say. It were that shocking. The poor mistress."

Taking a leaf out of Mrs. Draycott's book, Francis smiled at the girl in a friendly way.

"I daresay it was quite a cacophony."

The maid looked mystified. "A what, my lord?"

"There was a lot of talk? Everyone talking at once?"

A trifle of excitement showed in her eyes as she nodded vehemently. "Yes, my lord, and some bust out crying. Sukey were sobbing fit to bring the roof down and Cook had to give her a slap." Recalling perhaps to whom she was speaking, she hastened to add, "Cook sat her down after and give her a drink of port special, for it were poor Sukey as had been in the chamber to light the fire and the mistress dead in her bed all the time. I'd have been took bad myself if it'd been me."

Astonished at the looseness of the girl's tongue, Francis reflected on the far-reaching effects of the ghastly events of the day. Everything and everyone was in disarray. Apart from those such as Mrs. Thriplow, whose long service and position in the household allowed a little licence, few servants would dream in the normal way of pouring out such a torrent of words before one of the family. Or was it, Francis wondered, because he was not inclined to encourage it? But the reference to Sukey was useful. He must apprise Mrs. Draycott, who would no doubt wish to speak to the girl.

"Thank you, er —"

"Jane, my lord," supplied the maid, bobbing again.

"Jane, of course, yes. Thank you, Jane. Run along now. Oh, and don't forget about Mr. Jardine."

"No, my lord."

The girl vanished through the doorway, and Francis followed more slowly, feeling as if he trod on ice which might at any moment give way and plunge him into the depths. The press of things that must be done was overwhelming.

In the dining parlour he discovered seated at the table, which was spread with a selection of sliced pies alongside a loaf of bread and several cheeses, his mother, Mrs. Draycott, and Colonel Tretower, who had returned from an official errand. The dowager, who was looking hangdog, hailed him with a demand to know what had kept him so long.

"I have but just finished my letters," he told her, feeling a trifle guilty. He should never have allowed her to come here. Had there been more said to dispirit her? Before he could enquire, Jardine was ushered into the room.

There was, on the face of this man of law, Francis noted, an incipient scowl that accentuated his usual appearance of unrelieved severity. The fellow's cold eyes had ever caused Francis an inward twinge of distaste, despite a thorough knowledge of Jardine's incomparable competence at his calling. He was as shrewd a man as one could wish, and it was far better to have him in one's corner than supporting an opponent.

The lawyer paid his respects first to the dowager, executing a small bow and offering his condolences in the clipped manner habitual to him.

"A sorry affair, my lady. I have every sympathy with your loss."

The dowager eyed him balefully, and Francis recalled how little his mother liked the man. "It's to be hoped you can do more than sympathise, Jardine. For one thing, you can tell us where my son has gone."

The lawyer pursed his lips, but his face gave nothing away. "I would tell you if I knew."

"You need not dissemble. Polbrook was making for the coast, and we must suppose he has set sail for France. If anyone knows where in that present hellhole he may be going, it is you."

The mention of France caused the faintest twitch of a muscle in the man's cheek, Francis noted. His mother was right. Jardine did know. But if she thought he would reveal it, she had a deal to learn of the man. He was as close as an oyster.

"Jardine," he cut in, "will you take these letters, if you please? This for my nephew, that for my brother. I rely on your messengers to locate both and bring them back here as speedily as they may."

Taking the letters, the lawyer looked at their inscriptions, turned them over, and inspected the seals. Then his keen glance came back up to Francis's face.

"Anything else, my lord?"

"Not at present. The others are to persons situated within the country, so it will not tax my ingenuity to have them delivered. Colonel Tretower is assisting us with the authorities. If there is anything else, I will —" A thought occurred to him. "Stay! There is the matter of the will. You have it, of course?"

Jardine nodded briefly. "The reading must await an inquest."

"But you can tell us what is in it," said the dowager.

His lips pursed once more. "I am not at liberty to divulge anything prior to the reading, but I think you will find no surprises."

"Pardon me, sir."

Francis had forgotten Mrs. Draycott. If she was planning to question Jardine, he had best pave the way. Without knowing her interest in the matter, the fellow would likely refuse even to answer. But much to his surprise, the lawyer turned at once.

"Yes, Mrs. Draycott?"

Her special smile appeared, but Francis could not see that it had any visible effect upon Jardine.

"Is there anything in her ladyship's will that could provide a motive for murder?"

The lawyer's brows drew together, increasing the sternness of his expression. "You interest yourself in this affair, ma'am?"

Mrs. Draycott's chin went up, and Francis saw, with a stirring of interest, a light in her eye that was positively martial.

"My dear sir, would you expect Lady Polbrook's companion to do otherwise?"

"She is acting for me, Jardine," cut in the dowager irritably. "I wish you will not stand upon your dignity, man, in such an extremity as this."

Typically, Jardine chose not to respond to the last, although he addressed himself directly to the dowager as he answered. "I cannot suppose one could make out a case against anyone from the contents of the will. Since your ladyship presses me, I will look into the matter further."

"Do so, if you please."

Jardine bowed, and looked back at Francis. "If that is all, my lord?"

Feeling compelled, Francis asked if he cared to share their repast. To his relief, the lawyer refused the offer.

"I have other business waiting, and I must attend to your letters instanter."

With which he nodded to the rest of the company and withdrew.

No sooner had the door closed behind him than the dowager exploded. "I loathe and detest that creature! It was just the same with your father, Fanfan. I never could worm a single secret out of Jardine." She flicked a hand towards the companion. "I doubt even you could prise him open, my dear, and you are singularly expert. Francis, do you know she got that foolish maid of Emily's to tell us everything she knew? Not that I am happy to have heard it, for a more damning set of statements one could scarcely imagine."

Francis instantly demanded enlightenment, and as the company set about consuming the cold collation provided for their sustenance, he was regaled with the tale

Mrs. Draycott had extracted from Hunt-shaw.

Dismay swamped him. "Lord! To my mind, that augments the case against Randal." He looked across the table at Colonel Tretower. "George?"

His friend chewed thoughtfully for a moment. "I am bound to agree it looks bad. Have you any notion what he did after he left his wife's bedchamber on the last occasion?"

He turned as he spoke to Mrs. Draycott, who was seated with her back to the window. Francis focused on the woman's eyes. They really were quite free of guile, he reflected. Unusual in the females of his acquaintance, and therefore refreshing.

"Not as yet," she replied. "But I have not yet had time to talk to the other servants. I have every hope we will be able presently to piece together the marquis's movements."

"And the disappearance of the fan?" pursued Tretower.

This was news to Francis. "What in the world are you talking of? I thought you said Emily and Randal had been arguing over it."

"Yes," agreed Mrs. Draycott, "but although Mary Huntshaw saw it in the morning, left carelessly among the pots on the dressing table, I did not."

"What? You mean it had vanished?" Francis set down his fork with a clang. "The devil! It was I who forgot to lock the dressing room door."

"But the footman was guarding it," his mother reminded him.

"Yes, but the window was open," Mrs. Draycott pointed out. "I remarked it when we went into the room. Had you opened it, Lord Francis?"

He shook his head. "No, it was already open. One of the servants must have thrown it wide before I reached the place."

"Do you seriously imagine someone might have scaled the wall and climbed in the window?" asked George, his tone sceptical. "Difficult and dangerous, I think. And he might have been spotted."

There was a pause. From the faces of the others, Francis knew he was not the only one who found it perplexing. Almost without thought, he looked again at the companion.

"Mrs. Draycott?"

Her open gaze met his, and her tone was meditative. "Difficult, but not impossible — to climb the wall, I mean."

"Next you will be suggesting this fictitious

lover came and went by that route," George cut in.

Francis almost snorted. "What, like Romeo? Even I, desperate as I am to believe in the lover, could not support that notion."

"On the other hand," said Mrs. Draycott, apparently indifferent to this interchange, "someone might have slipped past Abel. Like everyone else, he was suffering from shock. How long were you at your toilet, my lord?"

Francis shrugged. "I scarcely know. Diplock provided me with a much needed brandy when I got back to my room. I had to shave, but I did not waste time about the rest. I suppose it may have been half an hour or so before I got back to Emily's room."

"When you locked the dressing room door," suggested George.

"Yes, because it had only just occurred to me to recall the connecting door into the bedchamber."

"Time enough," snapped his mother. "For my part, I would trust no servant to be vigilant at all times. I daresay any number of curious others came to Emily's room in the interim."

Tretower laughed. "Only too likely. And this footman of yours, being one of the privileged, might well have taken his eye off the game in a bid to puff off his own importance. It is a failing I have had to check in several of my men, I can tell you."

The dowager was in agreement, and the conversation ran upon these lines for several moments before Francis realised that Mrs. Draycott was bearing no part in it. A faint crease sat between her brows, and she looked to have her attention otherwhere.

"You seem in a brown study, Mrs. Draycott," Francis ventured at the first lull.

The companion blinked, looking at him as if she had just noticed his presence. "I beg your pardon?"

"I say you looked as if you had not been attending."

He saw withdrawal in her features, but she gave a quick shake of the head. "It is nothing. A random thought."

Oddly dissatisfied, Francis eyed her. "Has it to do with the business at hand?" She seemed uncomfortable, as if she did not wish to pursue the matter. Francis felt impelled to press her. "We are all on the same path, are we not?"

At this, Mrs. Draycott seemed to throw off her abstraction. "Indeed. The case is, I was wondering which of the household to talk to next."

If he had been challenged, Francis could not have given a reason, but he felt certain this was a blind. Something she did not wish to share was in her mind.

CHAPTER 5

Mrs. Draycott's words, however, had reminded Francis of the maid Jane. "I can tell you just whom to talk to next. One Sukey, a chambermaid, who must have been the first into the room this morning. I recall you expressly stated someone must have made up the fire."

"Why, thank you, that is most helpful, my lord." She gave him a bland look. "And you, sir? What is your next move?"

Francis sighed. "I must leave in the morning to fetch my niece home."

"But it will take you all of two or three days to reach Bath and come back again," his mother cut in.

"Longer perhaps," suggested Mrs. Draycott, "for the roads are despicable at present."

"Worse yet," his mother complained. "How shall we do without you?"

"I will leave you in George's capable

hands. And Mrs. Draycott will doubtless have enough to do in questioning the household."

"What of the household? With no one to direct them, the servants will be at sixes and sevens at a time like this."

"I have no choice, Mama. It is not a task one can leave to a stranger, when all is said and done."

His mother's dissatisfaction was plain. Francis felt oppressed. It was not as if he desired to go upon the errand. Left to himself, he would infinitely prefer to remain in London and do what he might to scotch the coming scandal, besides unravelling the mystery of last night's hideous events. His eyes strayed towards Mrs. Draycott. Not that he supposed she could offer any palliative to alleviate his troubles. He caught her glance and her warm smile appeared.

"I wonder, my lord, if it might answer for Lady Polbrook and myself to take up residence here — temporarily, I need hardly say."

The notion was anathema. Leave his mother in situ, prey to remembrance and every sort of imagined nightmare? "I hardly think that would serve —"

"An excellent suggestion, Mrs. Draycott," said his mother, cutting him off. Light entered her face, just as if the horrors of the day had been nonexistent. "You may work uninterrupted upon your investigations, while I supervise the workings of the house."

"You cannot stay here, ma'am," Francis protested with vehemence.

"Why not?"

"With all that has occurred in this house in the last few hours, you can ask that? The whole notion is morbid in the extreme."

"Then the sooner a semblance of normality is restored, my lord," came the soothing tones of Mrs. Draycott, "the better it will be. And now that the body of the unfortunate deceased has been removed, thanks to the offices of Colonel Tretower —"

"I don't see what difference that makes," Francis snapped. "It is still morbid."

"But it is not a matter of wishing to be here, sir. It is pure expediency."

"True, but it is the last place I could wish my mother to be at such a time."

"On the contrary, it is just where I ought to be. It will not be thought odd under the circumstances. And when the news breaks, as it undoubtedly will, I shall be far better suited to be here. I was dreading a positive siege in Bruton Street, but I cannot think the most inveterate scandalmonger will venture to approach this house."

About to refute his mother's reasoning in no uncertain terms, Francis paused. "There is something in that, but I cannot like it. George?"

Thus called upon, his friend gave him the singular look of one male to another in a stand against the other sex. "I believe there is little purpose in arguing the point, Fan, if Lady Polbrook has made up her mind."

"How wise of you, Colonel Tretower," said the dowager. "I am glad Francis chose to appoint you his deputy."

Francis threw up his hands. "I am silenced. On your own heads be it. But I might point out that my object in fetching Candia was not to thrust her into misery by placing her where she can only be distressed by memories, not to mention a lively imagination."

His mother nodded. "I have been thinking about my granddaughter, and you need not fret. I have an excellent solution in mind."

With the departure of Lord Francis a settled thing, Ottilia found the dowager's spirits considerably reduced, despite her determination to remove to Hanover Square. Either repugnance of the grisly event was catching up with her, or the prospective absence of her younger son left her bereft in light of the apparent loss of the elder.

Colonel Tretower went off shortly on various missions of his own, including an arrangement for the retrieval of Lord Polbrook's chariot and horses from Portsmouth, but promised to return upon the morrow to see how they did. Lord Francis accompanied him in his way to the post office to despatch his letters in time for the night mail, and it was left to Ottilia to persuade the dowager to repair to her own house, where her son had promised to sup with them.

"We can do no more here at present, ma'am, and indeed I think you have endured enough for one day."

At that, the elder lady's eyes fired up. "There can be no limits to endurance in this extremity."

"Agreed," Ottilia said patiently. "But why subject yourself to unnecessary pain? With what lies before you, it will be well to recruit your strength, do you not think?"

A grim smile curved the dowager's mouth. "Unanswerable. But I will have none of Pellew's draughts, and so I warn you."

Ottilia raised her brows. "I was thinking more of hard liquor, ma'am."

This forced a reluctant laugh from the dowager, and she at last consented to leave

Hanover Square. Relieved, Ottilia had the butler call up a hackney, for daylight was fading.

In the event, there was little rest to be had, for the dowager could not remove without imparting a deal of unnecessary instruction to her staff on running the house in her absence and supervising her woman's packing. Ottilia was glad she'd had no time to unpack her own trunks, for it left her free to think. She took time to sit at the dowager's writing table and draw up a list of her findings. This exercise left so many questions that she was obliged to list these separately and decide on a plan of action to find means to answer them.

Her employer interrupted her at this work to complain of being hardly used, for Lord Francis had sent a note to say he could not after all join them for supper, which was to be served immediately.

"It is too bad of him, when he knows how hungry I am for news."

"Perhaps he has none," said Ottilia pacifically.

"And now I shall not see him at all," pursued the dowager, ignoring this suggestion, "for he means to be off to Bath at first light."

"Then he will be back the sooner, ma'am."

Her employer refused to be mollified. Through the meal, of which the dowager partook sparingly, eating perhaps three mouthfuls from each of the two modest courses, her voice became increasingly querulous, warning Ottilia that shock was at last catching up with her. She abandoned any attempt to bring the dowager to a better frame of mind, instead allowing her to talk herself to a standstill. At which point, Ottilia got up and rang the bell, drawing the elder lady's instant attention.

"What are you about?"

Ottilia smiled at her. "I think you stand in crying need of a restorative, ma'am. Oh, not the doctor's remedy, be sure."

A trace of amusement drove the tetchiness from the dowager's face. "I daresay I might not refuse a glass of port."

"Then port it shall be."

While the dowager drank, Ottilia attempted to divert her mind by talking lightly of everyday things until she saw her employer's eyelids drooping. Satisfied, she ceased speaking and sat for a while, contemplating the remains of the ruby liquid in her own glass.

Her first day in office and how the world was turned inside out! She had come here expecting a life of tedium, and very likely drudgery. Her brother had deprecated her decision, but Ottilia could not feel content to continue to live on his bounty now that she had no longer any employment by which she might return his kindness. With the boys gone, she had become restless and impatient of life in a country village. Taking the temporary post of companion had been an experiment, if truth be told. Or so she had represented it to Patrick. He had agreed to it only on condition that she would return immediately, should she feel dissatisfied. How he would laugh now, were he to learn how his sister had become embroiled almost instantly in just the imbroglio to tax her ingenuity to the utmost.

Though it was, to be sure, no laughing matter. And her immediate desire to be of assistance had been prompted not by curiosity, but by the very real distress occasioned to the dowager and to her remaining son. What a monster she would be to allow them to suffer, if by any effort of hers she could alleviate something of their trouble.

Glancing at the dowager, the marks of anxiety were there even as she dosed. Her features were pallid and drawn, tiny muscles twitched in her cheeks, and the hollows beneath her eyes had darkened a little.

Wrung with pity, Ottilia got up quietly and slipped out of the cosy little dining parlour in search of her ladyship's maid. Miss Venner was better acquainted with her and would know how to persuade her into her bed. For herself, Ottilia was more than ready to get between sheets. The day's events, coming atop yesterday's journey, had tired her out.

The morning found her refreshed and ready for action, but although the dowager was lively, she located a number of items left unpacked and had so many additional instructions for her household that it was near noon before a hackney deposited them in Hanover Square.

Mrs. Thriplow, who was even more upset than upon the previous day, Ottilia judged, had been unable to arrange for the new arrivals to be accommodated near together. The dowager, to her immediate chagrin, had been assigned the back room next door to that of the marchioness.

"I'd no choice, my lady," the housekeeper apologised, sounding harassed, "for you wouldn't want to be up on the second floor, where I've put Mrs. Draycott. And Master Francis is only across the passage, my lady."

The dowager remained dissatisfied, giving a little shiver as she cast a glance over her shoulder towards the fatal room. "I should prefer to negotiate a second set of stairs than sleep in here behind poor Emily's bedchamber."

"That would be ineligible, ma'am," said Ottilia. "But if you should be nervous, I can very well sleep in a truckle bed alongside you."

But this her employer would by no means agree to, saying that Venner could very well perform that duty. "At least until Francis returns."

"I'll get Abel to fetch one down, my lady, and I'm sorry as the beds ain't been made yet, but the sheets is still airing and, what with the washerwoman vowing as she'll never set foot in the house again and the maids having hysterics every time they come within ten foot of my late mistress's chamber, I don't know if I'm on my head or my heels."

"Oh, for heaven's sake, what a set of ninnies," said the dowager, just as if she had not one moment since expressed much the same sentiment.

Ottilia smothered a laugh and made haste to soothe the housekeeper's lacerated feelings. "I have every sympathy with you, my dear Mrs. Thriplow. It must be hard indeed for you to keep any semblance of order and direction under these terrible circumstances."

"Well, it is, ma'am, and I'm that put about over it, for I promised Master Francis as I'd see all went along as normal as possible."

"To the devil with Master Francis," stated his fond mother. "Does he have the least notion what it takes to run a household? Of course he has not."

"That he ain't, my lady, and no mistake. If it ain't one thing, it's another, and if Cook manages to produce a dinner fit to eat, what with young Betsy shrieking like a moonling at every sound and spilling half the fat off the roast all over the kitchen floor so's no one can't take a step without slipping in it, I'll take leave to call the woman a saint!"

This was too much for Ottilia, and she struggled to contain her amusement under the housekeeper's affronted gaze and the dowager's stony stare.

"Oh, pardon me, Mrs. Thriplow," she managed at length, "but I could not withstand the picture you conjured up in my imagination. I'm afraid it is one of my worst faults to be merry at the wrong moment."

"Well, it's better than screeching, I suppose," said the housekeeper, consenting to be mollified.

"Forgive me, pray. And I am sure Cook

need not fret over dinner. We will be content, I am persuaded, with the simplest of fare, will we not, ma'am?"

She cast an imploring look upon the dowager as she spoke, and was relieved when her employer rose nobly to the occasion.

"I have little appetite in any event, Thriplow. Let Cook do what she may and that will suffice."

The housekeeper's relief was patent, and by way of help, the dowager asked her personal maid to superintend the preparation of the rooms, thus freeing Mrs. Thriplow for other duties. Feeling that the two women would do better without them, Ottilia suggested to the dowager that they repair to the front downstairs parlour they had occupied yesterday.

"It is the least grand of the rooms," said the dowager, standing in the centre and looking about at the pale green papered walls with a once-fashionable stripe, the gilt-edged chairs and sofas with prettily cushioned seats, the little escritoire in one corner, and the Adam fireplace where a cheerful blaze had been encouraged by an unseen hand. "I was in the habit of using it daily when I lived here, but Emily preferred the Blue Salon across the hall. She likes

formality." A shadow crossed the older dame's features. "*Liked,* I should say. How hard it is to become accustomed."

Ottilia went to her and led her to one of the sofas set against the wall, obliging her to be seated and taking a perch at her side. "There is no hurry on that score, ma'am."

"But there is on the score of discovery. Should you not be questioning the servants?"

"It can wait."

"But they will forget, or worse, supply incorrect details from their imaginations. Servants thrive on these lurid affairs."

"On the contrary. In a day or so, I imagine they will recall events more clearly," Ottilia said. "By the sound of things, I should get very little sense out of them today. It is evident they are all suffering an inevitable paralysis of the mind. Besides, I would much prefer to embark upon questioning in a less formal way than we did yesterday. And there are other matters to consider."

She came under a suspicious stare from the dowager's dark eyes. "What other matters?"

"Nothing to concern you, ma'am. I would like, for example, to familiarise myself with the layout of the house, if you permit that I wander about unhindered."

"Francis gave you carte blanche. Do whatever you need to do, my dear. I suppose you will be hunting for a particular door."

Ottilia laughed. "Well reasoned, ma'am. That and other things. Lord Francis yesterday gave me the key to the late Lady Polbrook's bedchamber so that I may take another good look around before we allow her ladyship's maid to — well, to clean and tidy."

"Yes, that must be done." The dowager sighed deeply. "What a lowering thought. One forgets the necessary business of disposing of everyday belongings. Emily's wardrobe will naturally go to her daughter, unless she has bequeathed any items of costume elsewhere. Jardine will know. We had best pack it all away until the poor child is sufficiently composed to deal with it herself."

Ottilia applauded this suggestion, realising that the busier the dowager could be kept, the better. Not only for her own peace of mind, but to prevent her interference when Ottilia undertook interviews with the staff. If one thing was more certain than another, it was that she would get a deal more out of the servants unhampered by the dowager's presence.

"It will be for Mary Huntshaw to do the actual packing, but I daresay it would be best if you were to supervise it, ma'am. We cannot have her ladyship's maid in danger of being accused should anything go missing in addition to the fan."

Lady Polbrook agreed to this, but the reminder of the fan's loss led her to inquire how Ottilia proposed to set about finding its present location.

"I have no notion," said Ottilia frankly. "I doubt there is very much to be done about that until we have Lord Francis back with us."

"Francis? What in the world can he do in the matter?"

Evidently Lord Francis remained unforgiven for last night's lapse. Ottilia wisely did not refer to it, but said instead, "Did I not suggest that we must carry our investigations further afield? I depend upon Lord Francis to go out into the world to find Emily's lover."

The hour being advanced and the afternoon dark and dismal, Ottilia felt there was little to be gained in setting off on a tour of the house. The dowager being anxious to know what she intended to do next, Ottilia took time instead for the hour or so before dinner to go over the lists she had made up the night before, to the accompaniment of much comment and discussion.

The promised visit of Colonel Tretower coincided with the dinner hour, and the dowager invited him to partake of the meal in their company. She was amply rewarded when he referred without prompting to Lord Francis's failure to attend his mother the previous evening.

"My fault, ma'am, I'm afraid. I asked Fan to sup with me instead, for I wanted to give him an account of my dealings with Bow Street."

Ottilia started. "Bow Street? Did you go there then?"

"Indeed, for I deemed it best to go myself," he said, nodding to the butler who was ready to ladle a portion of steaming broth into his bowl, "having learned from Mr. Satterleigh that it was his duty to lay his information there. The justices were shocked, of course, but I am relieved to report that they were reluctant to set the blame at Lord Polbrook's door. I did what I might to encourage this attitude, saying that it was believed his lordship's journey had been premeditated."

"But it hadn't been," objected the dowager, beginning upon her soup. "Or at least we don't know that it had."

"Precisely. We don't know. It is therefore entirely possible that it was, and serves our purpose better than to discourage the notion. I also told them that Fan has already sent after his brother."

Ottilia eyed him over her bowl with amusement. "But you did not, I take it, suggest that Lord Francis does not in fact know where his brother has gone?"

Tretower grinned at her as he took up a spoon. "Well spotted, Mrs. Draycott. I could not feel it would serve any useful purpose for them to know that."

"You are a better conspirator than I gave you credit for, Colonel," said the dowager approvingly. "Do you suppose the justices will be satisfied to await Randal's return?"

His features became grave. "I will not conceal my doubts from you on that score, ma'am. But I did stress the need for discretion in light of the imminent scandal. I am assured that Bow Street is not in the habit of disclosing its beliefs and actions to anyone connected with newssheets, in particular the more scurrilous rags devoted to gossip."

"Not that it will stop them printing anything they choose," said the dowager bitterly, taking a sip of her wine. "Nor do I imagine we can rely on every member of

Polbrook's household to be immune to the offer of a bribe."

The butler, under instruction, was serving the company himself without the services of the footman or one of the maids, a precaution instituted by the dowager in order that they might talk freely. At this juncture, he coughed delicately. Lady Polbrook looked round at him.

"Well, Cattawade? Can you vouch for all of them?"

"Not all, my lady, but I venture to hope that none will be as disloyal as you suggest."

"A vain hope, my friend," said Colonel Tretower on a dry note. "Show me the fellow who will not be swayed by the sight of a fistful of gold, and you will show me a saint."

Ottilia noted the look of deep offence in Cattawade's features and resolved to tackle the man as soon as she might. At least she might trust to one account being as accurate as the man could remember it. Meanwhile, she deemed it politic to change the subject.

"I have been wondering, ma'am, about mourning clothes."

The dowager looked startled. "Lord, if I had not forgotten that!"

"It is not urgent, I suppose, but perhaps it would be wise to prepare."

"I will send Venner to fetch my seamstress.

Not that I need go into blacks until I am receiving, but as you say, it is well to be ready. Apart from offending people, I could not wish to show Emily the slightest disrespect. Little though we saw eye to eye, she did not deserve such a death."

Ottilia was well satisfied to have found another matter to take up the dowager's attention. Mention of the lady's maid reminded her that she was hoping to find an opportunity to talk to the woman, but without alerting her mistress. Venner had been tight-lipped with reluctance upon hearing of the removal to Hanover Square, and Ottilia was anxious to discover the reason. It had been borne in upon her that Venner regarded the late Lady Polbrook with scant approval, for she'd apparently had no sympathies to offer when news of the murder had been broken to her the previous morning.

Ottilia had met the woman when she had fetched her warm cloak from upstairs. Venner had been requested to bring down the dowager's pelisse, but a moment's conversation made Ottilia realise she had not been apprised of the morning's events. Thinking to save the dowager an unpleasant task, she delivered the information herself.

"So she's dead, is she?"

"I am afraid she was brutally murdered, Miss Venner," Ottilia had said as lightly as she could manage.

The woman's eyes had widened a little, but her features had remained taut. "How?"

"She was strangled."

Venner's stare had remained fixed for a moment, and Ottilia could read nothing in her face either of pity or indeed shock. At length, she'd given a wriggle of the shoulders, as if to shake off the fixing of her attention.

"I'll fetch her ladyship's pelisse to her," she'd said curtly, and had turned away into the dowager's bedchamber.

Ottilia came back from this recollection to find that Colonel Tretower was speaking of his further actions today. "I enquired of the coroner when you may be able to hold the funeral, and he has no objection to a burial being arranged as soon as may be. I imagine you cannot wait upon Lord Polbrook's arrival, ma'am."

"We cannot possibly do so, since we have no notion when he might return. Or indeed *if* he will return."

"I beg you won't dwell on that possibility," said Tretower, taking the words out of Ottilia's mouth. "I have been thinking it over, and I believe he must return, regardless of the circumstances. He cannot remain abroad forever. How would he live? And who would take his place?"

"The burden would devolve upon Giles," said the dowager. "And if it came to it, I daresay Jardine would be able to arrange to send money to him wherever he is. I had rather that than to see him —"

She broke off, leaving a depressed silence around the table. The slice of beef Ottilia was in the process of consuming became abruptly nauseating to her palate. Laying down her fork, she drank a little wine in hopes of damping the rise of discomfort in her stomach. Delayed shock? If the business could have this effect upon a virtual stranger, how much worse it must be for members of the family. The sooner she could set their minds at rest, the better pleased she would be. She had been dilatory today. No stone must be left unturned. No more time could be wasted.

The lateness of the hour was far less than it must have been upon the night when the dismaying events had taken place, but Ottilia was nevertheless conscious of an eerie sensation as she trod the empty spaces of the mansion. Strange shadows were thrown ahead and behind the light of her single candle in its silver holder, and when the flame swayed threateningly as she pushed open the door to the Blue Salon, she began to wish she had instead appropriated a candelabrum.

There was little to be noted in this, the grander of the two receiving rooms, situated across the hall from the parlour. The house being double-fronted, the two rooms were much of a size, but as Ottilia held the candle aloft, the sparse and austere furnishings set around the walls made this one appear much the larger. A door to one side led back into the dining parlour, cosier than it might have been due to the smallness of the table with its rounded ends. With its leaves extended, it would no doubt render the space as formal as the salon.

Ottilia left it by its main door and found herself back in the vestibule for the main staircase. She passed it and found the smaller lobby with the meaner stairs for domestic use and came to the last room on the ground floor, which proved to be a wood-panelled library. This was no doubt where Lord Polbrook conducted his business affairs, for a large desk dominated the room, which was otherwise lined with glass-fronted bookshelves.

Ottilia left it and contemplated the two

sets of stairs. She had been up the main staircase, of course, but not down, so she chose to follow this route first, in preference to the darker, and thus less welcome, staff stairway. One flight set her on a small landing with a door to the outside. There was no key. Peering through the window into the gloom beyond, she discerned the outline of a balustrade upon part of a stair. Shadows indicated the presence of one or two trees and a hedge.

A pulse began to thrum in Ottilia's throat. Here was a likely entrance point for a lover. He might be visible, but at that late hour of the night, would it matter? Who was to see him enter?

So far, so good. But she must not discount the other possibilities. Which meant she must brave the darkness of the basement and penetrate into the domestic quarters. Most of the servants were already abed, in preparation for an early start in the morning. Ottilia might count on making her exploration without interruption.

The thought of a lonely visit below stairs was not encouraging, however, and she was obliged to summon every ounce of that determination to achieve a swift resolution before she found courage to descend into the depths.

She looked downward from the landing on which she stood and drew a steadying breath. Come, what was so difficult? It was merely a copy of the floors above, and she already knew how they were laid out. There would be one door to the back, one to the front. She had only to traverse the corridor to each and that would be the end of it.

But when she reached the bottom of the main stairway, Ottilia immediately saw she was mistaken. She was confronted with a lobby, but a door separated her from the domestic staircase. She was facing a corridor, which appeared from this end to be devoid of doors to either side.

It was narrow and very dark. Ottilia's logic told her it must be in daily use and its appurtenances would be obvious by day. But logic played no part in the riffle of unease that travelled through her veins. This was precisely the sort of clandestine byway through which a lover might enter, and the thought that such a one might have made his escape down this very corridor after committing his brutal assault was disturbing in the extreme.

Ottilia was obliged to give herself a stern reminder that it was in the highest degree unlikely that any such marauder would return to the scene by this means, or indeed any other, before she found courage to proceed. Indeed, she very nearly turned tail, thinking to come back on the morrow. Only the reflection that very little daylight could penetrate here, rendering the place as unprepossessing by day as it was now, kept her from abandoning the project. Her mouth a little dry, she urged herself onward and slowly made her way along the passage, holding the candle high to throw the light as far ahead as she could.

Nothing untoward occurring within the first few yards, she grew bolder, stepping along smartly and keeping an eye out for any means of exit there might be. As it chanced, the only door lay ahead of her, and Ottilia paused when she saw it.

Ridiculous as it was, she had an almost overwhelming feeling that there was some-one on the other side. Without intent, she went on tiptoe to conceal her footsteps along the bare wooden boards. Creeping forward, she transferred her candle to the other hand, and gripping the handle of the door, turned it smartly and jerked it wide open.

A massive shadow on the passage wall ahead showed the figure of a man.

CHAPTER 6

Ottilia's heart jerked and her startled eyes shifted to the smaller silhouette that formed the origin of the shadow. She smothered a shriek, forcing herself to call out.

"Who is there?"

For an instant, before his candle went out, Ottilia caught his features.

"Abel!"

Then the door handle slipped from her grasp and the heavy door swung shut. For what felt like an age, she stood benumbed, struggling to recover herself, feeling the thrumming of her heartbeat. Presently she rallied, calling on common sense. Come, it was but a trick of the light. There was nothing to fear.

Gathering her forces, she reached out to the handle again and pulled the door open with a force engendered by fright. The solid body of a man confronted her, his bulk directly in the way. She flinched, but stood her ground. There was a brief pause, and then the man moved into the light of her candle. It was the butler.

"Is that you, madam?"

Ottilia stared at him blankly. "Cattawade?"

"Yes, madam." The butler coughed. "I did not expect to see you here, madam."

"Nor I you," said Ottilia with feeling. Had her senses so deceived her? She saw the holder in his hand with a candle half burned down, the wick of which was smoking. "Why did you put out your candle?"

"It was blown out by the draught when you opened the door, madam."

Blown out? At that distance? A tiny seed of confusion settled at the back of her mind, but she put it aside for the moment.

"Well, I beg your pardon for that, but I was so sure there was someone behind this door — and you see I was right. One should always trust one's instincts."

She offered him a light from her candle, and the additional glow was comforting. She discovered the horrid passage ended past the door, and she was in a roomy vestibule, from which several doors led off in each direction.

"May I ask what you are doing here, madam?" Cattawade asked, not without a touch of austerity.

"I wanted to check on the doors to the outside," Ottilia told him. "Where is the nearest to here?"

"The one at the front, madam."

"To the area?"

"That is correct, madam."

Ottilia eyed his rather puffy features in the semigloom. "Could you show me, if you please?"

The butler turned and gestured towards a heavy door behind him. "I have just locked it for the night, madam."

Ottilia did not miss the disapproving note in his voice, but she ignored it. "Well, perhaps you would be kind enough to unlock it again?"

He hesitated but an instant, and a resigned look came over his features. Turning, he went to the door, and Ottilia followed. It was a heavy door of coarser wood than the one leading to the garden, and it was unpainted. Cattawade turned the key and undid a couple of bolts. Then he opened it and held it for Ottilia to go through.

The little yard outside contained little besides a coal hatch and a narrow set of steps leading up to the street. This would be the easiest entry for a lover but for the bolts inside, which would require an accomplice within the house. Who but Mary

Huntshaw, in that case? But she had been told not to wait up that night.

Not dressed to face the elements, Ottilia shivered in the chill of the night. She came quickly back inside and watched the butler shoot the bolts and lock the door again. He turned to her.

"May I escort you back, madam?"

"You may not," said Ottilia flatly. "What other outside door is there down here?"

"Only the one to the yard."

"Lead me to it, if you please."

Cattawade hesitated. Then he bowed slightly and, turning, led the way through a different door than that through which she had arrived, revealing a second and much more open corridor, with doors leading off. One was ajar, and Ottilia caught a glimpse into the large kitchen. In a very short space of time, the space widened and she recognised the narrower of the staircases within a small lobby. The butler took a path that led directly past the stairway towards an outer door.

Holding her candle high, Ottilia noticed an opening in the stairwell. She halted, discovering a horrid-looking iron spiral stair that seemed to descend into the bowels of the earth.

"Where does this lead, Cattawade?"

The butler was in the act of unbolting the door, but he turned and looked where she pointed.

"The cellar, madam."

"Is there a door to the outside down there?"

He looked surprised. "Yes, madam, but it leads only to a small area below ground level."

Ottilia's heart skipped a beat. "I should like to see it, if you please."

The butler did not move, and the austerity of his features intensified. "I should not advocate it, madam."

She stared him out. "Why not?"

"The area merely contains the outside facilities for the use of the staff, and a narrow alleyway for the night soil men to carry away the refuse from the pit."

Ottilia understood his reluctance, but she continued to meet his gaze. "I should still like to see it."

Without further argument, but with a look that said clearly she had only herself to blame, Cattawade turned and led the way down the horrid iron stair. Ottilia had to steel herself to follow. She had to forego an instinct to cling tight to the railing, for she needed her free hand to hold up her skirts, and not for anything would she have abandoned her candle. Both sets of feet clanged on the steps in a manner hardly conducive to any clandestine intent.

At the bottom, the butler set down his candle and wrestled with several bolts. Once again, an accomplice in the house must leave the bolts open. But, Ottilia reasoned, a determined intruder could wait his moment for one of the servants to come out to use the privy or deposit a bucketful of ordure into the cesspit. There were enough dark corners down here for a man to lurk unseen.

The stench as the door opened was distinct, and Ottilia wrinkled her nose and held her breath. She stepped out behind Cattawade and immediately saw what he meant. The area was a mere square patch of gravelled ground, containing only a wooden shed, the purpose of which was obvious. Running down the side of the garden, an extremely narrow pathway led off towards the street, and from the look and smell of it, anyone venturing down there could expect to trail unpleasant debris upon his shoes. Hardly conducive to an amour with the lady of the house.

Spreading the light of her candle about, Ottilia saw that the area itself gave onto the yard above, or perhaps the gardens, but a surround of high iron railings with pointed tops looked to provide a substantial deterrent. It would take an agile and determined lover to scale them.

"Thank you, Cattawade."

Turning back into the house, Ottilia waited for the man to bolt the door again. Then she mounted the stairs ahead of him and stood aside for him to unlock the back door. A wide yard was revealed with a plethora of domestic accoutrements round about and two doors into a lean-to shed. The railings seen from below surrounded it on all sides. An iron gate opened onto a path that adjoined the gardens, and the lower railings to one side must, Ottilia reasoned, let into the alley she had just seen.

Three doors, and each had possibilities. In truth, any one of them might have been used, given particular circumstances. Which supported the notion of a lover having been with Emily on the fatal night.

The butler was waiting by the door, and Ottilia came inside and retraced her steps to the lobby. She eyed the narrow stairs with misgiving, and turned impulsively to Cattawade.

"Are you on your way to bed? Would you escort me? I have no mind to traverse the stairway on my own, and I must go all the way to the second floor."

The butler unbent a trifle. "Certainly, madam. It is very dark tonight."

Ottilia could not but feel that this escapade had lost her ground with Cattawade. She sought in her mind for an olive branch, for she needed the fellow in her camp. Useless to attempt to converse while he walked ahead of her up the narrow stair. To her relief, when they reached the ground floor, he led her through to the larger vestibule and started up the main staircase.

"Ah, this is better. Thank you, Cattawade. I am sorry to have incommoded you."

"Not at all, madam," said the elderly man, and there was less stiffness in his tone.

Ottilia halted as they arrived on the first floor vestibule and turned to the butler with a confiding air. "If I seem to you to be prying, I hope you will understand that I am merely trying to piece together the events of the other night."

Cattawade bowed. "So I have been informed, madam."

"You could help me a great deal."

A wary look came into his face. "In what way, madam?"

"Who knows the household better than you, Cattawade? Indeed, whose opinion of the marquis could I better trust? I sometimes think those long in service are more fully acquainted with their masters than are the immediate family."

In the harsher glare from a large candelabrum set on a small table in a corner of the vestibule, Ottilia was able to note the look of gratification that entered the butler's features. It always paid to credit people with more than their share of knowledge.

"I have known his lordship for a very long time," Cattawade conceded, a gracious note in his voice.

"Just so." Ottilia smiled at him, and then gave a start, as if she had recalled something. "If I had not forgot! Lord Francis thought you might be able to enlighten me as to what happened that morning before he came upon the scene. When were you first aroused, Cattawade?"

"I hardly know now." The butler thought for a moment. "I remember I was in the process of dressing myself, madam, when I heard Huntshaw's screams."

"What did you do?"

"I proceeded without delay down to this floor and discovered several persons outside her ladyship's bedchamber there."

"Who were they?"

"Huntshaw herself, madam. There were also Abel the footman and Diplock, my lord

Francis's valet."

"Was the housekeeper there, too?"

"Mrs. Thriplow arrived a moment or two after, I believe, along with the kitchen maid and the boots. For by the time I had gone in to ascertain the cause of Huntshaw's distress —"

"So you were the second person to see her ladyship's body?"

A faint look of doubt crept into the man's features. "I cannot be certain, madam. There were, as I say, others present already."

"Very well. And what did you do while you were in the bedchamber?"

"I opened the shutters and the windows, madam."

"Why? To bring light to the scene?"

A spasm crossed his face. "To let out the stench. I could see well enough."

A diminution of pallor told Ottilia he was not as composed as she had thought. Even the memory had shaken his urbanity. He must have been severely affected by what he had seen. She forbore to press the point.

"Did you touch anything else?"

"No, madam."

"And you did not go into the dressing room?"

"It did not occur to me to do so. The immediate necessity, it seemed to me, was to

151

apprise a member of the family of what had occurred. But my lord Francis came upon us before I had opportunity to do so."

Ottilia probed carefully. "Was it to Lord Francis you intended to carry the news?"

The butler nodded. "Yes, madam."

"Why not to your master, the marquis?"

Cattawade showed hesitation for the first time, his gaze sliding away from her. Then he shifted with surprise. Flicking a glance in that direction, Ottilia saw the dowager standing quietly in the doorway of the back bedchamber, attired in a dressing robe with a nightcap on her head. Ottilia went quickly across.

"My dear ma'am, I beg your pardon. Did we wake you?"

The dowager stepped out into the vestibule before Ottilia could reach her. "I was awake, but never mind that." She had evidently been there for several moments, for she approached the butler, upon whom her gaze was fixed. "Why did you not go straight to the master with this news, Cattawade?"

Ottilia rejoined them in time to note the butler's resumption of the rigidity of manner reserved for his calling. His answer was couched in the expressionless tone that gave nothing away.

"Because I knew his lordship had left the house, my lady."

The dowager sprang on this. "How did you know? Did you see him go?"

"No, my lady. But Foscot had roused me earlier. His lordship had called for two bottles of brandy to be taken to his chaise. There were none in the pantry, and I have the key to the wine cellar."

Ottilia tried to recover lost ground, speaking with exaggerated courtesy and friendliness. "Tell me, Cattawade, had you any idea of the time of night?"

To Ottilia's regret, the butler did not unbend in the slightest. He merely gave a fractional shake of the head. "No, madam. I took it to be some time around three or four, but I could not say for certain."

"Very well, let that pass. So you got up to fetch the bottles. Did you take them to your master?"

"No, madam. Foscot accompanied me and took them himself."

"That will not do, Cattawade," snapped the dowager. "I know your habits. You would consider it your duty to hand the bottles personally to his lordship. What should induce you to do otherwise?"

The butler did not flinch. "The knowledge, my lady, conveyed to me by Foscot,

153

that his lordship was in a foul temper."

"He was, was he?"

"Yes, my lady, he having quarrelled violently, according to Foscot, with her ladyship."

Ottilia eyed him with new interest. "And in the morning you discovered her ladyship murdered. What did you suppose, Cattawade?"

His eyes went to the dowager, and the mask slipped a little as his jowls reddened. "I confess, madam, I thought what anyone might think. It was not a welcome notion."

"It was a false one," the dowager returned on a harsh note.

"I am in hopes of so proving," Ottilia said, and gave the man her warmest smile.

For the first time in their dealings, the butler showed real emotion. The rims of his eyes gleamed and his mouth quivered. "I hope and trust you will, madam, for the horror of that suspicion haunts us all."

"I will do my best. And I am so grateful for your help, Cattawade. I am sure we will have occasion to talk again."

Her words, she was glad to see, had silenced the dowager, who shot her a sharp look. Ottilia hurriedly nodded dismissal to the butler, who bowed and circumspectly withdrew. She turned to her employer with a smile, ushering her back towards her bed-chamber, from which the glow of many candles set the vestibule alight.

"I am sorry to have been so thoughtless as to talk outside your chamber."

"I am only too glad to hear another voice," said the dowager, leading the way into the room. "Come in with me, my dear."

Ottilia entered behind her and saw at once that the truckle bed set up beside the four-poster was empty. "But where is Miss Venner?"

The dowager was climbing back into bed. The curtains were not drawn and there were candles burning on the mantel, on the night table, and in one of the wall sconces.

"In the dining parlour, I trust. I sent her to fetch me a glass of port." She settled herself against the pillows and patted the bedclothes beside her. "What have you been up to this late in the night?"

Obediently, Ottilia perched on the edge of the bed. "I thought it as well to seize opportunity at once and begin upon my explorations." She gave a brief account of what she had found. "Although I cannot think Colonel Tretower will do anything but pooh-pooh the suggestion that a lover came by any of these ways. Nor can I blame him, for each has its drawbacks."

To Ottilia's dismay, the dowager shivered. "Are you cold, ma'am?"

"To the bone," came the reply, "but not from lack of heat."

Her glance shifted, as if she tried to penetrate the wall separating this chamber from that of the late marchioness.

"Dear me, is it so very uncomfortable, ma'am?"

"To lie behind Emily's chamber? It is perfectly morbid, just as Francis said." Abruptly, she hit the pillow beside her with a clenched fist. "Why had this to happen? It is so cruel. Who could have done it? Who would be so vicious? Oh, it does not bear thinking of!"

Ottilia reached out, taking hold of that fist and cradling it. "Hush, ma'am. We will discover him, I promise you. The truth will come to light."

For several moments the dowager did not speak, her anguished gaze remaining fixed upon Ottilia's face. She bore the scrutiny without protest, aware that her employer's eye was concentrated rather on the inner turmoil of her emotions than on herself. At last the dowager spoke, and with weariness.

"I see that image of her ruined features and feel nothing. It is as if there is no reality in it, as if I dwelled in a dream."

156

Ottilia said nothing. This was the expected stupor, catching up at last with the elderly dame. It was perhaps merciful that the overburdened mind should close down for a while, leaving one numb. She was no stranger to the phenomenon.

"What is your given name?" asked the dowager abruptly. "It is absurd, after all that has passed, to be addressing you as 'Mrs. Draycott.' I feel as if I had known you forever."

"I know just what you mean," she returned warmly. "I would be only too happy if you will call me Ottilia."

The dowager's brows rose. "Yes, I remember now. Unusual. But I like it. It suits you."

"Why, thank you, ma'am."

"And you may address me as Sybilla."

Ottilia was startled. "Oh, I could not."

"I don't see why not. Teresa does so, and you are my companion."

"Yes, but Miss Mellis has been with you for many years, while I —"

"Have insinuated yourself into an intimacy unequalled by the wretched creature in all that time. No, I will hear no more argument, for my mind is made up."

Ottilia felt utterly discomposed. "But, my dear ma'am, it is scarcely respectful. In the circumstances —"

157

She was cut off without ceremony. "The circumstances are unprecedented."

Then, to Ottilia's great distress, the dowager's face crumpled and she leaned forward, holding out trembling hands.

"Oh, my dear child, can you not see how desperate I am for a friend?"

A tear slipped from under the dowager's lashes, and Ottilia could bear no more. "Sybilla! Oh, my poor dear."

And then her arms were enfolding the woman, who clung to her, dry sobs racking her thin body. Ottilia rocked her, hushing gently, much as she had done when one of her nephews had needed comfort. But this was a collapse she had not anticipated. The dowager appeared so strong, so assured. But to find her vulnerable after what she had endured should come as no surprise.

Within a few minutes the dowager's sobs abated, and Ottilia felt her resist the encircling arms. Releasing her, she hunted in her pocket for a handkerchief.

Sybilla took it with a word of thanks. "I am glad we are alone," she said a trifle shakily. "I should hate Francis to have seen me behaving like a watering pot."

"I am sure he would much dislike to see you distressed, ma'am."

"No, and I would not add to his troubles,

poor boy. This has brought a deal of unpleasant work upon him."

"Indeed," agreed Ottilia, relieved to note how Lord Francis had returned to favour. She added with deliberate cheer, "But he has been a soldier, I gather, and will know how to stand to battle."

"We must all do so, Ottilia."

"Very true. But for the present, dear Sybilla, I think you have stood enough, do not you?"

She had expected an argument, but the sound of the door opening forestalled it. The dowager contented herself with a sigh.

"Here is Venner with my port."

"In good time," said Ottilia, and rose to give place to the lady's maid by the bedside. "Good night, ma'am. Don't let the nightmare fright you too much, I beg."

Sybilla took the glass from her maid and sipped. "It will be well if we both sleep, Ottilia. We must needs conserve our strength."

Ottilia was relieved to hear the more normal acerbic note returning to the dowager's voice.

"Not only must we face the gossips in due time, but there is Candia to be thought of."

Venner started, catching Ottilia's attention, and she saw a flash of some violence

159

of emotion in the woman's face. But in a second, her customary sour expression returned. Ottilia's response to the dowager was made without thought as she continued a surreptitious survey of the lady's maid.

"Candia?"

"My granddaughter."

"Of course, I had forgot."

"The poor child will be distraught at losing her mother," said Sybilla. "I shudder to think what it will do to her to learn the manner of Emily's death."

Sleep was fitful, disturbed by strange dreams wherein dark passages and contorted faces juxtaposed with a series of odd conversations and a coach hurtling into the night with a clatter of hooves upon the cobbles. This last clashed so loudly in Ottilia's head that she woke, staring with unseeing eyes into the enclosing darkness of the bed-curtains. The clatter came again, transposing itself in her mind into something near at hand.

An instant later, she identified its source. No horse this, but the ordinary household sound of the chambermaid working at the grate in the fireplace. The happenings of the past couple of days tumbled into Ottilia's mind, and she fastened upon one piece of information she'd been given. Without thought, she reared up in the bed and flung back the curtains on one side.

"Sukey!"

The girl cried out, dropping her tools with a clang as she tried to turn sharply. Crouched as she was, the chambermaid lost her balance, threw out her hands to save herself, and ended up on all fours, staring up at Ottilia with starting eyes.

"Oh dear, I am sorry," exclaimed Ottilia, throwing herself out of bed and going quickly across. "Let me help you up."

Sukey allowed herself to be assisted to her feet, but she was clearly unsteady, her breathing shallow and fast, so that Ottilia felt obliged to keep a hand under her elbow to prevent her falling again.

"I am so very sorry," she said again. "I did not mean to startle you."

The girl found her tongue. "Ooh, miss, you give me a terrible fright! I thought it were the mistress, large as life again."

How this might be so in a chamber set in a separate floor of the house and on the other side to boot, Ottilia forbore to enquire. It was evident Sukey was a girl with a vivid imagination. She was a plump child, little more than fourteen or fifteen, Ottilia judged, with a quantity of bouncing dark

161

hair escaping from under the regulation cap and a pair of expressive pansy eyes that were undoubtedly destined to get her into a great deal of trouble. She was just the sort of girl to draw the opposite sex like a magnet.

"What a horrid thought," Ottilia said, with just that touch of drama to induce the chambermaid to develop her theme.

The girl nodded and sniffed, dragging her sleeve across her nose. "It give me the shivers, miss. I thought I were back in my lady's room, and her lying all cold and dead in the bed."

She sniffed again, but there were no tears in the wide eyes, and it was borne in upon Ottilia that she was suffering from a cold in the head.

"Goodness, how dreadful! I am sorry to have reminded you of such an experience."

Sukey gave an artistic shudder. "Summat awful, it were, miss. To think of my lady lying there all cold and stiff while I made up the fire! Fair makes my hair stand on end, miss."

"I am not at all surprised. It must have been quite shocking." She released the girl, confident the chambermaid was sufficiently recovered to stand on her own. "I don't suppose you heard anything while you were in the chamber, did you, Sukey?"

escaping from under the regulation cap
. pair of expressive pansy eyes that were
ubtedly destined to get her into a great
of trouble. She was just the sort of girl
aw the opposite sex like a magnet.

hat a horrid thought," Ottilia said, with
that touch of drama to induce the
bermaid to develop her theme.

girl nodded and sniffed, dragging her
across her nose. "It give me the shiv-
iss. I thought I were back in my lady's
, and her lying all cold and dead in the

sniffed again, but there were no tears
wide eyes, and it was borne in upon
that she was suffering from a cold in
ead.

odness, how dreadful! I am sorry to
eminded you of such an experience."

y gave an artistic shudder. "Summat
it were, miss. To think of my lady ly-
ere all cold and stiff while I made up
e! Fair makes my hair stand on end,

m not at all surprised. It must have
quite shocking." She released the girl,
ent the chambermaid was sufficiently
red to stand on her own. "I don't sup-
ou heard anything while you were in
amber, did you, Sukey?"

poor boy. This has brought a deal of unpleasant work upon him."

"Indeed," agreed Ottilia, relieved to note
how Lord Francis had returned to favour.
She added with deliberate cheer, "But he
has been a soldier, I gather, and will know
how to stand to battle."

"We must all do so, Ottilia."

"Very true. But for the present, dear Sybilla, I think you have stood enough, do not
you?"

She had expected an argument, but the
sound of the door opening forestalled it.
The dowager contented herself with a sigh.

"Here is Venner with my port."

"In good time," said Ottilia, and rose to
give place to the lady's maid by the bedside.
"Good night, ma'am. Don't let the nightmare fright you too much, I beg."

Sybilla took the glass from her maid and
sipped. "It will be well if we both sleep,
Ottilia. We must needs conserve our
strength."

Ottilia was relieved to hear the more
normal acerbic note returning to the dowager's voice.

"Not only must we face the gossips in due
time, but there is Candia to be thought of."

Venner started, catching Ottilia's attention, and she saw a flash of some violence

of emotion in the woman's face. But in a second, her customary sour expression returned. Ottilia's response to the dowager was made without thought as she continued a surreptitious survey of the lady's maid.

"Candia?"

"My granddaughter."

"Of course, I had forgot."

"The poor child will be distraught at losing her mother," said Sybilla. "I shudder to think what it will do to her to learn the manner of Emily's death."

Sleep was fitful, disturbed by strange dreams wherein dark passages and contorted faces juxtaposed with a series of odd conversations and a coach hurtling into the night with a clatter of hooves upon the cobbles. This last clashed so loudly in Ottilia's head that she woke, staring with unseeing eyes into the enclosing darkness of the bedcurtains. The clatter came again, transposing itself in her mind into something near at hand.

An instant later, she identified its source. No horse this, but the ordinary household sound of the chambermaid working at the grate in the fireplace. The happenings of the past couple of days tumbled into Ottilia's mind, and she fastened upon one piece of

160

information she'd been g
thought, she reared up in th
back the curtains on one sid
"Sukey!"

The girl cried out, droppin
a clang as she tried to
Crouched as she was, the cha
her balance, threw out her
herself, and ended up on al
up at Ottilia with starting ey

"Oh dear, I am sorry," ex
throwing herself out of b
quickly across. "Let me help

Sukey allowed herself to be
feet, but she was clearly
breathing shallow and fast,
felt obliged to keep a hand u
to prevent her falling again.

"I am so very sorry," she
did not mean to startle you."

The girl found her tongue
you give me a terrible frigh
were the mistress, large as life

How this might be so in a
a separate floor of the hous
other side to boot, Ottilia forb
It was evident Sukey was a g
imagination. She was a plun
more than fourteen or fi
judged, with a quantity of b

161

Sukey shook her head vehemently. "I've a cold in me head, miss, and me ears weren't working good."

"I don't suppose you saw very much, either?" Ottilia surmised, crossing to the door to retrieve her dressing robe from a hook and shrugging it on. It was cold, the chambermaid having been interrupted before she could get the fire going properly, but this was not the moment to draw her attention to the fact.

"I didn't see nothing but the bed-curtains, miss. Closed they were, like always." Her eyes grew rounder. "But I felt summat."

"What did you feel?"

"Ooh, it were like the time me little brother shoved a piece of ice down me back, miss." She shuddered again. "Like as if I knowed there were summat wrong."

Ottilia knew the propensity of people to be wise after the event, but she saw no reason to doubt the girl. A lively imagination did not preclude the possession of a sixth sense. She shifted tack.

"Can you remember what time it was when you were doing her ladyship's room?"

The question seemed to throw Sukey, who blinked owlishly. "I start at six, miss."

Ottilia smiled. "Yes, but I take it you do not start in her ladyship's room."

163

"Oh no, miss. I've the downstairs parlours to do first, so's they're warm when anyone comes down."

"Very well, what time do you usually finish?"

"After seven, miss, depending."

"Depending on what?"

"Who's in the house, miss. But I've to be back downstairs afore eight to help Jane get the dining parlour ready for breakfast."

"Then you must have been in her ladyship's chamber somewhere between, say, half past six and a little after seven?"

"Yes, miss." The reminder proved unfortunate, sending her back to a familiar theme. "Ooh, miss. To think she were lying dead there all the time while I were poking flinders in the flames!"

"It was horrid for you," Ottilia soothed as patiently as she could. "It would be better to try not to think of it."

"I can't help it, miss," Sukey protested. "It's like as if I knew. Only I couldn't do nothing for her if I had. It were too late."

A note of hysteria had crept into the child's voice, and Ottilia gentled her tone. "There is no need to distress yourself. You could not have known, Sukey."

The girl struck her hands together and her whole face brightened, as if a sudden

164

thought had attacked her.

"I did know, miss, I did. I never thought it before, but I couldn't hear her, miss. I couldn't hear her breathing."

Ottilia stared. Of course! The chambermaid performed the same chore, day after day, like clockwork. She would not have realised how every sound and sight must be imprinted in her memory. She had no need of a sixth sense. The lack of one item in the familiar pattern had penetrated without full awareness.

Sukey stood like a stock, as if lost in her own recognition. Then a change came and her pansy eyes widened.

"I heard the clock. On the mantel."

Intent now, Ottilia eyed her. "When, Sukey?"

"When I were outside the door, miss. I were that glad to get out, I stood a minute for me heart was beating so fast, I was afeared as I'd swoon."

"And you heard the clock. Did it chime?"

The girl nodded wildly. "It ain't nowise loud. It's like a little tinkle, chiming the hour."

"Seven o'clock then."

"Must have been, miss. It don't chime but the once. When I hear it of a morning if I'm in there, I know I'm near finished."

"Oh, well done, Sukey. That is most helpful."

Sukey beamed. That she understood the significance of her words was doubtful, but she blossomed under the praise. Ottilia thanked her profusely.

"I am sorry to have kept you. I'm afraid you will finish late this morning."

"It don't matter, miss," said the chambermaid airily, kneeling to the fire again. "I've only the range to do after, and it ain't going nowhere."

Ottilia laughed and, throwing back the curtains around the bed, climbed into it again, wondering if it was too early for a maid to bring hot water for her ablutions. Since she was now wide awake, she could fill in the time until breakfast by resuming her exploration of the house, although she did not wish to get in the way of the servants who would be busy at this hour. Undecided, she nevertheless stopped the chambermaid as she was about to leave the room.

"Sukey, would you be kind enough to ask one of the maids to bring my hot water up early?"

"Yes, miss. If the copper's been set on the fire, which ain't nowise certain," said the chambermaid frankly. "The whole house is that upset, Mrs. Thriplow says as how it'll be topsy-turvy for days." On which ominous note, the chambermaid bid Ottilia a cheerful good morning and retired, armed with her bucket of coals.

Proof of the housekeeper's prophecy was rapidly evident. The copper had undoubtedly been nowhere near the fire at its usual time, for no hot water appeared in Ottilia's chamber until past nine o'clock, and she had perforce to abandon her scheme of checking the rest of the house. It was going on for ten by the time she joined the dowager in the dining parlour, where a small round table set between the two windows had been covered with a cloth and laid for breakfast.

"If you are hoping for sustenance," said Sybilla by way of greeting, "you may find yourself disappointed. I have been waiting more than half an hour already. Thriplow was not exaggerating. The whole place has gone to pieces."

"So I have been led to believe," agreed Ottilia smilingly. "Inevitable, in the circumstances."

"I'll give them inevitable," promised the dowager fiercely. "There is no reason in the world for such slackness."

"Come now, ma'am. Do you expect the

servants to be any less discomposed by these events than ourselves?"

"No, I expect them to be more so," came the tart response. "They thrive on such happenings."

"Well, yes. Despicable as it may seem, I daresay it brings excitement into lives otherwise drab beyond bearing."

Ottilia came under a glare from the dowager's black eyes. "Must you always stress the very thing I prefer to ignore?"

Laughing, Ottilia begged her pardon. "Do I do that? How very irritating it must be."

Sybilla flicked a hand at her. "There you go again. It is for me to speak of my irritation, not you."

Ottilia eyed her narrowly. "You slept badly, ma'am?"

The dowager sighed deeply and her pose of injured defiance collapsed. "Appallingly. I could not swear to it that I closed my eyes at all, but I suppose I must have done."

"Oh dear," said Ottilia, contrite. "Did not Venner's presence help? Perhaps I should not have suggested the move."

"Yes, you should," snapped Sybilla. "Do you suppose I cannot endure a few sleepless nights?"

"Not if even one makes you as crotchety as this," said Ottilia frankly.

A faint laugh escaped the dowager. "My dear Ottilia, if you have a fault, it is in being so ruthlessly right all the time. Are you never at a loss?"

Ottilia smiled. "Frequently, ma'am. At this moment, in fact, for I have been awake since seven and I am ravenous. But I feel it to be grossly unfair to the domestic staff to be complaining of it."

"Well, so do I not," stated Sybilla, reaching for a silver hand bell set in the middle of the table and plying it with some violence. "That should shake them up a bit."

The door did indeed open within a very short space of time, but not to admit the butler, as might have been expected, or even one of the maids. Instead, a well-dressed matron sailed into the dining parlour like a perfumed whirlwind, flinging herself upon the dowager in a flurry of passionate words and hugging the elder dame to her bosom.

"Oh, Mama, it is so dreadful. I was afraid you would be prostrate. I was ready to swoon myself when I read Fanfan's letter. How terrible it all is!"

CHAPTER 7

Sybilla struggled to extricate herself. "Let me go, Harriet, I cannot breathe."

The visitor released her, only to throw her arms wide in a gesture of despair. "There is no bearing it. Poor Emily, what a horrible way to die!"

The dowager waved her towards an unoccupied chair. "Sit down, child, for heaven's sake, and stop fidgeting me."

Ottilia was obliged to suppress a sneaking amusement at the other's look of slight deflation, but as the creature shifted to take the indicated chair she caught sight of Ottilia and halted abruptly.

"But who is this?"

"My new companion," said Sybilla shortly. "Did I not write to you of Teresa breaking her leg?"

"Oh, of course, I had forgot."

Ottilia was treated to a bright smile, which instantly reminded her of Lord Francis and gave the lie to the visitor's harrowed air. Not that Ottilia supposed her insincere, but it was immediately apparent she was a flighty piece with a butterfly mind.

"Delighted to make your acquaintance," she said blithely, offering her hand.

"My daughter, the Countess of Dalesford," supplied Sybilla.

"I come between Randal and Francis." Ottilia took the hand and introduced herself. "I take it Lord Francis wrote to you?"

"Yes, and I set off at once, as you may imagine, and arrived late last night," responded Lady Dalesford, seating herself in a whirl of silken petticoats. "Dalesford wished me to wait upon his escort, for he had business to attend to before he could leave the estate, but I would not hear of it. 'How could I leave poor Mama to bear this alone for one more day?' I said, and Dalesford supposed she had Francis for support, but I knew he had the intention of fetching poor Candia, so that would not answer, and so I told him."

"You need not have rushed," interpolated the dowager, taking advantage of her daughter's drawing breath, "for I have Ottilia, who is more than adequate for my purposes."

"Oh, I am sure she is everything that is

desirable," uttered the creature, waving expressive hands, "but a stranger is not the same."

"Very true," said Ottilia before the dowager could cut in again. "I am sure her ladyship will be the better for your support, Lady Dalesford."

"I will need it if I have sunk back to 'her ladyship.' "

Ottilia laughed. "I do beg your pardon, ma'am, I had forgot."

At this point, the door opened again to admit the butler, accompanied by the footman and a maid. All three were laden with trays, the contents of which they proceeded to set out, while the countess resumed the direction of the conversation.

"What in the world possessed you to come here, Mama? I went directly to Bruton Street this morning, but Gipping told me you had removed. Could anything be more macabre?"

Lady Dalesford gave a shudder, which Ottilia found quite as artistic as Sukey's. She had disposed her elegant person in a picturesque fashion that Ottilia guessed had become a habit. But her advent was opportune, providing the dowager with a distraction from the tardiness of the servants that Ottilia at least welcomed.

It provided Ottilia equally with an opportunity to subject Abel the footman to a surreptitious examination. The glimpse she'd had of a face behind the door before Cattawade was revealed had been fleeting, and since Ottilia had seen the footman but once before, she could not be at all certain of having identified his features. She had learned to trust her senses, but at this fresh sight of Abel she fell prey to doubt.

"I had a very good reason for removing from Bruton Street," the dowager was saying. "Someone had to take control of this household with Francis away and Emily gone."

A utensil she was just about to set down fell from the maid's nerveless fingers. Ottilia quickly reached to pick it up and hand it back to her, glad that Lady Dalesford's immediate response prevented Sybilla from noticing.

"I declare, I could weep to think of Emily now, little though we cared for each other."

"Pray do not go about telling that to the world," said her mother roundly. "Bear in mind that we are all in deep mourning."

Lady Dalesford threw up her hands. "Gracious heaven! I never thought to bring my blacks, such a rush as I was in. You are perfectly right, Mama. But what about you?

Why have you not gone into black?"

"Venner is going to fetch my sewing woman tomorrow."

"But it will be days before she can make you a gown."

"She can make over one of my old ones," said the dowager dismissively. "Since I am not receiving, it is not yet of moment."

"Well, I cannot possibly be seen like this," declared the countess, nodding to Cattawade who had placed a cup for her and had the coffee pot poised. "What in the world would people say? I shall have to have Celeste make up a suitable gown immediately. I declare, I loathe wearing black, but I daresay it may not be so bad if she will fashion it up to the minute."

Her mother cut in sharply. "Save yourself the trouble. I have an excellent scheme in mind, and it will spare you the cost of a new gown." She turned to the butler, who had just filled her cup. "Thank you, Cattawade, we will serve ourselves."

As the butler signed to his minions, Ottilia glanced rapidly from his face to the footman's. Was there any slight resemblance? Could she possibly have seen in Cattawade's jowled features the vibrant good looks of the younger man?

And then Abel, letting the maid precede

him, was through the aperture, and the butler withdrew behind them both. Ottilia stared at the closed door, still trying, with scant success, to fit one image on top of the other.

"When Francis returns, Harriet, you will go home and take Candia with you."

Over the rim of her coffee cup, the countess's face fell. "Oh no, must I? Yes, I suppose I must, poor child."

"You are better placed than I to take care of her," pursued the dowager, reaching for a breakfast roll and requesting Ottilia to pass the butter.

Ottilia thrust her problem to the back of her mind and concentrated on Sybilla's discourse.

"And the presence of her cousins will help to divert Candia's mind."

Lady Dalesford shivered and waved away the basket of bread rolls Ottilia was offering. "No, I thank you, I could not possibly eat a thing. How could anything divert Candia's mind from this horror? I am sure I shall not sleep for weeks."

Ottilia was beset by unseemly amusement and had all to do to hide it. Everything the countess said and did had a flourish that attracted interest. But if it had once been so by design, it had clearly become so much a part of the creature that Ottilia did not believe it was studied affectation. It was decidedly endearing, and she warmed to the woman.

"You are not in question," said her mother flatly, spreading butter on her roll with a lavish hand. "And the horror of the situation is precisely what we wish to minimise, as far as Candia is concerned."

"Yes, yes, I see that," instantly returned the other, sipping her coffee. "We must strive to behave as normally as possible. Oh, and what of her come-out?"

"It will have to be put off for another year."

"Gracious, yes! But even then, with Emily gone —" She broke off, suddenly setting down her cup. "Lord, I will have to do it myself!"

"Well, there is nothing to concern you in that," said her mother. "You may bring her out with your own daughter. What could be better?"

Lady Dalesford waved a dismissive hand, a mannerism wholly reminiscent of her mother, Ottilia noted as she began upon her own repast.

"That, yes. I may as well bring out two girls as one, and my Lizzy can have no objection. But have I to take Emily's place in all things? Oh, Mama, I don't feel as though I can."

Ottilia could not refrain from entering the lists. "Of course you cannot be all things to the girl. But you can be her loving aunt, as I am sure you are. She will very soon become accustomed to depend upon you just as much as she needs to do. Young people are very adaptable, do you not find?"

Looking quite astonished, Lady Dalesford stared at her in silence for a brief moment. Ottilia was relieved to hear the dowager chuckle.

"You will have to get used to Ottilia. She has a keen mind and cannot help exercising it at the expense of everyone with whom she comes in contact."

"Why, thank you, Sybilla," Ottilia returned on a dry note. "I am sure that will reconcile Lady Dalesford in an instant."

The countess gave an embarrassed little laugh. "You must forgive me. I am so used to Teresa, who never says boo to a goose, that I was surprised just for the moment."

"You may as well prepare to be bowled over, for we are relying on Ottilia to uncover the murderer." The dowager swallowed down a portion of bread roll. "Which is another reason why we cannot be doing with Candia on the premises. She will hamper our investigations."

Lady Dalesford's mouth dropped open. "Investigations? What in the world can you mean?"

Ottilia, biting into a roll liberally laced with a delicious blackberry jam, glanced across at the dowager. Did she mean to enlighten her daughter? The fewer people to be apprised of their purposes, the better. Particularly a creature whose discretion might be suspect. Not that she was likely to let anything fall on purpose, but her tongue was clearly not under her full control.

The dowager was frowning. "How much did Francis tell you?"

"Oh, the bare bones, I imagine. That poor Emily was dead." A little shiver shook the countess as she added, "Strangled in her own bed. And that matters were complicated because Randal was away. Oh, and that he was going to fetch Candia."

For a moment the dowager did not speak, only sipping thirstily at her coffee. Ottilia thought she was weighing what she might say. At length she set down her cup and sighed.

"There is no point in keeping it from you, but you must be careful not to give Candia an inkling of what we suspect."

Her daughter's eyes grew round with apprehension. "Suspect? Suspect what?"

"Randal departed for France in the early hours of that very morning. And Emily was killed, as far as we know, around the same time."

The implication hit, and Lady Dalesford drew in breath sharply. "No! Oh no, Mama. He cannot have done it. Not Randal. It isn't possible."

"Unfortunately, it is quite possible. Not that I believe it for a moment. But until we can prove the contrary, Randal remains suspect."

The flat tone had its effect. It occurred to Ottilia that the reality of the situation had not fully penetrated Lady Dalesford's mind until this moment. Which accounted for the superficial response she had hitherto demonstrated. Her features blanched and anguish showed in her eyes. When she spoke, there was a tremor in her voice.

"Oh, poor children. Poor, poor children. Yes, I will take Candia away. She must not know of this. And Giles?"

"Francis has sent for him. I don't know what he wrote, but Jardine is pledged to have a messenger find Giles and bring him home."

Ottilia quietly rose and refilled the countess's cup. "A little more coffee, ma'am?"

There was a blind look in her eyes as they found Ottilia. Dark eyes in a vibrant face, framed by locks of a darker hue than her brother's, but with the same rich texture.

"Coffee? Oh — yes, thank you."

Returning to her chair, Ottilia took care to adopt a matter-of-fact tone. "I am glad you are come, Lady Dalesford, for there is much to be done. Is it your intention to stay here?"

"No, I —" She seemed to have difficulty concentrating. "I had not thought."

"Harriet has a very good town house of her own," the dowager interposed.

"No doubt, but I wondered if perhaps her ladyship might be willing to assist you with the disposal of the marchioness's effects."

The countess had lifted the refilled cup to her lips, but at these words, her fingers shook perceptibly and she was obliged to set it down. There was a distinct quiver at her lips as she spoke.

"Meddle with Emily's things? Oh, I had rather not."

Sybilla pounced on this. "Don't be such a ninny, Harriet. If I can bear it, so can you. Besides, I had far rather trust to you than that featherbrained Huntshaw. She may do the heavy work."

Lady Dalesford looked decidedly mulish.

"But surely it is for Randal to —"

Her mother snorted. "We cannot possibly wait for Randal. And I am perfectly certain he will want nothing to do with such an enterprise. You know very well how distant were relations between those two."

"Then that is settled," said Ottilia, taking up her discarded roll again and turning to the dowager. "Why do you not go with your daughter to her house, ma'am, while she removes? I am sure you must have much to say to each other. And it will do you good to be an hour or two out of this atmosphere, do you not think?"

"Oh yes, Mama, do come with me. I am sure I should be the better for your company, for I am so overset, I scarcely know what I am doing."

But Sybilla had no attention to spare for her daughter. Her keen gaze raked Ottilia. "And what are you proposing to do once you have me safely out of the way?"

Ottilia preserved her countenance. "My dear ma'am, I cannot imagine what gave you the notion that I wanted you out of the way."

"You need not dissemble. I suppose you will be off questioning the servants without me."

The accusatory tone made Ottilia smile.

"To be frank with you, ma'am, I believe I may make more headway on my own." She was obliged to interrupt an indignant retort. "Do not bite my head off, ma'am. All I meant was that the servants are more likely to open up when they are not confronted with the marquis's mother."

A reluctant sigh was drawn from the dowager and her little spurt of defiance died. "That I cannot deny. Very well, do as you wish. But I will want a full report."

"Of course. But in any event I will question no one today, for I must take a last careful inspection of the marchioness's bedchamber to ensure all is safe to be removed and packed away."

Ottilia became aware that Lady Dalesford, apparently recovering from her stupefaction, was looking in puzzlement from one to the other.

"Do we seem to be talking in riddles, ma'am?"

The countess did not answer this directly. "You are questioning the servants?"

"Of course she is questioning the servants. How else are we to find out what happened?"

"But if Randal —"

"We are not dealing in 'if,' Harriet. We must proceed on the assumption that Randal did not kill his own wife."

Lady Dalesford covered her eyes with one hand. "How can you, Mama?"

"Did you expect me to be mealymouthed? Nothing is to be gained by refusing to look at the thing squarely."

"Yes, but —"

"But nothing. Emily is dead. Randal has vanished. If Ottilia cannot find evidence to support the view that her death has nothing to do with his departure, I may live to see my son tried by a jury of his peers. I have faced that, and so must you."

The countess, surging up from her chair, brushed this aside. "What I am trying to ask you, Mama, is why this burden falls upon Ottilia — oh, I beg your pardon, Mrs. Draycott."

"Pray don't. We need not stand upon ceremony."

"No, well, be that as it may, if Randal has gone, why in the world is Francis not the one to undertake these investigations?"

"Because your brother, competent as he has shown himself in dealing with the aftermath of this horrible affair, has not Ottilia's genius."

Here Ottilia felt bound to intervene. "I wish you will not say such things, ma'am. You will give Lady Dalesford an entirely erroneous impression." She looked directly at the countess. "Your dismay is perfectly understandable, ma'am. Your mother exaggerates. If I have a knack, it lies perhaps in observing what others might not. And in this particular, as I have already had occasion to explain, I can more readily observe because I am not intimately involved."

Lady Dalesford did not appear to be convinced. Her brows went up. "My dear Mrs. Draycott, if you have impressed my mother enough for her to be calling you a genius, I am ready to believe you possess far more than a 'knack.' " All at once she smiled, reaching out across the table to grasp Ottilia's hands. "I must thank you. If you can indeed find out the truth and clear my brother of suspicion, I shall join in singing your praises to the skies."

Ottilia laughed and pressed the hands holding hers before releasing them. "I must beg you will do no such thing. And although I am satisfied there is sufficient evidence to support the belief that your brother is innocent, I cannot persuade myself that it will convince a jury."

"Then pray do all in your power to change that view."

Ottilia thanked her, and refrained from pointing out that until another suspect had been discovered, nothing would avail to determine Lord Polbrook's complete innocence.

It was no bad thing, Ottilia felt, to send mother and daughter off together. There must be a deal to say upon the event that was not for the ears of a virtual stranger. She hoped Sybilla might be encouraged to unburden herself of the distresses that had come upon her these few days. Hard to believe so little time had passed, so eventful seemed the period.

As she climbed the stairs on her way towards the late marchioness's bedchamber, Ottilia wondered whether Lord Francis had yet reached Bath. He had opted to drive his own curricle and four, saying it would make for better speed, despite the disadvantage of having to secure suitable teams at the various stages. The marquis kept no horses on that route, although Lord Francis had said that he believed his brother stabled pairs all along the road to Portsmouth. Which confirmed the likelihood of his having gone by that way, since it was clearly a route he took frequently. Ottilia made little headway in calculating how long it might take Lord Francis to get back with his niece, especially taking into account the likely condition of the roads, and was dismayed to discover in herself an eagerness for his return.

This was absurd. She must suppose it to be mere impatience to communicate her findings. Not that these were in any way substantial. Indeed, she could hardly be said to have found out very much at all. The potential entry point for a lover was spurious, to say the least. And all one could take from what Sukey had told her was the certainty that at seven o'clock the marchioness was already dead. Which was substantially proven, according to the doctor's calculations.

Ottilia found it in her to be glad, after all, that there was little likelihood of seeing Lord Francis for a day or so, giving her more time. It would be decidedly embarrassing, after the buildup she had been given, to have so little to show for her efforts.

Arrived at the fatal chamber, she slipped a hand through to the pocket beneath her gown and groped for the key. Fitting it into the lock, she hesitated briefly before going in, unable to resist a glance back into the vestibule to check she was not observed. There was no one in sight, and she swiftly turned the handle, removed the key, and entered, locking the door again from the inside.

Turning, Ottilia noticed the bed-curtains had been pulled open on three sides, no doubt by the undertakers to facilitate the removal of the body. The bed linen had been drawn down the bed, but was otherwise undisturbed. She glanced across to the chaise longue. The silken dressing robe was just where it had been left. Looking to the mantel, she found the clock to which Sukey had referred: a small gilt case clock with an ornately decorated face. To either side were delicate china figures. Emily, Lady Polbrook, had been a woman of feminine taste, it seemed.

This notion was borne out by a painting above the fireplace of an idyllic country scene of nymphs upon a picnic, a charming set of miniatures upon one wall, and the ornate and gilded design framing the long mirror. The bed-curtains, which Ottilia had not taken in upon her previous visit, were of deep blue velvet, but the posts and tester were painted white and covered in gilt. Ottilia began to suspect that the occupant of the room, despite the gruesome ugliness of her corpse, had been in life a handsome creature. There must, Ottilia thought, be somewhere a portrait of the dead woman. She would seek it out.

Meanwhile, there was work to be done. There was nothing to be gained by inspecting the bed. The soiled linen must be thoroughly scrubbed, although Ottilia might suggest to the dowager the advisability of burning the sheets, or giving them away to the poor. She was not easily dismayed, but the thought of using them caused a riffle of disgust she was certain would be echoed by anyone in the house.

The chest at the foot of the bed boasted many pairs of shoes set neatly side by side and one atop the other, with several parasols laid behind them. Ottilia made a cursory inspection of the night table cupboard housing the chamber pot, and turned her attention to its single drawer above. This proved to contain little more than a bible, a few discarded hairpins, a large key that excited her immediate attention, the stub end of an old candle, and a few oddments of paper, scribbled with notes. Ottilia had no hesitation in reading them, but found nothing incriminating. The flowery hand that had written them was of interest, and there was but one of potential significance.

It was a scrap torn from a sheet, and on it had been written a single letter and three numbers: Q230.

Ottilia stared at it for several moments.

There was nothing to say it had any bearing on the night in question. Indeed, it almost certainly had not, since it was buried under a selection of other notes, most of which appeared to be matters relating to the household, reminders — one to speak to Thriplow, for example, or a list of ladies' names perhaps for an invitation. But this was a curious item. Ottilia pocketed it, slipping the rest of the papers back into the drawer.

Shifting her attention to the key, she turned it over and over in her hands, recalling the dowager's notion that an enterprising woman might supply one to a lover. Was this a key to an outer door? It appeared heavy enough, yet was not so bulky that it could not be concealed in a pocket beneath a gown, as Ottilia found when it followed the slip of paper into her own. She debated whether to keep it there, but decided it was safer where she had found it and slipped the key back in the drawer. She must warn the dowager to leave its contents untouched.

She shut the drawer and headed for the dressing room, which was where she expected at least to find more clues to enable her to form a clearer picture of the late marchioness's character. The underclothing flung with haste upon the floor still lay where it had fallen, and Ottilia let it be. Also untouched was the open drawer of the dressing commode, with its collection of glass pots, several left open with their silver lids scattered and flecks of colour spattering over everything. The marchioness, it was evident, had been a woman of untidy habits.

Not so her personal maid. Ottilia opened the larger clothes press, one of a set veneered, like the dressing commode, with oriental lacquer. She found gowns, bodices, and petticoats folded with meticulous care and laid up in perfect order, each item in its allotted place in the trays lined with marbled paper. She would swear the late Lady Polbrook's impatient fingers had touched nothing here that night.

Turning to the second, Ottilia found a similar pattern of order, where her ladyship's bonnets were carefully stowed together with a selection of pelisses and scarves. In the drawers under the press cupboards were found her ladyship's undergarments: stays, shifts, and stockings, together with her night attire and those accoutrements necessary to a lady's complete appearance.

Finally there was a modest old-fashioned chest of drawers. As Ottilia opened the top drawer, it was immediately apparent that within it a hasty hand had rummaged, throwing out of kilter a selection of frivolous accessories.

Ottilia looked without touching, noting gloves with strings tangled about them, handkerchiefs thrown pell-mell, indeterminate articles of silken sheen twisted about one another. Poking through the mêlée was a satin garter, one of an embroidered pair of pockets, and the edge of a bejewelled mask.

Had the fingers that wrought this shambles belonged to the marchioness? What could she have needed in this motley collection? If her purpose was an assignation with her lover, these seemed scarcely the sort of accessories through which to be hunting. A garter? Ottilia conjured the image of the woman's dead body into her mind. She'd worn no stockings. Had they been discarded along with the other undergarments? She looked across to the untidy pile on the floor. Had Emily taken them off at that time they would be on top, and no such accoutrement was visible. No, they must have been removed later. In which case, where were they? And where indeed were the garters that had held them up?

Crossing swiftly through to the bedchamber, Ottilia pulled the bedclothes down. Wrinkling her nose at the revived odour and the myriad stains, she gingerly twitched the sheet. Nothing. With a mental note to make a thorough search for the missing stockings before delivering the room up to the dowager's ministrations, she went back to the dressing room to study the drawer again. Dismissing the notion of the marchioness needing a garter, she looked over the rest of its visible contents.

Were there fans in here? No, that made no sense, for had not Mary Huntshaw seen the fan that was a Polbrook heirloom discarded among the paints and powders? Without rummaging herself, Ottilia could see nothing that might aid a woman in the expectation of entertaining a man in her bedchamber. Yet if Emily had not hunted through this drawer, who had?

There was only one way to find out. Going through to the bedchamber, Ottilia looked about for the bellpull. Seeing it, she crossed and tugged upon it with vigour. Then she went back into the dressing room to check the other three drawers of the chest. There were fans aplenty, knots of ribbon, gloves and strings, mittens and muffs, fur tippets, feathered headdresses, knotting-bags, artificial flowers, girdles, and trinkets.

In a word, all the little accessories indispensable to the lady's needs. But everything was neat and orderly, nothing out of place.

Ottilia was about to return to the dressing commode to examine the glass pots when footsteps sounded without and an unseen hand tried the door handle. The key to the dressing room was still with Lord Francis. Ottilia went into the bedchamber and unlocked the door. Opening it, she found Huntshaw at the dressing room door in the little lobby outside the chamber, looking white and fearful. She let out a sighing breath, clapping a hand to her bosom.

"Oh, it's you, miss."

"Indeed it is," said Ottilia lightly. "What, did you suppose your mistress had risen from the dead?"

The woman shivered. "I didn't know what to think, miss. It gave me such a turn when the bell went."

"I hope you will pardon me for having startled you, Mary, but I need your help."

The maid's mouth drooped. "Is it — is it time to be sorting my lady's things?"

"Not now," Ottilia said gently, laying a hand on her arm. "And you need have no apprehension. The task is to be undertaken by the Dowager Lady Polbrook and Lady Dalesford. You will merely assist them."

These tidings made Huntshaw look, if anything, even more fearful. "Then what do you want of me, miss?"

"Come with me, if you please."

Ottilia led the way to the dressing room, noting how Mary shuddered as her glance fell upon the disordered bed. The sooner it was cleared up and the memories laid to rest, the better. But the open drawer proved an immediate distraction.

"Lordy, what a mess!"

"Just so, Mary." She put out a restraining hand as the woman's fingers reached towards the drawer. "Don't touch it! At least not yet."

Huntshaw looked at her. "I hope you don't think I left it in that state, miss."

Ottilia smiled her reassurance. "I have seen enough of your handiwork to know you could not have done. What I wish to ask is whether you think her ladyship might have searched for something in this drawer."

"Not she," said Mary without hesitation. "If my lady had been in there, she would have left the drawer open and the things all strewn about, and I'll stake my life it weren't open when I came in that morning."

"That is rather what I suspected. Besides, I cannot think what she could have wanted among this stuff, can you?"

"Nothing, miss. Nor I don't think she'd have been wishful to have put on any jewellery, for I'd already laid up what she was wearing that night."

Ottilia's heart skipped a beat. "Jewellery? She kept jewellery in this drawer?"

Mary's mind had obviously leapt to the same conclusion that was jangling in Ottilia's. A horrified expression came into her eyes and she reached out immediately towards the drawer. Remembering, she looked to Ottilia.

"Shall I — ?"

"Yes, for heaven's sake, look!"

She watched in rising trepidation as the woman pulled the drawer out further, thrust aside the intervening articles with trembling fingers, and reached deep into the back. Ottilia could tell by the changing expressions on her face as her arm swept back and forth that her worst fears were confirmed.

Huntshaw withdrew her hand, staring blankly at Ottilia. "It's not there, miss."

CHAPTER 8

Ottilia gazed at the woman. "Do you mean a jewel box?"

The maid nodded, her eyes becoming frantic, as she once again thrust her hand into the drawer and hunted with increasing panic as she spoke.

"It's a wooden box but covered in velvet so's no one would think anything of it. My lady kept the key on a chain around her neck. Except at night. She put it in the little drawer beside her bed."

"Well, it's not there now," Ottilia said grimly, "for I have already looked through that drawer."

"Stolen!" Tearful now, Huntshaw once more removed her hand from the drawer. "The box is gone, miss. And if the key's not there —"

"Stand aside," said Ottilia curtly. "Let me try."

Seizing a handful of items from the

drawer, she instructed the woman to set them aside. Before long there was a pile of articles laid higgledy-piggledy on top of the press and the drawer was empty. Ottilia stood back with a defeated sigh.

"There is no box."

Huntshaw peered into the drawer, as if she might conjure the box back into its place. "But who would steal it? Who would know it was there?"

"Evidently someone did."

"But only my lady and myself knew where her jewels were kept. Besides, they weren't always in that drawer. We were used to move them every few weeks. Sometimes my lady would even have me take some out of the box and secrete them between the folds of her gowns."

Ottilia eyed her absently, her mind roving possibilities. "But not on this occasion?"

"No, miss. They were all in the box. And I put back the necklace and the crescent for the hair that she was wearing."

"Then we can be sure the box was in place when you went off to bed."

"Yes, miss."

"What we can't know is whether the jewels were taken before or after her ladyship was discovered."

Huntshaw gaped at her. "You don't think

197

— but who would — ?"

Ottilia did not mince her words. "Either the murderer, or a sneak thief who had prior knowledge of the whereabouts of the jewels and took advantage of the chaos of the hour."

The maid looked frankly appalled, and no wonder. Then a horrified gasp escaped her and she clapped a hand to her mouth.

Ottilia frowned. "What is it, Mary?"

"You don't think —" The woman broke off, swallowed, and tried again. "You don't think it was me, do you, miss?"

A faint laugh was surprised out of Ottilia. "If it were, you have shown yourself an actress of calibre, Mary. No, I think we may safely acquit you. But we may not say the same for others."

Before she would dismiss the lady's maid, Ottilia went through the pile of undergarments on the dressing room floor, shaking out each item and handing it to Mary Huntshaw. No stockings, no garters. But when she picked up the dressing robe from the chaise longue, the woman gave a sudden cry.

"There, miss. Underneath."

Ottilia looked where the woman pointed and saw what the trail of silken material had concealed. A pair of spangled garters lay half coiled under the chaise. Then the stockings had been removed here. Her mind painted an image of the scene, which was all the proof Ottilia needed that a lover had indeed been in the chamber.

"But the stockings. Where are the stockings?"

She spoke almost absently, throwing glances about the room. From the puzzlement in Mary's face, it was evident she had made no such jump as Ottilia's imagination had furnished. It was time and past she examined the extent of the maid's knowledge.

"Mary, do you not see what this means?"

The woman began to look apprehensive. "How do you mean, miss?"

"Come, Mary, you are no fool. Her ladyship was not alone that night."

A red stain mantled the woman's cheek. "I did wonder, miss."

Ottilia pressed her advantage. "Have you not wondered in the past? You were involved in Lady Polbrook's intimate concerns, as her personal maid must be. And you have often heard her quarrel with the marquis on the subject of unfaithfulness, have you not?"

Mary nodded, looking deeply miserable. "But I never saw it, miss. If — if my lady had a lover, I never knew it for certain."

"She was discreet where you were concerned, is that it?"

"She never mentioned no one. She never said."

The maid bit her lip, but Ottilia continued to regard her, knowing her own silence would work more in her favour than any amount of probing. Sure enough, within a moment, the dam burst.

"Oh, I wish I could say it wasn't so, but I can't. What else was I to think when she'd send me to bed before ever I'd done what was needful? Just as she did that night. And the bedclothes all rumpled in the morning! Times I saw the imprint of two heads on the pillows, and I knew his lordship never come next or nigh my lady of a nighttime. What else was I to think?"

Unregarded tears were trickling down Mary's cheeks and Ottilia was satisfied. The woman's distress was genuine. She had not been in Emily's confidence, and the little deceits had dismayed her.

"Dry your eyes, Mary," she said gently. "No blame attaches to you, be sure. Speak of this to no one, if you please."

"I wouldn't, miss," averred the woman, sniffing as she applied her pocket-handkerchief to the wetness at her face.

"I've never said nothing to nobody, no matter what I thought."

"I believe you. And pray keep silence over the disappearance of the jewel box as well. We would not wish to add to everyone's upset with such a tale."

"No, miss. You can trust me, miss."

Ottilia smiled at her. "Thank you. Now let us see if we can find those stockings."

But a thorough search failed to turn up any sign of them. Ottilia sighed with discontent. Little though stockings counted in value against the momentous loss of the jewels, the mystery of their disappearance niggled. While the fan and the jewel box were both susceptible to several ready explanations, she could not account for anyone removing the stockings from the scene. They had not been used for a ligature, for the imprints of a man's fingers had been clearly marked on the marchioness's neck. No other reasonable excuse offering for their disappearance, Ottilia was obliged to lay the problem to one side for the time being.

Impatient now for the dowager's return, for it was imperative she was told about the missing jewels as soon as may be, Ottilia sought to distract her mind with an examination of Emily's portrait. Learning from

Mary that this was to be found in the Blue Salon, she released the lady's maid at last and repaired thither to discover the likeness displayed above a sideboard where the light from the window struck it into prominence.

Ottilia studied it with interest. If the painter had been faithful to his subject, the late Lady Polbrook had been a magnificent creature. She was pictured in the romantic style of an earlier decade, with high curled and feathered hair of a soft shade of brown and ringlets caressing her white neck, about which a jewelled circlet hung, reposing upon a full white bosom. Her nose was straight, her lips prettily curved, and a pair of vivacious green eyes smiled upon the world in a look captured by the artist, perhaps unconsciously, that gave at a glance the reason for the sitter's popularity. It was a look both flighty and serene, as if its wearer possessed supreme confidence in the efficacy of her own attractions.

The marchioness must have been years younger at the time the portrait was painted, but Ottilia could not suppose the inner being to have changed, even if the flesh had shown signs of aging. The inevitable comparison between this and the wreckage she had contemplated in the bedchamber could not fail to incite a resurgence of dismay in

Ottilia, together with a surge of sympathy. Whatever she had been, no woman deserved a death so monstrously unpleasant.

She found herself thinking with sadness of the unfortunate marriage in which Emily had been entangled. Was it any wonder her unhappy alliance had driven her to a life of degradation? What a pity she and the marquis could not have found in each other that felicity of domestic content which might, in the end, have saved her from a fate as tragic as it was horrific.

Ottilia's determination redoubled to discover the man who had thus ended the poor creature's life, even should it prove to be the husband. In her heart of hearts, she was convinced it was not so. But she must establish it beyond reasonable doubt. Yet that was not enough. She must find out the true culprit and have him answer for his deeds.

Sounds of an arrival distracted her, and she went into the hall to find at last the dowager and her daughter just entering from the street, with Cattawade and the footman Abel exiting by the front door to fetch the countess's portmanteaux and bandboxes under the direction of that lady's personal maid.

Leaving the servants to their labours, the

ladies put off their cloaks, which Venner took from them, and were ushered into the parlour by Ottilia.

"You were in the right of it, Ottilia," said the dowager, sinking into her favoured chair by the fire. "I feel the better for the change. Though we are decidedly late, due to my daughter's fuss and bother about her luggage."

"And then we took tea, for Mama was parched," said the countess.

"We might have been later still," said Sybilla, ignoring this, "for Harriet would have had me to church, but nothing will induce me to show myself abroad until matters have been resolved."

"I daresay the Almighty will forgive you, ma'am," said Ottilia with a smile.

"Well, on second thought, I did not care to go myself," put in Lady Dalesford, "without being habited properly. How shocking if we had been seen out of mourning in St. George's on a Sunday!"

"Worse, to have had all the fools of London gaping at us and daring to offer condolences when we know full well they are dying of curiosity."

"Very true, ma'am," Ottilia agreed. "But I have matter here, unfortunately, that will inevitably return your attention to the difficulties of your situation."

Sybilla flung up a hand. "Oh, what now, pray?"

The story of the disappearance of the jewel box put all thought of the opinions of the outside world out of court. The countess appeared even more perturbed than her mother.

"Great heavens! Who in the world could have taken it?"

"Don't be a widgeon, Harriet. Ottilia has just told you the options."

"But why should the murderer make off with Emily's jewels?"

"That is a very good question," cut in Ottilia before the dowager had an opportunity to squash her daughter once more. "But if it was the murderer, we can be even more certain he was not your brother."

Lady Dalesford brightened. "No, indeed."

"On the other hand," put in the dowager, "there is also the possibility that the jewels were taken after Emily was found dead. Which means we have a thief on the premises."

"One of the servants? Surely not," protested the countess. "Why, they would know one of them must be immediately suspect."

"I am inclined to agree with you, Harriet.

Any servant making off with the jewels would be wise to run away altogether."

"Just so," said Ottilia, "which is why I have warned Mary to keep silent about the loss."

This move being approved, Ottilia held her tongue on her own thoughts. Unlike the other ladies, she could not dismiss the notion of the theft having been perpetrated by a member of the domestic staff. She was most perturbed by the clear indication that whoever took the jewels knew very well where they were. Even assuming someone had got past Abel, which she had yet to ascertain, that someone would have had very little time in which to abstract the jewel box. Even more difficult to escape Abel's eye with it on their person, never mind where they might secrete it afterwards.

Lady Dalesford was standing at the mantel, resting an elbow upon it and leaning her chin on her hand. Abruptly she straightened.

"Stay! Could Francis have taken the jewel box?"

Sybilla snorted. "Francis has as little need to be stealing his sister's gems as Randal himself."

"I don't mean he stole them. But might he not have removed them for safekeeping?"

Ottilia gave this short shrift. "It is a good

thought, Lady Dalesford, but no. For one thing, Lord Francis was not in a state of mind to be thinking as clearly as that. For another, he probably has no notion where the marchioness kept her jewels."

"Only too likely," agreed Sybilla. "Why in the world should he?"

"Besides, I have it on the authority of Mary Huntshaw that the hiding place was changed from time to time."

The countess nodded. "Yes, I do the same thing."

"And even if Lord Francis had taken them," pursued Ottilia, "I am sure he would have mentioned it, or given them into the dowager's keeping."

"I begin to wish it had been so," said Sybilla on a sour note. "The alternative quite sinks my spirits."

"Why?"

"Because, Harriet, I had far rather believe poor Emily was strangled by her lover in a fit of rage than for the sake of a fistful of jewels." She glanced suddenly at Ottilia. "Can it be the same man who took the fan?"

"The fan?"

Ottilia explained how Emily's personal maid had seen the Polbrook heirloom in the early morning, but that it had not been there when Ottilia first went into the dressing room. "Which means it need not have been the same perpetrator, for the fan was definitely taken after the marchioness was found. We do not know when the jewels were taken."

Lady Dalesford uttered an exasperated cry. "Lord, it is all so muddled and difficult! How will we ever unravel it?"

"Piece by piece," Ottilia soothed. She smiled. "Meanwhile, I have told Mary Huntshaw to be ready to assist you both tomorrow. I think we may safely put the room in order now and lay up the marchioness's effects."

The countess shuddered. "A prospect which has effectually ruined my appetite."

"Poppycock," said the dowager on a bracing note. "You must be excessively hungry, for you ate nothing for breakfast."

"No, and I doubt I can eat anything now."

"I daresay you will find," said Ottilia, "if you force yourself to begin with, that your appetite will swiftly return. It must be close on the dinner hour. Shall I ring the bell?"

She spoke in a tone of deliberate cheerfulness, which in no way reflected her own state of mind. The discovery of the theft of the jewels had set up a train of speculation, the import of which was decidedly unnerving, particularly now that Ottilia had seen

208

the portrait. With every encouragement to think of the late marchioness as an adulteress, she was yet reluctant to impugn her with the possibility of the unsavoury liaison that was running in her head.

Breakfast upon the following morning was enlivened by a conference with the dowager's favoured seamstress, who had been fetched by Miss Venner. By the time Ottilia came down, the discussion was already in full swing. That the dowager's efforts had been hampered by the interventions of her daughter was evidenced by Sybilla's ruffled temper and Lady Dalesford's decidedly sulky air.

Having waved Ottilia to a chair, the dowager turned back to the elderly little creature who was standing alongside the taller lady's maid.

"Then that is settled, Biddle. You will go back to Bruton Street with Venner. She will unearth the two gowns from the attics, and you may take them away to make the alterations."

"I still think you ought to have gauze or silk," put in the countess in a petulant tone.

She was seated opposite, partaking of a hearty breakfast — despite her avowed distaste for food — of baked eggs flanked by buttered bread rolls and a plentiful supply of coffee. From the spread of viands set out to tempt the ladies' appetites, it was evident Mrs. Thriplow had succeeded in restoring some vestige of normality.

"It will be thought very odd if you appear in that dreadful bombazine."

"Bombazine is perfectly acceptable wear for mourning," said Sybilla tartly. "Besides, one of the gowns is crape."

"Crape! Could anything be more old-fashioned?"

The dowager ignored this. "That will be all, Venner. Thank you, Biddle. As quick as you can do the thing, if you please."

The sewing woman curtsied. "Yes, my lady. It won't be more'n a couple of days, my lady."

"That will be satisfactory. Off you go with Venner."

The maid was holding open the door, and the little woman waddled out. Lady Dalesford did not wait for the door to be shut.

"I declare, Mama, you are as obstinate as a pig! We shall be the cynosure of all eyes in no time at all, and it will not do to be dressed in a manner as disrespectful as it is inferior."

"Be silent, Harriet," Sybilla snapped. "I have no intention of parading myself in public, and you, if you have forgotten, will be safely immured at Dalesford Hall."

"Do you suppose there is no society around Dalesford Hall? I am sure we shall be inundated with visitors from the moment of my return. Well, I shall insist upon Candia at least sporting something fashionable. Black satin and velvet is the coming thing, I hear."

"No doubt Candia will have her own views," suggested the dowager. "She is as headstrong as Emily herself."

"I will say for Emily," returned the countess roundly, "with all her faults, she had excellent dress sense. She would not have been seen dead in bombazine."

The moment the words were out of her mouth, she realised what she had said. Her eyes flashed quick remorse, and she instantly put out her hand across the table.

"I did not mean to say that. Pray forgive me, Mama."

Sybilla took the hand and gripped it, her tone gruff. "Of course you did not mean it. Forget it. One cannot be minding one's tongue for every little common expression."

Consuming a sustaining meal on her own account, Ottilia reflected how momentous events were apt to draw families together. Tempers became frayed, but rifts were more

211

readily mended than in the ordinary way. She adopted a tone of deliberate cheer, throwing Sybilla a glance of mischief.

"I must admit I am glad to be bearding Mrs. Thriplow, instead of joining the two of you in your labours in Emily's bedchamber. I can imagine no more fruitful task to engender a positive barrage of bickering between you. I pity poor Mary Huntshaw."

Both ladies burst into laughter and Ottilia was relieved to have lightened their moods. There was enough, heaven knew, to fret them. She resolved to keep her latest suspicion to herself.

Mrs. Thriplow poured ratafia into a glass for herself, handed a cup of tea to Ottilia, and then she seated her bulk in the comfortable chair on the other side of a round table. Ottilia waited while the housekeeper settled, putting her feet up on a low stool situated precisely for the purpose. She took a sip from her glass and let out a contented breath.

"That's better. It ain't no manner of use trying to answer a lot of questions if a body ain't comfortable."

"Quite right," said Ottilia, looking round the housekeeper's inner sanctum.

It was a small room, stamped with the

woman's personality, if a trifle overfull of knickknacks alongside the cupboards and heavy ledgers necessary to her duties, and a single window let in a modicum of light from the street above. Like all long-serving retainers, the housekeeper evidently did herself well, reserving to her own use a motley collection of pieces of old china no longer serving the family by reason of some small chip or crack, and a respectable selection of expensive beverages. Ottilia had been offered a choice of tea from a locked store, coffee — no doubt liberally laced with sugar — and a variety of wines. Wishing to keep a clear head, she had settled for tea while her hostess excused herself from joining her and opted for ratafia.

"How are you coping, Mrs. Thriplow?" Ottilia asked by way of an opener.

Mrs. Thriplow sighed deeply. "If I'd only myself to think of, ma'am, I'd be back on my feet in no time. But half the girls seem to find reasons to fall into hysterics for naught, and the other half can't keep from gossiping with every Tom, Dick, and Harry who comes to the area door. I'm trying to keep their minds on the work in hand, but it ain't nowise easy, and I can't say as I blame them, poor things."

"What an excellent person you are, Mrs.

Thriplow," said Ottilia, seizing the opportunity to butter the woman up. "I can tell you take your duties towards the female staff to heart."

A red stain rose to the woman's cheeks and she puffed them out. "Kind of you to say so, ma'am, I'm sure. I like to think I've learned a trick or two over the years."

"I imagine your late mistress must have found you invaluable."

Mrs. Thriplow pursed her lips at that, looking dubious. "As to that, there's no saying what she thinks — thought, I should say. She'd her standards, like any lady, and it paid a body to learn them and abide by them."

This was intriguing, to say the least, and Ottilia took the cue. "She was exacting?"

Watching the changing expression on the woman's face as she hesitated, Ottilia guessed she was struggling between the urge to speak out and a sense of loyalty. Ottilia applied a spur.

"I hope you will forgive my blunt speaking, Mrs. Thriplow, but if I am to unravel the mystery behind her murder, it behoves me to learn as much of Lady Polbrook's character as I can. And you are very well placed to help."

A moment more the housekeeper's resistance held. Then, with an air of reckless abandon, she tossed off the contents of her glass and reached out a pudgy hand for the bottle.

"Well, if it's the truth you want, Mrs. Draycott, the mistress was a worse tartar than old Lady Polbrook, and that's saying something."

"Ah, I wondered."

"You might well, for you're at the old one's beck and call. But the bigger difference between them, ma'am, is you couldn't speak your mind to my late mistress as you could to t'other. It were 'yes, my lady' or 'no, my lady' and she wouldn't stand for nothing else."

Ottilia smiled. "I find it hard to believe you were able to abide by that."

The housekeeper let out a guffaw. "Well, I weren't, of course. I'd tell her what's what if I had to, never mind she didn't like it. I knew she wouldn't shoot me out the door, for I run the house like clockwork and it ain't easy with a place this size."

"And I daresay she recognised that such a good housekeeper is hard to come by."

Mrs. Thriplow chuckled, setting several chins wobbling under the ties of her cap. "More like she didn't want the bother of doing too much herself. Hated being obliged to think of domestic affairs, did my lady. Unless it were for one of them soirées, as she liked to call them."

"She was fond of entertaining?"

"Not if it meant she had to work at it. But in her position my lady was obliged to entertain. She'd name the day and give out a list for the invitations. Then she'd say how she wanted it to be and that was all. But woe betide you if it weren't just how she'd said."

"Dear me, it sounds as if she had a temper," Ottilia opined.

"Tantrums more like. Neither Cattawade nor me took no account of them, but she'd put the fear of God into some of the maids. Such a one for throwing things. Poor Mary was terrified of her. Kept everything in apple-pie order for fear my lady would ring a peal over her."

Ottilia thought of Huntshaw's meticulous care and her mistress's careless abandon and had a silent curse for the departed Lady Polbrook, who demanded what she was not willing to give. She sounded a spoilt and pampered creature. Little wonder both the dowager and Lady Dalesford had disliked her.

"Did you think her beautiful, Mrs. Thriplow?"

The housekeeper blinked. "Ain't you seen the portrait?"

"Yes," said Ottilia, noncommittally, stirring her tea.

"It was done a long time ago, but she hadn't changed much. Used to be in his lordship's library, but it was moved to the Blue Salon years back. Striking, that's what people used to say."

"Yes, that was rather my impression," said Ottilia. "But it is difficult to relate the portrait to life. How was she striking?"

Mrs. Thriplow took a swig from her glass and smacked her lips. "She was that kind who'd walk into a room and have everyone looking at her."

"Gentlemen especially?"

A sharp glance came Ottilia's way from the housekeeper's intelligent eyes. "Why yes, ma'am. But she'd a way with her for the ladies, too, had the mistress. She'd one of them laughs that tinkled like a chandelier. If you ask me, it were there for show most of the time."

Much to Ottilia's gain, the woman's tongue was loosening. No doubt the ratafia was partially responsible. Ottilia sipped at her tea and dared a little further.

"Did you despise her, Mrs. Thriplow?"

The housekeeper pursed her lips. "It

weren't my place to judge her ladyship, ma'am."

"Come, Mrs. Thriplow," Ottilia said gently. "You are scarcely a nobody in this house. Why, you were here long before the late Lady Polbrook. For my part, your opinion is one to be wholly relied upon."

The woman eyed her with suspicion, but the flattery had done its work. She sighed gustily. "This ain't to go no further, ma'am."

"Nothing you say to me will go outside these four walls, Mrs. Thriplow."

For a moment the housekeeper hesitated. Then she set down her glass and took up the bottle with a determined air. With her drink again replenished, she settled back and surveyed Ottilia in a considering way.

"You'd not have liked her one little bit, ma'am, I can tell that. Highty-tighty was my lady, every bit the marchioness. The likes of me weren't nothing to her. Just part of the background that kept her where she was. Always astonished her ladyship when I answered her back, you could see that."

"Then I really am surprised she didn't turn you out."

A smug look crept over the housekeeper's face. "She daren't. For all her temper tantrums and high-and-mighty ways, my lady was afraid of his lordship's mama. She knew the old one would cut up something terrible if she were to try to be rid of Cattawade or me. And for why? His late lordship, the dowager's husband that was, left us both a home on the estate and a lifetime annuity to be paid when we was to leave service with the Polbrook family. She knew the old mistress wouldn't have stood for them wishes to be laid aside."

The housekeeper took a defiant swallow from her glass and fairly glared at her visitor.

"I am sure you are right," Ottilia soothed, and shifted direction. "What of the relationship between her ladyship and the marquis? I have gathered there was some bone of contention between them."

Mrs. Thriplow snorted. "Bone of contention? If you ask me, they hated each other."

"Dear me, as bad as that?"

"Almost from the start, barring a year or two. Well, you know how it is with them as is born high. They've to marry to suit, not from choice. And from what I heard, my lady was promised to the master from her girlhood."

Ottilia could appreciate this. Marriage at the Polbrook level of society was a matter of business. Affection must be counted a bonus, although many couples, she believed, grew into a degree of mutual tenderness through sheer propinquity. Evidently this was not so with the marquis and his wife.

Following the housekeeper's example, Ottilia fortified herself with a swallow of tea before tackling the most important aspect of her investigation.

"Pardon me, Mrs. Thriplow, but I have to ask you this. To your knowledge or belief, was the marchioness involved with another man?"

The other's plump features became suffused and for the first time she looked discomfited. Her gaze drifted away from Ottilia's face. Why, when she'd spoken freely up to this moment? Ottilia pressed the point.

"I would not ask you if it did not promise to make the difference between Lord Polbrook's possible guilt or innocence."

The housekeeper gasped. "You ain't never going to say he done it? I'll stake my life the master wouldn't, not for fifty lovers!"

"But if it was not he, Mrs. Thriplow," pursued Ottilia ruthlessly, "it must be another. Whoever it was, there can be no doubt that he and the late Lady Polbrook had been amorous together."

The woman's hand shook, and she was obliged to set down her glass for fear of spilling its contents.

"No, ma'am, no. I'll not believe the master done it. If he's been next or nigh my lady's bed for such a purpose these many years, you may call me a dunce and welcome."

"Then who, Mrs. Thriplow? Who could it have been?"

The housekeeper put her hands together and wrung them, setting them at her lips and then down again. Ottilia noted these signs of discomfort with growing suspicion. Without doubt the housekeeper knew, or suspected, something. Someone?

CHAPTER 9

"Mrs. Thriplow?"

The housekeeper's eyes were now desperate as they looked into Ottilia's. "I don't know, ma'am. Oh, I wouldn't discount what you say. I daresay there may be more than one man to be looked for. But I couldn't tell you no name."

Couldn't, or wouldn't? "You have your suspicions perhaps?"

She got nothing but a violent shaking of the head. Ottilia affected to accept this.

"Well, it can't be helped. I daresay your path would not run in the direction of finding out such a thing."

Mrs. Thriplow fiddled with the stem of her glass. "Was there anything else, ma'am?"

The gruffness of the tone told Ottilia she had lost the woman, for the time being at any rate. She gave her a warm smile as she rose.

"Nothing at all, Mrs. Thriplow. I will not

trespass on your time any longer. I must thank you for being so extremely helpful."

The housekeeper looked a little mollified, not to say surprised, and she thawed a little. "Was you meaning to talk to anyone else?"

"Why, yes. I am extremely anxious to interview Abel the footman."

Mrs. Thriplow's glance met hers. Was that a frown in her eyes? And did her lips tighten a fraction?

"Abel, is it?"

Was there a matter of conflict here? Some servants' hall tiff?

"He was guarding the bedchamber door, if you remember," Ottilia said mildly.

The housekeeper's face cleared. "Ah, I'd forgot that."

"I asked him at the time if he would talk to me and he agreed."

"He'd better," muttered Mrs. Thriplow, belligerence surfacing once more. "Likely if anyone knows who came and went that night, it's him."

Ottilia noted this without comment. "Can you suggest somewhere as cosy as this where I might pursue these enquiries?"

Mrs. Thriplow cast her a sharp look, but Ottilia, not unhopeful, kept her expression blandly questioning.

"I don't know as there is anywhere, Mrs.

Draycott. But I'm sure you're welcome to stay here. I've duties to attend to." She hoisted herself to her feet and picked up the bottle. "I'll just lock this away." Recalling her role as hostess, she offered to replenish Ottilia's cup from the little silver pot she'd made.

Ottilia declined and thanked her with every appearance of gratitude and pleasure. "Would it be possible to send for Abel?"

The footman stood in an attitude of stiff attention. He had refused the proffered chair, regarding Ottilia with a mixture of hostility and suspicion. She felt at a distinct disadvantage being seated, lessening the possibility of putting the fellow at his ease. She tried what a soft approach might achieve.

"You do remember that you consented to talk to me, do you not, Abel?"

He did not shift, nor did his eyes waver from hers. "I remember, madam."

Ottilia hesitated. Should she weigh in at once, or would it serve her better to break down his resistance at the outset. She opted for attack.

"Then why are you looking at me as if you thought I represented some danger to you?"

At that he flinched and looked quickly away. His eyes darted about the room and came back to her. With reluctance?

"It's not you, madam. It's this place."

Ottilia recalled the housekeeper's belligerence towards the man. "You mean Mrs. Thriplow's room? You do not get on with her, I think."

His mouth set in a straight line, and he did not answer. Ottilia assumed a confidential air.

"I assure you, Abel, she is not within earshot. I understand she is busy in the still room."

There was a fraction of relaxation in the set features. He eyed her briefly, then suddenly went quickly to the door and flung it open, looking up and down the corridor outside. Apparently satisfied, he closed it again and came back to the table. Ottilia noted the drop at his shoulders. Now they were getting somewhere.

"Do sit down, Abel," she said in a friendly way. "You are giving me a crick in the neck."

A faint laugh was drawn from him, and he drew out the only other chair besides the large comfortable cushioned affair that was reserved for Mrs. Thriplow. Setting it a little way apart from the table, he perched on its edge, clearly still ill at ease.

"That's better," Ottilia encouraged him. She sought for a way to loosen his stiffness.

"Do you think the household has calmed down a little? I know everyone was dreadfully stunned."

Abel frowned. "I don't think anyone has calmed down, the reason being they won't talk of nothing else."

"We had hoped the presence of the dowager would serve to keep them busy."

"They're busy all right, busy as market day. You'd suppose everyone in service in London has business in this part of the town."

Ottilia smiled. "Visitors to the area door? Yes, I gathered as much from Mrs. Thriplow."

The footman shook his head in a disapproving fashion. "They won't be satisfied, they won't, not 'til they see the master hang."

Ottilia seized upon this. "Do you think he did it, Abel?"

His gaze shot back to hers, and Ottilia could not interpret the hard look within it. "If he didn't, who did?"

"That is precisely what I am trying to establish."

"But there weren't no one else. Least, if the voice I heard weren't his lordship —"

Startled, Ottilia threw out a staying hand. "What voice?"

The man looked puzzled. "In the bed-chamber, madam."

A flurry of apprehension started up in Ottilia's chest. "Whose bedchamber? Her ladyship's?"

The frown deepened on the footman's forehead. "That's right."

Ottilia drew a breath. "Let me understand this, Abel. You heard a voice in her ladyship's chamber, which you think belonged to the marquis."

"That's what I said."

She eyed him. "At what time was this?"

He looked away from her, seeming to ponder, biting his lip. "It was before Foscot came for me."

"Then you were up already? At four o'clock in the morning?"

Abel shook his head. "I was stood in for the porter that night. I'd been asleep in the hall, waiting for the master and the mistress to return from their engagements. He came in last, and after I'd let him in —"

"At what time?"

Abel scratched his head. "I've been trying to remember, madam. I'd heard the watch call two of the clock, I know that, but I must have slept again after, so I can't be sure."

"But it was before three?"

"I can't say, madam. I went straight to my

bed, only then I couldn't get off to sleep. And I don't hear the watch from my side at the top of the house."

"Very well. What happened then?"

The footman shrugged. "I hardly know, I was that befuddled. I tossed and turned, trying to get off, for I'd to be up again at six."

"But you got up out of your bed?"

For the first time, Abel's eyes showed a tendency to shift. Embarrassment? Or was he lying? To what purpose, if he was?

"The case is, madam," he said at length, "I had such a thirst on me, there was nothing for it but to go down to the pantry. But I never reached there, for as I was going downstairs I heard this — this noise." He moved restlessly in the chair. "I suppose I now know what it must have been, but at the time it was just — odd, madam."

Odd indeed. Odder still that he had failed to mention this in the first place, Ottilia thought with a surge of annoyance. She held it down, forcing herself to speak calmly, without a vestige of reprobation in her tone.

"Can you describe the noise, Abel?"

Something like a spasm crossed his face. "Sort of gargling."

"What did you do?"

"That's just the trouble, madam," he

returned, dismay growing in his eyes. "If I'd done more — if I'd thought —"

Ottilia carefully remained silent, intent upon forcing him to push through to the end of his tale. She knew he would feel impelled to continue if she said nothing.

"I went back up the stairs and crept through towards my lady's chamber. I'm ashamed to confess that I listened. That's when I heard his voice."

"Did you hear any words?"

Abel shook his head. "I couldn't make anything out, madam. But it was a man's voice all right."

"Could you make out something of the tone? Was it angry perhaps?"

He thought for a moment. "Gruff, madam. Not shouting or anything."

"I see. And then?"

Now there was definite embarrassment. "After a bit, I thought I heard the door handle being turned. I didn't want his lordship to catch me there, so I scarpered, madam. Made the best of my way back to bed. I was just dropping off when Foscot came for me to get round to the stables."

Ottilia digested this information in silence for a moment, aware of the footman's eyes upon her, a trifle of anxiety in his aspect. As well there might be. There was little point in postponing the inevitable question.

"Why did you say nothing of this to Lord Francis?"

He let fall a great sigh. "I knew you'd ask that. You'll scarcely believe me, madam, but I never thought. What with the panic and the shock, and I'd had so little sleep, it was clean swept from my mind. I remembered it yesterday. I've been troubled ever since, for if there's one thing more certain than another, it's that her ladyship might still be alive if I'd not been such a coward. I can't help thinking of that noise and what it must have signified. And to think I could've stopped it fair has me rattled, madam."

"I imagine it might," Ottilia said, with a calm that in no way reflected her state of mind. "But I doubt your intervention would have achieved the objective of saving the marchioness. We might, however, have known the identity of the murderer."

Abel looked miserable. "I'd not swear on oath against his lordship, madam."

"But you did think it was the marquis."

His hands clenched on his knees. "I'm between the devil and the deep blue sea, madam. If I say it wasn't, I'm condemning the mistress."

Ottilia surveyed him in silence. Was it common knowledge in the household that the marchioness had been entangled outside the marriage bed? Could Abel be ignorant, or was this disingenuous? She decided to let it go for the present. She produced a friendly smile.

"I'm glad you told me all this, Abel. There is just one other thing you may be able to help me with."

He looked eager now. "Anything, madam."

"While Lord Francis was dressing, did anyone come into the vestibule? Anyone at all?"

Abel hesitated. "Well, yes, madam. Several, as it happens. And not only those as hadn't been there at the start. Morbid, I call it. But I didn't let a soul go in."

"But you were alone there for some of the time?"

"Oh yes, madam. I didn't like it, knowing her ladyship was in there like that, but Lord Francis was depending on me. To tell the truth, madam, I was glad of company when it came. And once the coroner had been, I was released at last."

"You are sure you did not leave your post, even for a moment?"

He looked affronted. "When his lordship had asked me special to take care and see no one didn't go in?"

"Then you had your eye upon the doors

the whole time?"

A faint look of puzzlement came into the man's face. "Yes, madam. The bedchamber door, madam."

Ottilia noted the particularity. "Lord Francis came back to lock the dressing room door, did he not?"

"Yes, madam," said Abel, frowning now. "But if you're thinking someone went in there beforehand, madam, I must have seen them. It's but a step away from the bedchamber."

"Of course."

Ottilia decided to leave it at that for the present. The fewer people who knew about the disappearance of the jewels and the Polbrook fan, the better. She was inclined to doubt the footman's assertion that he would have seen anyone enter the dressing room, for he might well have shifted into the vestibule to conduct any conversation with other members of the staff. But she preferred to keep her own counsel. It would not be politic to alienate the fellow with searching questions on this point.

She thanked and dismissed him, but just as he reached the door, a half-remembered puzzle leapt into her head. She obeyed the impulse.

"One moment, Abel."

He halted with his fingers around the handle and looked back. Ottilia was a trifle surprised to see a rough frown in his features. Was that a hint of fear in his eyes? If so, it vanished with the frown and his face took on the bland look of service.

"Madam?"

"Late the other night, when I was down here in the basement, could I have seen you in the corridor?"

"Which night, madam?"

"The night before last, was it?" So much had happened, Ottilia felt a distortion of time. "Saturday, I think. Yes, I believe it was."

The footman gave a faint smile. "No, madam, I was not in the house. It was my evening off and I slept out."

Ottilia returned the smile. "Then I must have been mistaken. Thank you, Abel. You have given me considerable food for thought."

The man bowed and withdrew. Ottilia stared at the closed door without seeing it, recalling the shadow in the passage. It had been but an instant, a mere flash of recognition. She was forced to acknowledge the likelihood of error. She'd seen the fellow but briefly before that moment. But the conviction that the first man she'd seen had not been Cattawade refused to be uprooted. Worse, she could not rid herself of an impression — possibly unfounded — that Abel had lied.

For what reason? If he had been there, he must have hidden himself from Cattawade's eyes. Which could only mean his purpose in the domestic area at such an hour had been nefarious. Unless it had indeed been his evening off and he had but just returned. Slipping in ahead of the butler's locking and bolting the back door? Then why not advertise his presence?

Concluding that she must indeed have been mistaken, Ottilia banished the matter to the back of her mind and returned to the voice Abel said he'd heard. It provided but a slim hope, and was a double-edged sword. If it opened up the possibility of another suspect, it equally put Randal, Lord Polbrook, back into the picture, setting the time of the murder squarely ahead of his departure.

The arrival late in the afternoon of Lady Candia Fanshawe coincided with a visit to Hanover Square from the family's man of business, Mr. Jardine, who was just concluding a punctilious greeting when a series of unmistakable sounds took the dowager's attention. She interrupted without ceremony.

"Is that not a carriage, Ottilia? Take a look out of the window. Is it Francis at last?"

Doing as she was bid, Ottilia peered through the glass in the near parlour window, looking into the street where a bustle was going forward. She was afforded a view only of the hooded back of a carriage, but a servant was standing to one side and a groom was already at the horses' heads.

"It looks like a curricle, but I cannot see —"

She broke off, for a pair of booted feet landed on the road on the other side, and in a moment a man rounded the carriage and Ottilia caught a glimpse of his features under the beaver hat.

"Yes, I believe it is Lord Francis." She saw him throw open the low door and reach up a hand to someone inside. "There is a female getting out of the curricle."

"Candia! The poor child. Where is Harriet? Ring the bell, Ottilia."

As she went to comply, the lawyer moved towards the door.

"You will wish to be alone, Lady Polbrook."

"No, you don't," snapped the dowager. "Stay just where you are, Jardine. Francis will be as anxious as I for your news."

"It is nothing that cannot wait."

"That is immaterial. You will oblige me by remaining, if you please."

Mr. Jardine, whether in deference to the dowager's wishes or to avoid further argument, gave in with an obvious ill grace and retreated to the window. Ottilia wished she might hint to him that he was wise, for her employer's temper, uncertain since the distressing event, had been exacerbated by Ottilia's various findings. To Sybilla's mind, the introduction of a mysterious voice served to blacken the case against her elder son, and Ottilia had been obliged to remind her about the garters and reiterate her conviction of there having been a lover involved.

Presently the bustle in the hall beyond the door indicated that the travellers had entered the house. Ottilia caught the butler's voice and the light fresh tone of Lord Francis in answer. A ripple disturbed the even tenor of her pulses and she was conscious of a rise of anticipation that signalled a distinctly unwelcome development. The effort to suppress it took all her attention, and by the time she had succeeded in recovering at least a semblance of her habitual calm, the party was entering the parlour.

The youthful creature who halted on the threshold, despite blotched cheeks and a pair of tragic eyes, was breathtakingly lovely. She was tall, and the family resemblance was marked — dark eyes, high cheekbones, glossy brown hair — but a straight nose and a mouth finely sculpted as by the hand of a master set her apart from the rest and caught a resemblance to the portrait of the marchioness.

The large eyes darted from face to face, catching on her grandmother's features. Sybilla rose and held out a hand towards her.

"My poor child."

Lady Candia took a few steps into the room, but Ottilia noted reluctance in the girl's face. Then she found herself quite unable to keep her eyes on the girl, for Lord Francis entered behind her. Her breath caught. She had not recalled him as attractive as this. He did not notice Ottilia's fixed regard as he put off his hat and greatcoat and threw them carelessly upon the nearest sofa. She was relieved when thereafter, without looking about the room, he crossed to the dowager and dropped a chaste salute upon her cheek.

"We came as speedily as we could, Mama. Candia was anxious to arrive. I hope you have not been unduly oppressed."

His mother's answer was forestalled by the entrance of Lady Dalesford, who no sooner saw her niece than she cried out, "My dear, dearest girl. Oh, I am so very sorry."

Lady Candia turned quickly, catching sight of her aunt. She let out a wail of despair and flung herself headlong into the countess's welcoming arms.

So much for Lady Dalesford's worries, Ottilia thought, watching as she received her niece in a comprehensive embrace, sobs bursting from her throat to match Lady Candia's grief. Ottilia could not forbear casting a glance at the dowager, and was not very much surprised to note the faint look of exasperation that crossed Sybilla's features. Being herself of an undemonstrative disposition, she had evidently little patience with displays of naked emotion. It struck Ottilia that the only one of her children to take after her in this respect was Lord Francis.

Looking across at him as he moved to close the door the countess had left wide, she found in his features a mixture of indulgence and irritation. She was relieved to discover that her own nerves had settled while the little drama was in play. Without thought, Ottilia crossed to his side.

"Do I detect a trifle of impatience in your aspect, Lord Francis?" she murmured. His gaze came swiftly round, a startled look in his eye. "The task of conveying a grieving niece all the way from Bath has tried you pretty high, I think."

The dark gaze crinkled at the corners and his lips twitched. "As usual, you are perfectly in the right, Mrs. Draycott. I could readily have thro—" He broke off, consternation leaping into his face. "No, I don't mean that."

Ottilia smiled her understanding. "I daresay the thought of the gallows was a sufficient deterrent."

He laughed out at that. "Mrs. Draycott, you are the most outrageous female."

"Not at all," she countered. "Flippancy is always an efficacious remedy against the dramatic happenings of life, do you not think? One must fight back somehow."

"It is certainly preferable to indulging in settled gloom. But how have you fared here? Any news?"

Ottilia met his eager glance. "Nothing conclusive, but I think we have made a little progress. Your sister's advent was fortuitous, for it has given me rein."

His eye gleamed appreciation. "You mean Harriet has kept my mother occupied."

"Most usefully," she agreed, smiling. "They have done wonders together in sorting the marchioness's effects."

Lord Francis cocked an eyebrow. "You set them to that, did you? Masterly, Mrs. Draycott. I will not ask if you had done all you needed in the chamber first."

Ottilia was insensibly encouraged by the clear indication that he understood her so well. But she felt obliged to put out a warning finger. "We may be overheard. Let us reserve this discussion until your niece is safely out of the way."

Lady Candia had been perforce passed to her grandmother, whose hug, though eloquent, was brief. The dowager held the girl away, gripping her shoulders.

"Come now, my child, you must be brave. Your Aunt Harriet will look after you. And you will have all your cousins about you."

The young girl sniffed dolefully. "What of Papa? Has he come home?"

Sybilla shook her head. "Jardine has sent to him. He will be home presently."

The pretty features crumpled. "Where is Giles? I want Giles."

As Lady Candia dissolved into tears again, the dowager threw a harassed glance at her own daughter, who at once came to the rescue.

"There, there, my pet," she soothed, taking the young girl into her arms again and drawing her away. "Let us go and put off your travelling costume." Over her shoulder, she called back to her mother as she drew her charge towards the door. "Pray ring for your woman to come to me, Mama."

"An excellent idea," said the dowager, relieved. "Ottilia, ring the bell. Venner can make up a calming drink for Candia."

"It wouldn't hurt to put a dose of laudanum into it," suggested Lord Francis as the door shut behind the two females.

"I would not recommend it," Ottilia said, tugging at the bellpull. "The stuff is addictive. Hartshorn or a tisane of herbs would be far safer."

The dowager waved her hand at Lord Francis, who seemed about to say something. "Venner will know how to do, and she disapproves strongly of laudanum." A loud cough brought her head round to the window embrasure. "Jardine! I was forgetting you were still here. I made him wait, Francis, for I imagine you will wish to hear anything he has to say."

Lord Francis went across to the lawyer. "I certainly will. What news, sir?"

"Nothing of moment, my lord. Her ladyship bade me examine the late marchioness's will, which I regret to say I cannot read except in the presence of her immediate family."

"You are saying we must wait for my brother and my nephew?"

Jardine gave a slight bow of assent. "I can, however, confirm that there are no beneficiaries other than the immediate family."

"What, nothing to any of her own kin, let alone Randal's?" exclaimed Sybilla. "Nothing to any servant?"

"The late Lady Polbrook's personal fortune is tied up in the funds, my lady. It cannot be separately apportioned unless the beneficiaries choose to sell out."

"I daresay, but she has personal items of value. It is customary to reward one's faithful retainers, even if she did not see fit to assist individual relations."

"The deed is hardly likely to come home to any of Emily's family," cut in Francis. "Nor can I suppose she would be quite so crass as to leave a sum to a person who might fit the criteria belonging to the particular murderer for whom we are looking."

The dowager gave a grunt of dissatisfaction. "I suppose not. I had hoped the will might have given us a lead."

"So had I, ma'am," Ottilia put in, "but at

least we now know that there is only Lord Polbrook to consider in that light, and he, as no doubt Mr. Jardine can confirm, would have no need to murder his wife for money."

She came under the lawyer's penetrating glance, but he merely nodded and then turned back to Lord Francis. "I think you may be glad to know, my lord, that my messengers have been despatched these three days."

"Excellent." The lawyer's thin brows drew together, and Ottilia was unsurprised when Lord Francis demanded the reason. "There is something else?"

Mr. Jardine cast a glance from Lord Francis to the dowager, who had passed from a species of disgust at her erstwhile daughter-in-law's apparent lack of generosity to a look grimly anxious.

"I feel it my duty to inform you, with regret, of what has come to my attention," said the lawyer.

"Well, out with it, man," came testily from Sybilla. "No need to make a meal of it."

The severe look intensified, but the lawyer made no demur. "Hard upon the heels of my fellow in his way to France, I understand there is a Bow Street Runner."

CHAPTER 10

A hasty exclamation escaped Lord Francis, and the dowager glared at her man of business as if he were to blame. Ottilia put her oar in without ceremony.

"Is your man capable of staying ahead?"

For the first time, a muscle twitched at the corner of Mr. Jardine's mouth and his usually stern eye gleamed. "I choose my tools with care, Mrs. Draycott. No mere redbreast can hope to outfox my fox."

She had to laugh. "I am relieved to hear it. How many days before we may expect to hear?"

He did not hesitate. "Up to a week, I imagine. At most, ten days."

Ottilia eyed him for a moment, and then cast a swift look towards the others. Lord Francis was regarding the lawyer with a thoughtful expression, but the dowager was watching Ottilia.

"If you are going to come out with one of

your revelations, Ottilia," she said irritably, "pray do so and stop checking to see whether the rest of us can stand it."

"I was rather wondering if one of you might have leapt to the same conclusion."

Lord Francis's eyes turned towards her. "That Jardine knows precisely where my brother is to be found?" He looked back at the lawyer as he spoke, but the man's face gave nothing away. Nor did he speak. "I have long believed you know far more about his lordship's affairs than we do, Jardine, and I can only applaud your integrity. In Polbrook's place, I should wish for a similar reticence on your part. However —"

"All very well," interrupted the dowager, her eyes flashing at the lawyer, "but when my son is suspected of murdering his wife, it is not the time to be reticent."

The lawyer gave a small bow. "I appreciate your ladyship's point of view. No doubt his lordship, when he returns, will give a satisfactory account of himself."

"In other words, your lips are sealed," fumed Sybilla.

He bowed again, not wasting words in denial. Ottilia, watching Lord Francis, guessed he at least realised there was no future in argument.

"Is it 'when,' Jardine?" he asked, changing

tack. "Can you be certain of that?"

The lawyer drew in breath and gazed briefly at the ceiling. "No, my lord, I cannot." He interrupted a hasty exclamation from the dowager. "I can offer one assurance. If Lord Polbrook has followed an intention he had before the distressing event, then it is certainly his design to return."

"Whereas if he ran off after strangling his wife, it is only too possible that he will keep on running," said Lord Francis with sangfroid, drawing Ottilia's admiration.

"Why in the world cannot you tell us this intention?" demanded Sybilla with heat. "What if it has a bearing on the case?"

"Improbable, my lady."

"How do you know? And I should infinitely prefer to judge for myself."

"Leave it, ma'am," Lord Francis interposed. "Jardine has his instructions. Besides, anything he might be able to tell us can lead to speculation only, and we want facts."

"What I want is my son," retorted his mother, a note of hysteria in her voice.

"And you shall have him," soothed Ottilia, going across to lay a hand upon the elder dame's shoulder. "Do not forget that Mr. Jardine has set his recovery in train. There is much we may do meanwhile."

The lawyer threw her a look in which she might have read a modicum of gratitude, should she choose to believe him capable of such an emotion. He looked to Lord Francis.

"If there is nothing further, my lord, I shall take my leave of you."

"By all means. No doubt you will keep us informed of any developments."

A nod, a bow to the dowager, and Mr. Jardine was gone. The dowager barely waited for the door to close behind him.

"Wretched man! You should have insisted upon his telling us all, Francis."

"To what end? You know as well as I that he would never betray Randal's confidence."

"Indeed." Ottilia moved to take a seat opposite the dowager. "And you will gain nothing by alienating his willingness to serve you."

"Then what are we to do?" Sybilla demanded. "You have already said there is likely little more to be learned from the servants."

"We must look elsewhere."

Lord Francis threw himself onto one of the sofas, his eyes going to Ottilia. "Had you no success while I was away?"

"Indifferent, but a couple of worrying facts have come to light."

"Such as?"

Ottilia thought she detected a resurgence of anxiety in the dark gaze, and wished she might have had better news to impart. There was no point in withholding what there was.

"I'm afraid we have discovered that your sister-in-law's jewel box is missing."

A faint groan escaped him. "As if the fan was not enough. With all its contents?"

"I presume so. Mary Huntshaw is convinced it was not abstracted by the marchioness herself, for she claims the drawer — which was considerably disordered — would have been left open. We cannot place the time of the theft except that it occurred after the point when Mary put away the items Emily was wearing that night."

"Which leads one to suppose they were taken by the murderer."

"Or by the same person who took the fan, which we know occurred after Mary had discovered the body and before you locked the dressing room door."

Lord Francis dropped his head in his hands with a groan. "Lord help me, but that mistake looks like to cost me dear!"

"There is nothing to be gained by sinking into a slough of self blame," said the dowager tartly. "You did what you did and there's an end."

Raising his head again, his lordship shot a fulminating glance at his mother. "If I am not even permitted to indulge in a moment of protest —"

"Save it for the rest, boy. We are by no means out of the woods."

His eyes returned to Ottilia. "Don't spare me, will you?"

She was obliged to smile. "I should not dream of it. I am sure you can stand a knock as well as your mama."

To her delight, he broke into laughter. "A knock? A battering might better describe it. But go on, pray. What other alarms have you in store for me?"

"Well, although I have discovered several possible means of entry and exit, one is so insalubrious that I find it difficult to believe it was used. And there must needs to have been assistance from within the house to accomplish the others."

She explained in a few words her excursions through the basement and the location of the door that led to the outside privy for the use of the domestic staff and the pathway used by the night soil men.

"The devil! I had hoped the lover theory would yield results."

"It may yet. I have been too occupied to pursue the matter. Furthermore, although the other doors seem more likely, it is one of the ways into the house and should not be altogether discounted."

Lord Francis sighed. "What else?"

His tone provoked Ottilia into a mischievous mood. "I wish I had something worthy of such resigned fatality. But alas, there is only Abel's mysterious voice."

"Mysterious voice? Oh, dear Lord! Enlighten me, I beg."

A gurgle escaped Ottilia, but she caught sight of the dowager, who looked as if she might explode at any moment, and hastily swallowed her mirth.

"Pardon me, ma'am. It is no matter for laughter, I know. The case is, Lord Francis, that Abel has belatedly recalled that he left his bed in the small hours for the purpose of going to fetch a glass of water. He never reached the kitchens, it appears, for he heard an odd sort of gargling noise and a man's voice."

"For pity's sake!" Wrath had succeeded the resignation. "Why the devil could he not have spoken of this before?"

"It seems he had little sleep that night, and in the press of the morning's events, it escaped his memory. He was aware that this would cause a degree of censure."

"I imagine he might well have been. Tell

me it all, if you please."

Ottilia gave him the gist of her interview with Abel, and was relieved that he chose to take an opposite view to that of Sybilla.

"It could be damning, I daresay. But we may equally suppose this mysterious voice of Abel's belonged to another as to Randal. Especially taking into account your observations upon the scene. What of the timing? Does this point to a later hour than we suspected?"

"Unfortunately we are unable to pinpoint the time," Ottilia said regretfully. "The best Mary Huntshaw could do was to suggest it was after one in the morning when the marchioness came home. Abel puts the marquis's arrival after two. We can therefore say only that the quarrel must have taken place somewhere between two and three, at which point your sister-in-law was still alive. She was definitely dead by the time Sukey left the chamber as the clock struck seven. Although Cattawade is uncertain about the time he was asked to fetch brandy from the cellar, from the testimony of Abel and Turville in the stables, I think we can assume the carriage was sent for around four or a little later."

"Which means there is a good clear hour between three and four during which Emily could have received another man in her chamber," said Lord Francis eagerly.

The dowager snorted. "Who then killed her before walking calmly out of the room, according to Abel."

"We do not know he was calm," said Ottilia. "Abel merely stipulated the turning of the door handle. There were no footsteps. Therefore our murderer must have crept to the door as quietly as he could. That does not necessarily suggest a calm state of mind."

"It suggests a guilty one."

"Perhaps."

Lord Francis suddenly slapped a hand on the arm of the sofa. "One moment! We are placing the time of the murder between Randal's leaving Emily and his leaving the house altogether. Why should the lover not have been in her room after that?"

"Regretfully," said Ottilia, "because it does not square with Abel's voice, which came before. Recollect that he was the one to be sent to rouse them at the stables, after which he made no attempt to go back to bed."

"And let us not forget," added the dowager, "that Pellew says the time of death could readily have been earlier than four."

Lord Francis's disappointment was so obvious that Ottilia felt impelled to comment upon it. "Pray don't despair, sir. I am sure we have a trick or two yet to play."

He nodded. "I am too tired to think clearly. Is this all of your current findings?"

"I'm afraid it is." Although it was not quite all of her thoughts, but these she preferred to keep to herself for the moment. Remembering her interview with the housekeeper, she added, "Oh, except that Mrs. Thriplow gave me to understand that the marquis and his wife had never enjoyed an affectionate relationship."

"You may say so with confidence," Sybilla said with candour. "I had reason enough to regret that Polbrook — my late husband, I mean — made the alliance, but it was a settled thing for years. Randal could not have wriggled out of it, even had he wished to."

"Did he ever express such a wish, ma'am?"

The dowager shrugged. "Boys can always be counted upon to wish to marry some quite unsuitable creature, but there was nothing serious."

Ottilia glanced quickly at Lord Francis, wondering that he kept silent. She tried to read his expression but found it bland. Perhaps his plea of tiredness was indeed to be taken at face value. He had driven a great distance. If he knew anything, on the other hand, he clearly had no intention of revealing it before his mother.

"Meanwhile," he said, as if he had been thinking of something quite other, "what is our next move?"

Ottilia could not resist. "*Your* next move, my lord. You cannot expect your mama and me to do all the work."

Francis eyed the companion with misgiving. "I mistrust that look in your eye, Mrs. Draycott. Just what is in your mind?"

An unmistakable look of mischief crept into her features, and Francis was conscious of the oddest sensation to which he could not have put a name. As if a jug of warm water had been trickled onto his chest.

"I think it is time to go out into the world to hunt out suspects. Do you belong to a gentleman's club? Of course you must. White's?"

"Brooks's," he countered. "You are suggesting I visit my club. And do what? Ask around to find if anyone there has been so careless as to make Emily his mistress and strangle her?"

"Don't be an imbecile, Fanfan."

"Well, dear Lord! All I will get is half the fools of London gaping, and the other half offering commiserations to which I have no notion how to respond. I won't do it."

"I hope you will think better of that decision, my lord, for it is imperative that we shift our ground."

There was no reproach in Mrs. Draycott's voice, but her clear gaze made him feel churlish. Yet he was reluctant still. "How will it help?"

She smiled then. "If there is a killer out there, he will approach you. He will not be able to resist."

Francis was disappointed. "Surely you are not naïve enough to suppose that every man who attempts to make his condolences to me must be suspect?"

"I was just thinking the same thing," his mother cut in. "What in the world are you thinking of, Ottilia?"

She looked from one to the other. "I expressed myself badly perhaps. Of course you must take note of what is said and of the manner of any approach."

"Discounting, I presume, my immediate circle of friends who are bound to speak of the matter?"

Mrs. Draycott's eyes opened wide at him. "By no means. Can you swear to every one of your friends?"

"I would like to think so, but I daresay not. How very unsettling."

"What must he look for, Ottilia?"

Francis began to be interested. Had his mother gauged the measure of this woman more readily than he? He waited while she frowned in thought.

"Most people," she said at last, "will be reticent, perhaps embarrassed. Or they may speak eloquently, but say very little. It is in the nature of genuine feelings for people to have difficulty in expressing them. Be wary of those who are effusive. That may denote a gossipy disposition, but you will already know who has that tendency. Otherwise, it is likely the effusion is insincere."

"Ingenious," Francis commented. "Anything else?"

"It may be too much to hope for, but it is possible someone may hint at your brother's involvement. Delicacy must keep the subject closed for most, but a guilty man will wish to assure himself that the finger is pointing elsewhere."

"Gracious, Ottilia, how in the world do you do it?" asked his mother in accents which mirrored his own grudging admiration. "I should never have thought of that in a million years."

Mrs. Draycott's laughter caught at some distant chord inside him, one that had not been touched for many a year. He almost missed what she said.

"I assure you there is nothing miraculous in my reasoning. Whenever I wish to analyse human reactions, I think back to the conduct of my nephews. It is like viewing the world in microcosm, but in high relief, for children are much more obvious than their adult counterparts."

"But you have made a study of adults, too, anyone can tell that," said the dowager, echoing Francis's thought.

Then he found Mrs. Draycott was regarding him with amusement in her features. "I am naturally curious, as Lord Francis divined at the outset."

"Did I so? But I had not supposed you had an ambition to become the prime mover in an investigation of murder when you chose to take up this appointment." The ripple of laughter sent a wave of warmth through him and a new thought struck. "However," he added, eyeing her with suspicion, "it has more than once occurred to me that you are taking an uncommon delight in the proceedings."

A guilty look crossed her face, but mischief leapt in her eyes. "Dear me, am I so obvious? Then I must freely confess that, ghoulish as it may seem, and particularly indelicate of your own and Sybilla's feelings, I am indeed enjoying myself immensely."

For the life of him, Francis could not suppress a burst of laughter. For the first time since the start of these horrific proceedings, his mood lightened.

Dinner was enlivened by the presence of Colonel Tretower, who greeted Lady Dalesford with every evidence of pleasure. Ottilia, watching the access of gallantry in the colonel's manner and the flirtatious response, was highly entertained, despite the dowager's evident disapproval. Whether this was due to a general tendency to deprecate her daughter's conduct or to an idea of it being inappropriately lighthearted in the circumstances, Ottilia did not know, but she thought it an excellent thing if it had the effect of dissipating the prevailing atmosphere of gloom. There could be no doubt the countess beguiled the male element wherever she went, for a lively air coupled with her scatterbrained impulsiveness was just the combination to set gentlemen's heads in a whirl. Added to which, Lady Dalesford was a handsome woman, safely married, and therefore perfect prey for a little harmless dalliance.

It was fortunate, Ottilia felt, that young Lady Candia was not as yet equal to joining the company, for her presence must have cast a damper over this lighter mood.

"I told her she should have a tray in her room," disclosed the countess in accents of sympathetic concern as she took her place at the table. "The poor child has been weeping her heart out."

"And you left her?" demanded Sybilla.

"Oh, she is asleep now. Besides, Venner insisted upon sitting with her. You know how she dotes on Candia."

"None better. She is positively maudlin about that child."

This caught Ottilia's attention. "Pardon me, ma'am, but how is this?"

The dowager was engaged in deciding between a dish of chicken and a pie, but she looked round. "How is what?"

"Is it not a trifle odd for your maid to be so very fond of your granddaughter?"

"It would be," chimed in the countess, "but that Venner was Emily's personal maid when she came to this house."

Ottilia was conscious of a leap of hope. "Was she indeed?"

"Oh yes. Venner was in support of Emily when Candia was born. She had no part in the nursing of her, of course, but she became excessively attached to the child."

From across the table, Lord Francis

caught Ottilia's eye. "What is in your mind, Mrs. Draycott?"

She put out a staying hand. "Presently, if you please, my lord." She turned to the dowager. "When did Venner come to you then, ma'am?"

Sybilla, having settled upon a portion of pie, looked up from controlling how much Cattawade was laying upon her plate. "I cannot recall exactly. She has been with me these five or six years."

"At the least, Mama," put in Lady Dalesford. She leaned towards Ottilia across the colonel, placed between them. "She fell out mightily with Emily. I believe their final quarrel could be heard all over the house."

"Harriet!"

As the countess turned enquiringly to her mother, Sybilla put a finger to her lips, indicating with a jerk of her head the continued presence of the servants. Ottilia was not much surprised to see Lady Dalesford cast up her eyes, as if the indiscretion were of no account. She was evidently of that order of being, much prevalent in Society, who thought of domestics as so much furniture at any moment when she did not require their services. Which was the main reason, Ottilia reflected, that servants were so well informed about their employers' affairs. It was an unconscious arrogance, but it dimmed the lustre of the countess a trifle.

She felt indebted to Lord Francis for introducing a less controversial subject.

"How have you fared, George?"

Colonel Tretower gave a little sigh. "Not so very well, I'm afraid." He glanced from the butler to an attendant housemaid, and hesitated, evidently picking his words with care. "You've heard about Bow Street's move, I take it?"

"Yes, Jardine told us."

"I tried to dissuade Justice Ingham, saying we had the matter in hand, but he was adamant. I must suppose he is looking to cover his own back."

"How, pray?" asked the dowager.

"By being seen to have done something, should anyone choose to call him to account, I don't doubt," Lord Francis cut in, an edge to his voice.

"Exactly so," Tretower confirmed.

Sybilla's look persuaded Ottilia that she was with difficulty suppressing an angry retort. Hardly surprising, for the implication presumed guilt upon the part of her elder son.

"What of the carriage and horses?" asked Lord Francis, changing the subject.

"Ah, there I may reassure you all. They are coming by easy stages and should be here within a day or two." The colonel paused to take a sip of wine, and when he spoke again it was in a tone carefully neutral. "Now you are returned, Fan, you may wish to arrange for the burial as soon as may be."

Lord Francis gave a curt nod, but Lady Dalesford was seen to shudder eloquently, while the dowager faltered as she was about to partake of a mouthful of food. Ottilia watched her set it back down upon her plate and press her napkin to her lips, as if to prevent a rise of nausea. She hastened to fill the breach.

"You will be interested to learn, Colonel, that there are several possible ways a lover might have entered the house." She looked quickly about and found the housemaid had disappeared. "I need not scruple to speak before Cattawade, for he showed me the doors."

She went on to elaborate upon her discovery and was relieved to find the atmosphere lightening again as Colonel Tretower fell into immediate discussion with Lord Francis as to the likelihood or otherwise of a man having come into the house by any of these routes, in which Lady Dalesford and the dowager soon joined. By the time this had been exhausted, all the dishes had been set upon the table and Lord Francis dismissed the butler.

"We will serve ourselves, Cattawade. I will ring when we are ready for the remove."

The butler bowed and withdrew, leaving Ottilia at last able to satisfy her curiosity as regards the woman Venner.

"What happened after the quarrel, Lady Dalesford? Did the marchioness turn her out?"

"Gracious, no," exclaimed the other. "Venner had been with Emily from her girlhood. She would never have dreamed of dismissing her. But Venner refused to remain in her employ. Not that Emily believed she would really leave her, but she did, and you've never heard such a rumpus as Emily kicked up. Talk about tantrums. I heard she threw herself on the floor and drummed her heels on the carpet."

"Poppycock," snapped the dowager. "Do stop talking twaddle, Harriet."

"It isn't twaddle, Mama. You know very well Emily had a temper like the fiend. I for one am quite ready to believe she indulged in just such a temperamental display."

Sybilla shrugged and gave her attention to

her plate. "If you will listen to servants' gossip."

"It isn't mere gossip," protested the countess hotly, and turned to her brother. "Francis will bear me out. He has spent enough time in this house to see just how shockingly Emily behaved upon occasion."

Lord Francis threw up a hand. "Hold me excused, Harriet. Beyond the odd quarrel she had with Randal, I was able, I thank God, to remain ignorant of Emily's tantrums. Besides, when these events took place, I was probably in America."

"Yes, carousing with George, I expect," returned his sister, turning with mock recrimination upon Colonel Tretower.

He grinned. "Pray don't set Fan's excesses at my door. In any event, we were far too taken up with fighting the locals to be indulging in carousals."

Ottilia interrupted a laughing rejoinder, addressing herself to the dowager again. "How came it about that you took Venner on, ma'am?"

Sybilla swallowed a morsel of pie before replying. "My own woman was upon the point of retirement. I daresay Venner knew it, for she came to me and asked to be considered for the post."

"Did you not question her motive?"

"You may be sure I did. All she saw fit to tell me was that she had fallen out with the marchioness, but that she preferred to remain with the family, if I was agreeable to taking her on."

"From what I understand of the late Lady Polbrook," Ottilia said on a dry note, "I cannot imagine she was best pleased."

"Oh, you must not suppose Mama did not make every attempt to persuade Venner to return to Emily," chimed in Lady Dalesford. "Indeed, she went to Emily upon the matter, did you not, Mama?"

The dowager nodded. "She made no demur, rather to my surprise. If she had kicked up a dust, there was no sign of it when she spoke to me."

"Of course not," put in her daughter irrepressibly. "Emily was terrified of you, Mama. She would never have objected to your face. But I'll wager she gave Randal snuff afterwards."

Lord Francis laughed shortly. "Now that is more than likely. She was apt to set all the foibles of the family at his door."

"I should not say so now, I suppose, but she was the most quarrelsome wretch," said Lady Dalesford. "We never did see eye to eye, and she was not in the least afraid of me."

"Did you quarrel openly with her, then?" Ottilia asked.

"Oh, we had words now and then, but I know that whenever we did so, Emily took it out on Randal, for he told me so."

"Let us not forget, my dear sister," put in Lord Francis dryly, "that Randal gave as good as he got."

"Very true. I declare, it would not have surprised me to hear that Randal beat her."

Sybilla suddenly slammed the flat of her hand upon the table. "Be silent! Next you will say you are not surprised if he strangled her."

Lady Dalesford looked struck for a moment, and then dissolved into hiccupping tears as she protested. "That is grossly unfair, Mama. I never said it. Never thought it. I know Randal would never —"

She broke off, sniffing desperately as she attempted to stifle her distress. Colonel Tretower, looking decidedly embarrassed, addressed himself to his plate, and Lord Francis silently handed his sister a pocket-handkerchief.

Ottilia was once more prompted to pour calm on troubled waters.

"It does sound to have been a most uncomfortable marriage. I have been wondering whether Lord Polbrook has been in the habit of taking off at random. I seem to recall your saying, Lord Francis, that he has been a frequent visitor to Paris?"

It seemed to Ottilia that he dragged his attention to the question with an effort.

"Paris? Yes, I did say so. At least, he went often to France. I would not swear to his ultimate destination, but he was fully conversant with everything that was happening in the capital. The turmoil over there was increasingly a worry to him."

Ottilia heard this with a leap of interest. "Now, why?"

Beside her, Colonel Tretower took up the question with obvious relief. "Is it not the part of us all to be concerned? Apart from a general empathy with those being victimised, it is surely setting a precedent that must trouble landowners everywhere."

"Yes, but why so particularly?" Ottilia pursued. She looked across the table to Lord Francis. "Would you say your brother's interest was beyond that of most of his acquaintance?"

The dark eyes were studying her, she thought, as if he sought to fathom where she might be leading. He did not answer at once, but appeared to consider the question with care, until his mother grew impatient.

"Well?"

He appeared undismayed by the snap in her voice, merely taking a meditative sip of wine. "I think so," he said at last. "I should say his concern was inordinate. He raised the point in the House several times, calling for action from the government."

"I had no knowledge of this," complained the dowager.

"Nor had I until it was brought to my attention."

"Who brought it to your attention, sir?" asked Ottilia swiftly.

"Why, Randal himself. A few days ago, now I think of it. He was beside himself with fury, declaring that if those in authority would not make a move, he would be obliged to act."

"He did not say what form of action he had in his head?"

Lord Francis looked regretful. "Unfortunately not. I took it for one of his ranting threats. He is prone to make them and then do nothing. To be truthful, I lent but half an ear to the tirade."

"Well, why should you do otherwise?" chimed in his sister, who had recovered her composure. "I declare, he was apt to give me a headache when he began upon those rampages of his."

Ottilia was almost betrayed into laughter.

"Rampages?"

"Well, stamping about and roaring like a beast," said his fond sister dismissively. "He was like it from a child, you must know."

Ottilia glanced at Sybilla, fearing another outburst. But the dowager remained silent, sending only a flicker of irritation from the black eyes towards her daughter.

"What significance can you draw from all this?" Colonel Tretower enquired of her, saving the day.

"I am not sure I can draw one, but I recall Mr. Jardine speaking of an intention Lord Polbrook had in his mind. Indeed, Mr. Jardine appeared wholly unmoved by his lordship having left the country. I cannot help feeling that this intense interest in the welfare of the disenfranchised French gentry has some bearing upon the matter of Lord Polbrook's departure."

"An inference much to be preferred to the alternative," said Lord Francis feelingly.

Ottilia looked at him, and had spoken the thought in her mind before she could judge the wisdom of letting it out.

"Yes, but I am not at all certain that it may not provide exactly the motive we are seeking to avoid."

Since the lady's maid Venner had not been

on the premises upon the fatal night, it had not seemed politic to Ottilia to attempt to question her on the same basis as the other domestics, which would inevitably put up the woman's back. She racked her brains for an opportunity to no purpose during the rest of the evening, and then fortune favoured her just as the countess pronounced she was ready to take to her bed.

"I will look in on Candia on my way. I was thinking to offer her to share my bed, for I daresay the poor child would prefer not to sleep alone."

"An excellent notion," approved Sybilla. "Otherwise we shall have Venner wishing to remove the truckle bed from my room to sleep in there with her, and I need the woman in a fit state to serve me."

"Are you going up now, Mama? Shall I send her to you?"

"No, for I wish to talk to Francis."

The countess left the room and Ottilia immediately rose. "You will wish to be private, ma'am."

That this was patently the case was borne out by a look exchanged between Lord Francis and his friend Tretower, who instantly also got up to take his leave.

"It was kind of you to feed me, Lady Polbrook."

270

"It is the least we can do." The dowager held out her hand to him. "I have not said so, but I am indebted to you, Colonel."

"Not in the least, ma'am." He bowed over her hand, kissing her fingertips lightly. "I am only too happy to be of service."

Ottilia, having said good night, was about to follow him from the room when Sybilla stayed her.

"One moment, my dear. Will you be so good as to warn Venner that I will be up within the half hour? Pray ask her to fetch me a cup of hot milk and to be sure to see the sheets are warmed."

"Certainly, ma'am. Good night."

Ottilia hurried up the stairs, passing the first flight and carrying on up to the second floor, where her own room was situated and where Lady Dalesford had perforce also been accommodated. But the other two chambers, she understood, were assigned to the younger members of the household. It was not difficult to catch the muted voices that must lead her to Lady Candia's room, and once there she put her ear to the door with the hope of identifying them. Hearing the countess's light tones and a deeper response reassured Ottilia that her hope the lady's maid had not yet left the chamber was not misplaced.

271

Standing back, she waited in the vestibule. Within a few moments, she heard footsteps within and the door opened. Venner's thin features were illuminated by Ottilia's candle and she saw them overlaid with distress. It vanished as she caught sight of Ottilia.

"Mrs. Draycott!"

Ottilia kept her voice low. "I beg your pardon, Miss Venner. I did not wish to disturb Lady Candia, but I have a message for you from her ladyship."

She delivered the communication, and then turned deliberately as the woman started down the stairs and kept pace just behind her.

"How is Lady Candia?"

"How could she be?" countered the lady's maid sourly. "The poor dear dove."

"Yes, indeed," agreed Ottilia warmly. "It is so very sad for the children."

"Sad?" uttered the other in accents peculiarly savage. "Oh yes, sad enough to be losing your mother. If only she were worthy of the name!"

She then put a hand to her mouth as if she regretted having spoken, but Ottilia seized on the slip.

"I think you were not over fond of the marchioness, Miss Venner." The maid halted in the middle of the next flight and her eyes flashed. Ottilia hastily added, "Forgive me, Miss Venner, if I am taking a liberty. I would not mention it for the world, if it were not pertinent to the cause."

The woman's gaze narrowed as the wrath died out of it. "Cause?"

Ottilia sighed with exaggerated care. "You cannot be ignorant of the fact that everything points to the marquis in this unhappy affair."

The maid looked startled. She put up her hand and a couple of fingers ran over her mouth in a gesture betraying her unease. Then she turned and went quickly down the rest of the flight.

Ottilia hurried after her. "Miss Venner!"

The woman stopped in the vestibule and looked back. "Not here." It was a harsh whisper. She jerked her head as if to indicate that Ottilia should follow and slipped into the dowager's bedchamber. Moving to the chest below the bed, she took a taper from a silver container and begged a light from Ottilia's candle.

"My lady likes the place as bright as day," she said as she began putting the flame to the wicks in the wall sconces. "Not like my lady Emily. Preferred the dark, she did. Darkened rooms for darkened deeds."

Ottilia kept her station by the door, feeling strangely disquieted by the creature's manner. But the questions must be asked. She went for an attack direct.

"Miss Venner, why did you leave her late ladyship's service?"

The woman paused in her task, and the taper in her hand, which was poised towards a wick, trembled a little, setting the flame adrift.

"How could I stay?" The tone was low and vibrant. "How soothe my conscience? Bad enough to be cajoled into conniving, party to her deceits and lies. But to stoop below her station? And then expect me to pretend I did not know? To be a laughing stock among my colleagues, yea, even to the lowest kitchen maid or the boot boy? No, I could not."

A shudder ran through her and the taper burned out. Ottilia kept silent, her thoughts whirling. She longed to ask for enlightenment, though enough had been said to add fuel to a suspicion that had been burgeoning these few days. To gain time, she set down her candle and went to the chest for another taper. Lighting it, she moved to complete the work the lady's maid had started.

Venner did not appear to notice. She went to the bed and drew the curtains around one side and the foot, leaving the point of entry open. Then she turned and sat plump upon the bed, watching Ottilia's motions.

"I would have left her long since, but my heart misgave me." The tone was quieter now, a deadness within it that wrung Ottilia's sympathy more than had the passion. "I promised her mother I would look after my lady. And, God help me, I loved her dearly! And how was I repaid?"

The bitter note entered in at the end brought Ottilia across to sit near her on the bed in a companionable way.

"You were not appreciated." She made it a statement.

The woman's head came up, a fierce look in her face. The harshness returned to her voice. "What did I care for that? I knew what she was from the first. I expected no return of my affection. I was, after all, merely her personal maid, a servant. My lady Emily had no feelings to spare for servants. Nor indeed for anyone, bar the boy. Oh, the boy!"

"You mean Giles? Her son?"

Venner nodded. "He could do no wrong. Giles this, Giles that, until I wanted to scream. 'What of your daughter? Is she nothing to you?' And here is the poor sweet babe, weeping her little heart away, and all for the sake of that harlot."

CHAPTER 11

Ottilia held her breath. This was dangerous ground. And she half feared the lady's maid was a trifle unhinged. Hard to know if it was habitual or induced by the press of events. She ventured to pursue the matter.

"Harsh words, Miss Venner. Was her ladyship so very bad?"

"Worse. Oh, they'll think me evil to say so." Who would, Ottilia wondered? The other servants? But she reserved the question, unwilling to risk closing off the woman's tongue. "But they had not to set the candle in the window when the house was all abed. They had not to wait in the shivering dark for the furtive knock at the door and draw the bolts to let him in. Nor rise again before the lowest menial ceased his snores and creep to shut the secret out that none might know who came and went."

"Who came, Miss Venner?" Ottilia asked, low-voiced, her imagination painting a vivid image of the marchioness's clandestine amours. "Who came and went?"

Venner emitted a noise of disgust, shifting her whole upper body as if to shrug the memories from her. "Oh, they changed with the years. She tired of them soon enough. First one, then another when the first was out of favour."

"Did any of them come back into favour?"

"Only the bully Quaife. He'd battle with her once too often and be dismissed. But the months would pass and she'd forget and take him back again."

Gently, Ottilia probed, hoping the woman was too lost in reminiscence to be aware of being questioned. "There were others, you said?"

"I knew them only as shadows."

"You did not know who they were?"

"She'd greet them by name when I took them up, but I paid no mind. Do you think I wanted to know?"

"Memory is a wayward thing," Ottilia said. "We do not always realise how much we remember."

The maid looked at her, the eyes sharp and urgent. "You'd like to think one of them killed her and not his lordship. I've not been next or nigh my lady for six years. How do I know who came and went?"

"Who would know? Mary Huntshaw perhaps? Do you suppose she performed the same offices for her ladyship?"

A scornful snort came from Venner's mouth. "What, that mouse? If my lady had dared trust her!"

"Then how could she entertain if she had not means of introducing the gentlemen?"

"Gentlemen! I've a word better than that — even for them as had legitimate title to it."

"But how could they enter, Miss Venner?" Ottilia persisted.

A sullen expression entered the woman's features. "She'd keys enough. I know. She made me go to the locksmith for 'em. I told her it was a danger, but I wouldn't put it past her to give one over."

"Keys to which door? And how many?"

"There's only one door safe enough in the night hours. She used it herself to go out in secret, that's why she wanted the key."

"You said there was more than one."

"Two, in case she lost one. She was never tidy."

Ottilia was about to ask for the specific door again when the maid suddenly grasped her arm.

"If you're wise, you'll leave this. They'll not hang his lordship. What does it matter who killed her? It won't bring her back."

"No, but I'm afraid you are too sanguine. If Lord Polbrook is tried by his peers in the House of Lords, as things stand there is little doubt he will be found guilty."

Venner's stare became intent and her grip tightened. But she said nothing. Ottilia held her gaze.

"I need your help. I need names. You have mentioned Quaife. But the others? Please think, Miss Venner."

The lady's maid released her arm and sat back. She gave another dismissive shake of her shoulders. "I don't know. Theo, I think. Another may have been a Jeremy. But you'll not find the man you look for among these, not if I know it."

"Why not?"

A peal of laughter broke from Venner's mouth, a mirthless sound akin to the screech of a madwoman. Ottilia flinched a little, setting her teeth against a surge of revulsion.

The noise stopped as suddenly as it had begun and the maid rose smartly from the bed and headed for the door.

"I've to fetch the milk and send up a maid with the warming pan."

Her manner had reverted to the normal sour reserve. She opened the door and pointedly stood back from it, looking towards Ottilia.

Ottilia got up, feeling as if she had been granted an interview that was now at an end. There seemed nothing for it but to take her departure. When the two of them were outside the door and Venner had closed it, she turned.

"I must thank you, Miss Venner —"

"Don't." The fire was back in the creature's eyes. "Do you think it gives pleasure to me to revile her? She's been punished. That is enough. It is not for me to judge if she came by her deserts."

With which the woman thrust her head down between hunched shoulders and went on her way with rapid gait. Ottilia was left wondering how in the world Sybilla bore with the creature.

Lurid dreams disturbed Ottilia's repose, peopled by unnamed shadows, flittering candle flames, and sensual groans arising from a tangled panorama of shifting shapes within a curtained interior from which the ghastly bulging features of Emily, Lady Polbrook, rose in disembodied form.

Ottilia strained awake and lay panting in the dark, her heart pounding, her body sluggish and heavy. The contorted visage of the woman Venner, mouth open in maniacal laughter, hung like a pall in her mind's eye as Ottilia slowly came out of the torpor of sleep. Common sense tapped on the walls, and even as she recognised the origin of the unquiet dreams, the image began to fade. A clink outside her immediate environment sharpened her senses, and a memory leapt into her head.

Keys! Venner had spoken of keys.

Emily had two keys to a convenient door. Ottilia cursed inwardly as she remembered she had forgotten to ask which door. But there was a key. She must test for a fit, but which door?

A horrid thought threw her into near panic. In the commotion over discovering the theft of the jewel box, she had forgotten to ask Sybilla to leave the drawer of the night table intact. Heaven send the key had not been thrown away!

The clink sounded again and Ottilia realised she had woken once more to the chambermaid's dawn wanderings. Recalling the last time, she took care to advertise her wakened state with a gentle cough or two before calling out.

"Is that you, Sukey?"

There was a brief cessation of sound. Then the girl answered.

"Yes, miss."

Ottilia rose onto her elbow, groping for the break in the curtains. By the time she threw them open enough to let in the welcome light of day, albeit grey and dim, Sukey had risen to her feet and moved towards the bed.

"Fire's going nicely, miss," volunteered the girl, bobbing a curtsy.

"So I see. Thank you. How are you faring, Sukey? Is all well?"

"Well as can be expected, miss, though we ain't none of us as bad as poor Miss Candy. Sick as a cat she is, though that ain't no surprise."

"No, indeed," agreed Ottilia, pulling herself out of bed.

"Mrs. Thriplow is that cross, miss, as she'd like to poison him as done it, she says, to be giving our poor Miss Candy such a heartache."

Ottilia reached for her dressing robe and tugged it on. "I take it Lady Candia is a favourite in the household?"

"Oh yes, miss. There ain't no one don't dote on our Miss Candy. She ain't toffee-nosed, she ain't. Knows us all by name, does our Miss Candy, and she never forgets to say 'please' and 'thank you.' Nor she don't like giving no trouble to anyone."

"With the result," smiled Ottilia, "that everyone takes the greatest trouble about her."

Sukey nodded vigorously. "Oh, yes, miss. Why, even yesterday when I went in to make up the fire in her chamber, for she come unexpected like and I hadn't done it afore, and our Miss Candy were crying fit to bust herself, but she ups and greets me and says to me straight off, 'Sukey, have you a cold?' I said as it were nearly done now, but our Miss Candy says as how I should take care of myself, but I told her not to worry herself none over me for she'd enough trouble of her own, and she thanked me pretty like and you could see the poor dear were trying not to cry no more only she couldn't help it."

The rush of words were delivered with the passionate effusion typical of the chambermaid, but the encomium impressed Ottilia. She replied suitably but could not help the sneaking thought that the demise of the marchioness might not prove uniformly disastrous.

Meanwhile, she was itching to be up and doing. "Sukey, how long do you think it might take to have my hot water sent up today?"

The chambermaid exhibited consternation. "Ooh, miss, I'm that sorry it took so long that day. Things is getting more like normal, for Mrs. Thriplow ain't best pleased as the household is going all to pieces and she's been a-chivvying like a regular lion she has."

"Ah, has she? Well then, may I hope to have hot water within, shall we say, the hour?"

Sukey looked affronted. "The hour, miss? I should think Jane'd do better nor that."

"Half an hour then."

The girl nodded. "I'll tell her meself, miss." Then her eyes grew round again. "That is, if she ain't still hollering about that there jewel box and crying out as we'll all be taken for thieves and transported."

Ottilia's mind jumped. Her instant thought was that Mary, despite her warning, had let the cat out of the bag. But it did not ring true, for she had formed a good opinion of Huntshaw's reliability. Which meant someone had been listening at doors. The theft had been discussed both in the marchioness's bedchamber and in the parlour. She gave the chambermaid a sharp look.

"Who told Jane about the jewel box, Sukey?"

The girl looked scared suddenly. "I don't

know, miss. I couldn't say as anyone did, for it's all as any is talking of this morning."

Smothering a spurt of annoyance, Ottilia let it go. Small chance of discovering who had begun such a tale, she knew well. Tongues wagged so readily in domestic circles, she doubted even the redoubtable Mrs. Thriplow could trace it down. But the notion revolving in her head was disquieting. Suppose it was the thief who had set the story going in a bid to divert attention? If so, the finger pointed inevitably to one of the staff, for the news could not have come from outside the house.

Dismissing the chambermaid, she moved to warm herself by the fire. Sukey's final revelation did not encourage her to suppose that the hot water would indeed make its appearance in under an hour, and in the meanwhile she was wasting precious time. She must get that key — if it was still there. There might be a few servants about, but the family would be abed for an hour or two yet. Besides, her mission was too important to be set aside for mere convention, Ottilia reasoned.

The decision made, it was not long before she stood in front of the late marchioness's chamber door with the key turning in the lock.

Daylight spilled into the room from the unshuttered windows and the blinds were up. The chaise longue had been moved out of the way and several open trunks were set in a row along the wall to one side. Ottilia gave each a cursory glance, enough to see that Sybilla's orderly hand was behind the organisation. Although she and Lady Dalesford had, with Mary's help, made an excellent start on the disposal of Emily's effects, there was still a great deal to do.

The bed had been stripped, and the bare mattress had a poignancy that threw the loss of its former occupant into high relief. Ottilia was relieved she had insisted upon the doors remaining secured and the key in her possession. There was no chance Lady Candia might wander in to be ripped apart by this distressing scene.

The bed-curtains were securely tied at each post, and as Ottilia came around, heading for the night table, she was struck by an oddity that had gone unnoticed when the curtains had been drawn about the bed. The back drapes behind the headboard had also been pulled back and tied, and Ottilia could clearly see that the four-poster was not flush against the back wall. Moving up to the head, she looked behind the near post. There was a gap of several inches.

Distracted from her mission, she stared at it for several moments, a picture forming in her startled mind and filling it with question. If the possibility had any substance, it put a vastly different complexion on the whole premise.

"Ottilia?"

She looked swiftly across the bed. Lord Francis stood by the door, attired as she was in his nightclothes, a dressing gown over all. He had spoken softly and his look was questioning. It came to her belatedly that he had used her given name, and a cascade of warmth rushed into her bosom, throwing her off-balance.

"Oh, it's you."

She knew she must sound foolish, but her wits seemed to have deserted her and she could think of nothing sensible to say.

"What in the world are you doing in here at this hour?"

A laugh escaped her at that, and her tongue leapt into action. "I might ask you the same question."

The smile lit his face and Ottilia's breath vanished.

"Touché!" He came into the room, casting a look over the trunks. "I was in my brother's room and heard the lock turning."

"And thought I might be the murderer

returning to the scene of the crime?"

Lord Francis eyed her, his expression unreadable. "Something of the sort." He glanced back at the open door. "Let us hope none of the servants takes it into his head to look in on us."

"Indeed," she managed, breathlessness returning. "A highly improper encounter."

He cast a rueful glance down at his night clothing, and gave a sudden grin, which affected her not a little.

"Then we had best keep the matter strictly between ourselves. But I am yet in the dark. Why are you in here?"

Instead of answering, Ottilia gestured towards the back of the bed. "Do you suppose a man might conceivably conceal himself behind the back drapes?"

An arrested look replaced the humour in Lord Francis's face as his glance moved to the back wall. He did not speak, but moved to the head of the bed on his side and in his turn looked behind it.

"Shall we essay it?"

"By all means."

Ottilia watched as he inserted himself, not without some difficulty, into the space behind the headboard.

"It's not particularly comfortable," he

commented, bracing his back against the wall.

"I doubt comfort was the first consideration." Ottilia moved to the bottom of the bed and turned to look again. "I cannot see if you create a bulge or not."

"That is easily remedied."

He pushed his way out again and began untying the bands holding the folds of the drape together. Ottilia immediately moved up the other side of the bed again and performed the same office. She was obliged to get onto the bed to pull the drapes fully across. Then she sat back on her heels and inspected the result.

"Try now."

Lord Francis's dark eyes raked her in a fashion oddly disturbing. Ottilia became doubly conscious of her unconventional attire and her hair lying unkempt and loose about her shoulders. Heat stole into her cheeks.

His eyebrow quirked. "Are you going to stay there? You are bound to see me if you are on the bed."

"Very true," Ottilia agreed, conscious of an inexplicable feeling of disappointment. She banished it, concentrating on the task in hand. "Also, I imagine the bed's occupant would already know that you were there."

By the time she had managed to drag herself off the bed and resume her position at the foot, Lord Francis had inserted himself into the place of potential concealment. His voice came to her muffled.

"Well? Can you detect my presence?"

She surveyed the drapes, a pulse beginning to thrum as excitement mounted. "If I stare intently, I think there is a bulge. But I doubt I would notice anything at all if I was not expecting to see something."

"And some of the other curtains might well be drawn," came the indistinct response, "which would —"

"— undoubtedly make you far less easy to detect."

Lord Francis's head reappeared around the side. "Have you seen enough? Can I come out now?"

"Pray do." She watched him force an exit. "You realise what this means?"

He was busying himself with pulling the drape on his side open again and retying it, but he looked up at that. "I can hazard a reasonable guess."

"I had not before considered the notion that a lover might already have been in the chamber when your brother and his wife quarrelled."

Lord Francis finished his task and looked

at her with a gathering frown. "Without witnesses, how the devil could we prove it, Mrs. Draycott?"

The resumption of her title caused Ottilia's spirits to slump, but she answered with composure. "We can't prove it, not without discovering who it might have been."

He let out a groan. "Impossible."

Ottilia clicked her tongue. "Must you give up before we have even made the attempt?"

He stiffened. "I am hardly likely to give up with my brother's life at stake!"

Ottilia instantly backtracked. "Of course not. I spoke without thinking."

The spark in his eye lessened. "It makes no matter."

Feeling awkward and self-conscious, Ottilia tried for a softer approach. "There is hope, my lord. I have already three names."

The effect was immediate. He looked at once alert and incredulous. "Three names? How in the world did you come by them?"

Ottilia could not resist. "Did not your mother stigmatise me a genius?"

To her delight, his lips twitched. "Don't tease, Ottilia."

Her heart swelled, and she felt heat rise to her cheeks. To cover it, she broke into rapid explanation. "I had them from Miss Venner last night. The only one of real use is Quaife.

The other two are merely Christian names, and uncertain at that."

But Lord Francis's brows had drawn sharply together. "Quaife? Then rumour does not lie."

Ottilia lost all shyness in immediate interest. "His name has been coupled with Emily's?"

He nodded. "Frequently. I know he was at one time her most assiduous cicisbeo, but it was never certain whether it had gone further than that."

"According to Venner, he came in and out of favour over time. She called him a bully."

The dark eyes burned. "Did she so?"

Ottilia put up a warning finger. "Do not let us leap to conclusions. What sort of a man is he?"

"The Baron Quaife? I am barely acquainted with him. He is years older than I." Lord Francis shrugged. "He is a heavy-set fellow, not a bonhomous type, but courteous enough."

"A large man?"

He eyed her with question, and then glanced to the shallow place behind the bed he had lately occupied. "You are thinking he would not fit the hiding place? It is a consideration." He sighed in a disappointed fashion. "Who were the others?"

"She mentioned Theo and Jeremy."

Lord Francis cast up his eyes. "That is no help at all. Unless you choose to pore your way through the peerage."

Ottilia laughed. "I do not so choose. However, a little enquiry may elicit something."

He was looking at her with a frown in his eyes.

She raised her brows. "What is it?"

"How was it you thought of this hiding place?"

She smiled. "I didn't. I came in here to fetch a key." Recalling her mission, she clicked an impatient tongue. "If I had not forgotten all about it again!"

"What key?"

Ottilia made a face. "I am afraid you will not like to hear it, but there is no point in keeping it from you."

She gave him an unvarnished account of her conversation with Venner, and secretly rejoiced to see how his disgust increased with every word. It was not uncommon for gentlemen to condone the sort of intrigue in which the marchioness had indulged. Whether his disgust was due to an offence of his moral sensibilities, or whether it was merely because Emily had been related to him by marriage, Ottilia had no means of knowing. But she was cheered nevertheless.

"I came in here because I remembered I had found a key in that drawer," she finished.

She moved to the bedside table as she spoke and drew open the top drawer. To her relief, it had not yet come under notice in the attempt to dispose of the marchioness's effects.

As she rummaged within for the key she had seen, she suddenly recalled the scrap of paper she had removed from this very drawer. Her hand stilled.

"Q230. *Q* for Quaife."

"What are you talking about?"

She found, to her consternation, Lord Francis just behind her, and she half turned, conscious of a spurt of speed in the rhythm of her pulses.

"I found a note among others in here. But this was the only one that looked to be significant. Just the letter *Q,* and the numbers two, three, oh. I think now it must have been an assignation."

His eyes widened. "Quaife at two and thirty? In the early morning, one supposes."

Ottilia nodded. "It seems likely."

"And the key?"

Turning again, Ottilia hunted about the drawer with a hand that was not quite steady. Her fingers closed on the coldness of metal. She brought them out, a large key clutched within them.

Lord Francis took it from her and examined it. "It looks vaguely familiar, but I don't know what door this might fit."

"Then we must try them all until we find the right one."

She would have moved to begin, but Lord Francis stayed her, one hand resting lightly on her arm.

"You can't wander all over the house dressed like that."

Acutely aware of his touch, Ottilia's brain froze and she could not answer.

"Besides, there is no saying this fits into a door to the outside. It does not look heavy enough to me."

Ottilia swallowed on a dry throat. "Nevertheless, we must try. We know Emily used a door secretly, for Venner told me so."

He removed his hand, shifting past the bed and out into the room. "It will keep. You would be better employed at this moment in helping with my own search."

Ottilia was breathing more easily, but this last arrested her attention. "What search is that, sir?"

He looked at her, a glint in his eye that Ottilia strongly suspected to be ironic. "You have not asked my purpose in being up at this hour, and so improperly dressed."

Ottilia laughed. "I rather had my attention elsewhere."

"I was searching Randal's room for something to tell us why he went away."

Interest burgeoned in Ottilia. "Did you find anything?"

He shook his head. "I had only begun when I heard you. I should be glad of your help." An eyebrow quirked. "Assuming you dare to continue to risk being compromised?"

Ottilia hoped the heat did not show in her face. "Oh, I hardly think a widow of my years need be troubled by such fears," she said lightly. "Besides, our purpose is sufficient, should anyone call our activities into question."

He said no more, but merely nodded and crossed to the door. Slipping the key into the pocket of her dressing robe, Ottilia began to follow, and then her eye fell on the bed. She checked.

"One moment, sir. I forgot to retie the drape on my side."

She went up to the headboard again as she spoke and leaned to pull the velvet drape back. It eluded her grasp and Lord Francis came back and knelt on the mattress, reaching over to flick it towards her. A fold of his dressing gown fell away, and Ottilia was treated to a glimpse of bare leg. Flustered, she lost her grip upon the tie and it slipped to the floor behind the night table.

"Drat!"

Dipping down to her haunches, she felt about behind, her pulse out of kilter and a resurgence of burning in her cheeks.

"Here, allow me."

Ottilia looked up to find Lord Francis directly above her on the bed, his untied lush hair falling about his face. Unable to move for an instant, she stared up at him, conscious of fluttering in her stomach. He grinned down at her and her mouth went dry.

"Are you going to get up? I don't wish to tread on you."

She threw herself to her feet with more haste than elegance and moved quickly aside as Lord Francis dropped lightly off the bed and swept a long arm out of sight by the night table.

Ottilia's hands were shaking, and she thrust them into the folds of her dressing robe. A grunt of triumph came from his lordship and he pulled his arm back. The band was in his fingers and he drew it forth.

"But what is this?"

She hardly heard him, her startled gaze taking in the silky white article that had become attached to the fringes on the end of the tie. Lord Francis detached it and held it up. Ottilia gasped as the crumpled garment fell to its length.

"Her stocking!"

All embarrassment forgotten, she stepped forward and took it from his grasp, letting it slide through her fingers. Her mind alive with conjecture, she regarded first the stocking and then the back wall.

"Is the other there?"

Lord Francis, who had been watching her with his brows drawn together, looked first under the bed, and then rose quickly and looked over the headboard.

"Not that I can see."

Ottilia went quickly around the bed to the other side and squinted down at the floor behind. There was nothing there. He was watching her across the divide of the bed.

"What are you thinking?"

"That there was a man there. Or perhaps not, and the stocking fell behind the bed during the activities within it. It might have been thrown aside, perhaps. It might even be an old one, lost months ago."

"You are saying it proves nothing."

She gazed at him, troubled by a nagging

doubt. "Mary Huntshaw and I searched high and low for any sign of the stockings. And here we have one. I would give much to know what happened to the other."

Lord Francis drew in a sharp breath and let it go. "There is nothing to be gained by conjecture at present. Let us hope we may be as lucky in my brother's chamber."

Ottilia had forgotten that other task. She bundled up the stocking and tucked it into the pocket of her dressing robe, preparing to follow Lord Francis, who was already moving to leave the chamber. She paused outside to lock the door behind her, but Lord Francis was already moving through the open doorway opposite. Ottilia checked on the threshold, taking in the marquis's room.

It was a mirror of the other in shape, but a little larger, the four-poster with its plush dark curtains placed in a similar position. But here were none of the feminine curlicues that graced the marchioness's chamber. The whole was strictly masculine, its contents solid and austere.

Lord Francis had gone directly to a chest where the second drawer was already open, and had evidently resumed his interrupted scrutiny of the articles within.

"What are we looking for?" asked Ottilia,

moving into the room and looking round for a place to begin.

Lord Francis turned where he stood. "Do you not wish to know why my mother wanted to talk to me last night?"

Startled, Ottilia gazed at him. "It is none of my concern."

"Oh, I think you will be interested."

"Indeed?"

"Since you provoked her thoughts with a remark you made last night." He left the chest and moved a little towards her. "She is severely exercised by the puzzle of what Randal is doing in France."

Ottilia's mind leapt to the conclusion she had made at dinner and so foolishly blurted aloud. Wary, she eyed Lord Francis.

"Had she any suggestions?" He hesitated, looking away and back again. Ottilia gave a light laugh. "Come, sir, you cannot be shy of mentioning it to me when you know my propensity for frankness. Let us not beat about the bush. Does Sybilla suspect your brother may have a mistress over there?"

He gave a sigh, as if of relief. "I have long suspected it. There have been too many visits, and the concern he exhibited over the welfare of the unfortunates over the Channel has made me believe the woman in question may be an aristocrat, and likely married."

"And so he fears for her safety."

"My mother has taken the notion into her head from something Emily's woman said."

Ottilia nodded. "About your brother threatening an end to Emily's tenure as his wife."

"Yes, and you may imagine how black it will make him look."

"Indeed." Ottilia looked briefly about the room. "Letters, then? Perhaps a love token of some sort?"

He grinned. "There now, I knew you would be useful to me."

But the most thorough search through every drawer and cupboard failed to turn up anything that could point to the existence of a mistress. Lord Francis groaned with frustration.

"I shall have to go through his desk in the library, something I was hoping to avoid."

"I imagine it is more likely to yield results." Ottilia closed the last drawer in the dressing table she had been checking. "What a pity there is nothing here."

"I can't imagine the library will yield any incriminating piece of evidence, either," said Lord Francis irritably. "I could have sworn Randal's affections were engaged, so assiduous has he been in trying to benefit these dispossessed French."

Arrested, Ottilia stared at him. "Where have our wits gone begging?"

"I beg your pardon?"

She waved a dismissive hand. "Oh, I don't mean to denigrate you, sir, but I have certainly shown myself remarkably foolish."

He was frowning. "How so?"

"Picture to yourself, my lord. You are passionately in love. Where do you secrete your keepsake?"

Lord Francis gave an eloquent lift of his shoulders. "I have not the remotest conjecture. I have never cherished a keepsake."

Ottilia threw him a darting look of mischief as she moved to the bed. Leaning over it, she pulled aside the coverlet and slipped her hand beneath the pillow, sweeping from one side to the other.

"You surely don't think —"

She cut him off with an exclamation of triumph and brought her hand out again. A small oval frame was revealed. She looked at it briefly and held it up, showing Lord Francis the miniature depicted there.

"A handsome creature, I think you will agree."

He came to take it from her, amazement writ large across his countenance. "Dear Lord, woman, you really are a genius!"

She gave a mock curtsy. "I thank you, my lord."

"This alters things indeed," he uttered, still staring at the lovely face shown in the tiny portrait with its cascade of fair locks. "What in the world do we do now?"

"We must find this lover of Emily's," answered Ottilia briskly, retrieving the miniature and tucking it back where she had found it, "and with speed. I cannot think the justices at Bow Street will be slow to seize upon the implications of this as the perfect motive for murder."

CHAPTER 12

Francis was never more glad to have his friend George's support as he entered the portals of Brooks's. The very first pair of gentlemen he encountered in the hallway broke off their conversation to stare at him. Feeling intensely conspicuous, Francis busied himself with handing his greatcoat, hat, and cane to the porter, throwing Tretower a look designed to convey everything he felt.

"Sheer bad manners," said George in a voice loud enough to be heard. And in a lowered tone as the two other men shuffled swiftly about, displaying their backs, "A pair of gaping fools, Fan. Don't mind them."

"I am minded to let Mrs. Draycott go hang, if that is a sample of what I may expect," Francis rejoined savagely, smoothing sleeves ruffled by the exercise of removing his greatcoat.

George laughed. "Run the gauntlet, dear

boy. You will rapidly become accustomed."

"I've a good mind to cut and run."

George took hold of his elbow in a companionable way. "No, you don't. I am pledged to keep you up to scratch, you know."

"Yes, I heard the dratted woman ask you before we left the house."

"That 'dratted woman' is merely serving your purposes, Fan, as well you know."

Francis blew out a frustrated breath. "Do you suppose I would be here if I didn't know that?"

"Come, my friend. Recollect that your funereal garb will afford some degree of protection."

True enough, Francis reflected. He had donned the severest black for this excursion, his sister having reminded him, before returning to the care of her prostrate niece, that he ought to be in mourning attire if he meant to appear in public. He straightened his shoulders and gestured towards the door that led into the Club rooms.

"So be it. Lead me to the scaffold."

But his emotions upon entering the saloon centred less, to his surprise, on the embarrassment of his position than the oddity of being obliged to regard his erstwhile friends and acquaintances with suspicion. A number of gentlemen were present with whom he would, but a few days ago, have enjoyed a convivial evening. Today he looked from group to group, variously engaged in desultory or eager conversation, or merely reading the latest newssheet or sporting magazine, and saw only candidates for the role of Emily's paramour. It was distinctly unsettling.

He had not failed to notice the sudden hush that fell upon each couple or group as they caught sight of him, and it was only George's firm hand at his elbow that enabled him to retain a pose of nonchalance and appear unaware.

Only half-conscious of where he moved, he allowed Tretower to steer him to a position to one side of the large saloon. He watched his friend signal a waiter.

"Ale, Fan? Or would you prefer wine?"

"I will have coffee," Francis said, firmly squashing a desire to demand brandy. He needed his wits about him. He looked about for a convenient chair.

"Don't sit," advised George, low-voiced. "It will discourage people from approaching you."

"I don't want them approaching me," said Francis acidly.

George's brows rose. "Come, Fan, is this

the man of spirit renowned throughout the regiment for the iron in his backbone?"

"At this moment, my backbone feels filleted. I had rather face fifty cannon than the avid curiosity of my peers."

His friend's smile was sympathetic. "I don't altogether blame you, dear boy, but needs must as I understand it. Now, what was it? Beware the effusive, ignore the gossips?"

"I can't recall." Francis's eyes wandered as he spoke and caught upon a thickset man standing apart across the room. "Lord, there's Quaife!"

"Where?"

Francis allowed his gaze to lead his friend where to look, and quickly turned away as he saw the quarry's eyes were on him.

"He's coming over," George warned. "We're off."

Francis felt a rise of panic and struggled to suppress it. At all costs he must not exhibit any hint of suspicion or an iota of his allotted task. All too soon, the Baron Quaife had reached them. His manner was brusque to the point of rudeness.

"Fanshawe! In good time, sir. Rumour is rife about the town. Is it true?"

Considerably taken aback, Francis did not answer immediately. This was hardly the approach he had anticipated. Useless to pretend to misunderstand.

"If you mean, is it true that Lady Polbrook is dead, I am desolated to be obliged to affirm it."

"Yes, yes, but the other. Slain? And brutally so, if the word flying around town is to be believed. Tell me it is not so!"

A vibrancy of dismay rang so true that Francis answered without thought.

"I cannot."

Quaife looked as if he had been struck in the face. "Then it is so? Thunder and turf! But I saw her, spoke with her, only the night before. How is it possible?"

"An impossible question, sir," cut in George, loyally sparing Francis the necessity of answering. "You may believe the shock to the family is as severe as your own."

Quaife stared at him, a species of blankness in his eyes. Then his gaze returned to Francis. "Your brother is out of town, I gather?"

"Temporarily," Francis said. And if the fellow thought he would elaborate, he was destined to be disappointed.

Quaife lifted a hand and ran it over his face in a gesture redolent of confusion. "I still cannot believe it."

George took the comment. "No, sir, nor

can all those intimately involved."

This seemed to penetrate. Quaife gave an odd frown, glanced from George to Francis, and then looked as if he was suddenly enlightened. He bowed from the neck.

"My condolences, Fanshawe."

With which he turned on his heel and headed directly for the door. Francis watched him until he had left the saloon.

"He is either a very good actor or he is not our man," suggested George quietly.

Francis shook his head. "I think it was genuine."

There was no time for more. It seemed the baron's approach had broken the ice. One after another, Francis received words of regret from his acquaintances. It gave him the oddest feeling of alienation to be watching each with unanswered questions in his mind. It was apparent Mrs. Draycott knew what she was talking about. The majority moved in and spoke their piece briefly and to the point. Francis found himself mentally reviewing their Christian names.

"Do you see anyone who answers to Theo or Jeremy?" he asked his friend during a lull.

"Not that I recall. But I am dubious about that altogether. The information from this previous lady's maid appears sadly out of date."

Impatience gnawed at Francis. "This is useless. I believe we are wasting our time. No one has so much as hinted at Randal's involvement."

"Except Quaife."

"Obliquely, yes."

He finished the last of his coffee and looked about for a waiter to ask for his cup to be replenished. Abruptly he became aware of being under scrutiny. A pair of eyes in a youthful countenance were darting towards him and away again. He nudged Tretower.

"Do you know that young fellow over by the fire?"

George glanced round. "The pretty little fop with the yellow hair standing alone?"

Francis would not have described the boy as a fop, but he was undoubtedly a devotee to fashion. His green coat was moulded so tightly to his slim form, one must suppose it required the efforts of a couple of men to remove it. His breeches clung to a pair of shapely thighs, and his boots were polished to perfection. The epithet "pretty" scarcely did justice to a face made for the sculptor's art, though it wore just now an expression of severe anxiety.

"He looks worried to death and he's been

watching me. Not now, of course, but he was."

While he signalled the waiter, Francis kept a surreptitious eye upon the young man, aware that George did likewise.

"What do you think of him?"

"Behaving like a cat on a hot bakestone," said Tretower, interest in his voice. "Shifting from foot to foot and keeps clenching a hand, did you notice?"

The waiter took his request and Francis turned, giving his profile to the boy. "If we affect not to notice him, we may force him to come up to us."

"I doubt he has the courage," said George, "though he is making it obvious that is precisely what he wants to do."

By the time the waiter returned with his second cup of coffee and another tankard of ale for Tretower, Francis was growing restless.

"Does the wretch mean to make his move or not?"

"Patience, my friend. He does not know either of us, which complicates matters for him."

"I've a good mind to go over and ask him what he means by staring at me."

"You will ruin all if you do."

Francis looked at him. "Then you think it

significant?"

"Don't you?"

He sighed. "I think our minds are so full of this event that we can think of nothing else. For all I know, there may be a perfectly legitimate reason for his conduct, utterly unconnected with Emily's decease."

As if to confound him, at this moment the young man started across the room. Francis turned to await his approach. The boy came up, his cheeks reddening as he coughed with obvious embarrassment.

"I beg your pardon, my lord, but I — I wished to — to offer my heartfelt condolences on your — on your loss."

His hesitant speech, interrupted by a battery of swallowing and dipping of the head, argued an unquiet mind. Francis eyed him with acute suspicion.

"I have not the pleasure of your acquaintance, sir."

The boy shook his head with vehemence. "No, my lord. But I — I knew her ladyship. Lady Polbrook, I mean. She was — she was excessively kind to me."

"Indeed?"

Francis felt himself bristling. Was this meant for euphemism? The fellow was half Emily's age. Disgust roiled in his gut.

"I am but newly come to Town, my lord.

Emily — Lady Polbrook — was kind enough to — to smooth my path a little."

George was noticeably silent. Francis glanced at him and found him studying the fellow. Was he making the same assumptions? He shifted his gaze back to the young man.

"You still have the advantage of me, sir."

The boy looked perplexed. And then flushed deeply. "Oh! I beg your pardon. My name is Bowerchalke, sir. Jeremy Bowerchalke."

Francis all but exclaimed aloud. And then confusion beset him. Six years? It could not be the same man. He broke into speech.

"You are new in Town, you said?"

Bowerchalke nodded. "These three weeks."

"How did you meet Lady Polbrook?" asked George, entering the lists for the first time.

"Through my godfather, sir."

"Ah. Is it possible you share the same name?"

The young man's eyes widened at Tretower. "How did you know?"

George gave his peculiarly teasing smile. "It is a common courtesy. Who is your godfather?"

"Sir Jeremy Feverel."

314

"And Sir Jeremy felt Lady Polbrook would be a useful acquaintance, I take it?"

Red chased into the boy's cheeks once more and he stuttered cruelly in his response. "She — he — it was a matter of — of introduction. The marchioness knows everyone. She was — she was graciously pleased to — to present me. I am indebted — wholly indebted. I cannot bear to think — a hideous thing! It has utterly overset me." He thrust a hand into the interior of his coat and brought out a pocket-handkerchief, pressing it tightly to his lips. "I must beg — excuse . . ." came muffled through the cloth.

And then he turned quickly, thrusting wildly through the chattering groups and out into the smaller saloon beyond.

Francis fairly gaped after him, feeling stunned. Beside him, Tretower clicked a ruminatory tongue.

"Well, well. Fascinating, wouldn't you say?"

Francis turned to face his friend, speaking the immediate thought in his mind. "He couldn't have done it. He's far too slight a man. He wouldn't have the strength."

George nodded slowly. "But he knows."

Arrested, Francis eyed him. "Knows what?"

315

"A great deal more than he is saying. Did you remark his aspect at the finish? I believe he was about to be violently ill."

Shock ripped through Francis. "You mean he saw it?"

"Hideous, he said. Now wouldn't you say that fairly describes the sight we have all been obliged to witness?"

Having lain in wait unseen in the Blue Salon while the servants cleared away the remains of breakfast and tidied the dining parlour, Ottilia seized her moment to catch the butler alone, hissing at him through the connecting door.

"Psst! Cattawade!"

The elderly servant visibly jumped, turning quickly from his position at the round table by the window and dropping the cloth he was in the act of folding. At sight of who called him, his brows beetled and an austere look entered his face. Ottilia became impatient.

"Do not frown at me, if you please, but come in here for a moment. I must speak with you alone."

Cattawade cast a brief glance towards the door to the vestibule, which remained firmly closed, and crossed in his stately way to where Ottilia awaited him. Without ceremony, she grasped his sleeve and pulled him through the aperture, closing the door behind him. His severity intensified.

"What can I do for you, madam?"

"Keep your voice down, for heaven's sake! And come away from that door."

Thus adjured, he followed her into the centre of the room. Ottilia turned back to him and was relieved to note a glimmer of change in his aspect. The urgency of her manner must be affecting him at last.

"What is the matter, madam?" he asked, in a lowered tone.

"A great deal," Ottilia answered at the same level, "but this will suffice. Have you any notion whence came the story of your mistress's missing jewel box?"

His brows parted and lifted sharply. "How did you know the news had broke, madam?"

"From Sukey. She could not tell me who had begun the tale, however."

Cattawade eyed her warily. "I take it the story is true?"

Ottilia nodded. "Mary Huntshaw and I discovered the theft on Sunday. But Mary promised to keep mum, and I believe she did. Indeed, she came to my room this morning while I was dressing expressly to assure me she had said nothing of it."

"You may trust to that, madam. Mary is a

very truthful girl."

"Then who is not, Cattawade? Who could have set the story about?"

The butler looked grave. "I cannot tell that, madam. This is a large household."

"I am aware. And a great deal goes on behind the scenes, no doubt, to keep everything afloat."

"Precisely, madam. Mrs. Thriplow and myself encourage the staff to be about their business as unobtrusively as possible."

Ottilia let out a frustrated breath. "Which means anyone might have been within earshot of the marchioness's dressing room when Mary and I were in there. I have not overlooked that possibility, Cattawade. But why wait until now to pass on such a piece of news?"

The butler looked struck, and his frown reappeared. "Because it affects each one of us, do you mean, madam?"

"Just so." Ottilia watched the implications sink in and reinforced them. "It smacks less of indignation than of mischief-making, do you not think?"

From his expression, Ottilia saw that her words had gone home. She thought she read a trace of alarm in the man's eyes and judged the time ripe to pounce.

"By the by, Cattawade, was it Abel's

evening off that night you found me downstairs? Saturday, was it not?"

Something flashed in the butler's eye, but it was veiled so swiftly that Ottilia could not be sure she had seen it. She waited, letting her steady regard remain upon his. Cattawade endured her scrutiny for several seconds and then averted his gaze, flicking across the room and back.

"Saturday, madam?"

"The first night Lady Polbrook and I stayed here. Was Abel off that evening?"

The butler now looked frankly puzzled, as if he wondered why she asked. Ottilia did not enlighten him. He appeared to have difficulty adjusting his mind to the change of subject.

"Let me think, madam. The routine having been thrown out of kilter, Mrs. Thriplow and I have been obliged to make adjustments." He was silent for a moment, and then his face cleared. "It should have been Abel's evening off, madam, yes. I don't recall as I sanctioned it, but if he took it, he was within his rights."

Ottilia digested this. "I see. And does he sleep out on such occasions, do you know?"

"I've known him to do so, madam, yes. His mother resides at some little distance from the metropolis."

"But he is usually back at his post in the morning, I take it?"

"I have never had reason to complain of his absence, madam."

An evasive answer, but Ottilia thanked him with a smile, adding, "I am sure you will keep your eyes and ears open, Cattawade."

The butler assented to this, if with a degree of bewilderment, and Ottilia allowed him to return to the dining parlour, while she whisked herself out of the salon via the door to the hall where she stood for a moment in silent contemplation.

It was conceivable, then, that Abel had spoken the truth. In which case Ottilia had to have been mistaken in thinking she saw him that night. She was obliged to concede that her nerves had been on edge, and she could think of no perceptible reason for the footman to have concealed himself had he been there. Was she grasping at straws to lend to the suspicion there was a thief in the house rather than outside it? She chided herself for clinging to suppositions that failed to play out and thought how willingly she would lull such unwelcome thoughts to rest, if only Lord Francis was able to supply a satisfactory alternative.

She was about to cross the hall to join the

dowager in the parlour when a heavy tread stomping up the servants' staircase caught her attention. It was followed by several lighter feet, which so surprised Ottilia that she moved towards the vestibule to investigate.

The housekeeper presently hove into sight, halting as she reached the top of the stairs, one hand clutching the banister rail, the other at her weighty bosom. She was red-faced and panting and had clearly taken the stairs at a pace unsuited to her girth. Ottilia saw several peeping capped heads, perforce brought up short on the stairs behind. She took a step towards them.

"What in the world is this, Mrs. Thriplow? A deputation?"

The housekeeper drew a painful breath and surged forward, closely followed by her acolytes, among whom Ottilia was glad to note the absence of Mary Huntshaw.

"That it is, Mrs. Draycott, if you've a mind to call it so."

"Dear me," said Ottilia mildly. "May I ask the nature of your complaint?"

A vigorous shake of the head was accompanied by the setting of the woman's arms akimbo. "It's for her ladyship to hear, ma'am, not you."

"I am her ladyship's companion, Mrs.

Thriplow, and I must partake of anything that promises to distress her, particularly at such a time."

The housekeeper glared. "Well and so you may, if you choose, but I'll speak to her ladyship and that's that."

Ottilia raised her brows. "I see. Then let us repair instantly to the parlour."

With which she turned at once for the hall, knowing Mrs. Thriplow, the wind taken out of her sails, would follow with a lessening of belligerence.

Entering the parlour, Ottilia left the door open and approached the dowager, attempting to signal with her eyes as she spoke with exaggerated calm.

"Here is Mrs. Thriplow, ma'am, with a matter she feels bound to take up with you. Oh, and several of the maids have come along in support."

Sybilla's black eyes snapped dangerously, but she had evidently taken note of Ottilia's silent warning, for she did not immediately break into her customary harangue. Instead, she surveyed the housekeeper from her head to her heels and allowed her gaze to take in the three maids at her rear — Sukey, Jane, and a third unknown to Ottilia — who were now looking a trifle apprehensive.

"Well, Thriplow?"

The housekeeper put up her chin. "I take leave to tell you, my lady, I'll not have my girls put in fear of being took for thieves."

To Ottilia's delight and approbation, the dowager's stare was a masterpiece of incomprehension. "Who has so taken them, Thriplow?"

Discomfited, the housekeeper fidgeted a little. "Well, no one ain't, not yet. But that ain't to say as they won't, and I tell you straight, my lady, as none of my girls would dream of touching them jewels. Nor none wouldn't go snooping in the mistress's chamber to look for 'em, neither."

"How did you know the jewels were missing?" asked Sybilla, wholly ignoring this protestation.

"I didn't know it, my lady. But someone did, and everybody does now. And if suspicion is to fall upon —"

"Peace!" The dowager flicked a hand towards the three young women. "Have you anything to say?" Three pairs of eyes exchanged agonized glances. "Any of you?" There was a biting of lips and an assiduous studying of the carpet. "Has anyone accused you?" Three heads shook denial. "Very well, you may go. I have no doubt Mrs. Thriplow will speak for all of you."

From her stance by the mantel, Ottilia watched the clearly thankful maids shuffle out as fast as they could, closing the door softly behind them. But the dowager's gaze darkened as it fell once more upon the housekeeper. Her voice was vibrant with anger, but her tone was level.

"How dare you, Thriplow? What do you mean by it?"

Ottilia expected a violent comeback, but instead the housekeeper's shoulders drooped and she let out an overwrought breath.

"I had to, my lady. There weren't no other way to quiet them. I thought as I'd have a riot on my hands if I didn't. I knew they wouldn't say nothing of it to you, but I've had my ears dinned from the moment I got up out of my bed."

For an instant, the outcome held in the balance. Then the dowager let out a cackle. "Serves you right, you crafty old besom!"

Mrs. Thriplow's broad features broke into a grin. "It's well for you to be calling me names, my lady, but it's tried enough I've been these past days."

"Goodness, I should think you have," said Ottilia. "I am so glad to know it was a ruse."

Trouble entered the housekeeper's face. "Aye, but there's truth enough to the business, ma'am. If them jewels has gone, what else is to be thought but they've been took by someone in the house?"

Conscious of a frowning glance from Sybilla, as if she sought guidance on what might be said, Ottilia took an ambivalent stance.

"It would seem to be the natural explanation."

Mrs. Thriplow sighed gustily. "Never did I think to see the day I'd be shamed by one of our own." Her distressed gaze sought her erstwhile mistress. "I'd have sworn myself black and blue for the honesty of my girls, my lady, but now . . ."

"Temptation may attack anyone, Thriplow. We are none of us immune."

"Yes, for a pretty paste gewgaw or a bit of discarded lace, my lady. But them jewels is a hanging matter."

The housekeeper was a good deal upset, but Ottilia decided it was impolitic to palliate her distress with the notion of the murderer having perpetrated the theft. She returned to the nub.

"Mrs. Thriplow, can you remember who first mentioned the matter this morning?"

A pair of chubby hands were thrown in the air. "I couldn't tell you, ma'am. They was all talking at once, and it took a deal of trouble to understand what the fuss was about in the first place."

"Were any of the male servants involved in the discussion?"

"All of them, barring the outdoor fellows, though Jem and Turville came in from the stables in the midst."

Sybilla let out one of her impatient snorts. "You will never get to the bottom of it, Ottilia. Let it be. Anyone might have overheard us talking of it."

"My lady's in the right of it," said the housekeeper. "I'd have vouched for my girls as honest, but I'd not put it past one of them to be listening at keyholes. Nor Cattawade's lot, neither. If I catch them at it, they know as they'd get a box on the ear as they'd listened with, but I can't be everywhere at once."

"Very true."

With reluctance, Ottilia let the matter slide. It would be a waste of time to question every servant. Particularly since it was outside the interest of all to admit to foreknowledge of the theft. But she disliked the puzzle of it, which forced on her conflicting conclusions. A faint sense of desperation crept over her, and she fastened her hopes upon the result of Lord Francis's mission.

■ ■ ■ ■

Retelling his experience, Francis discovered, had a beneficial effect. Whether it was the calm attention with which Ottilia Draycott listened, or the fact that he was no longer the cynosure of a collection of interested eyes, he was insensibly soothed by the necessity to relate what had happened at Brooks's. What had felt momentous at the time acquired in the retelling a lessening of significance, and Francis began to think he had read too much into the matter. Mrs. Draycott speedily disabused him.

"We must find out more about this fellow," she said when he had finished. "If the marchioness had taken him under her wing, it must have been remarked."

"You think he might be the lover we are looking for?"

A snort of derision came from his mother. "Lord in heaven! I thought I had known the worst of my daughter-in-law, but it seems I was mistaken. How old was this boy?"

Rather to Francis's relief, George chose to take up the question. "No more than two and twenty, if that. He looks as if he has barely reached his majority."

"Disgraceful! Had Emily no shame?"

Mrs. Draycott put up a finger in that way Francis was coming to recognise, when she wanted to impart a caution.

"We do not yet know that she did indeed entertain this young man with intimacy."

"Oh, don't we just," muttered his mother. "What other interpretation is to be put upon the matter?"

"It may have been quite innocent," said Mrs. Draycott in the mild tone she used when she wanted to pour oil on troubled waters. Francis felt a surge of admiration. So capable a female, and yet she possessed a capacity for empathy with everyone with whom she came in contact, or so it appeared.

His mother, he knew, was in a mood to be ready to believe the worst. The discovery of the miniature under Randal's pillow had upset her more, he thought, than any other piece of evidence as yet uncovered. Fortuitously, she had not called into question the fact of himself and Mrs. Draycott being alone together, and Francis had been careful to omit any hint of their both having been inadequately dressed at the time. His mother's temper had been further ruffled when Mrs. Draycott had revealed that word of the jewel box theft had somehow spread amongst the staff, a complication which she had rightly foreseen would only add to the present disorder of the household.

"What did you think of this man Quaife?"

Francis dragged his attention back to Mrs. Draycott and the matter at hand, glancing briefly at his friend. "George was more inclined than I to regard him with suspicion because he asked after Randal. I thought he was sincere. He may have been fond of Emily."

"Well, Venner did say he had been her most favoured — er — companion."

"Don't be mealymouthed, Ottilia," snapped the dowager. "We all know what was the relationship between them."

"Yes, if we are to take Venner's word."

George was quick to seize on this. "You doubt her?"

Mrs. Draycott's mischievous look appeared, and Francis felt brighter for the first time that day. "To be truthful, I think the creature is more than a little mad. She might exaggerate, perhaps."

Francis was conscious of severe impatience. "Then who are we to believe? I had it settled in my mind that the Jeremy we looked for was this young fellow's godfather, Sir Jeremy Feverel."

His mother started. "That is only too likely. I remember that fellow was used to hang around Emily. We must ask Harriet. She did not run with Emily's set, but she knows everyone."

"Better still," said Mrs. Draycott slowly, "we will widen our net even further."

"How, pray?"

"I think you may readily assist, ma'am. Only think how much Lord Francis has found out by venturing forth."

"Do you imagine I am going to show myself in public?"

His mother's indignation did not appear to trouble Mrs. Draycott. She merely smiled, and Francis marvelled at her inexhaustible tolerance.

"You need not go so far. But perhaps you may allow some select individual to visit you. Preferably one with a long tongue."

His mother burst into laughter, in which George readily joined.

"You are quite unscrupulous, Mrs. Draycott," Francis told her, but he could not help smiling.

"No, why? I am merely trying to discover the answers to pertinent questions."

"What questions precisely?"

She spread her hands. "So many. Who spoke or danced with Emily at the ball that night? Did she have the fan or not? Did anyone take it from her, or were they given it? Whom did she see? Whom did she talk to? Whom, in a word, was she consorting with in the hours before she was killed?"

There was a silence. Francis supposed the others were thinking over these queries as he was.

"With discretion," she went on, "we may be able to discover whether this young fellow Bowerchalke was thought to be more to the marchioness than a mere protégé."

"Fanfan!"

He turned at his mother's sharp tone. "Have you a gossip in your head, ma'am?"

"No, but I aim to find one. Pray send someone to Bruton Street to bring back any cards that may have been left."

"Bravo, Lady Polbrook," approved George, laughing. "I'll wager you will have been inundated."

Francis was already by the bellpull and was about to give it a tug when the door fortuitously opened and the footman entered, evidently deputising for Cattawade.

"Lord and Lady Harbisher," announced Abel.

A suspended silence greeted this announcement, and Francis watched in numb dismay as a faded lady, only too well-known to him, tripped into the room, closely followed by the portly form and plainly irate features of Emily's elder brother.

"Ha!" he ejaculated, casting a fierce glance about the occupants of the room. "It's true then. Polbrook is not here. By God, but I'll see his head in a noose if it's the last thing I do!"

CHAPTER 13

The tempestuous entrance of the newcomers caused a momentary hiatus in the parlour. Ottilia was not much surprised when, the footman having retired, the dowager was the first to break silence, and in no very amiable manner.

"If that is the attitude you intend to take up, Harbisher, you will find no welcome here."

The gentleman addressed, who had trained his bulging eyes upon Lord Francis, swung round. His cheeks, already ruddy with anger, suffused the more.

"Lady Polbrook! I did not see you there." He emitted an unconvincing cough. "Your pardon, ma'am. But you will admit I have cause to be exceptionally put out."

"Put out?" echoed Sybilla in disbelieving accents. "I should better have sympathised in your emotions, my lord, had you exhibited transports of grief."

At this, the little wisp of a creature who accompanied him rustled forward, slipping past Lord Harbisher and putting out fingers as delicate as the pallid features.

"Oh, but poor Hugh has been quite bowed down with woe since he received the letter, dear Sybilla."

"So bowed down that he comes here threatening my son?"

"No, no, he only meant —"

"Be quiet, Dorothea," ordered her lord. "If rumour does not lie, I promise you I meant precisely what I said."

"Hugh, pray —"

The intervention was not attended to. Lord Harbisher turned on Lord Francis. "Where is Polbrook? Have steps been taken to find him?"

To Ottilia's unqualified approval, Lord Francis maintained a cool tone, despite a tightened jaw and a martial light in his eye.

"Rest assured we are doing all in our power to discover his whereabouts and bring him home." He held up a hand as the other seemed about to speak. "One moment, if you please, Harbisher. Do not imagine we have not all of us been exercised by the suspicion you have not scrupled to voice, but we have not been idle and we have reason to believe that your sister did not perish at the hands of her husband."

Ottilia, glad to have the matter of the relationship satisfactorily cleared up, was nevertheless unsurprised when the late marchioness's brother let out a derisive snort.

"It will not serve, sir. No doubt you are bound to make the best of him, but I know, none better, how little affection he bestowed upon my poor sister; how violent was his language towards her. It comes as no surprise to me that his rages ended thus. Try if you can to convince a jury, but you will never convince me!"

"Oh, this is intolerable," cried the dowager, pushing herself up from her chair.

Ottilia went quickly towards her. "Do not excite yourself so, ma'am. Do you not see that his lordship's grief has overset his common sense?"

She immediately regretted her impulsiveness, for Lord Harbisher's bile sent him streaking for this new target. Ottilia found herself pierced by the man's irate gaze.

"Hey? Who the devil are you to be pronouncing upon my state of mind?"

Seeing the snap of the dowager's black eyes and a hasty motion from Lord Francis, as if he would move to intercept himself between her and her attacker, Ottilia was relieved when Colonel Tretower instead stepped into the breach.

"Allow me to make you known to Mrs. Draycott, sir, companion to Lady Polbrook." He looked at Ottilia. "The Earl and Countess of Harbisher, ma'am."

"Companion?" Ottilia was arrested by the quavery voice of Harbisher's lady. "But where is Teresa?"

Again the colonel responded, a soothing note in his voice. "Miss Mellis had the misfortune to break a leg, I believe, Lady Harbisher."

The earl turned his fiery eye upon the colonel. "You have the advantage of me, sir."

Tretower bowed. "George Tretower, sir, of the Militia. I have the pleasure of serving as an intermediary between the family and the authorities in this lamentable affair."

Lord Harbisher's eye brightened. "You do, do you? Then you can tell me this: Why has Bow Street not acted? If the authorities do not see fit to find that scoundrel and bring him to justice, I will send the Runners after him myself."

"Will you have the goodness to control your tongue, sir?" Lord Francis shifted to confront the man. "I have every sympathy with your feelings, but I will not allow you to distress my mother. If you cannot speak with any moderation, I must ask you to leave this house."

Ottilia wondered briefly if these words might send the earl off in an apoplexy, but Lady Harbisher moved to put both those trembling hands upon her husband's arm, and clung to it.

"Hugh, pray be calm," she begged in breathy tones. "For the sake of dear Emily's memory. It is not becoming at such a time to continue in this strain, my dear."

Ottilia could not imagine this pathetic appeal would serve to turn Lord Harbisher's temper, but it proved immediately effective. The earl's high colour began to fade a little, and he puffed out his cheeks as he let out a sighing breath, patting his wife's hand.

"Very well, my love, you are in the right of it." He looked across at the dowager. "I'll beg your pardon, ma'am. Trust you'll make allowances."

Sybilla looked less than mollified, but she caught her son's eye and threw out a hand in one of her typically dismissive gestures as she subsided into her chair. "We have all of us been severely overset."

"Will you not be seated, Lady Harbisher?" Ottilia indicated the chair near the fire opposite Sybilla.

The woman darted an appraising glance at her out of the thin pointed face. "Oh!

That is very kind, thank you."

Ottilia retired to the window, not feeling it behoved her to invite the earl to be seated. Lord Francis stood back and Lord Harbisher settled on his heels. With a quick glance at his friend, the colonel once again stepped into the fray.

"If it will serve to calm your fears, my lord, I may tell you that Justice Ingham of Bow Street has indeed despatched a Runner to France."

At this, Lord Harbisher started. "France? France? By God, the fellow has fled the country!"

"Nothing of the kind," snapped Lord Francis, casting an anxious glance towards his mother. "It happens Polbrook had the intention of making the journey and there is no reason to suppose he did not do just that."

"Except that he left in the small hours and my sister was found dead in the morning," returned the earl, his voice rising again. "You may be sure I have ascertained that much."

Lord Francis fairly glared at him. "How? How have you ascertained it? I did not write as much to you."

"Ha! Of course you did not, Fanshawe. You did your utmost to cover up your brother's part in this. But I took care to question Jardine, and he was very well informed."

"That wretch?" uttered Sybilla furiously. "Traitor! I shall give him pepper for this."

A question leapt to Ottilia's mind, and as if he read it in her head, Lord Francis asked it.

"Jardine did not tell you about the Runner?"

For the first time, Harbisher looked taken aback. "He knew?"

"Undoubtedly he knew. Indeed, it was he brought the news and spoke of it in this very room only yesterday."

The earl looked decidedly put out. "Fellow's as close as be damned."

"Yes, I think we are all acquainted with Jardine's habit of saying just what he wishes and no more."

A muttered exclamation from the dowager proved the truth of this assertion. Lady Harbisher's limpid gaze turned upon her.

"You have felt it, too, Sybilla. One would suppose in such circumstances . . . but there was no moving him."

All eyes turned in question upon the lady, and her lord harrumphed a little in his throat, evidently intent upon silencing her from speaking any further. Ottilia wondered if anyone else had taken the same leap. It was an opportunity too good to miss, with its chance of drawing Lord Harbisher's fangs at a stroke.

"Mr. Jardine is indeed admirably discreet," she ventured with an air of innocence. "He would not disclose the contents of the marchioness's will even though it might serve to provide a motive for the murder."

She received a sharp glance from Lord Francis, but the earl's cheeks darkened and Lady Harbisher let out a gasp and went even paler. Sybilla looked from one to the other.

"So that is it. You come here blustering and hectoring like a man demented, but all you truly want is to find out —"

"Mama," came warningly from Lord Francis, cutting her off. He turned quickly to Lord Harbisher, who looked ready to explode. "No one doubts the sincerity of your grief, sir."

"So you say." He turned on the dowager. "Your insinuations, ma'am, are nothing short of insulting. But since you have brought the matter up, yes, I did ask Jardine about the will. Because if your misbegotten son had been mentioned, I'd take a case against his benefiting to the highest authority in the land."

"You would have no need to do so, sir," cut in Colonel Tretower before the seething dowager could respond. "If your suspicions of Lord Polbrook were proven, he could not benefit in any event."

"D'you think I care if they are proven? I'll not have the man profit by Emily's death whatever the outcome. He doesn't deserve a penny of her money and I'll see to it he won't get it."

Sybilla could no longer remain silent. "You mean to condemn Randal's treatment of his wife, do you not? Well, I am far from condoning it, but the faults were on both sides, sir. Without wishing to speak ill of the dead, I am bound to point out that Emily was not precisely blameless."

Ottilia saw Lady Harbisher's fingers flutter to her mouth, her eyes flying to her husband's face. True to form, the earl's temper was ruffled again.

"Ha! You mean to put it upon Emily now, do you? You'd have me think she drove him to it, I daresay."

"Nothing of the kind," broke in Lord Francis. "It is true there was a degree of estrangement between them, but neither party could take full responsibility for that — a common enough occurrence. Which is all my mother meant to imply."

This had the effect of reducing Lord Harbisher's ire, Ottilia thought. He was frustrated from making any comment, however, for the butler entered the room at this moment, with Abel at his heels bearing a tray of refreshments. The business of serving the company provided a welcome respite.

Watching the servants' motions, Ottilia was unaware of the approach of Lord Francis and was startled when he spoke close by her ear.

"What in the world possessed you to mention the will, you wretch? I would never have believed you could be so maladroit."

The familiar fashion in which he addressed her took the sting from the rebuke. Ottilia flashed him a look of apology.

"I'm afraid it was deliberate. I had hoped to confound and so disarm him, but I clearly mistook his motive."

His eye teased her. "And I thought you infallible."

"I hope not. Why, what a prig I should be."

He tapped his ear. "I must be growing deaf. Did you say pig?"

She chuckled, hastily suppressing it as Lady Harbisher, who had moved to converse with Sybilla, glanced round. "Will you be quiet? The atmosphere is supposed to be solemn," Ottilia said, admonishing him play-fully.

Lord Francis threw up his eyes. "I am sick of solemn. Would to God I could dump all this and take ship for Italy or somewhere bright and sunny."

"Speaking of Italy," said Ottilia, disregarding this rider, "how long do you suppose it may be before your nephew is able to return?"

He sighed. "That's right. Return me to reality. Have you no pity?"

"None at all," she told him merrily. "Besides, do you forget I am delighting in this game?"

"So am I not. And I have no notion when Giles may return. Nor do I care. His presence is neither here nor there until we have discovered the truth."

"I was only thinking he might be acquainted with his mother's friends, particularly if she had developed a penchant for young gentlemen."

He suddenly squeezed her arm. "Take care. Harbisher is approaching."

With which Lord Francis moved away from her towards the earl, leaving Ottilia feeling peculiarly bereft.

"If you insist upon Polbrook's innocence, Fanshawe," Lord Harbisher was beginning, taking immediate advantage of Cattawade and his minion having left the room, "what other explanation have you for my poor Emily's demise, I should like to know?"

His wife turned where she stood, her eyes dilating. "I was just thinking the same, Francis. If Randal did not do this terrible thing, who did?"

"That is just what we are endeavouring to find out," said the dowager from behind her. "Only today we have uncovered more than one possibility."

Ottilia held her breath, fully alive to the infelicity of these possibilities in the eyes of the marchioness's brother. The matter of the will was nothing to this. She cast an agonised look at Lord Francis and found him regarding her in much the same state. He had sprung to precisely the same conclusion. How to avert disaster?

Lady Harbisher's brow wrinkled. "But it does not make sense. We understand poor Emily was safely in her bed at the time. Who but Randal — ? Oh!"

The realisation struck her dumb, and a tide of pink entered her pale cheeks, while her eyes registered an all too vivid demonstration of her own opinion of the likelihood of her sister-in-law having entertained another man in her bedchamber.

It took a moment for the implication to register with her spouse, although Ottilia could see Sybilla was before him, recognising how her own words had led to this. Colonel Tretower was steadfastly regarding the ceiling, and Lord Francis's gaze signalled a frantic message. Ottilia grimaced in response. Too late!

"Hey? What's that you say?" uttered the earl, as if he could not believe his ears. "You dare tell me Emily played him false? Not while I live!"

"Oh, for heaven's sake," burst from the dowager. "Did you take the woman for a saint? How in the world are you to know what she may or may not have done in the privacy of her chamber? You are merely her brother, sir, not her keeper."

"I will not hear this," Lord Harbisher thundered. "I will not have my sister's name besmirched!"

"But you expect me to sit mute while you revile my son," Sybilla threw at him furiously. "Well, know this, Harbisher. Your sister's amorous dealings are a byword in the *ton,* and we are hunting down the culprit from among her favourites. There, it is said. Now let there be no more mealymouthed subterfuges between us."

This attack so stunned the earl that he

was evidently lost for words for the moment. To Ottilia's senses, the other occupants of the room held a collective breath, watching the protagonists holding stare for stare.

Lord Harbisher was the first to break. He jerked his gaze away from Sybilla's, looked intemperately about the room as if he hardly knew what he was looking at, and then fastened upon the glass in his hand. With a quick movement, he tossed off the wine it contained and moved to set aside the glass. It seemed to fortify him, for he looked directly at Lord Francis.

"Is this true?"

Lord Francis hesitated. Then he gave that shifting shrug Ottilia recognised as signifying discomfort with what he had to say.

"I can't confirm Emily's conduct as certain knowledge. But it is true that we have been led to the supposition that there may be a third party involved."

"Third party," scoffed the earl. "If you mean a lover, Fanshawe, then say so, since your own mother prefers to call a spade a spade."

"Very well, if you insist," Lord Francis said coldly. "So far as we can ascertain, there is a strong possibility that Emily was killed by a man she had expected and welcomed into her chamber. You will allow that Randal is unlikely to have been such a man."

"Oh, how truly dreadful, if it is really so," uttered Lady Harbisher in broken accents. "Poor, poor creature, to be so cruelly betrayed."

She set down her glass on the mantel and sank into her vacated chair. A pocket-handkerchief fluttered from her sleeve to her hand and was held to her eyes. Of the opinion that her emotions were genuine, Ottilia looked to her husband to see how he took this. The earl was surveying his wife with a frown creasing his brows, but Ottilia believed his thoughts were otherwhere.

Colonel Tretower stepped forward. "If you will furnish me with your direction, Lord Harbisher, I will be happy to keep you informed as to the progress of the investigation."

The earl started. "Eh? Progress? By God, I'll not have it progress an inch!" His now troubled eyes swung back to Lord Francis. "You'll not shuffle this off onto Emily, and so I warn you. D'you think I'll have every scandalmongering busybody on the town bandying her name in such a fashion? Saying she came by her deserts? For that's what they will say, sure as check. I'll not have it, I tell you!"

"That is past praying for," cut in Sybilla curtly. "The whole town has been buzzing these past days. What else can you expect?"

"Nothing else," came from Lady Harbisher in accents oddly bitter.

Ottilia glanced quickly at the woman and found her pallid features marred by an expression very like a scowl. The handkerchief lately held to her eyes was now jerking between unquiet fingers. She cast an anguished look at the dowager and her voice came low and very nearly vicious.

"Is it him they speak of? Is it Quaife?"

A pulse jumped in Ottilia's chest and her eyes flew to Lord Francis. He looked aghast, as well he might, his gaze trained on Lord Harbisher. The significance of his wife's words did not register with the latter at first. Then his cheeks suffused and Ottilia braced for the explosion.

"*Quaife?* Darby Quaife? What in thunder are you saying, Dorothea?"

Lady Harbisher paled still further and a gasp of fright escaped her lips. But she rallied, looking him in the eye in a manner either foolhardy or valorous, Ottilia could not decide which.

"Of what avail to pretend now, Hugh? You know well poor Emily's name has long been coupled with his. I know he is your friend, but —"

"Friend! A pretty friend to be ruining my sister's name."

"*Was*, then. Was your friend," said his lady, as one willing to make concessions. She hurried on. "None of us can know the truth of it, my dear, but in this predicament —"

She broke off, stuffing the wreck of her handkerchief against her mouth, as if she regretted having spoken, her eyes on the fulminating countenance of her spouse. To Ottilia's relief, Lord Francis leapt into the fray.

"Do not, I beg of you, Harbisher, go off at half-cock. George and I have spoken with Quaife this very morning and —"

The choleric earl turned on him. "Then you suspect him. By God, if that fellow is the villain who crushed the life out of my sister, he shall answer for it!"

Sybilla was on her feet. "A moment since you were threatening my son in like manner. What do you mean to do? Scour the town for Emily's lovers and call them all to account? You fool, man! Can you not see how your conduct must provoke the very talk you are desirous of scotching?"

"All?" Lord Harbisher's bulk shifted to

confront her. "What in thunder do you mean, *all*? How dare you make these insinuations, ma'am? How dare you impugn my sister's name?"

"By the same token with which you impugn my son's, sir."

"Let us have done with this," exclaimed Lord Francis, impatience lending his voice a note of authority that had the oddest effect on Ottilia's pulse, making it jump unevenly. "There is enough harm done without quarrelling amongst ourselves."

"Ha! Yes, and who is harmed?" demanded Lord Harbisher, seizing on this. "Who, I ask you, is the victim here?" Unexpectedly, his voice shook, awaking Ottilia's sympathies. "You none of you cared for her. Do you think I don't know it? Do you think I have not seen how little she was valued? There is not one in this house who held her in affection, who can speak of her with —"

The opening of the door interrupted him. Glancing round, Ottilia saw Lady Candia enter with Lady Dalesford behind her. The girl, who was looking composed but peaked, no sooner caught sight of the earl than she uttered an audible gasp and clapped a hand to her cheek.

"Uncle Hugh! Oh no. I thought —" She broke off, and bringing her hand down, clasped it tightly with the other. "I beg your pardon. I heard your voice and I thought — I thought Papa was come home."

A rustling drew Ottilia's attention. Lady Harbisher had risen and was moving lightly across the room, her hands held out, her eyes brimming.

"Poor, poor child. Dearest Candia, I am so very sorry."

Tears sprang to the girl's eyes and she accepted the proffered embrace with alacrity. Ottilia could not help but remark how the frail form of the countess all but disappeared into the more robust figure of the younger female. When she was released, the earl perforce went forward, expressing his condolences in the bluff manner that seemed to overtake him when he was overpowered by the emotions of the other sex.

"A narrow escape," came a mutter close behind Ottilia.

She turned, shifting her eyes from the reunion to focus upon Colonel Tretower's face. "The poor man is in a state to blame anyone he may. I should be careful what you tell him, sir."

The colonel's intelligent gaze regarded her with a lurking twinkle. "You think he may attempt to lay violent hands upon Quaife? Let me reassure you. The fellow is well able to hold his own."

"I was not thinking of fisticuffs."

A frown appeared. "You think Harbisher might call him out? The very thing calculated to worsen the scandal? Surely not."

"I suspect his desire for vengeance is too impatient for that." Ottilia glanced across at the earl, quiet now in the presence of his niece.

"What is in your mind, Mrs. Draycott?"

Ottilia turned back to the colonel. "Bowerchalke. You spoke of a slight youth, I think."

"Lord, yes! Harbisher would break him in two."

"Then I beg you will refrain from mentioning the boy's name to the earl."

Tretower nodded, casting a grim look at the earl's broad back. "I take your point."

The entrance of Lady Candia naturally put an end to the heated discussions that had occupied the inhabitants of the parlour hitherto, and the rest of the visit passed in a spurious atmosphere of peace. Anxiety nevertheless beset Ottilia. She kept a surreptitious eye upon Lord Harbisher and could not be satisfied with his demeanour. A certain rigidity in his pose, coupled with the motion of telltale muscles in his features, spoke of his underlying discontent. His intervention, should he be moved to take matters into his own hands, would likely blight any effort to discover the truth and clear Lord Polbrook's name.

It took some time for the effusions of sympathy offered by Sybilla's specially selected intimates to run down, but at length Mrs. Arncliffe's tongue ran dry and she took up her glass of proffered wine to wet it. The female who accompanied her instantly cast herself into the breach.

"You cannot imagine how much we have longed to be permitted to condole with you, dear Sybilla," said Mrs. Bucklebury, pointing her long nose at the dowager in a manner that reminded Ottilia irresistibly of an aristocratic dog on a delicate hunt for tidbits. "Such a nasty turn it gave me when I heard."

"I don't doubt it," returned the dowager.

The dry note did not escape Ottilia, though she guessed the visitors wholly missed it. She had been assured that the cousins, who had both come out in the same year as Sybilla, been married within a twelvemonth, and widowed these last ten years, had devoted themselves to an insatiable thirst for detail about the lives of everyone with whom they came in contact

— with particular attention to anything savouring of scandal. Ottilia was familiar with the type. It became a habit with them to take a vicarious pleasure in the misfortunes of others, adding piquancy to their own uninteresting lives. In other circumstances, she would have found them an entertaining duo as they sat together on the sofa by the windows, the one as plump as a Christmas goose, the other as skinny as its skeleton after the diners had eaten their fill.

"Horrible," pursued the latter with a shudder. "Poor dear Emily."

This last held so blatant a note of glee that Ottilia could not help butting in. "You were fond of the marchioness, ma'am?"

A tinge of pink overspread Mrs. Bucklebury's sallow features and a nervous tic attacked the false redness of the lips. "Who could not be? Dear Emily. Such a sociable creature. Always the centre of the crowd."

"A crowd of gentlemen, is what you mean, I don't doubt."

Mrs. Bucklebury stared wide-eyed at Sybilla and an O of surprise opened Mrs. Arncliffe's lips. As one, the two women turned to exchange a glance of question, and again as one turned back, the light of curiosity alive in both sets of eyes.

"A fascinating woman was Emily," ventured Mrs. Arncliffe. "She never wanted for beaux."

"Oh yes," agreed the other. "I imagine half the men in London were in love with her."

The dowager was correctly attired in severest black crape for the occasion, her sewing woman Biddle having been true to her word and completed her commission to make over two gowns. She looked from one to the other eager face and then nodded in a decisive fashion.

"Come, I have known you both long enough. Let us throw off the mask."

Puzzlement entered Mrs. Arncliffe's chubby countenance, but the other was sharper. "You asked us here for a purpose."

"A sufficient one. I will be glad if you will speak with candour. Were you at the ball Emily attended on the night of her death?"

"At Endicott House? Yes, we were both there."

"It is what makes it so particularly distressing," put in Mrs. Arncliffe. "Dreadful to remember poor dear Emily, so alive and vibrant all evening as she always was, and then — oh, it makes one mad to think of it!"

"Don't think of it," said Sybilla flatly. "Think only of the evening before. Who was there? By which I mean, who was in attendance on Emily?"

Mrs. Bucklebury sat back with a satisfied air. "Ah, I thought as much. It is not certain who did the deed, is that not so?"

Her stouter cousin looked a trifle shocked, and hastened in. "For my part, dear Sybilla, I could never believe it of Polbrook. Goodness knows they were no devoted couple —" She broke off, throwing a hand to her mouth as if to stuff the words back in. "I did not mean —"

"Spare your blushes," recommended the dowager. "Did I not request you to be frank?"

"You did," cut in Mrs. Bucklebury swiftly, "and if you are looking to pin the blame upon another, you would do well to look to Quaife."

Ottilia exchanged a glance with Sybilla, and her mind flew to the previous day's uncomfortable interview with Lord Harbisher. Little had been accomplished in the way of investigations since, due to Lady Candia's presence. But Sybilla, having received a swift acceptance to her invitation to the two gossips, had instructed her daughter to remove her granddaughter from the house for the morning. "Easy enough," had said Lady Dalesford. "I shall take her to Celeste. We must both arrange for

356

mourning clothes." Lord Francis and the colonel having gone off to begin upon the funeral arrangements, the field was left clear for Ottilia and the dowager to gain insight into Emily's last night upon this earth.

Mrs. Arncliffe seemed inclined to argue with her cousin. "How can you say so, Maria? Quaife was quite outside Emily's circle that night."

"Precisely so, my dear. But he was not absent. I marked him particularly, and if his aspect did not betoken jealousy, you may call me a dunderhead, and welcome."

"But he has been quite broken away from Emily these several years," objected the other. "No, no, Maria, you have it wrong, indeed you do. It is Feverel who has been most assiduous in hanging about her."

"But only for the purpose of thrusting that pretty fellow Bowerchalke upon Emily's notice. He is Feverel's godson, you must know, and as handsome a boy as you could well hope for. Anyone might have guessed what would come of it."

"Very true. Emily had ever an eye for a pretty youth. I daresay that is what first attracted her to Theo Rookes, for he was many years her junior at the time, although of course he broke with her upon his marriage."

"That is neither here nor there," argued Mrs. Bucklebury. "I am surprised you did not remark Darby Quaife's conduct, Phoebe, for I promise you, he looked fit to slaughter young Bowerchalke that night."

Ottilia listened to the swift give and take with concentrated attention, tinged with a touch of amusement despite the sinister trend of the conversation. Sybilla glanced her way once and she signalled with the faintest shake of her head that it was wisest not to intervene. So engrossed had the two ladies become, Ottilia thought they had sufficiently forgotten where they were to allow their tongues to run unchecked, which was all to the good. But consciousness returned in a moment, and Mrs. Arncliffe was the first to blush.

"Forgive me, Sybilla, I did not mean to run on so."

The dowager flicked her hand. "It makes no matter. Tell me, did either of you notice whether anyone had Emily's fan?"

Mrs. Bucklebury's sharp gaze widened. "The Polbrook heirloom? I did see the boy fanning her after a particularly energetic gavotte, I believe."

"Did he give it back to her?"

Mrs. Arncliffe took it up, leaning forward

in a confidential fashion. "You do not know, then?"

"Know what?"

The cousin sniffed. "Oh, it is only a romantic supposition of Phoebe's. I set no store by it myself. The fan is too valuable to be used in such a fashion."

Ottilia's senses were alive to a fresh possibility. "The fan was a signal? Is that what you are suggesting, Mrs. Arncliffe?"

The lady beamed and nodded, setting her chin wobbling. "That is it exactly. I don't know how many times I have seen her hand it over, with the prettiest of smiles and a whisper in the ear. What else could it mean?"

"And the gentleman in question was invited to return it in person to her bedchamber, I take it?" There was no reply, both ladies looking a trifle taken aback. Ottilia smiled. "Pardon my plain speaking, ma'am. I am pledged to assist Lady Polbrook in this matter, and the fan is highly pertinent in this instance."

Mrs. Arncliffe goggled at her, but her cousin's glance became keen. "How so?"

Ottilia spread her hands. "That I am not at liberty to divulge."

"Never mind that," cut in Sybilla. "Can you or can you not say whether this — this 'boy' gave the fan back to Emily at the ball?"

Mrs. Bucklebury turned to the other. "Do you recall, Phoebe? I do not remember seeing it in Emily's hands. But I could not swear to it."

"Let me think." Mrs. Arncliffe closed her eyes, as if she were reviving the scene within her mind. In a moment, she opened them again and her whole countenance brightened. "Do you know, I believe young Bowerchalke had it all the time. He was by her most of the evening, though she danced with others. Emily could dance the night away, I believe, and she never lacked for partners."

"Do you by chance remember what time she left the ball?" asked Ottilia, seizing a cue.

"I did not see her leave, for I had repaired to the card room."

"And you, Mrs. Bucklebury?"

The thinner woman looked regretful. "I am afraid I cannot help you on that score. She departed before we did."

"What time was it when you both left, then?"

"Not much after one, if that. I am past these late nights."

Ottilia exchanged a glance with Sybilla. It seemed Emily's maid had judged aright.

"You cannot tell, I daresay, if the boy escorted her?"

"Oh, he would not have done," said Mrs. Bucklebury positively. "Emily never left with a favoured suitor. I must suppose she had some idea of discretion. Or perhaps she was afraid of meeting with Polbrook."

"He was there that night, was he not?" asked Sybilla.

"Oh yes, but they spent no time together."

"They never did," averred Mrs. Arncliffe. "So sad. Indeed, Polbrook was rather like Quaife in that respect. Out in the cold, you know, obliged to worship from afar."

"Well, I am sorry to contradict you, Phoebe," said her cousin, "but I cannot support any claim that Polbrook worshipped his wife. For one thing, they came and went separately always. All the world knows they were estranged." She gave a little shrug. "I do not scruple to say it before you, Sybilla, since you have enjoined our candour. And, I may add, I would not attach such significance to Quaife, either. His was rather the attitude of a dog in the manger." She wagged an admonitory finger at the dowager. "You should not discount him, you know. I daresay he had been so much in the habit of regarding Emily as his property that he could not endure to see another man take his place. Particularly a young whip-persnapper such as Bowerchalke."

Mrs. Arncliffe was looking put out. "You might say the same of Jeremy Feverel."

"No, for you are forgetting he introduced the boy to Emily."

"Hardly in the expectation of her taking him into her bed," objected her cousin, indignation suffusing her cheeks. "I should think Feverel might be justly angered by such conduct."

"Enough to throttle poor Emily? I cannot think it possible. Quaife, on the other hand, has precisely the temperament." Once more, she belatedly remembered her company and apologised. "I never was used to mind my tongue, as you know, Sybilla. But I did not mean to prattle so indiscreetly of poor Emily's sad end. I could not wish that on anyone."

"No, indeed," agreed Mrs. Arncliffe, dabbing at her perfectly dry eyes. "It is utterly horrid."

There was an uneasy silence for a moment. Ottilia, with a view to bringing back into play the useful flow of words, broke it.

"You are quite certain, both of you, that there was no other man at the ball in whom the marchioness could be said to have an interest?" She saw both ladies frown as they

362

considered the question. "Anyone with whom she danced more than others? Anyone who caught her in private conversation?"

Mrs. Arncliffe looked dubious. "She was so very popular, you must know. You would see her all over the place, talking and laughing with many."

"Oh yes, Emily was everywhere at once," Mrs. Bucklebury agreed. Her gaze narrowed. "But no. As I see it, the only one who can be said to have been in close attendance throughout was the boy."

"That is true," agreed the other with vehemence. "Wherever Emily was, he hovered, even when she paid him scant attention."

Sybilla's glance returned to Ottilia. "Could it have been he after all?"

Mrs. Bucklebury stared. "You are not suggesting young Bowerchalke did the deed?"

"The thought had occurred to me."

"Gracious, Sybilla, banish it! That young man could not strangle a kitten. He has a palsy of the left hand. The result of an accident as a child, I believe. The fingers are near useless to him, poor boy."

Francis had barely begun swallowing his breakfast upon the following morning when he was beset by a series of interruptions. First came a message from Turville at the stables, announcing that Randal's travelling chariot had arrived back from Portsmouth at last. Next arrived the lawyer Jardine, who was requested to attend Francis in the dining parlour since Candia had chosen to breakfast in bed.

"Otherwise I should have had to see him in the book room, I suppose."

"You should have let him kick his heels," said his mother vengefully.

Francis shook his head. "He could not have sought me so early if his business were not of some import."

Across the table, Mrs. Draycott set down her cup. "Perhaps he has news of your brother."

This had the effect of changing his mother's tune. "If that is so, I can forgive him everything."

At which moment Jardine made his entrance. Francis waited while the fellow performed his punctilious greetings, noting that the severity of his countenance was accentuated with a preoccupied frown. The butler was hovering.

"Thank you, Cattawade, that will be all." When the man had withdrawn, Francis turned to the lawyer. "You have news, Jardine?"

"Information rather, my lord, which came to me by a circuitous route."

"Well?"

Jardine became austere. "You did not tell me, my lord, that the Polbrook fan had gone missing."

Before Francis could answer, his mother emitted an impatient exclamation. "Since you had no interest in anything beyond keeping Polbrook's whereabouts a secret, that is hardly surprising."

"How did you find out, Mr. Jardine?"

Francis looked at his mother's companion with increasing appreciation. As ever, she went straight to the point. He had no doubt it was due to her sagacity that so much had been extracted from his mother's cronies — as wily a couple of tabbies as one could hope to know.

"I am coming to that, ma'am," said the lawyer. "It appears, my lord, that someone attempted to dispose of the fan through the medium of a somewhat disreputable fence."

CHAPTER 14

Francis exchanged a startled glance with Mrs. Draycott, but his mother was sharper. " 'Attempted'? You mean he failed? I presume it was a man?"

Jardine permitted a slight smile to curve his lip. "Indeed he failed, my lady. And it was a man."

"How did the matter come to your attention?" asked Mrs. Draycott, pursuing her theme.

"The fence in question was too fly to take the thing without enquiry. Such a valuable item, in his opinion, might well prove an untenable prize. He fobbed the man off."

Hope leapt up in Francis. "He kept it?"

The lawyer looked regretful. "No, my lord. The man in possession would not give it up. But the fence described it to my informant, a jeweller of rather better moral standing."

"And he came to you?"

"My informant thought he recognised the description, and he had heard of the tragedy of the marchioness." Jardine's nostrils twitched distastefully. "I would not have you think it was altruism. I am known in certain circles as a man who will pay for useful information."

Which came as no surprise to Francis. A man of Jardine's stamp must inevitably maintain a wide network of sources. "I suppose it is too much to hope for a description of the would-be seller?"

Jardine shifted his shoulders. "It was dark and the man was masked. The fence spoke of a man of some height, but I fear that is unreliable as a guide, for the fellow is a snivelling little weasel to whom almost anyone would appear large."

The dowager snorted. "A lot of help that is."

"Quite so, my lady."

"Thank you, Jardine," said Francis. "No doubt you made provision in case the man should return a second time?"

The lawyer's response was forestalled. "He won't do that."

Francis looked at Mrs. Draycott. "Why won't he?"

"Because he must fear to be recognised, despite the mask. If he attempts to sell it again, which is doubtful, he will go elsewhere."

Jardine was looking surprised, and Francis concealed a smile. The fellow was unacquainted with the brilliance of Mrs. Draycott's mind. She was looking at the lawyer with that intent expression that signalled a pertinent question.

"Do you know when this attempt to sell the fan was made?"

"Very soon after the — er — after the marchioness died, ma'am."

"How soon?"

"Three or four nights ago?" The lawyer cast his eyes upwards as he considered, then brought them down with a decisive air. "Likely it was Saturday."

"I fail to see that it matters," said the dowager impatiently. "It is enough that the wretch dared to try to sell the thing."

Mrs. Draycott said nothing, and Francis wondered what was in her mind. He recognised that look. She'd had a reason for the question and it clearly did matter.

Having discharged his errand, Jardine was anxious to be gone and Francis made no attempt to detain him, intent as he was upon ferreting out whatever avenue Mrs. Draycott had been treading. But the opportunity was denied him, for the moment the lawyer left the dining parlour, Cattawade reentered it, bearing a silver salver.

"This arrived by the hand of a footman, my lord. From Berkeley Square."

He presented the salver and Francis picked up the folded sheet reposing upon the tray. His mother looked across at it.

"It must be from Harbisher."

"The footman said it was urgent, my lord," said the butler.

"I imagine so," put in Mrs. Draycott. "It is not even sealed."

"If it is not one thing, it is another," Francis complained, unfolding the note. He looked at the signature. "It is from Dorothea."

"Gracious heaven, what can have happened?"

He hardly heard his mother, for he was mastering the contents. An exclamation escaped him.

"Confound the fellow!"

"Harbisher?"

"He has gone after Quaife." As if it was instinctive, Francis looked to his mother's companion. "George said you suspected this might happen."

She nodded. "Particularly if he has chosen to make enquiries. After what Sybilla's friends told us —"

"Dorothea writes that he went to Endicott House yesterday and demanded an account of Emily's movements from her hostess."

Mrs. Draycott's brows rose. "Dear me. What a pity he should be intent upon acting alone. We might with advantage have made use of his services."

Francis uttered a short laugh. "Some hope."

"The man is mad," stated his mother flatly.

"Mad with grief, yes." Mrs. Draycott's wide gaze fixed upon Francis. "Do you think you can track him down?"

"I shall have to, shan't I?" He gathered his forces. "I will send a message to George and have him meet me at Quaife's residence. Cattawade!"

The butler had effaced himself, but he came forward at once. "At once, my lord. I will despatch the boots."

"What else does Dorothea say?" asked the dowager as Cattawade left the room.

Francis passed the sheet across to his mother. "Nothing of moment beyond that. As you see, she knows Hugh has gone in search of Quaife and she fears the outcome."

The dowager was running her eyes down the scribbled note. She gave a snort. "Trust Harbisher to make a friend of a man like

Quaife. No doubt Emily came to know the man through him."

"Which must naturally add to the earl's fury," said Mrs. Draycott.

"Why so?"

"My dear ma'am, there is no enmity so inimical as that of a broken friendship. And knowing himself to have been the instrument of their coming together must be doubly galling. His guilt now is pitiful to contemplate."

The dowager frowned. "You mean he cannot endure it?"

Francis rose to his feet. "Easier to shift the blame, I take it?"

"Just so." Mrs. Draycott's smile encouraged him. "This intervention is like to ruin all, if you don't stop it. Godspeed you, my lord!"

Francis bowed slightly. "Be sure I will do my damnedest."

The Baron Quaife inhabited one of the myriad narrow terrace houses along Maddox Street and it did not take Francis many minutes to walk there. He was obliged to waste a deal of time, however, arguing with a foolish manservant who refused to state whether or not his master was home. But when his representations were reinforced by the arrival of George Tretower, resplendent in the red coat and cream breeches of his chosen calling, the fellow was instantly over-awed.

"Thank the Lord you are come, George," Francis muttered. "Try if you can get any sense out of this fellow, for I have done with the brute."

Tretower raised his brows and focused upon the offending manservant, his tone deceptively mild. "My dear fellow, what is the difficulty? We are here to see Lord Quaife. I should be much obliged if you will inform him that Lord Francis Fanshawe desires a word."

A feeling of grim satisfaction entered Francis's bosom as he noted the immediate change in the man's expression. The under-lying steel in George's voice had its effect.

"My master is not in the house, sir."

"Indeed?" George eyed the man with a meditative look Francis knew well. "I wonder, are we not the first to enquire for him this morning?"

"Why, no, sir," the man blurted out, look-ing startled. "Lord Harbisher come asking for him not a half hour since."

"Ah. And where did you send his lord-ship?"

"Brooks's, sir."

Francis grunted his satisfaction. Barely tolerating the brief time it took George to dispense with the manservant's assistance, he set off towards St. James's Street at a cracking pace.

"Hold hard, man," his friend protested. "We will not fare the better for arriving out of breath."

"Harbisher is half an hour ahead of us, George. Lord knows what havoc he might have wrought by this time!"

"You don't think he may be hampered by the public nature of the venue?"

"I think he is in a mood to ignore everything but his thirst for revenge," returned Francis. "My only hope lies in his not being a member of Brooks's."

George was moved to grin. "Ah. He'll not easily get past the porter."

"He has only to wait for some willing member to accompany him inside, however."

His mind filling with hair-raising possibilities, all of which must increase the tide of gossip and speculation, Francis hastened his steps the more.

When they entered the hallowed portals of Brooks's, however, it was at once evident that Lord Harbisher's impatience had got the better of him. The altercation was taking place in the hall, in full view of a number of members who had clearly been drawn by the commotion to come out and watch the fray.

Quaife was facing them, his pose very much that of a creature at bay, his head down as if he wore horns readying for battle. The little that could be seen of Harbisher opposing him showed him at full growl, with his hands up, fists curled and ready.

"Hey? What do you say, scoundrel? Answer! Else I'll beat it out of you."

The other came back strongly. "You'll get naught of me, Harbisher, threaten how you will. Lay violent hands upon me, would you? Try if you can best me, you big-bellied poltroon!"

A roar of rage burst from the throat of Lord Harbisher, and he sprang for the man, attempting to seize him by the throat. Quaife's hands shot up, grabbing his wrists.

Mesmerised by the ensuing struggle, Francis only half heard Tretower's rapped-out orders.

"Don't stand there like a set of dummies! Take hold of Quaife! Fan, with me."

Francis snapped his attention back to his friend and found him already taking hold of the earl's shoulders. With a fluent curse under his breath, Francis raced to his aid, tugging at one side while George heaved upon the other.

The watchers on the other side having laid hands on Quaife, the two men were wrenched apart and dragged back, still spitting curses at each other.

Francis, his senses once more on full alert, addressed a goggling waiter over the top of the hubbub.

"A private parlour, fellow. And look sharp about it!"

Thus adjured, the man started. "Yes, sir. At once, sir."

He pushed through into the vestibule beyond, leading the way, and both combatants were manhandled out of the hall and through into one of the small apartments reserved for gentlemen who desired privacy.

By the time, with a brief word of thanks, the door had been firmly shut in the faces of those who had brought the earl's opponent, Harbisher had sufficiently recollected himself to be once more upon his dignity. Quaife, on the other hand, was in a rare fury.

"You'll answer to me, Harbisher. Name your friends, my lord!"

Francis threw up a hand. "None of that, Quaife. You will neither of you go out over this affair."

The baron turned a snarling visage upon him. "Who are you to interfere? He'll take my challenge and be damned."

Harbisher started forward. "I'll meet you, villain, when and where you will."

Tretower stepped between them. "Enough, gentlemen!" He addressed the earl. "To what end, sir, will you meet him? Have you forgot whose name will suffer by such conduct? Did you not, in the very house in which your sister met a violent end, decry the tattlemongers who bandied her name? Would you now add to that chorus?"

Francis, glancing from Harbisher to Quaife, saw how these commonsense words, delivered in measured tones designed to appeal to reason, were having an effect. Quaife's shoulders sagged and the lines of grief that had marked his features in their earlier encounter replaced the stiffened muscles of his anger.

"He is in the right of it." His tone was dull and heavy. "Our differences apart, I desire no more ill words to fall upon Emily's memory."

At that, the earl's ire sparked anew. "Do you dare speak her name, villain? You, who besmirched her vows to Polbrook and betrayed my trust?"

"Steady, man," said George, holding him off with raised hand. Harbisher thrust it aside.

"You need not fear. Though the scoundrel riles my breast, I have recovered my senses."

Francis cut in again. "As well, Harbisher. You do more harm than good, I promise you. Pray leave the discovery of Emily's murderer in our hands."

"So that is it," came forcefully from Quaife.

Francis turned quickly and found the baron was looking not at the earl, but from George to himself. Quaife hissed a breath and grunted.

"I am suspect. Damn your eyes! I thought nothing of Hugh's accusations. If he'd not made me so angry, I might see reason to excuse them. But this?"

Francis exchanged a glance with Tretower. Harbisher was now looking from one to the other of them, his brows drawn tightly together.

"Are you telling me you seriously believe he was responsible?"

Francis set his teeth. "I have not said so."

Quaife let out a fulminating oath. "You have no need to say so. What, am I held to be jealous, is that it?"

At this, Harbisher's nose went up, as if he scented a byway. "Jealous? Of whom, pray?"

Francis caught a frantic message from George's eyes, but before he could fathom the reason, Quaife was responding.

"I'll not sully her memory to please you, Harbisher."

George's relief was patent and Francis at once realised he'd been fearful of the mention of Bowerchalke. He had no time to ponder this, for he found himself once more the target of Quaife's wrath.

"I'll thank you to expunge my name from your damned list, Fanshawe! I'll not deny my involvement, why should I? But I cared for Emily. We'd long parted, but we were friends. Murder? I'd no more have harmed her than I'd take my own mother's life."

Again, Francis was struck by the note of sincerity. He glanced to see how Harbisher took this and found him tight-lipped and brooding. He caught Francis's look and his cheeks suffused.

"Ha! Then we're back to Polbrook. I tell you, Fanshawe —"

"Thank you, I have heard enough from you on this subject," Francis snapped.

"And you'll hear more, be certain. I'll not have done with this until I see him hanged."

"Polbrook?" It was Quaife's turn to frown.

"Then he has not returned?"

"Let him not do so," said Harbisher. "Let him but set foot in the country, and I'll have him, be sure."

"For the love of heaven," said Francis, losing patience. "Are you determined to make bad worse?"

"What of the whelp?" asked the baron suddenly. "Have you thought of him?"

"Giles? What has he to do with it?"

Under Harbisher's evident puzzlement, Francis heard George mutter at Quaife, briefly setting a hand to the baron's shoulder.

"Hold your tongue, man!"

"I've naught against the boy," the earl was continuing. "Never been one to visit the sins of the father upon the child."

Realising he had failed to hear George's utterance, Francis gave thanks that Harbisher had misunderstood Quaife's allusion. The baron was frowning, his eyes on George, who was now looking at the earl.

"May I suggest, sir, that you let these matters be? As I promised you, I will undertake to keep you apprised of any developments."

Harbisher glared at him. "You need not. I know who to blame." He transferred his irate gaze to Francis, who with difficulty held his tongue upon a heated rejoinder.

379

"Mind what I said, for I mean it. The moment Polbrook returns, I shall know it. And I shall know how to act."

With which he strode to the door and tugged it open too swiftly for the knot of persons gathered outside. They dispersed in a hurry, but Harbisher cursed them all soundly and stormed down the vestibule.

"Damn the man to hell," Francis muttered as George moved to close the door, throwing a warning glare upon the watchers beyond it.

Tretower turned back to Quaife. "You were about to mention Bowerchalke, I take it?"

Quaife nodded. "Wasn't thinking. It wouldn't do to deliver that whippersnapper up to Harbisher's wrath."

"Precisely," said George. "But have you reason to suppose him involved?"

Quaife's features took on a sneer. "Not he. Wouldn't have the nerve. But I know Emily and the cub had her fan."

"If ever there was a time for plain speaking, sir, this is it," said Francis briskly. "It is vital for us to know just what occurred that night."

He saw the man shift, as if he repressed a shudder. He shook his head. "I don't know that I can help you, though God knows I would, for her sake."

"Anything you saw. The smallest detail may be significant."

"What about this fan?" prompted George.

The man blew out a breath of scorn. "One of Emily's tricks. It was all a game to her. The luckless one was supposed to feel privileged to be given charge of the thing. He must return it to her carriage, in stealth and secrecy, don't you know? As if the world were blind. At the carriage, he'd be persuaded to ride inside. Then at the house —"

"He was given a key and told to enter by the back door."

Quaife's brows went up and he regarded Francis almost with amusement. "You have done your work well."

"Not mine, but let that pass."

"You think Bowerchalke was afforded this treatment?" George asked.

Quaife shrugged. "I was downstairs when he went out. I saw him get into the carriage. The inference is obvious."

Francis pushed for clarity. "Then you believe it possible Bowerchalke might have killed her?"

The man's features paled a little and sagged. "I don't pretend to know anything. Except that Emily is gone. Had I room for more than the desolation of this, I could only wish her end had been accomplished in some other fashion. I will bear the pain of it to my own grave." His tone was husky by the end, and he put out a hand as if he would stop either of them from speaking. Then he went to the door and paused there with his back to his auditors. "I can't think Polbrook would have rid himself of Emily by this means."

Then he dragged open the door and flung up his head to confront the group of apparently disinterested observers gathered in the vestibule.

Francis moved, by common consent with George, to follow him. But of a sudden, Quaife let out an oath and plunged into the knot of men beyond. Francis cast a glance of surmise towards his friend, but Tretower was already in the doorway.

"The deuce! He has Bowerchalke."

A moment later, Quaife was back through the door, dragging a terrified Jeremy Bowerchalke by the scruff of his neck and throwing him into the room before him. The boy stumbled forward, and Francis moved quickly to bear a hand as Quaife thrust inside and kicked the door shut behind him.

"There is the whelp. Ask him what he had

to do with Emily that night."

But the boy, trembling from head to foot and white to the lips, looked to be incapable of answering the simplest of questions. He leaned heavily on Francis's supporting arm, and his frightened gaze went from his assailant to George and at last fastened upon Francis.

"S-s-sir," he managed.

"Are you able to stand if I let you go?"

The boy nodded, but the instant Francis released him, he began to sink as if his knees were giving way. Francis grabbed him again, and George hastily fetched a chair. The lad dropped into it.

"What — what d'you — what — ?"

The stuttering ceased and the boy swallowed painfully. Francis felt his sympathy stirred and longed for Mrs. Draycott's presence. What would she look for? Remembering the palsied hand, Francis swept a glance down to Bowerchalke's left and found the limb reposing at his side, almost unregarded. As the lad twitched and shifted, Francis noted that his right hand shifted with him while the left remained still.

"Easy, boy, easy now," George said, as if he spoke to a half-broken horse.

It was a tone Francis had heard him use often enough with raw recruits, and the youth responded to it. His right hand came up and pressed against his chest as if he might by this means calm his erratic breathing. In a moment, he was able to form words.

"What do you w-want with me?"

Adopting George's example, Francis swallowed his own impatience and spoke gently.

"You have had a testing ordeal, have you not?"

The young man's eyes flew up, and the terror reflected in their depths told Francis much more than words could have done.

"What — what do you m-mean, sir?"

"I am talking of my sister-in-law's death, Mr. Bowerchalke."

He shied in his seat and his gaze shot back to where Quaife stood, his bulk against the door. There was a stage wait of several moments, and then the baron lost patience, striding forward.

"Damn it all, boy, I know you were with Emily that night! What happened?"

"Gently, Quaife, for the Lord's sake," protested Francis.

George came up to flank the baron. "He shall not touch you, Bowerchalke. My word on it."

Still the boy did not speak. Beads of perspiration appeared on his brow and he thrust a hand into an inner recess of his jacket. What he brought out he applied to his forehead, dabbing at the sweat.

Francis stared at the bundle in the boy's hand. It was white, and no doubt Bowerchalke imagined he had his pocket-handkerchief in his fingers. But as he dabbed, first one end and then another fell down over his face.

It was not a pocket-handkerchief. Francis almost cried his amazement aloud, but he held off as he heard the youth gasp. Bowerchalke brought his hand down and stared with disbelieving eyes at the offending bundle.

Then he uttered a cry and flung it from him. Next moment, he had risen from the chair and bolted precipitately past George and Quaife, who made a futile grab at him, and was gone through the door.

Tretower turned fast, but Francis, already stooping to seize the discarded bundle, stayed him.

"Let him go!"

Rising with the bundle in his fingers, Francis let it fall to its natural length. He looked up and found Quaife's eyes fixed upon the crumpled item hanging from his grasp.

As George returned, he regarded Francis's trophy with a frown. "What the deuce — ?"

"A lady's silk stocking. We found the other behind the bed."

Ottilia had possession of the key found in the late marchioness's bedside drawer, but time had overtaken her. She had begun upon her second tour of the outer doors while Lord Francis was chasing after Lord Harbisher. But when she set foot in the domestic facilities in the basement, she had been twice waylaid, by the boots and the kitchen maid, each anxious to disassociate themselves from the murder.

"Abel said as how Cattawade told you I were there, miss," said the boot boy, his anxiety plain. "Only I never come until I heard Miss Huntshaw a-screaming. And then my lord Francis come and he sent us all to the rightabout, miss."

Ottilia had no doubt the boy was not involved, but she made a show of questioning him for his pride's sake. "Did you enter the bedchamber?"

"No, miss. I weren't allowed in the mistress's chamber, not never."

"And you saw nothing?"

"Only them as were outside the door, miss."

"You did not return at any time?"

"Wot me, miss? With the mistress lying

there all stiff and cold? Not if I could help it, miss."

Ottilia smiled at him. "Then I think we may safely suppose you innocent of all blame."

The boots heaved a sigh of relief and went off with his head high. The kitchen maid was less easy to fob off. Ottilia recognised her as the third of the maids who had accompanied Mrs. Thriplow's domestic protest.

"Well, I do say as how I peeped round the door, miss, but I ain't seen nothing, for the bed-curtains were all closed like and my lady inside 'em, by all accounts."

"And after Lord Francis told you to return to your duties, did you come back again at any time?"

The kitchen maid, who had introduced herself as Betsy, shifted from one foot to the other, and a blush mantled her cheek. "Well, I can't say as I didn't, miss."

"You did come back?"

The girl nodded. "Abel were there, you see, miss."

Ottilia noted the wayward eyes, flicking this way and that. "He is a handsome fellow, is he not?"

The blush intensified, and Betsy fetched a

lovelorn sigh. "Oh, miss. Not as he'd look at me."

Ottilia eyed her with interest. "Why would he not?"

"Being as he's the footman, miss, and I'm only Cook's skivvy," said the maid frankly. "Too toplofty for the likes of me is Abel."

Which appeared to make no difference as far as Betsy's own sentiments were concerned. Although Ottilia suspected it was merely the footman's good looks and manly figure that had the kitchen maid sighing. She returned the girl to the matter at hand.

"When you went back, did you see anything more?"

"No, for Abel chased me off, miss. Said as how it were only him as was allowed near the place. Nor he wouldn't let me look in the chamber."

"Very proper," Ottilia commented primly, and dismissed Betsy with a word of thanks.

It was clear by this time that to check for the door to which the key fitted must advertise her activities to the staff and she was obliged to abandon the plan for the moment. It had best be done at night, she decided, once everyone was in bed, for the servants went to bed early and rose equally betimes. Accordingly, that evening she took to her bed armed with a book, intending to read until gone eleven.

The contents of the volume, a lurid gothic tale by Maria Edgeworth extracted from Lord Polbrook's library, failed to hold her attention, which kept turning upon the various pieces of the puzzle as she tried to slot them into place.

Lady Candia having chosen to abandon her own room and join the company these last days, it had proved testing to await the result of Lord Francis's excursion. She could see the dowager chafing and could not blame her. When the gentleman returned, clearly big with news, but obliged to bottle it, Ottilia had been forced to employ subterfuge and find an excuse to leave the room.

Lord Francis had picked up the meaning look she threw at him as she left the parlour, and within a few moments he came looking for her, accompanied by Colonel Tretower. They slipped into the deserted dining parlour, where Ottilia was regaled with the story of their adventures. She made no comment until Lord Francis extracted the stocking from a convenient pocket.

"Surely it proves something?" he asked as he handed it to her. "Is it the same as the other?"

"It seems so, but I have the other stowed

in my trunk, so we can soon check." Ottilia let the item sift through her fingers. "Assuming it is, I think we may safely place Bowerchalke at the scene."

"What I want to know is," said the colonel, "if it was Emily's, how in the world did the fellow get the thing?"

"Oh, I expect she encouraged him to remove it from her leg," said Ottilia. "Both stockings, probably. And when events became complicated, he stuffed them into his pocket."

"And in his agitation dropped one?" suggested Lord Francis.

"Just so." Ottilia sucked in a frustrated breath. "But it does not make him Emily's murderer."

"For my part," cut in Colonel Tretower, "I am by no means convinced that Quaife is not our man. He could have said all he did to throw suspicion off himself. He knew Bowerchalke had entered the coach. Why should he not have followed? He pooh-poohed the notion of jealousy, but what guilty man would not? He has a motive. He is physically capable of the deed, unlike Bowerchalke."

"But Bowerchalke was there, that much is plain," said Francis. "Unless we are to suppose Quaife planted the stocking on him."

"Less than probable," agreed the colonel, ignoring the ironical inflexion. "But even without the stocking, I am strongly of the opinion Bowerchalke was there that night."

"Why, if not because of the stocking?"

"His whole demeanour, his abject terror upon mention of the event, is enough for me."

Lord Francis looked to Ottilia, frowning. "What are your thoughts, Mrs. Draycott?"

She answered with her usual calm. "As I said, because he was there, it does not mean he committed the deed."

"No, and he has got a palsy. I took care to check upon that left hand of his and he does not use it at all."

"Which leaves us squarely at point non plus," said Colonel Tretower gloomily.

But Ottilia was not wholly despondent, although the problem nagged at her all day, fostered by an interview with Lady Dalesford. The dowager's frustration was patent, and Ottilia seized a convenient moment to delay her employer when the countess and Lady Candia left the room to dress for dinner.

"There is much to tell you, ma'am, but we have no time now."

"Don't talk to me about time," said Sybilla testily. "It has so dragged upon me today, I could scream. Why Candia must needs seek solace in company, I cannot imagine."

Ottilia reminded her that Lady Dalesford intended to take her departure upon the following morning, with her niece in tow.

"Then we may speak without reserve."

"Yes, but I wanted to sound out Harriet, for she knows all these people almost as well as did Emily."

"Nothing could be easier, ma'am. When the countess retires for the night, I will go after her and ask her to come to your chamber."

This notion being approved, and Ottilia's presence at the interview commanded — "for then you may give me all the news" — a short colloquy had been undertaken which had left Ottilia with food for much thought. Lady Dalesford had been brief but informative.

"Jeremy Feverel? I always suspected Emily had more than a passing interest in that man. But it was short-lived. If he did present his godson to her, you may be sure it was purely to give the boy the entrée into Emily's set. She ran with the best, I'll give her that."

But the countess could offer no opinion on Feverel's potential as a jealous lover upon finding his godson favoured far beyond common courtesy.

"I should think it highly unlikely, but who is to say how any man might act given sufficient provocation?"

On the subject of the Baron Quaife, however, Lady Dalesford was voluble and expansive.

"The man's a boor. Rough to the point of rudeness. It was a mystery to me how Emily could tolerate him."

"Some women relish the untamed beast," Ottilia suggested.

"Well, if Emily was of their number, I'll wager she gave as good as she got. She always did so with Randal."

"You don't think she cared for Quaife?"

"If she did, it must have been one of these love-hate affairs, where both parties are ill-suited but cannot overcome a mutual attraction."

This rang true to Ottilia. Had not Venner spoken of Quaife coming in and out of favour? Moreover, Lord Francis had reported his free confession of his feelings for the marchioness, intimating that a bond had still existed between them.

"It would not surprise me if Emily revelled in such a match, I must say," Lady Dalesford added. "Hers was a restless spirit, always seeking for sensation."

"Well, she got it," said the dowager on a dour note. "More than she bargained for."

The countess shuddered. "Don't, Mama. I am yet haunted by the thought of it. And I dread making a slip and letting fall some hint that might open the truth to Candia."

"You will be out of the house tomorrow," soothed her mother.

"Just so," agreed Ottilia encouragingly. "The chance of a mistake will rapidly diminish."

"I declare, I could almost wish she did know, except I would spare her the inevitable reflection that her father might have killed her mama."

"Yes, well we would all rather it were Quaife, if there were a choice," said the dowager.

Objectively, Ottilia thought there was a good possibility that it might be the baron. Lady Dalesford's opinion aside, one must not forget Mrs. Bucklebury's conviction of Quaife's jealousy, despite what the man himself had said. Gossip she might be, but she was witness to his presence at the ball and took a keen interest in everything she saw.

Yet Quaife's tenure was not current, and the marchioness had undoubtedly indulged in criminal conversation prior to her death. Unless the countess's theory held water and the baron was still occasionally master of Emily's bed?

Besides, it seemed certain now that young Bowerchalke was the lover involved upon the fatal night. Clearly, from the descriptions she'd had of him, the youth was slim enough to have escaped detection had he hidden behind the bed-curtains. But from whom? Lord Polbrook or the murderer? Or both?

Quaife then. Could he indeed have followed the boy to Hanover Square as the colonel had suggested? In which case, he had evidently not surprised Emily in the boy's arms, for a jealous lover would surely attack Bowerchalke rather than the marchioness. Supposing young Jeremy had heard an approach and hidden? Quaife, who knew how to enter the house unobserved, entered the room to find Emily abed and clearly post coitus. Enraged, he seized and strangled her.

But Abel heard a voice, did he not? Then Bowerchalke, cowering behind the curtains, must also have heard it. And recognised it. Why not denounce Quaife? He had been terrified in the man's presence. Was that significant?

A notion that he was shielding his god-father Ottilia dismissed even as it formed. Why should Sir Jeremy intervene, when his whole purpose had been to enjoin Emily's favour for the lad? Or had he not anticipated it would go so far? No, ridiculous. She felt it safe to discount Sir Jeremy Feverel as a possible murderer.

Which left the field narrow indeed. And no solution provided an answer to the problem of who had purloined the jewel box and the fan. She already had her suspicions on that score, and it did begin to look as if the thefts must be unconnected with the murder. Certainly she could not support the notion that Quaife had stolen either article. And Jeremy Bowerchalke's panic would not have permitted him the level-headedness necessary to abstract anything from the place.

Ottilia sighed and reached for her little gold watch. She was relieved to discover her musings had taken her well past her appointed hour. It was almost midnight. She ought by this time to be at liberty to check doors with impunity.

Rising from her bed, she put on her dressing robe and slipped the marchioness's key into her pocket. She lit a fresh candle, blew out the old one that had half burned down, and set the new one in its place. Taking the holder in hand, she slipped noiselessly from the room and embarked upon her search.

Her intention being to roam the domestic quarters unobserved, Ottilia headed for the main stairs, feeling reluctant to set foot upon the narrower staircase unless she must. Hardly had she turned the corner on the landing than she saw a glimmer of light beyond the first floor vestibule.

A feather brushed her heart and she stilled. Remembering her own candle, she cupped it, straining to see across the distance.

No shadow betrayed the presence of anyone in the lobby, and the gleam falling into it showed it to be empty. Then realisation filtered into her mind and the answering acceleration of her heartbeat pattered into her throat. Someone was in Emily's dressing room.

CHAPTER 15

Instinct warned her to retreat, but Ottilia paid it scant attention. She was alone, yes, but she had only to scream to bring half a dozen persons hotfoot to the scene, Lord Francis among them.

The last thought was curiously comforting. Ottilia took a grasp of the stick of her candleholder instead of its base, with a vague thought of using it as a weapon at need, and braced herself as she took the remainder of the stairs.

Gliding silently on tiptoe, she moved into the vestibule and slipped to one side, peeping around the jut of the intervening wall. The door to the dressing room was only partially ajar and she could not see inside. Listening intently, she thought she could make out a soft scrabbling sound, followed by a click and then a swish, as of wood against wood.

A premonition shot through her mind,

and she forgot caution.

Rushing forward, she called out softly, "Who is there?"

A startled gasp answered her. Then the gleam of light vanished. A shadowy figure lurched through the doorway just as she came close to it. She caught a glimpse of a masked face, and then a blow from the back of a man's hand struck across her chest, knocking her against the wall. The candle in its holder dropped from her hand and the light went out.

In the ensuing pitch of night, Ottilia could see nothing, but instinctively she reached out, grabbing at the man who had been there. Her fingers found only air.

A light thudding of footsteps sounded, and Ottilia remained perfectly still, trying to judge their direction. The sound changed, became hollow. Which staircase was he using? Then there was a thump. Had he missed a step in the dark and fallen?

Intent, she strained her ears, not daring to move for fear of coming to grief herself. She could hear nothing more, try as she would. The invader was gone.

Ottilia discovered she was trembling and leaned back against the wall. Her eyes were adjusting to the intensity of the dark and she could make out dim shapes for the walls and doors.

Oh, for her candle! But even if she could recover it, she had no means of lighting it. The thought of groping her way around the walls to the stairs and thence to her chamber caused a chilling sensation to sweep through her stomach.

Then she remembered that Lord Francis's bedchamber was a good deal closer.

The tapping entered his dreams. The puzzle of its intrusion lasted but a moment. As he woke, it resolved into a furtive knocking at his door. A hoarse whisper reached him.

"Lord Francis!"

The recognition was instant. Surprise as much as instinct caused Francis to thrust himself out of bed and patter to the door in his bare feet. He grasped the handle and pulled it open. The figure without was a mere shadow in the gloom, but he had no doubts of its identity.

"Ottilia! What the devil are you up to now?"

"Hush!"

She put out a hand and it touched his chest. It was cold and Francis instinctively grasped it.

"You're like ice, woman. What is the meaning of this?"

"I will tell you directly," she answered, her tone low, "but for the present, could you light a candle?"

"I should think I'd better."

With scant regard for the proprieties, Francis drew her into the room and closed the door. She remained where he left her as he crossed to the bedside and groped for his tinderbox. A light was soon struck and a glow sprung up in the room as he lit the candle. Then he turned with it in his hand and went up to Ottilia, holding it high so he could see her white face.

"You look like a ghost."

The characteristic gurgle was drawn from her. "I feel like one."

"Here, take this."

Francis handed her the candle and retrieved his dressing gown, shrugging it on. "That's better. Now, tell me all."

He watched her draw a breath and sigh it out, as if she had passed through a difficult experience and was only now relieved of it.

"I've just disturbed someone who was doing something in Emily's dressing room."

"What? Who?"

"That I don't know, but it was a man. I'm afraid he escaped and ran away. I could not tell which staircase he used, but I suspect the main one, as I heard his steps clearly.

Oh, and he had no time to shut the door, so we may readily discover what he was doing in there."

"We may, may we?" Francis eyed her in growing irritation. "What in the world possessed you to go wandering around the house in the middle of the night? And without a candle?"

"Of course I had a candle! I dropped it when the fellow knocked me to one side."

A sliver of ice traced a path down Francis's stomach. "He did what? Are you hurt?"

"Do keep your voice down," she begged. "The last thing we need is for someone to wake and find us together in this condition."

"Lord, yes," he agreed feelingly, his tone lowered. "We have scandal enough as it is. But did he hurt you?"

"I was a little jolted, but that is all. I am perfectly well, I assure you." Her fingers reached out and grasped his sleeve. "We are wasting time."

Francis shoved his feet into slippers and allowed himself to be shepherded into the lobby. He followed her to the vestibule, torn between indignation at her unorthodox wanderings and a lively anxiety for her safety. Impulse threw him into savage speech, albeit in a whisper for fear of waking his mother.

"If I do not end by shaking you unmercifully, Ottilia Draycott, it will be in no wise your fault."

A faint laugh reached him and she looked back. "What, because I encountered a marauder?"

"Because you are possibly the most infuriating female ever to cross my path," he returned. "Why must you venture into the night completely unaccompanied? A word would have secured my aid. Or don't you know that?"

She paused, turning to look at him and holding the candle up as she studied his face. "To be truthful, it did not occur to me to do so. But you will allow I lost no time in coming to fetch you when I found myself in difficulties."

Francis's annoyance melted. "True. But what were you about?"

"I wanted to find which door that key fits."

"Could you not have searched during the day?"

"Not in the domestic quarters, if I did not wish to advertise my actions to the servants."

He cast up his eyes. "What is so particularly maddening about you, Ottilia, is that you have an answer for everything." He grinned at her. "Lead on, then."

She turned again, moving quietly in the calm way she had. Francis reflected how often it had soothed his anxieties, if momentarily. As they reached the dressing room, its door still ajar, she spoke again.

"I am in hopes we may obviate the necessity to search the house, if we follow in the man's footsteps."

"You suppose he will have entered the house by that way?"

"It seems likely, don't you think?"

Francis mused on this as he followed her through the doorway. "Have you had any thought as to what the fellow was doing?"

"Yes."

She did not elaborate and Francis balked. "Well?"

Ottilia was standing before the neat chest of drawers, but she glanced over her shoulder. "I think that has just become obvious."

So saying, she indicated the top drawer. It had been left pulled open. He watched as Ottilia tugged it further out. Then she turned back with a smile.

"Would you hold the candle, if you please?"

Francis went up to her and took it. "What do you expect to find?"

She was rummaging within the drawer. Her hands stilled and she cast him a look of triumph.

"This." She brought out a velvet-covered box. "Emily's jewel box, I believe."

Francis set down the candle on top of the press and took it from her. "He returned it? And left the key in the lock."

Turning the little key, he opened the box. At the bottom, metal and stone winked and glittered in the candlelight. Ottilia's fingers reached in and drew out a necklace. Below it there was nothing bar a pair of ill-assorted earrings.

"This cannot be all."

"Obviously not," Francis agreed. "Our thief has seen fit to keep the bulk of it. Then why return the thing at all?"

"In hopes it might not be noticed?"

"He cannot have been so foolish."

"Or, if he originates from inside the house, since the theft is known amongst the staff, perhaps he thought it might avert suspicion from himself and spread it across a broader canvas."

"Then that hope is dashed, since you caught him at it. In which event, we may at least now eliminate the female staff."

Francis watched her examine the necklace, holding it to the light.

"Could this be mere paste?"

She held it out to him and Francis examined it more carefully, aware of a stirring at the back of his mind. At length he was obliged to concede defeat.

"I am no expert. But I can't imagine why Emily would have need of a paste bauble. She had funds enough."

As he was about to lay the necklace back in the box, his memory jumped. He paused abruptly and lifted it once again to the candle flame. Light dawned.

"This must be genuine. It is the one Emily wears in her portrait. I thought it looked familiar."

Ottilia peered closer and he held it for her to see better.

"I recall she was wearing a necklace, but I could not swear it was this one."

"You may take it from me that it is." He laid the necklace back in the box and allowed Ottilia to tuck it back in its place in the drawer.

"I will ask Mary about the rest. She will know precisely which jewels have been taken." Closing the drawer, she picked up the candle and gave it to Francis. "Now for the escape route."

Francis hesitated. "I'm sure I ought to refuse to let you come with me."

Her eyes lit with mischief. "And I am just

as sure you ought not. How can you prevent me?"

As he eyed her, he was aware of disturbance in the rate of his heartbeat and an unsettling shortness of breath.

"I can think of several ways," he responded without thinking.

Colour fluctuated in Ottilia's cheek. With an effort, Francis wrenched his attention away from the images crawling in his head.

"If we are going upon this adventure, we had best make haste."

Without a word, Ottilia turned for the door, and Francis felt abruptly distanced. He followed, reaching out to her shoulder to stay her.

"You had better let me go first."

She stood back in the lobby, and he passed her. "Shall we try the main stairs first?"

"Heading for which door, do you think?" Francis asked, starting off through the vestibule.

"Oh, Francis, wait!"

He halted and turned, regarding her with question. Then he realised she had left off his title and his mind froze momentarily. She began casting about on the lobby floor.

"Pray bring the light closer."

"What is it?"

"I wish to retrieve my candle."

Francis glanced down and saw a gleam of silver. He stooped to pick it up and in the narrow confines of the space his body brushed against her. The contact threw him back into confusion and he hastily rose, shifting back.

Ottilia got up from her knees, the candle in her hand. It hung crookedly. He gave up the holder to her but protested when she tried to fit the candle back into it.

"You can't use that. The candle is broken."

"The stub will serve. I have only to cut the wick."

His suppressed emotions found expression in irritation. "Yes, if you have a knife or scissors about you, for I have not."

She looked up at him. Francis read puzzlement in the clear gaze and regretted his tone. There was something in her voice to which he could not put a name.

"I will do it later. It need not go to waste. Besides, it will not do to leave the thing here for the servants to find and wonder about."

Finding nothing to say that would not prolong a pointless discussion, nor assuage his conscience, Francis merely nodded.

"Let us proceed."

Once upon the stair, Francis went ahead, holding the candle to the side to throw light for Ottilia.

"Can you see?"

"Well enough, I thank you."

He was relieved to hear normality in her tone once more. She was adept at recovering herself, he reflected, recalling instances when she had looked briefly disconcerted. It could be a tempting game to try to discompose her. But he had done enough tonight. Besides, he liked her too well for that.

The realisation filtered into his consciousness. He did like her, far too well. The question was, whether his liking was to any degree reciprocated.

Before he could lose himself in the agreeable recollection that Ottilia had shown herself to be at least enjoying his company on occasion, he arrived at the ground floor.

"Where now? The front door or the back?"

"The back, I think. It must be by far the fastest route."

As he started down towards the lower landing, Francis recalled adventurous forays of his own. A laugh escaped him.

"I used to creep out to the garden as a child to escape my tutor. I little thought I should resume such madness in my riper years."

"It just shows one never knows what one

may come to," said Ottilia from behind him, and the note of mischief Francis was coming to recognise struck him with pleasure.

Arrived at the landing, he paused before the door. "Have you the key?"

She produced it from her pocket and gave it to him, taking in its stead the candle as he handed it to her.

"Hold it lower."

He stood aside so the light fell upon the keyhole. The key fitted perfectly, and he turned it.

"Eureka!"

The door opened onto blackness and a whoosh of cold air. Francis hurriedly went to shut it again and found the wood warped so that he was obliged to thrust hard enough to make the door slam.

"The devil! Let us hope no one was awakened by that."

Ottilia said nothing and he turned to find her eyes fixed upon the door. Francis remembered the look. Her mind was otherwhere.

"What is it?"

She blinked and seemed to come back to him. "There is one mystery solved."

"You are to be commended."

She gave a light laugh. "Hardly. It was your mother who first suggested the possibility of the marchioness supplying a lover with a key. And if Venner had not alerted me, I should likely have dismissed this one I found in the night table."

"But you said at the outset there must be a way for a lover to get into the house without being detected."

"True. But by being supplied with a key? I can think of few more dangerous enterprises."

"Well, it certainly proved dangerous enough for Emily."

He saw a shiver shake her and felt instantly remorseful. But she spoke before he could voice it.

"I meant only that to be giving anyone access to your house is foolish. Suppose the key were to fall to some other hand?"

"According to Quaife, Emily only loaned the key long enough for the fellow to come in. I cannot think she would have given it wholly over to anyone."

"No, not if she was prone to change her lovers in the way she changed her clothes."

Francis was startled. He had never before heard her speak so acidly.

"If anyone kept a key," she went on, "it would be Quaife, for he appears to have remained longest in her affections."

"You don't approve of her, do you?"

She looked away. "I dislike any form of betrayal. Too many people take their marriage vows lightly. If one is fortunate enough to inspire affection, one should strive to deserve it, do you not think?"

He was struck by the passionate undertone, and a memory slipped into his mind. In just this way had she spoken that very first day, and upon this very subject. It seemed to Francis an age since that moment.

"Time has overtaken us, Tillie. I feel as if I have known you for weeks."

She was staring up at him, searchingly, he thought.

"What did you call me?"

Francis thought back and could not remember. He gave a self-conscious laugh. "I hardly know. I have fallen into the way of using your given name, though I should not, I know. It is as I said. I have lost track of time."

Still she gazed at him. "You called me Tillie."

Something in her clear eyes tugged at his senses. Francis was hardly aware of smiling at her. He wanted to set his hands either side of her face and hold her so.

"If I did, it was instinctive," he said, hardly aware that he spoke. "It suits you."

A moment longer her look held, and then a slow flush mounted into her cheeks and she drew away a little. Francis was conscious of regret for a moment lost.

Ottilia was looking down the stairs to the basement. "I am not convinced our marauder came this way."

"Why not?" he asked, vainly trying to banish a feeling of being dismissed.

Her glance returned to his face. "Because I would have heard the door slam."

Struck, Francis looked at the door again. His subsequent emotions had driven from his mind the difficulty in shutting it.

"It's you who have the head, Tillie."

He turned back as he spoke and caught her regarding him with a look unfathomable in her grey eyes. He was tempted to ask for her thoughts, but a barely acknowledged caution held him back. Instead, he raised a questioning eyebrow. Instantly the look was gone and her glance moved quickly away from his face.

"There is nothing more to be done here. I must go back to bed."

Without speaking again, he unburdened her of the extra candle and took the lead up the flight to the ground floor. A half-formed yearning came upon him to prolong this illicit idyll. He paused, holding up the candle to look into her face and gestured to the dining parlour door behind her.

"Would you care for a nightcap? To help you to sleep?"

Ottilia did not look at him. "I thank you, no. I had best go straight up."

"Then, since that candle is less than useless, I shall escort you."

At last her gaze found his. "We have a puzzle of identification, my lord. Tomorrow we must discover who did this."

"Bowerchalke?" Only half-aware of finding means to detain her, Francis worried at the puzzle. "In the press of events that night, suppose he had no time to return the key to Emily? There was Huntshaw, waiting to put her to bed. Then Randal entered when Emily was only half-undressed —"

He paused, struck by a sudden shift in Ottilia's features. Her eyes widened and she looked suddenly stricken.

"What is it? What ails you, Ottilia?"

She was staring at him, but Francis had the impression she was almost looking through him, as at some scene in her mind. Absently she spoke, a species of censure in her tone, which proved to be directed at herself.

"I have been unforgivably slow."

"How so?"

"To overlook a thing so obvious. Two o'clock? No, no. He must have been in the house well before that. What would Mary do for an hour or more?"

Confusion wreathed Francis's brain. "What in the world are you talking of?"

Ottilia blinked at him, and then a faint little smile crossed her mouth. "Francis, will you be so kind as to lock that dressing room door? I believe you have the key."

Acutely disappointed at her lack of response, and daunted by the matter-of-fact tone, Francis was thrown off-balance. "Certainly."

She started up the stairs and he followed, holding the candle high to light her way. Halfway up the second flight, she halted abruptly and he very nearly lost his footing. One hand upon the banister, she turned to confront him, eyes alight with eagerness.

"He did have a key!"

"Who?"

"The intruder. He had a key to the dressing room door."

No early opportunity was afforded to apprise the dowager of the previous night's discoveries, for which Ottilia was a trifle relieved. She could only hope the startling facts would serve to gloss over the impropriety of her having wandered around the house with Lord Francis in the middle of the night, and in her dressing robe.

Although the family foregathered in the dining parlour for breakfast, the imminent departure of Lady Candia with the countess formed the main topic of conversation. The girl was pale but composed, the focus of her pleadings to her grandmother falling upon her wish for her brother to post up to Dalesford as soon after his return as was possible.

"You will make him come to me, won't you, Grandmama?"

"Be sure I shall despatch him posthaste. But you must not expect him to remain long, for his duties are likely to multiply."

Lady Candia's large eyes showed apprehension. "What duties?"

Ottilia saw Sybilla throw a harassed glance towards her daughter and son. She evidently felt she had said too much. Lord Francis came to the rescue.

"There is more for a fellow to do upon an event of this kind than for a female, Candia. But you may depend upon having the comfort of Giles's presence for days at a time. Meanwhile, you have Aunt Harriet and your cousins. You will not lack for company."

Lady Candia did not look abashed. On

the contrary, her features took on a mulish look of rebellion.

"You are all keeping something from me, I know you are."

"Nothing of the sort," said the dowager with a little of her usual snap.

"Yes, but you are," insisted the girl. "You think I don't see it, but I do. You are forever whispering in corners. And whenever I enter the room, you fall silent and smile, as if you were speaking of something you do not wish me to hear."

A note of hysteria sounded in the child's voice, and Ottilia longed to intervene. She could not feel it her place, no matter the licence allowed her in the matter of discoveries concerning the murder. She withdrew her attention from the ensuing barrage of reassurance from Lady Candia's relatives and gave her mind up to secret contemplation of last night.

But it was neither the intruder nor the key that occupied her thoughts, which turned rather upon the strange conduct of Lord Francis.

She might have believed the sense of intimacy had been engendered by the atmosphere of the hour, for the night was apt to exaggerate and enliven one's imagination. But she could in nowise account in this way for that "Tillie" which had sprung spontaneously from his lips. There was no getting away from the fact that he had meant it for a nickname. And nicknames were either an insult or an endearment. She could not accuse Lord Francis of wishing to insult her.

In a night of much tossing and turning, Ottilia had relived those little moments of oddity in his attitude towards her, in between the business in which they had been engaged. She was ready to believe herself mistaken in reading more than she ought into a certain look in his eyes as they met hers, or a quality in his voice that caused an echo to resonate within her. But "Tillie" spoke deeply to a scarcely acknowledged hope.

She came to herself to realise that Lady Dalesford was making noises indicative of her wish to begin upon the journey. Almost Ottilia regretted it, for she hardly knew if she could maintain her composure in relating to Sybilla the adventures of the night. She dared not look towards Lord Francis, and was relieved to notice his attention concentrated upon his niece.

There was a flurry of hastening, a tinkling of the bell for the servants, and the travellers about to leave the breakfast parlour for their chambers to make last-minute preparations.

Then to Ottilia's ears came sounds without the room in the hall beyond that argued a similar jostle and fuss. Doors were opening and closing, there was a far jingle of harness and horses, as of a shifting of hooves upon the cobbles. She had not heard the knocker, but there were alien voices mingled with others she thought she recognised. Cattawade?

In a moment it was clear the hubbub had penetrated to the ears of the other occupants of the breakfast parlour. One by one they stilled. One by one, and speedily, they trod upon one another's words.

Lord Francis exchanged a glance with his mother. "An arrival? Surely it is not . . ."

His voice died, but Ottilia caught the instant mix of hope and apprehension in Sybilla's face. "I am sure it is only . . ."

The countess strained towards the door, a frown upon her brow. "Mama, you don't think . . ."

Then an unfamiliar and vibrant voice, raised in impatient accents, penetrated clearly through the walls.

"Let be, man. By God, but this officiousness is beyond what I may tolerate! Do you suppose I am about to escape from my own house?"

CHAPTER 16

Lady Candia was first to act, running to the door and shrieking as she went.

"Papa! It is Papa. Papa! Papa!"

She wrenched the door open and disappeared through it. Lady Dalesford was close upon her heels.

"It is Randal."

Ottilia saw the dowager clap a hand to her breast and seize the back of a chair. Quickly she moved to her assistance.

"Take my arm, Sybilla. Lord Francis, your mother is unwell."

He had begun to follow the others to the vestibule, from whence a cacophony of exclamation could be heard, above it all the sobbing of Lady Candia, still crying out for her papa.

Halting, Lord Francis looked back. "Mama?" He moved towards her, glancing briefly at Ottilia. "It's the shock."

The dowager, leaning heavily on Ottilia's

supporting arm, waved him away. "I am all right. Go on and I will follow presently."

Lord Francis looked dubious. "I am happy to wait."

Sybilla shook her head. "Go and greet him."

He disappeared with alacrity and Ottilia looked with concern at the dowager.

"Would you like to sit down, Sybilla?"

"No. Give me a moment only." Her breath drew heavily in and out, but she managed to speak. "I am so thankful, and yet I dread to see him. There is so much to be said."

"Presently, ma'am," Ottilia soothed. "Let the first greeting be one of pleasure, if it cannot go as far as rapture."

The dowager grasped her hand and held it tightly. "Sensible as ever. You are the greatest comfort to me, my dear."

Ottilia smiled. "I am glad."

But as Sybilla began a slower progress across the room than had her descendants, Ottilia could not help but wonder if anything she had to offer could afford the afflicted family any real degree of relief.

Francis stepped into the vestibule and rounded the corner into the long hall, where he halted, struck by the extraordinary number of persons assembled.

Candia had thrown herself on Randal's broad chest, still sobbing, and his brother held her, patting her back and murmuring soothing words, while his eyes signalled a harassed message to Harriet, hovering nearby. To one side of Randal's large frame and a little in his rear stood a burly fellow of stolid aspect, greatcoated and with a slouch hat pulled low over his forehead. His fixed gaze remained upon Randal's back and he seemed oblivious to the troop of servants shifting back and forth under the direction of his brother's valet, Foscot, and the stern eye of the butler, burdened with a multitude of bandboxes and portmanteaux.

Momentarily astonished at the quantity of his brother's luggage, Francis eyed the passing servants in bewilderment. Then a little coterie of persons caught at his attention. Standing against the wall to the unoccupied side of the open front door and looking as if they were desirous of shrinking into the background, stood a well-dressed female and two youngsters sheltered within her arms. Francis eyed the woman, a tenuous thread of alarm seeping into his gut as he caught a vague feeling of familiarity.

Before he could identify the source, his brother's glance found him.

"Fan, old fellow!"

Looking round, Francis saw that Candia had been transferred to Harriet's care. A rush of affection swept over Francis and he moved quickly to embrace his brother, holding strongly to the large form that had inspired in boyhood an awed fascination.

"You fiend, Randal," he managed out of the hoarseness of sudden emotion. "Where the devil have you been?"

His brother's arms tightened briefly and then let go. Randal stepped back a little, but his grip held on Francis's arms and the familiar quirky smile warmed his heart, though his brother's eyes were wet.

"D'you think I'd have gone, my boy, had I known? What, light out and leave you to pick up the pieces? You know me better."

Francis wished fervently he might never have wasted a second in the suspicions that had poisoned the past few days. His doubt must have shown in his face, for Randal's smile crumpled and a quick frown took its place.

"Devil take it, you did think it!"

Francis seized his hand and gripped it. "For a moment only. My God, Randal, if you had seen —" He broke off swiftly, recalling the press of persons about them, including his innocent niece. "Never mind that. You are here now, and we will very soon set everything to rights."

A look of dull misery crept over his brother's face. "Everything? I doubt it, old fellow."

Then, with his characteristic energy, he released himself from Francis's grasp and swept a wide arm towards the stolid individual behind him. Contempt was in both voice and eyes.

"For a start, try if you can dislodge our friend Grice here."

"Grice?"

The fellow indicated transferred his gaze and Francis was taken aback to find himself thoroughly appraised by the man's look as he nodded.

"Benjamin Grice, sir, and I've me duty."

This was said with the flat inflexion of one determined to stand his ground, come what may. An explanation for the man's presence leapt into Francis's head.

"Confound it, you are the Runner!"

"And he sticks as firm as a plaster."

Randal's bitter intonation excited Francis's sympathies, but his immediate reaction was against the family's man of business.

"So much for Jardine's boast. He swore his man could outwit any Bow Street minion."

"He did," said Randal, not without a note

of satisfaction. "By the time Grice caught up with us, we had already begun our journey home."

"Bow Street Runner?"

His mother's acid and infuriated tones, coming from the vestibule behind, alerted Francis to a fresh danger. He leaned to murmur a warning to Randal.

"Take care! Mama is like to skin you alive."

"Do you tell me a Bow Street Runner has had the temerity to enter this house?"

His mother's imperious tones immediately accomplished what Randal's contempt and his own dignity could not. Benjamin Grice did not quail, but his eyes showed definite apprehension as the dowager started forward. Rather to Francis's relief, his brother intercepted her, shifting quickly into the vestibule.

"You here, Mama? What, is the whole family residing in the house?"

Deflected, his mother halted. "I thank God you are come at last, Randal, but I shall soon be wishing otherwise if you mean to utter such foolishness. Naturally we are here at such a time."

She held out her hands to her elder son, who took them in his, kissing them one by one and then saluting her cheek.

"I might have guessed I could rely on you, ma'am. I imagine everything has been in uproar. Have they taken Emily?"

"Days since," Francis told him, stepping through to join the pair. "Tretower arranged everything."

"A good man, George. Well, I must arrange for the obsequies."

"It is all in hand."

By this time, the whole party, bar the servants and the newcomers, had followed into the vestibule, Grice the Runner resuming his station at Polbrook's shoulder.

"Randal!"

He returned his attention to his mother, and Francis's heart sank as he noted that, the way now being clear to notice them, her grim gaze was fixed upon the group of strangers near the door.

The dowager gestured towards the woman who had her arms about her two bewildered offspring. "What is this?"

"Ah."

For the first time, Randal's confident air faltered. Francis held his breath. His brother set an arm about their mother's shoulders and gently moved her into the hall in the direction of the trio.

"I must beg your indulgence and kindness, Mama. I know you will receive Madame Guizot and her unfortunate children with every sympathy." He paused a little way towards them and lowered his voice, and Francis strained to hear his words. "They are refugees, Mama. I got to them just in time. We were able to bring away but a handful of their effects, for we had need of haste. I beg you, Mama, on my life, do not repudiate them."

Francis knew by the rigidity of his mother's back that she was excessively angry. Had she guessed, as he had, the import of this invasion? But she shook off Randal's arm and moved forward, holding out her hand and greeting the lady in her own tongue.

"You are very welcome, madame, and your children also."

Madame Guizot, looking almost as fearful as her offspring, took the hand in a delicate one of her own and curtsied.

"Madame is very kind."

"Come, you must be tired after your journey. Let me arrange for your disposition. Then you may rest and refresh yourselves."

Turning with a magnificent assurance that drew Francis's appreciation, his mother motioned the butler.

"Cattawade, have Mrs. Thriplow come to

me immediately."

Then she ushered the forlorn trio of émi-grés into the parlour. For this they undoubtedly were, despite Francis's fears of their connection with his brother.

Candia was reclaiming her father's attention, the shrill note of panic echoed in her fearful eyes.

"What does this mean, Papa? Why have you a Bow Street Runner in your train? What does he want with you?"

Harriet, to her credit, attempted to brush the matter aside. "Is this a moment to be plaguing your papa with awkward questions, child? Let us come away, for we must begin upon our own journey, remember."

But his niece categorically refused to move. "You do not think I am going now? With Papa returned? No, Aunt Harriet, I cannot think of deserting him. Papa!"

Randal, who had half followed towards the parlour, looking highly troubled as if he feared what their mother might say to Madame Guizot, turned back at this appeal.

"What is it, child?"

The testy note should have warned her, and Francis marshalled himself to intervene if Randal was so thoughtless as to vent his no doubt confused emotions upon the poor girl.

"Papa, I was going with Aunt Harriet, but I want to stay with you. Pray let me stay!"

Randal received her impetuous advance with a worried frown, catching at her shoulders and holding her off from him.

"No, my dear. Matters are likely to prove extremely complex just at present. It is better for you to be out of the way."

Candia's face crumpled. "But I want to be with you. At such a time! It is not fair. There is something horrid going on and no one will tell me what it is. It is to do with Mama's passing, I know it is."

Randal's harried glance fell first upon Harriet and then swung towards Francis. He gave a tiny shake of his head, knowing his own eyes must echo something of the anguish in his brother's orbs.

"Candia, my dear, you must be sensible," Harriet pleaded, trying to extract the girl from the frantic clutch she had upon Randal's arms.

"No! I will not be put off."

"Candia, enough!"

Her father's sterner tones had only the effect of reducing the girl to noisy sobs. Francis moved in.

"Candia, pray be calm." He added sotto

voce, "Randal, for pity's sake, deal gently with her!"

And then, like a balmy wind, the cool tones he was coming to know so well poured gentleness into the maelstrom.

"Dear Lady Candia, you are perfectly right. We have dealt foolishly with you, for are you not a woman grown, endowed with common sense and practicality? Come, if you please, with me and let your father see to his affairs. Your aunt and I may tell you just how things stand, and then you will decide for yourself how best to help your papa."

How did she do it? Before Ottilia was halfway through this masterly speech, Candia's lamentations ceased as if by magic. Admittedly she was gazing at her grandmother's companion as if she might have descended from the moon. But such was the force of that calm personality that his niece allowed herself to be led, meek as a lamb, back into the dining parlour.

Harriet cast him an eloquent look as if to indicate her own astonishment, and Francis jerked his head to her to follow after the pair. He turned to his brother to find Randal staring, his mouth at half-cock, as if he had been caught a blow in the chest. His stunned gaze came around to Francis.

"What in Hades was that?"

Francis bristled. "That, my dear brother, is Mrs. Ottilia Draycott, officially Mama's companion, but in reality our saviour in this hideous predicament."

Randal's brows shot up. "You speak in riddles, my boy. Explain."

Francis took his arm. "I shall do so, but let us repair to a less public spot."

He began drawing his brother towards the library, but Randal held back, his anxious glance going to the parlour door, into which at that very instant was hurrying Mrs. Thriplow.

"Leave Mama to attend to them," Francis advised.

"Yes, but I am not at all sure —"

"You need have no fears. Mama is perfectly well able to behave with all the discretion in the world. You need not suppose her incapable of compassion."

"Yes, I daresay, but I am thinking of Violette. And the children are already overwhelmed."

Francis fairly pulled him into the smaller lobby. "Let them be settled, man. Did you not see Thriplow going in? There will be time enough for explanations."

At last Randal allowed himself to be shepherded to the library door, and it was

431

instead Francis who halted, realising they had a follower. He turned on the man Grice.

"What the devil are you at, fellow? Do you think my brother is going to make his exit via the book room window?"

Randal let out an exasperated breath. "He accompanies me everywhere, damn him!"

"Well, he is not coming in with us."

Benjamin Grice held his ground as Francis glared at him. "I've me orders, sir."

"I have not the faintest interest in your orders," Francis told the man, vainly trying to control a spurt of fury. Everything else, and now this! "I have private matters to discuss with my brother, and your presence can well be dispensed with."

The man did not even trouble himself to shake his head, but looked squarely into Francis's face. "I've to keep the quarry in sight at all times."

"Damn your impertinence!"

Grice did not even blink. Francis found his fixed stare peculiarly unnerving. His brother uttered a mirthless laugh and gave him a familiar buffet on the shoulder.

"No use, old fellow. Do you think I haven't tried to be rid of him by every means I could think of? I'll say this for Bow Street: They train their fellows well. Grice is up to every ruse in the book. Aren't you, Benjamin, eh?"

The mock familiarity and the jocular tone were so typical of Randal that Francis had the oddest sensation of his presence. As if he had only fully taken in the reality of his brother's return at this particular instant. He sighed defeat.

"Let him stay, then." And turning to Grice, "But you'll remain out of hearing at the window, if you please. The library, thank God, is a wide enough room."

With which he ignored any effect his words might have had, turned his back upon the Runner, and tucked his hand companionably into his brother's arm as he headed through the book room door.

Dinner was necessarily a stilted affair, the presence of Madame Guizot putting a stopper upon any freedom of conversation. Her children, Bastien and Lucille, who were respectively twelve and fifteen years of age, as Lord Polbrook informed the company, had been put into the charge of the housemaid Jane until such time as a French-speaking individual could be engaged. Whether this was to be a maid or a governess had already become, Ottilia gathered, a matter of altercation.

"Randal will have it that their education

433

must be continued in French," Sybilla had ranted in a brief interchange conducted in her bedchamber, whither the dowager had come to find her for the purpose, Ottilia suspected, of venting her spleen. "Of what use to teach them in French, said I, when they are destined to live in England? I might as well have spared my breath. It seems this Madame Guizot —" muttered in a tone of ill-concealed scepticism "— has no notion of settling in this country, fondly imagining the day will come when she may return to her homeland."

"I fear she is doomed to disappointment," Ottilia said mildly.

"Just what I said to him. But he is adamant the woman must be humoured. As if there were ever the slightest use in encouraging false hopes."

"Did you say so?"

"How could I, with the dratted female in the room? I have had no opportunity for private speech with Randal all day, for if she is not there, that wretched Runner must needs be like a shadow at his back."

Ottilia had commiserated with Sybilla's frustration, but a reprieve from this latter scourge at least had come just before dinner was to be served. A message had arrived for the man Grice from Bow Street, upon receiving which he had departed the Hanover Square mansion.

Amazed, Lord Polbrook had watched him leave the parlour where the family had foregathered and turned to his brother. "How did you manage it, Fan?"

Lord Francis had grinned. "I sent a note to George, begging his intercession with Justice Ingham."

"Good gad, then I am much in his debt!"

"More so than you know," had murmured Lord Francis, sending a glance across to Ottilia.

Randal had claimed his attention, grasping his hand. "And to you, brother. You have been sorely tried these past days."

"Randal, I must speak with you alone," said the dowager, urgency in her voice.

Lord Polbrook rubbed a hand across his chin. "Yes, presently, ma'am. But Francis has given me an account of events, you know."

"I do not wish to talk to you of events."

Lord Polbrook looked decidedly uncomfortable, Ottilia thought. And no wonder. She imagined everyone in the room, including Madame Guizot from the apprehensive expression in her eyes, was perfectly aware of the intended subject of discussion.

The Frenchwoman spoke very little English, but Ottilia suspected that, like all foreign language speakers, she understood more than she was able to express herself. Lord Polbrook was fluent in French, and both Sybilla and Lord Francis had a good command of it. Ottilia's was indifferent and she therefore bore little part in the dinner table chatter, although she gathered enough to know it was confined to innocuous subjects.

At liberty to indulge her own thoughts, Ottilia seized the chance to take stock of the gentleman whose absence at a crucial moment had caused all manner of difficulties to his relatives.

He was a much larger man altogether than Lord Francis, whose lithe figure had a grace wholly lacking in the brother. He was not nearly as good-looking, although the resemblance was marked. Both had the lush hair and dark eyes of their mother, although Francis's locks were much lighter than those of either of his siblings, but the elder brother had heavier jowls and his cheeks were broad. Ottilia judged him to be of mercurial temperament, for a peevish tone often underlay his apparent good humour.

This would scarcely surprise Ottilia under the circumstances, was it not patent Lord Polbrook was not in mourning for his wife.

The irony of his returning one week to the day of a departure made in ignorance of Emily's violent and tragic death had clearly passed him by. His attention seemed to be taken up primarily with the plight of Madame Guizot and her children, and if it were not for the nuisance of the marchioness having met her end in a manner that enforced a priority of interest upon him, was Ottilia's cynical thought, she was ready to believe he would have welcomed his newfound freedom.

Barely had this thought passed through her mind than a thunderous knocking was heard upon the front door. The Frenchwoman started more nervously than the rest of the company, and Ottilia reflected that the events of the past days had done much to inure them all to sudden shocks. Possibly in response to Madame Guizot's reaction, Lord Polbrook chose to take a high-handed attitude, turning to the butler.

"What the deuce is that infernal row? Cattawade, go and tell whichever fool is battering on the door that we are not receiving. And if it is that fellow Grice back again," he called after the butler, who was making his stately way towards the door, "let him kick his heels in the street until we are finished."

Almost without her realising it, Ottilia's

eyes went to Lord Francis. She found him tight-lipped, his dark eyes burning. Was he angry at his brother's insouciant resumption of his position as head of the family, just as if nothing had happened? She could sympathise, for he had been left to deal with the calamity, and his life had been turned inside out. Though to be sure Lord Polbrook had not known what was to happen within hours of his departure.

The dowager was uncharacteristically silent, but Ottilia saw her with eyes trained upon the wall, as if she sought to see through into the hall beyond, from where the sounds of an altercation were springing up. She could hear Cattawade's deep tones against a high-pitched feminine wail, both of which were overborne by a voice that began at once to be familiar. Evidently Lord Francis recognised it also, for he started up from his place.

"Hell and the devil!"

His brother's eyes turned swiftly towards him, a frown creasing his brow. "What's to do, Fan?"

But there was no opportunity for Lord Francis to respond, for hasty footsteps sounded without, the door was wrenched back, and Lord Harbisher thrust through the aperture, closely followed by his wife, the butler bringing up the rear.

The earl's violent glance swept the room and fixed upon Lord Polbrook seated at the head of the table.

CHAPTER 17

Lord Harbisher started forward. "Ha! I knew it. Murdering fiend! You dare show your face, do you? Damned if I don't smash it to pieces!"

The marquis, plainly astonished, sat blinking under the onslaught until Harbisher, with a howl of rage, launched himself at the man.

"Hugh, *no!*" shrieked his wife.

Polbrook had no time to do more than half rise from his chair before the earl was on him, fists pounding wildly. The victim fell back, raising his arms in an attempt to fend off his attacker, grunts of protest issuing from his throat.

Ottilia shot out of her seat with no very clear idea of what she could do, but Lord Francis was already in the fray, yelling at the footman who had been assisting the butler to serve dinner and was hovering by the sideboard.

"Abel, don't stand there like a stock, you fool! Help me seize him."

A cacophony of voices, one distinctly French, added to the hubbub as the two rescuers heaved at Harbisher's shoulders. Lady Harbisher darted about them, alternately hectoring and pleading. Ottilia went to the woman and pulled her apart without ceremony.

"They will do better alone, ma'am. Pray calm yourself."

"I tried to stop him," she uttered tearfully, "but the moment the message came, nothing would do for him but to come round at once."

"What message, Lady Harbisher?" asked Ottilia, trying to make herself heard above the grunts and growls issuing from the male element still locked in combat.

The wispy creature had her eyes still on her struggling spouse, and there was a breathless quality to her voice.

"He set a man to watch the house."

"This house?"

Lady Harbisher nodded. "The fellow was to bring news of Polbrook's arrival. Hugh would have been here long since, but that he was out of town."

At this point the earl was successfully detached from his brother-in-law's person,

441

but Lord Francis and Abel were obliged to hold him back. He was panting, and his voice was hoarse, but he continued to revile the marquis.

"Dastard! You killed her. Assassin!"

The marquis rose, flinging out his arms. "Have you run mad, Hugh? Of course I did not kill Emily."

"You hated her. You wanted to be rid of her."

"Even if that were true —"

"You admit it!"

"Nothing of the sort, I merely —"

"By God, Polbrook, you'll answer to me!"

"That is enough!"

Startled into silence, both men turned as one to stare at Lord Francis. Ottilia was no less astonished at the harsh fury of his utterance. She had not supposed him capable of so thoroughly losing his temper.

"If you don't cease this ridiculous charade this moment, Harbisher, I will have you conveyed to Bedlam for a lunatic," he pursued, the deadly calm of his voice in no way lessening its effect. Then he turned on his brother. "As for you, Randal, you would do well to keep your mouth shut. If neither one of you has the common decency to observe a little dignity in the face of Emily's demise, then I recommend you look upon the gruesome ravage of her features, as we had no choice but to do. If that does not bring you to your senses, nothing will."

Ottilia could have applauded. Lord Polbrook dropped into his chair, looking shamefaced, and took refuge in his glass. The earl, a dull colour seeping into his cheeks, fell back, his shoulders drooping. His mouth worked, and then his hand went out and grasped Francis's arm.

"I am well rebuked." A bitter note crept into his voice. "But do not suppose me content. I will have justice." He cast one last glance of loathing upon his brother-in-law and turned to look for his wife. "Come, Dorothea."

The frightened woman hurried up to him. "I am here, Hugh."

With pity, Ottilia saw the man stagger a little as he set a course for the door. Lady Harbisher, slight as she was, took his weight, supporting him to where the butler was holding open the door. He looked back.

"Let him look to his lawyers, I say, for I will have justice."

His departure left an atmosphere one might slice with a paring knife. Ottilia sought in vain for a way of breaking it without worsening the mood. Then Sybilla, who had remained mute throughout the altercation, rose magnificently to the occasion.

"Be so good as to serve the remove, Cattawade. And replenish the glasses, if you please."

Galvanised, the butler immediately set the footman to removing platters, despatched Jane to the kitchens, and himself went round with the claret. The dowager addressed a commonplace remark in French to Madame Guizot, who bravely attempted a response as close to normal as possible. Ottilia watched Lord Francis go around the table and resume his seat. He did not look at his brother, and stealing a glance towards the head of the table, Ottilia saw that the marquis was likewise avoiding eye contact. He had tossed off the contents of his glass and was watching the liquor splashing into it from the decanter in the butler's hand. He drank deeply of the replenished supply, downing half the contents at a gulp. It had not escaped Ottilia's notice that he had imbibed freely throughout the meal. A habit of drowning his sorrows? If so, it was not an uncommon method.

From what Lord Francis had told her, in a swift exchange seized earlier in the day, the marquis's indulgence was understandable. In their discussion in the library, Lord

444

Polbrook had admitted the violence of his quarrel with his wife that fatal night, but had vehemently denied any intent of harm. His memory of time was less than useless, Lord Francis complained, for he could not precisely place his homecoming from the ball nor his leaving the house, averring he'd been in no state to be consulting his watch. But he was adamant that Emily had been alive and well when he had last slammed himself out of her chamber. On the subject of the fan, he had become voluble and incensed enough to corroborate Mary's recollection, declaring his right to withdraw it from his wife's possession and his anger at her practice of using it as a lure, of which he was fully aware. Ottilia could not think him a reliable witness and believed it would go hard with him should the matter come to trial.

By the time dinner finally came to an end, a semblance of good relations had been restored, the brothers addressing one or two innocuous remarks to each other. It was well they had a moment alone with the port, Ottilia thought, as she followed Sybilla and Madame Guizot to the parlour.

When the gentlemen joined them, the Frenchwoman excused herself on the score of seeing to her offspring. She added, with a nervous flicker of her eyes towards the dowager, that she hoped they would understand her tiredness from the journey. Once she had seen the children, she would go to bed.

The dowager sent her on her way with every expression of goodwill, but added a sharp rider, in English, to her elder son as he made to escort Madame Guizot.

"Do not forget, Randal. In five minutes, in the library, if you please."

Lord Polbrook threw a harassed look at his brother, which augured well for a better understanding between them, but agreed to present himself at the rendezvous and departed after the Frenchwoman. The moment the door closed, the dowager broke out in a fury.

"Madame Guizot! I'll warrant the creature has scant right to such a title. How dare he! How dare he bring her here?"

Lord Francis rolled his eyes at Ottilia and attempted to mitigate the onslaught. "He saved her life, Mama. Not to mention the lives of those innocent children."

"I do not forget that, but he need not have insulted Emily's memory by bringing them into her house. Why could he not have deposited the creatures in a hotel somewhere?"

"I daresay that is just what he would have done, had circumstances been otherwise. Recollect, ma'am, that Randal must have had this in mind when he left for France. It is not his fault that fate struck Emily down at the same moment."

Sybilla showed no sign of softening. "Not his fault? Pray, how is it not his fault that he became entangled with this woman at the outset?"

Lord Francis sighed. "That is neither here nor there. I hope you do not mean to approach him in this spirit, Mama, for I doubt he will listen to you with any degree of patience."

The dowager's glare was directed upon the luckless Lord Francis. "Do you suppose I care about that?" She drew a shuddering breath, clenching her fists in her lap. "I should not mind it so much if he had shown the least vestige of remorse or sorrow. There is poor Candia, distraught, and all he can think of is this — this harlot!"

Moved, Ottilia came quickly to kneel beside the dowager's chair. She covered those unquiet hands with her own. "Dear Sybilla, it is very upsetting for you, but do pray think a little."

She saw she had the elder lady's attention, the distress receding a little as the dowager's eyes turned upon her.

"Think? Of what would you have me think, Ottilia? Try if you can offer me a modicum of mitigation, for I can see none."

She was close to tears, and Ottilia took hold of one of her hands and held it between both her own.

"Dear ma'am, Lord Polbrook has not been here. As Lord Francis earlier pointed out, neither he nor Lord Harbisher have seen the ugly sight to which we have all been witness. It is perhaps unreal to him, even the fact of Emily's death, let alone the brutality with which it was accomplished. Yes, his disinterest is callous, but let us rather suppose him to be thoughtless than uncaring. Had he been the one to find his wife, instead of Lord Francis, I cannot but believe that his sensibilities must have been as harrowed as your own."

She saw that her words were having an effect. The dowager's high colour began to die and the shallowness of her breathing lessened. Her fingers released themselves from Ottilia's and reached out. Ottilia felt her cheek stroked with a hand that shook, and Sybilla's voice came husky and low.

"My dear, dear friend. You will never know how great a comfort you have been to me. Without your calm good sense, we had all of us been in danger of going to pieces."

With which she put Ottilia gently aside and stood up. Her step was a trifle shaky, and Lord Francis saw it.

"Will you take my arm, Mama?"

She waved him away. "I can manage perfectly, I thank you."

Still kneeling where the dowager had left her, Ottilia watched her walk out of the room, her back straight and determined, her control magnificent.

"Bravo, Tillie!"

Turning, Ottilia discovered Lord Francis holding out a hand. She took it and allowed him to help her to her feet. Only then did she take in that he had once more used the nickname he had bestowed upon her last night. Her heart glowed.

"By the by," he went on lightly, "I have had no chance to congratulate you on your handling of Candia. What in the world did you tell her to make her go off with Harriet as meekly as you please?"

Ottilia let out a laugh. "And here I had expected one of your scolds."

"No, why?"

"I thought you would have objected to my interference, especially when you had all agreed that it was best for Candia to be kept in ignorance of the whole."

"On the contrary, I was immeasurably grateful to you. None of us knew how to do, though I confess I had qualms about how much you might feel it incumbent upon you to reveal."

Ottilia sat down in the dowager's vacated chair and looked up at him where he stood, leaning one arm along the mantel.

"I revealed as little as I could get away with, you may be sure. But it did seem to me to have gone past the point where the poor girl could be kept completely in the dark. She had sensed too much."

He sighed. "I am to blame. I should have packed Harriet off with her upon the following day."

"You could hardly have done so, my lord. She was not fit to travel, such a state as she was in."

He grinned. "Thank you. I stand corrected and can only be glad of it. What did you tell her?"

"That her mother had died an unnatural death and that we were doing everything we could to find out who had killed her. She was horribly stricken, of course, but I think also relieved."

"Relieved?"

"It is not so surprising, my lord, for —"

With an impatient gesture, he flung away

a little from the fireplace. "If you don't stop 'my lording' me, woman, I will not be answerable for the consequences. We have surely moved too far for that."

Too far toward what? But Ottilia did not say it. She could feel her heart beating unnaturally fast. She strove for calm.

"Very well, if you desire it. In private at least, I will address you by name, but you must excuse me if I keep to formality in the presence of others."

His dark gaze was upon her, its expression unfathomable. "Afraid of scandal, Tillie?"

Ottilia's breath stuck in her throat. Would there might be cause! She essayed a nonchalance she was far from feeling.

"It would scarcely be seemly, as your mother's companion, to be seen to be upon terms of — of —"

The word would not leave her tongue. Lord Francis supplied it.

"Intimacy?"

She let out a faint gasp. "I was going to say 'friendship.' "

"Were you indeed?"

Ottilia felt her breathing to be quite as shallow as that of the dowager so recently. She controlled its passage as best she could, and firmly brought the subject to an end.

"We are wandering from the point."

For a moment he did not answer. Then he withdrew his gaze from hers and threw himself down into the chair opposite.

"Yes. You were saying?"

As Ottilia had not the remotest recollection of what precisely she had been saying, she was nonplussed. "What was I saying?"

Lord Francis eyed her coolly. "That Candia was relieved on hearing of the murder."

"Yes, just so," Ottilia said quickly, feeling relief herself. "She had sensed there was more to her mother's death than she knew and perhaps it was of benefit to her to know she had not imagined it."

He nodded, his manner seeming more normal. "That I can appreciate. And the Runner?"

Ottilia shrugged. "There I had little choice. I had to tell her that as her father's departure had coincided with the event, he had naturally been put under a false suspicion. I made out that it was all a mistake and would very soon be sorted out. But it provided the perfect excuse for her departure. Indeed, your sister jumped upon it, suggesting that while her father's attention was taken up with this matter it would be less of a worry to him to know his daughter was well taken care of."

"Oh, that was well done of Harriet! Bless

her, she has not a tithe of your talent, but she was ever quick."

This encomium of the brother for the sister amused Ottilia. She suspected the bond between the two was greater than that felt by either for their older brother.

The thought of Lord Polbrook recalled Ottilia to the matter at hand. She jumped up.

"Francis, what are we about? We shall miss the half of it, if we do not hurry."

He had risen at once, but at this he frowned. "What are you talking of?"

"Your mother and Randal. I take it this room adjoins the library?"

For a moment he stared at her, and then a delighted grin split his face. "Have I not said time and again that you are an atrocious wretch? You mean to eavesdrop."

Ottilia giggled. "Well, of course. How else are we to know just what was said. Do you forget we are pledged to prove your brother's innocence? How can we do so if we don't witness his statement?"

At this, Francis jerked towards the inner wall and turned, throwing out a hand. "After you."

She went towards him and took a place at the wall, putting her ear against the wallpaper. A faint murmuring came through the intervening stucco and brick. Sighing, she shifted back.

"This will not do. A door will work better."

Francis frowned. "You can't stand with your ear to the door in the lobby."

"Why not?" She was already crossing to the door. "Pray bring a candle, if you please, Francis."

She saw him hesitate, but continued on her way. A muttered expletive reached her and Ottilia let out a laugh as Francis flung over to the escritoire in the corner and seized a candelabrum that stood there.

"I feel like a conspirator," he said as Ottilia preceded him from the room.

Ottilia threw an amused look back at him. "Well, you are one."

"Yes, and I can see that association with you is rapidly undermining my moral sense." His eye gleamed. "It is well for you to giggle, woman, but there is no doubt you are a debilitating influence. Ah, here we are."

Slipping into the vestibule, Ottilia put a finger to her lips and tiptoed into the lobby, where a short wooden settle was placed in the alcove opposite the servants' staircase. Ottilia indicated it and lifted her brows in question.

"A convenience for persons engaged to see Randal on business," said Francis, his voice low.

Wasting no more time, Ottilia crept up to the door and leaned in, setting her ear to the woodwork. She could hear the murmur of voices, but could not make out the words. Pulling back, she stared at the door, thinking.

"Well?"

Ottilia looked round. "Francis, I am a little thirsty."

He frowned. "Why did you not say so before we came?"

She shrugged. "I was not thirsty then."

"Can't it keep?"

Ottilia smiled at him. "Would it be too much to ask you to fetch me a glass of water? A tumbler, if you will."

He looked disconcerted. Ottilia waited.

"Are you trying to get rid of me, by any chance?"

She laughed, and quickly smothered the sound with her hand. "Of course not."

He eyed her with suspicion, she thought. And then capitulated, turning towards the dining parlour. Then he checked and came back, speaking low.

"If I return and find you gone, Tillie, I shall be very much displeased."

"But why should I go anywhere?"

"Heaven knows! Why do you do anything mad? I don't trust you an inch."

But he went off to the vestibule and disappeared through the dining parlour doorway, and Ottilia once again put her ear to the door, pressing flat and covering her other ear with one hand. It was better, but not good enough.

From what she was able to hear, it was clear Sybilla was holding a tight rein on her temper, for her tones were taut and clipped. The marquis, on the other hand, sounded alternately blustering and wheedling. Striving to make out words, Ottilia mentally urged speed upon the absent Francis.

When she heard his step, she shifted back and looked round. Francis was possessed of a little silver tray, upon which reposed an empty tumbler, a small jug of water, and a glass of wine.

His brows rose as her gaze came back up to his. "If I am to act the part of a spy, I require fortification."

"I quite understand." Her demure tone deserted her, however, as Francis set down the tray on the settle and lifted the jug. "No, don't pour!"

Darting to the tray, Ottilia seized the tumbler. Throwing him a look brimful of

456

mischief, she returned to her post and set the tumbler's open maw carefully to the door. Then, aware of Francis's astonished gaze, she put her ear to the flat glass end.

Instantly, the voices within the room beyond became audible, albeit of an oddly echoing quality.

"At least you admit this woman is more to you than a mere acquaintance," the dowager was saying. "Will you then have me believe that these children are not?"

"I don't care what you believe, ma'am," came in anger from her son.

Sybilla's tone sharpened. "Randal, are they your children?"

There was a perceptible pause. Then a rough, long-drawn sigh. "Yes."

Ottilia jumped, her shock tinged with satisfaction. Had she not guessed as much? She glanced towards Francis, ready to convey this intelligence, and found him shaking with suppressed laughter.

Startled, she abandoned her position. "What in the world is the matter?"

Francis's eyes danced. "Can you ask? Unscrupulous is what you are, Tillie. But sheer genius! How did you think of it? And why not say so instead of pretending to be thirsty?"

He spoke in a whisper and she responded

457

in like manner. "I thought you might refuse to fetch the glass if I said what I really wanted it for."

"Only too likely, you wretch. How do you come to know this boys' trick?"

She had to control a spurt of laughter. "Precisely through boys, of course. My nephews."

He struck a couple of fingers to his forehead. "I had forgot them."

Ottilia put out a finger. "I must listen. Your brother has just confessed the Frenchwoman's children are his."

"What?"

"Hush!"

He lowered his voice. "Are you sure?"

Ottilia already had her ear back in place. "Your mother asked him outright and he admitted it."

Out of the corner of her eye she saw Francis look at the glass in his hand and then toss off the wine in one quick motion. But her attention was reclaimed by the discussion going forward on the other side of the door.

"Don't you see, Mama? That's why I went. I knew they were in danger, for Violette had written of the unrest in the area and her fears for their safety."

"I understand so much, but could you not

have spoken of it?"

"I had the intention of telling Emily that night. I knew I must bring Violette and the children to England. I could not see how it was to be done with the same secrecy I was able to maintain while they were in France. An establishment had to be set up, and —"

"Wait one moment. You intended to tell Emily? Distress her? For what? What was your intention, Randal?" Suspicion ran rife in the dowager's tone.

"I have told you. I meant to fetch my family out of France."

"Your family? And what of your legitimate family? Don't tell me. You had it in mind to abandon them, didn't you? *Didn't you?*"

"Abandon? No!"

"What, were you going to live a double life as you have done these many years?"

"And why should I not?" The marquis's fury erupted and Ottilia had a glimpse of what must have occurred during his quarrels with his wife. "What sort of life have I had with the woman you and my father picked out for me? Why should I continue to suffer the indignities of her faithlessness?"

"*Her* faithlessness?"

"I did not conduct my amour in the full light of public scorn. Yes, if you will have it,

459

I wanted to leave her. I was going to tell her so that night."

"Desertion! Oh, Randal, how could you?"

In the pause that ensued, Ottilia lifted her head with the intention of passing the gist of this information to Francis, but found him close beside her, his ear glued to his wineglass, which was fastened tight to the woodwork. She could not think his glass would prove as effective as her tumbler, but the grim look in his face told her he had heard enough.

Her heart reached out to him. She wanted to cradle his hurt and croon him to comfort. Instead she applied her ear to her improvised listening device as the voices started up again.

"To think of dragging your name, your children's names, through the mire! What had you in mind, divorce?"

"Separation rather."

"I am sick to my stomach."

Sybilla's voice had sunk, and the desolation in it caused Ottilia to look quickly to Francis. That he was cut to the heart was patent. Without thinking, Ottilia reached out a hand to him. He saw it, took it, gripped it as might a drowning man. But he did not shift from his position.

"There is no need to take it so, ma'am,"

the marquis was saying, his voice rough and strained.

"Is there not? I tell you, boy, if it were not for the despicable manner of poor Emily's death, I could almost wish her joy of being spared all this. And you! You stand there, self-righteous in your sins, without a vestige of realisation of the consequences of your deeds."

"I know, I know," came with impatience. "But I would risk all for Violette's life."

"And what of your own, my poor deluded son?"

His mother's acid note had the effect of altering his tone.

"What do you mean?"

"I am talking of your life. You appear to have little understanding of your own danger."

"Pooh! What danger? Oh, you're talking of that officious little Runner, are you? I'll soon send him to the rightabout."

"And will you send your peers to the rightabout? Will you have an answer for them when they know you meant to put aside your wife for the sake of your French mistress? You may as well have set the noose about your neck yourself!"

In the deadly silence that followed, Ottilia could almost feel the thickness of the stupor that enwrapped the marquis. She came away and looked at Francis, only then realising he had released her hand.

"He has taken in at last the danger in which he stands," she said quietly.

Francis nodded. He shifted away from the wall and set the wineglass down on the tray. Then he slumped into the settle beside it, his shoulders hunched, his chin sinking half to his chest.

Ottilia, all too conscious of his distress, had for once no words of comfort. Everything that came into her head she dismissed for a platitude. She would have liked to offer her hand again, but a foolish fear of rejection held her back.

At length Francis looked up. He tried to smile, but it went awry.

"Come, Tillie, have you nothing in your armoury?"

She shook her head. "I must fail you on this occasion."

Francis sighed. "Well, so be it."

Then he got up in a restless way, shifting into the vestibule. Compelled, Ottilia followed him.

"Say something," he whispered urgently. "Make me laugh."

At that, Ottilia was surprised into merriment herself. "To order? But you laugh only at what you consider my eccentricities."

His lip quirked. "Do I so?"

The effort to overcome his lowering mood moved her even more than the mood itself. Ottilia forgot caution and held out her hands to him.

"If I cannot make you laugh, I can listen."

Francis took the hands and held them. His dark eyes looked deep into hers.

"You are too good, Tillie. I am ashamed to think how much we have put upon you. Not once have I heard you complain."

She controlled her voice with an effort. "I could scarcely complain when I brought it on myself. No one asked me to interfere at the first. And though I am sorry for your distress, on the whole there is still much to entertain me."

His eyes lit and his grip tightened. "There now, I knew you had it in you to lighten my load. Entertain you, forsooth, you wretch!"

Ottilia could not prevent her happiness in the moment bubbling over into mirth. Francis let go one of her hands and reached up a finger, brushing it lightly across her mouth.

"Of all your eccentricities, I think I like that gurgling laugh of yours the most."

"And I like —" She broke off, appalled at what she had been about to say.

Question was in his face as he prompted, "And you like — what, Tillie?"

"You, Fan."

It was out before she could prevent it, the endearment of his nickname slipping naturally into the confession. She felt heat in her cheeks and knew she was flushing.

The dark eyes gleamed in the candlelight. Softly, so softly he spoke.

"Do you know, that is the kindest thing you have ever said to me."

Kind? No, she had not meant to be kind. Disappointment swept over her in a wave, and Ottilia released her hand from his, shifting away.

"We are neglecting our duties."

With shaking fingers, she hunted for her tumbler, spied it on the settle where she had unthinkingly set it, and seized it up. But when she put it to the door, there was no sound to be heard. She moved away again.

"They are silent. We will be remarked. You take the tray back and I will go to the parlour."

With which she set the tumbler on the tray and slid past him without meeting his gaze. That he did not speak, nor make any move to prevent her leaving seemed to Ottilia to bear out her conviction that she had wholly misinterpreted both his words and his actions.

The necessity to dispose of the tray and its contents afforded Francis a much-needed opportunity to compose his unquiet mind. Whether his brother's duplicity or Ottilia's inexplicable withdrawal rankled most, he was unable to decide.

Only when she had left him did it occur to him that he had been within an ace of kissing the woman. Without intent and wholly out of the blue. Or so it seemed. But in truth it did not take a deal of wit to trace the path that had led him thus far. Having begun with admiration, his esteem for her had imperceptibly grown until it had taken off on a sudden and plunged him into wholehearted affection.

Yes, affection. Francis balked at going further, falling into a commitment that must turn his life upside down. Besides, he was loath to dare to suppose that Tillie's "liking" masked a warmer feeling. Her precipitate exit argued otherwise.

Depositing the tray on the sideboard in the dining parlour, he recalled her little subterfuge and laughed out. Whatever came, he had at least the satisfaction to know that Ottilia's presence, quite aside from her genius in divining what had occurred, was responsible for leavening the bitter pill the family had been obliged to swallow. That he must ever regard with gratitude.

In this more settled frame of mind he reentered the parlour that had become their headquarters to find his mother seated, Randal noticeably absent, and Ottilia in the act of pulling the bell. She smiled at him, as composed as if the little scene between them had never happened.

"We are going to have in the tea tray. Sybilla is tired. And no wonder, for it has been quite a day."

"A masterly understatement," Francis returned.

He glanced at his mother, dismayed at the drawn look in her face. She had aged all in a moment. He longed to offer words of comfort, but remembered he was not supposed to know what had passed between her and his brother.

"Has Randal gone to bed?"

She lifted her bowed head, with an effort, it seemed to Francis. "I have no notion." She fiddled with her fingers for a moment, and then looked up at him. "We quarrelled."

Francis strove to sound nonchalant. "I expected no less. Did he give you any satisfactory assurances?"

"If you mean concerning the woman now residing in this house," said his mother with something of her accustomed acid, "he gave me nothing beyond the headache which plagues me now."

Francis could not refrain from glancing across at Ottilia, seeking either her advice or opinion, he knew not which. She met his eyes and flashed him one of her warning looks. Dangerous ground? Undoubtedly.

He was just wondering whether he should probe further or leave it until the morning when the knocker sounded at the outer door. His mother started and Ottilia looked round, as if she might see through the wall.

"A strange hour to be calling," Francis said, and made towards the parlour door.

"It must be urgent," Ottilia said from behind him, and he realised she, too, had risen and was following.

He reached the door, pulled it open, and found Abel already walking down the hall. Remembering Ottilia had rung the bell in the parlour, he must suppose the footman had been responding to it. Vaguely he wondered at Cattawade's absence, but forgot it at once as the front door opened and a well-known voice spoke.

"Ah, Abel. Is Lord Francis here? I must speak with him without delay."

"George!" Francis strode forward as his friend entered the house. Tretower saw him and came quickly up. "What's to do?"

George seized his outstretched hand. "I will tell you directly. Let us go in. How do you do, Mrs. Draycott?"

Francis waited only to instruct the footman to bring the tea tray and followed his friend into the parlour. George was bowing over the dowager's hand.

"What brings you here so late, colonel?"

His mother was looking as apprehensive as Francis was beginning to feel. "Out with it, man. What fresh disaster is about to befall us?"

George faced them all, his back to the fire. "I have just come from Bow Street. Justice Ingham has issued a warrant for your brother's arrest."

CHAPTER 18

Disbelief swept through Francis, and he barely heard George continue.

"Ingham intended to carry it through tonight, but I managed to persuade him that nothing was to be gained by incarcerating the marquis at such an hour. But he intends to come himself in the morning to administer the warrant and take Polbrook into custody. Meanwhile, there are Runners stationed front and back outside the house."

His mind blank, Francis saw the colour draining out of his mother's face. Instinctively, he looked to Ottilia, hardly aware if he expected succour from that quarter. She stood tensely, her features painful with enquiry.

"But on what grounds, Colonel Tretower? There has been no interview, no questioning. What can Justice Ingham know that justifies his taking this action?"

Francis looked automatically to his friend

and found Tretower setting his teeth. His heart lurched. "What is it, George?"

George drew a breath. "I don't know how to say this, but say it I must. There has been an information laid against Lord Polbrook."

"An information?" Francis echoed. "What sort of information?"

George shook his head. "Ingham would not tell me."

"By whom was this information laid?"

Ottilia, as ever, asking the most pertinent question. Francis almost dreaded his friend's answer.

"He would not tell me that, either."

"The devil!"

In the silence that followed, Francis sought options. Who could it have been? His mother gave a sudden cry.

"Harbisher! He left here baying for justice. He must have gone directly to Bow Street."

George's frown intensified. "Tonight, you mean?"

"He interrupted dinner with the declared intention of smashing Randal's face in," supplied Francis, an edge to his voice.

"Then it cannot have been he. Whoever laid this information did so earlier. He spoke to the fellow who went after Polbrook — Grice, was it?"

Ottilia's gaze was fixed upon George, but

Francis noted that faraway look in her eyes that meant she was thinking of something else. Before he could enquire the reason, she spoke up.

"Just what did Justice Ingham tell you, Colonel Tretower?"

George thought for a moment. "That an information had been laid which gave him reason and witness to Lord Polbrook's culpability in the crime."

"Witness? But that must mean Bowerchalke."

His mother's tone expressed astonishment and Francis looked to see how Ottilia took this notion. She was frowning, but she did not speak. Francis mustered his own resources.

"If it was Bowerchalke," he said, thinking aloud, "then it would explain why he put back the jewel box. He would wish to disassociate himself from the theft."

Both George and his mother gazed at him with blankness. He recalled there had been no opportunity to report on the find.

"Ottilia and I discovered it last night. She caught the fellow in the act, but did not see who it was in the dark."

George glanced curiously from one to the other of them, and a gleam of amusement crept into his eyes.

"You two have been busy, it seems."

Francis brushed this hastily aside as his mother's puzzled eyes flicked across at him. "Never mind that. We were driven by sheer necessity."

He could only suppose his mother's attention was concentrated upon the matter at hand, for she said nothing.

"Ottilia," he pursued, "don't you think it possible?"

She had been lost in a brown study, but she looked at him then. "That Bowerchalke was the one who returned the jewel box? I can't believe he stole it in the first place. Nor does it seem politic to endanger himself by laying an information."

"Why should he endanger himself?"

Ottilia's glance went to the dowager. "Because I am certain he was still in Emily's bedchamber when she was murdered, concealed behind the bed-curtains."

"Indeed? Then it would be to his disadvantage to go to Bow Street."

"Exactly so," Francis agreed. "I imagine the notion of persuading the justices that he had seen and heard all but had taken no hand in the proceedings would terrify Bowerchalke."

"And he is probably the only witness," said his mother despairingly. "I daresay, if

472

we only knew, he could readily exonerate Randal."

"The only witness we know of." Francis struck his hands together in frustration. "Who the devil could have laid that information?"

"I thought of Quaife," offered George, "but it seems unlikely."

"For the same reason as Bowerchalke?" asked the dowager.

"No, ma'am. Because if Quaife had been involved, he would have more sense. Bowerchalke is an untried and very nervous pup. I am ready to believe any folly of him."

A silence fell. Francis felt sorely in need of a restorative and bethought him of the tea tray. "Where in the world is that wretched footman? I told him to bring the tea an eon ago."

Ottilia's eyes turned towards him, and Francis saw an odd look flash in them. Without thought, he moved towards her.

"What is it? Why do you look like that?"

Her face cleared abruptly and she smiled. It was not the warm smile he treasured. It looked forced.

"Perhaps you had best ring the bell again."

The puzzlement did not leave him as he crossed the room to do as she suggested. "I never thought it would come to this."

"If an information had not been laid, I don't suppose it would have," George said. "Without a witness there really is nothing to place Polbrook on the spot. It must be all supposition."

"Not entirely."

Francis caught the dry note in his mother's voice and for a moment he forgot Ottilia's odd conduct. "What do you mean, ma'am?"

"The servants, Fanfan. Huntshaw heard Emily and Randal quarrelling. Both Cattawade and Turville in the stables can place him still in the house at a convenient time. And there is Abel's word, too, both on time and —"

"That cursed mysterious voice? Yes, I remember."

Ottilia had been watching his mother during this recital, and her gaze continued upon the dowager. But Francis could swear her thoughts were otherwise.

"Ottilia!"

She started and looked round. "Yes?"

"You say nothing to the purpose." He gave a little smile, half hoping she would respond with a more natural one of her own. "Come, we are accustomed to have you set us all to rights."

Her clear gaze remained on his face,

disconcerting in its intensity. "You are forgetting the key to the dressing room door."

His mind jumped. He had forgotten it. "What of it?"

"Why should any lover be in possession of that key when he had the one to the outside?"

"Well, to get into the chamber, I imagine," George offered.

Ottilia's glance went to him. "He would not go to the chamber when Emily was out of it. He did not need a key to get in."

Francis was beset by a conviction that she was holding back, as if she might say more if she chose. His mother saved him from having to ask.

"Remember we have not your insight, Ottilia. What do you imply?"

She looked round at them all, and Francis saw reluctance in her face. "We must look within the house."

George uttered a short laugh. "Now you have lost me altogether, Mrs. Draycott."

"Yes, I am quite in the dark," agreed the dowager.

Francis saw the discomfort under which Ottilia laboured and wondered at it. What had she in her mind that she could not reveal before them all?

"Oh, you must pardon me," she said, as if goaded. "Until I have made further enquiry, it is best I keep my own counsel."

Francis was not surprised to see his mother's evident displeasure. "Why? Can you not trust us, Ottilia?"

There was now apology in both face and voice. "It is not a matter of trust. I fear to malign where it may not be deserved. If I voice my thoughts, I may cause irreparable damage."

George's puzzlement was plain, but he was too polite to press her. Not so the dowager.

"But I will not have this. Can there possibly be anything worse to hear than that we already know?"

Without intent, Francis leapt to Ottilia's defence. "Leave her be, ma'am. We have no right to tangle with Ottilia's ethical considerations. We have burdened her enough."

He looked at Ottilia as he spoke and the warm gratitude in her eyes rewarded him. She smiled briefly — a real smile this one — and her gaze went back to his mother.

"Sybilla, forgive me. I may be wrong, quite wrong. Let me but make enquiry tomorrow, and I promise I will speak. If I am right, I will speak."

For a moment, his mother eyed her, and

Francis hoped she would leave it. Then she took his breath away.

"You know who did it."

His eyes flew to Ottilia in mute question. She met them, looked again at George, who was gaping with lively astonishment, and then her gaze went back to his mother's face.

"I think I know, yes." She drew a breath. "But I must be certain. I have also a task for you, Francis. You and Colonel Tretower together."

Francis had relied upon his friend to discover the whereabouts of Jeremy Bowerchalke's lodging, but as he tooled his curricle in the direction of Pall Mall, it was Tretower who wanted clarification of their purpose.

"What is it we must discover?"

Mindful of his instructions, Francis went over what Ottilia had said.

"If she is right that the fellow was hiding behind the bed-curtains during the murder, he is the only witness. We are to extract his confession of his presence, and have him tell us precisely what occurred."

"And if he refuses?"

Francis laughed. "We are to bully him into speech, poor fellow. Ottilia was specific on that point."

Tretower sat back in his seat. "That explains why she wanted both of us to go. I can't see the fellow resisting, can you? I don't imagine much bullying will prove necessary."

Neither did Francis. "I will own myself astonished if he does not capitulate immediately. Assuming, of course, he can be made to be coherent for the space needed to tell his story."

"Almost I feel sorry for the fellow," George commented. "Or I would do if we had not been obliged to witness your brother being carted off to gaol."

Francis could not forbear a shiver of distaste. It had indeed been a harrowing moment. More for Randal's bewilderment than anything else. His brother had clearly not believed he could seriously be accused. Ingham, it had to be admitted, had been both courteous and apologetic, but inexorable nonetheless.

Francis knew his mother had slept badly, and in truth his own rest had been fitful. Had it not been for Ottilia's schemes for the day, he must have despaired. He knew she meant to question a member of the household, which was presumably what she meant by saying they must look inside the house, and he was determined to carry out his part.

"I suppose there is no chance the fellow will be out?" asked George, scanning the windows of the house as Francis brought his horses to a standstill outside Bowerchalke's abode.

"I hope it is too early," Francis answered, for he had set out with Tretower very soon after the Bow Street party had departed from Hanover Square.

The groom leapt down and went to the horses' heads and Francis was able to descend. George had gone on ahead and was already plying the door knocker with energy.

It was several moments before any response came, and Francis began to wonder if they should have waited for the hour to advance. But at last footsteps were heard within, and there was the sound of a bolt being drawn back. The door opened a crack and a frightened face peered round. George put a hand against the door, a precaution Francis instantly approved.

"Is Mr. Bowerchalke at home, if you please?"

The girl, a maid by the mobcap sitting awry upon her head, gave a gasp of fright and looked even more terrified, her eyes popping.

"Mr. Bowerchalke?" George repeated.

"He can't see no one," said the girl in a quavery voice and tried to shut the door.

George pushed it inwards. "No, you don't."

The maid shrieked and backed hurriedly away as Tretower walked calmly into the narrow hallway.

"He can't see no one," repeated the girl, cowering by the stairway.

George was about to speak, but Francis, whose ears had caught the sound of muffled crying somewhere above them, put out a hand to stay him.

"Listen!"

Tretower's head went up for a moment. Then he threw a troubled and suspicious glance at Francis before turning back to the girl.

"What has happened here?"

For answer, the girl burst into sobs. Francis exchanged a glance with George and jerked his head upwards. In a moment, he was leading the way upstairs, followed by Tretower. Francis made short work of the stairway, chasing the sounds of lamentation.

They were coming from a room at the front of the house, outside of which several persons were gathered. A stout dame was leaning against the doorjamb, her apron over her face, helpless whimpers escaping from beneath it. Two young men, clad only in nightshirts, their hair tousled and their faces white with horror, were poised, one on the stairs leading on up, the other in the open doorway to the room at the side.

Both strained faces were pointed towards them as Francis and George reached the landing. Taking advantage of his friend's wearing full military rig, Francis waved him ahead and was grimly satisfied to see the youths shrink back, looking first at each other and then to the doorway from whence the sound of weeping emanated.

"What the deuce is amiss here?" George rapped out. "Is that Bowerchalke's room?"

The boy by the door nodded. "Aye, sir, but he's — he's —"

The fellow on the stairs gripped the banisters and thrust his head over the rails. "He's dead."

Francis froze. "Dead?"

"Murdered!"

"Oh, dear God! Clear the way, George, for pity's sake!"

Tretower's commanding figure filled the hallway. "Stand aside, if you please."

Both the young men shifted with alacrity, leaving him access. But the woman, who appeared to have heard neither their approach nor the brief exchange, was blocking the door. George towered over her.

"Madam, stand aside!"

"It's the landlady, sir. She's in shock."

This was the fellow on the stairs again. He at least had his wits about him.

"You'll have to move her bodily, George," Francis advised in an under voice.

Nothing loath, Tretower took hold of the landlady and shifted her willy-nilly out of the aperture. She hardly noticed, merely sinking down heavily. George took her weight as he lowered her to the stair. He spoke to the fellow standing above her.

"Look after her."

His path now free, Francis pushed past and into the chamber beyond. One glance told its tale. In a far corner, a second maid was crouched, her racking cries echoing mournfully around the chamber.

On the bed, lying in his own blood, lay Jeremy Bowerchalke, death white, with a scarlet gash across his throat.

The housekeeper was in a belligerent mood, and Ottilia's patience was failing.

"Mrs. Thriplow, do you understand that his lordship has been removed to Bow Street? This is no time to be getting up on

482

your high ropes."

"And do you understand, Mrs. Draycott," returned the woman, arms akimbo and face red, "as I've got a clutch of girls half in hysterics for the master's fate?"

"Then help me to change it, Mrs. Thriplow," said Ottilia, exasperated. "All I want is to talk to Mary Huntshaw about the contents of the jewel box."

"Mary has been troubled enough, ma'am. As it is, the poor girl is afeared as she'll be accused."

"I have no intention of accusing her. I am quite sure she did not take the jewels. But I must know what I'm looking for, can't you see that?"

Mrs. Thriplow sniffed, and Ottilia could see her working her way around to find some other objection. She hastened to intercept it.

"I see I will have to confide in you, Mrs. Thriplow. I do not scruple to do so, for I know I can trust your discretion."

The woman visibly softened, preening a little. "Well, it's true as I know how to keep me tongue between me teeth."

"Just so."

Ottilia made a play of going to the door of the housekeeper's sanctum and checking to see if anyone could be listening. Then she came back and confronted the woman across the barrier of the table.

"You see, I know who took the jewels. I also think I know where they are hidden. But what I do not know is what jewels were in the box. Mary can supply me with that information."

The housekeeper sniffed again, but she clearly had no more weapons to produce. "I'll have to send for Mary. Her ladyship set her to maiding that there Frenchie his lordship took and brung. And I know what I think of *her*."

"Yes, well, that is by the by. Please send for Mary at once."

She allowed the woman to waddle as far as the door before she stopped her. "Oh, Mrs. Thriplow?"

The woman halted, frowning back at her. "Yes, Mrs. Draycott?"

Ottilia assumed her best confidential manner and sidled up. "There was one other matter."

She paused, but Mrs. Thriplow looked merely puzzled. The ruse was working. She was lulled, believing Ottilia's real business lay in the jewellery.

"Do you remember when we first had our little talk?"

"Yes?"

"I asked you if you thought her ladyship had been involved with another man, do you recall?"

Yes, there it was again. The housekeeper looked instantly discomfited, a tinge of pink creeping into her cheeks. Ottilia seized her advantage.

"You look now just as you did that day, Mrs. Thriplow. Pray don't attempt to turn away from me. You know, don't you, just who it was?"

The housekeeper's fingers curled around one another and her lip trembled. "I don't — I don't —"

Ottilia grew stern. "Mrs. Thriplow, it is too late. You can no longer plead ignorance. I know, you see, that he did it. He killed your mistress."

The woman's eyes met hers in stark distress. "No. No. He couldn't."

"He couldn't, but he did. Oh, he didn't plan it. I expect he was provoked. But he strangled her, Mrs. Thriplow."

The housekeeper's gaze wavered and she staggered slightly. Ottilia caught her and guided her to a chair, inducing her to sit. Her eyes were wild.

"I didn't want to believe it. I knew he'd been favoured, the cocky little upstart."

"Yes, it had been going on for a long time,

had it not? Miss Venner alerted me to that. Oh, she named no names," Ottilia added, seeing Mrs. Thriplow's head rear up, "but it was the reason she left the marchioness's service. She could not approve when her mistress took up with a servant."

The housekeeper's mouth pursed. "Venner weren't the only one. Not that it was proven, mind. But I guessed it, and I should think Cattawade did, too."

"But neither of you said anything."

Her head came up again at that, defiance in her gaze. "Why should I? How should I? What could I do, tell the master? He'd not have believed it. Nor I didn't dare try to remonstrate with the fellow himself, for he'd have denied it all."

"No, I can see how awkward was your position," Ottilia soothed. "But when her ladyship was killed, you had your suspicions, did you not?"

Mrs. Thriplow dropped her gaze, her cheeks suffusing. Her tone was gruff and resentful. "I might have. But I dursn't think of it. Nor I didn't have no reason to think it, excepting as I knew he'd been welcome in her bedchamber."

"But not recently, I fear."

The housekeeper's head shot up, quick understanding in her gaze. "That's why?

She'd booted him?"

Ottilia nodded. "So I suspect." She became businesslike. "Now, Mrs. Thriplow, I need your help. You send for Mary as arranged and get that list written down for me. In the meanwhile, have you seen him this morning?"

Before the housekeeper could answer, a violent knocking came upon her door and the butler's voice was heard behind it, urgent and breathless.

"Mrs. Thriplow, do you have Mrs. Draycott in there?"

Ottilia went swiftly to the door and jerked it open. "What is it, Cattawade?"

The butler's urbanity had deserted him. "It's my Lord Francis, ma'am. He says to come immediate, quick as you can."

A tattoo started up in Ottilia's breast, but she lost no time in speeding through to the servants' stairs, which were nearest, and calling back as she went. "Where is Lord Francis?"

"In the front parlour, ma'am."

The butler was following gamely behind, but Ottilia outstripped him, her mind racing this way and that, as if she might fathom the reason for this urgency. What in the world could have happened?

She was not left long in mystery. As she

came up to the ground floor and moved quickly to the vestibule, she saw Francis hovering by the parlour door. One glance at his face gave her the seriousness of his news.

"Ottilia! In here, now."

He seized her as she reached him, hustling her inside. The dowager was there, sunk in a chair, her hands covering her face. A shaft of sheer terror cut through Ottilia.

"What is it, Fan? Tell me quickly. Did you see Bowerchalke?"

He caught her hand and held it tightly. "We were too late. Bowerchalke is killed. Murdered."

"Oh no! Oh, poor boy."

"The villain cut his throat."

Ottilia uttered a cry, releasing herself and throwing a hand to her mouth. "Oh God! He heard us speak of him. He knew young Bowerchalke could prove his undoing."

Francis was staring at her. "Who? Who is it you mean?"

The time was past for prevarication. Ottilia felt the quiver in her voice and knew her hands were trembling.

"Abel."

For a moment Francis only stared at her, his expression thunderstruck. "*Abel?* The footman?"

"Yes."

He could not seem to take it in. Ottilia became aware that the dowager was on her feet.

"Then that is why you would not tell us last night?"

Ottilia moved past Francis a little towards her. "That is why."

"But *Abel?*"

She turned. "Is it so hard to believe, Francis?"

"Yes," he said with emphasis. "I could believe many things of Emily. But that she would take up with the footman? I would never have imagined such a thing!"

Ottilia was seized with a hysterical desire to giggle and knew she was close to the end of her tether. She moved to a chair and sat down, setting her elbow on the arm and sinking her face into her hand.

"Fanfan, get her a drop of brandy."

She found Sybilla at her side. The dowager took her other hand and began to chafe it. "My poor child, you have borne too much."

Ottilia tried to refute this and could not speak. Sybilla's black eyes reproached her.

"You could have told me your suspicions. Why did you not?" The dowager's gaze softened and she threw out one of her dismissive gestures. "You need not tell me. You thought you would repel me, that I could not believe Emily would sink so low. That was naïve of you, Ottilia. But then you have not moved in the circles in which I have lived."

A glass appeared in front of Ottilia and she looked up to find Francis holding it out, a worried frown in his eyes.

Sybilla took the glass and urged it upon her. "Drink it, my child. It will recover you."

Obediently, Ottilia took it and put it to her lips, sipping gingerly. The golden liquid burned her lips and sent fire down her throat. She coughed.

"Finish it."

That was Francis, a peremptory note in his voice with which he had not previously addressed her.

"Let her take her time," Sybilla said, and gave a dry laugh. "Francis is almost as shocked as you, my dear. It is not nearly as uncommon as you suppose, Fanfan, for ladies of high birth to amuse themselves with a handsome footman. Decidedly immoral, of course, and grossly unfair upon the victim. It takes him out of his proper sphere and gives him ambitions which can never be fulfilled."

"Is that what you think happened to Abel?" Francis asked.

Ottilia, reviving a little, chose to answer

this herself. "I think she gave him his congé, and perhaps she did not fulfil her promises to him."

"What promises?"

She shrugged. "I cannot tell that. But the theft of the jewels and the fan suggests it. For some while I believed that was all he had done."

"You think he took both?"

"Not at the time. I am sure then he thought only of escape. But in the morning, when the opportunity presented itself —"

"And I left the man to guard the door!"

"You are scarcely to blame for that, Fanfan. You could not have known. Besides, did you not suggest he had a key to the dressing room, Ottilia?"

She nodded and sipped a little more of her restorative. "I daresay he stole that, too. I doubt Emily would have given it to him."

"But I have the key," Francis objected.

"Yes, but Abel had been Emily's lover for years. On and off, I daresay, like Quaife. And if the key was lost, she had only to have another cut. She had done it for the back door for a key to give her lovers."

The dowager made a derisive sound in her throat.

"In any event, I am certain Abel took only the fan to begin with."

Francis jumped in. "He must be the man Jardine heard about, who tried to sell the thing to a fence."

"Just so. When I encountered him in the basement that first night, I suspect he had just come from there."

"The man was masked, Jardine said. Then was it Abel you met last night in the dressing room?"

"Without doubt."

The dowager was looking grim. "Do you say he only went for the jewels when he discovered the fan was too well-known to be saleable?"

Ottilia nodded. "But it may be he had it in mind for some time, before the murder even, for he certainly knew where the jewels were kept. They were moved from time to time, but he may well have kept track of them. When he thought he had succeeded in throwing us off the scent, he seized his chance, making us take the view that the murderer made off with the jewels."

Francis let out a grunt. "He appears to have acted with remarkable coolness under the circumstances."

"Oh no. He made several mistakes," Ottilia said.

"Which is how you came to suspect him," suggested Sybilla.

Ottilia shivered a little. "I did so almost from the first."

"How?" demanded Francis. "You said nothing of it."

"It was so distasteful, I found it incredible. Which is why I foolishly dismissed my suspicions." She sighed. "At least, I tried to. But the possibility kept forcing itself upon my notice. There were little things, unexplained, that did not fit."

"The mysterious voice?"

"For one thing, yes. Abel was guarding the door when the fan was abstracted. He made a point of hinting his eye was on the bedchamber door."

"In hopes of making you think someone had slipped past?"

"Just so. Abel introduced discrepancies in the time. He was in the hall when his master came home. But a full hour after Emily? When Polbrook had been to the same ball and he clearly meant to accost her? I missed badly with that one, for Mary Huntshaw was witness to their quarrel, and she could not have taken so long to undress her mistress."

Francis's dark eyes lit with understanding. "That is what you meant last night when you blamed yourself. Do you say Abel lied about the time?"

Ottilia nodded. "He set the whole pattern on that lie. I now think it likely your brother began his preparations for departure no later than three. I suspect he was gone from the house by four or shortly thereafter. Abel said he went to the stables and did not think it worthwhile to go back to bed. Where did he go, then? What did he do? Then, too, Abel was 'too toplofty' for the kitchen maid. Abel's name had an odd effect on Mrs. Thriplow, and her manner showed she knew the identity of Emily's lover. Venner also gave me to understand that Emily had taken up with a servant. And Abel denied having been in the house the night I saw him in the basement."

Ottilia realised her breath had shortened and saw that her free hand had curled tightly into a fist. She straightened it fastidiously and looked up to find Francis looking dumbfounded. When her eyes shifted to Sybilla, the latter threw up her hands.

"You make it sound obvious."

A little laugh escaped Ottilia. "Sometimes it is the very thing that stares us in the face that we find hardest to see."

"But it wasn't obvious," said Francis flatly. "You have put it together piece by piece. But it fits. He must have panicked several times. Why invent the mysterious voice unless he supposed Randal's guilt would not hold water? Especially if he overheard Pellew's supposition of the time of death. And then he must have put about the news of the jewel box disappearing in order to sow unrest and cast suspicion upon the other domestics."

"But why put the jewel box back in the drawer?" asked Sybilla. "That seems inexplicable."

"In a bid to puzzle me and muddle my thinking, I believe. He would have succeeded had I not caught him at it."

"And yesterday," pursued Francis, "it was Abel who laid the information, was it not?"

Ottilia nodded. "That was the last piece in the puzzle. He knew I suspected him, and when your brother came home, he took a last-ditch stand to try to throw the blame where it stood most chance of holding."

"But why go after Bowerchalke?" asked the dowager, mystified.

"Because Abel listened to us talking in here."

Francis started. "He answered the door to George."

Sybilla looked horrified. "He heard it all?"

"And knew the game was up," said Francis grimly.

Ottilia sighed deeply. "His last hope lay in

silencing Bowerchalke. Without a witness, it is all supposition." Then her mind leapt and she pushed herself up, setting her glass down on the mantel. "Except that he went to Bow Street. Grice will remember him. Francis, we must act! Where is Colonel Tretower?"

"I dropped him at Bow Street. I imagine the justices will have sent their men posthaste to Bowerchalke's house."

"But they don't know about Abel," Ottilia said, a rush of panic lending her wings. "It cannot be in doubt he disposed of the boy, in which case it is doubtful he will dare return to this house. But we must make sure."

Francis was already making for the door. "I'll do that. Cattawade will lead me to his chamber."

"And then we will see if he has already removed the jewels from their hiding place."

The dowager started. "You know where they are?"

"I think so."

"Then wait here for me."

With which Francis left the room precipitately, shouting for the butler. Ottilia found her knees weak and sank back into her chair. She looked up to see Sybilla regarding her with concern.

"Are you yet fit to go on with this, my dear?"

Ottilia sighed. "I must. Justice Ingham will at least know that Lord Polbrook could not have murdered Bowerchalke, for he was in this house and under guard. But until Abel is found, your son's innocence cannot be proven."

CHAPTER 19

The odour was atrocious. Francis whipped out his pocket-handkerchief and clapped it over his nose. He glanced back to the doorway where Ottilia stood on the single step, well away from the noisome little area, and saw her with fingers against her nostrils to cut down the stench.

"Are you certain of this?"

She nodded. "It will possibly be wrapped in paper or rags, somewhere out of sight. In that little ditch along the wall perhaps."

Francis eyed the noxious buckets with acute disfavour. They were set next to the cesspit wall, awaiting the coming of the night soil men. Bloodied and mutilated bodies were one thing; effluent from all the chamber pots in the house was something else entirely.

"Francis, you need not look inside the buckets."

The mischievous note, which he had half

thought quenched forever, caused him to throw Ottilia a fulminating glance.

"Do you care to assist me, Tillie?"

She chuckled. "No, I thank you."

"Then be so good as to refrain from petty morsels of advice."

To his mingled irritation and amusement, Ottilia covered the lower part of her face entirely, but the laughter was not wholly smothered.

"If this is the one occasion when you prove to be wrong, my girl, I promise you signal vengeance presently."

But there was no help for it. The foul search must be effected. Tugging his gloves securely and holding his breath, Francis stooped to grasp the first of the buckets with the intention of moving them out of the way.

"Allow me, my lord."

Francis stood up abruptly. "Cattawade? No, no, stand back, my friend. This is young man's work."

The butler drew himself up. "Quite so, my lord, which is why I have fetched Stibbs."

The marquis's groom was standing at Cattawade's shoulder. He did not look to be enamoured of the prospect in store, but Francis was so glad to be relieved of the task that he moved aside with alacrity.

"You leave it to us, me lord," came a fresh voice.

Turning, Francis beheld his brother's head groom, turning in from the street and approaching down the narrow alley.

"Turville! In a good hour, man. For this reprieve much thanks, though I am sorry to burden you with such a mean task."

"It ain't nowise a burden, me lord, to aid in setting his lordship free. Now, what is it we're looking for?"

Francis relayed Ottilia's instructions and went to join her on the step, watching the burly grooms heave the buckets with their evil contents to one side.

"It is at times like this that one appreciates one's position in life, Mrs. Draycott."

Ottilia's dancing eyes met his over her protective hand. "How very true, my lord. A lucky escape."

"Luck has nothing to do with it."

"What then?"

"Merely the advantage of having about one ancient retainers who have known one from the cradle. Cattawade would not suffer me to perform a task so ill-suited to my station."

She laughed. "I suspect Cattawade is trying to make amends. He knew, like Mrs. Thriplow, but he dared not believe his own senses."

Francis reflected a moment. "Now you mention it, I wondered at a look of remorse I thought I detected in his face when I told him the position of affairs."

"What could he have done, poor man?"

Ottilia's attention returned to the grooms, who had now cleared the wall of obstructions and begun upon their search. For several agonizing minutes nothing was found. Francis began to be restive.

"I'm beginning to be sure you are wrong. I can't imagine why anyone would hide jewels in such a disgusting place."

Ottilia's clear gaze came around to his. "Would you think to look in such a place?"

"Not without the prompting of a madwoman."

"Just so," she said, ignoring the jibe.

"But what made you think of it?"

"Remember when we discovered the door to the garden must slam if you wanted to shut it? I think Abel escaped down the passage below. It was then I realised he must have followed me that night when Cattawade brought me down here."

"And that gave him the idea?"

"Not then. He had not yet taken the jewels. But when he needed a secure hiding place, I suspect his mind jumped to that memory."

"As yours did."

"My lord!"

Francis looked quickly towards the men and found Cattawade's pointing finger. Stibbs was holding up a dun-coloured roll. Excitement stirred in his breast as Francis heard Ottilia's quick exhalation of breath beside him.

He jumped off the step and strode towards the groom. "Let me see."

Stibbs held the thing up. It was bespattered with dirt and stank of its resting place. Francis refrained from touching it.

"Open it."

The groom brought the thing to the step and laid it down. It was sausage-shaped, tied in several places with tapes, presumably to keep the contents from slipping out. Francis dropped to his haunches to watch, aware of the other men crowding round. He could feel Ottilia's tension from where she stood above them all.

It took effort for Stibbs to undo the ties and Francis was tempted to tell him to cut them. But at last the tapes came loose. He thought the entire group held its collective breath as the groom carefully unrolled the cloth. Within there was a further, cleaner wrapping.

"Don't open it!"

Stibbs looked up at Ottilia just as Francis did. "But they're in there, miss. I can feel 'em."

"Yes, but your hands are dirty. Let Lord Francis take it."

Francis at once reached out. As Stibbs had said, the package was all unevenness and bumps and cold to the touch. He unfolded it with care and the mess of metal and stone winked and glittered in the weak sunshine.

A hissing of breath bore witness to the awe of lesser men at sight of such wealth. Discomfort ran through Francis and he quickly covered the jewels and stood up.

"Pray don't move anything," Ottilia said quickly. Her eyes went to Francis. "They must find stones and earth, enough to seem as close as possible to what you have in your hands. Then wrap it up and tie it, just as it was discovered."

Francis was ahead of her. "And put it back? A trap?"

"Just so. We are fortunate he was too panicked to take them last night when he went after Bowerchalke."

Francis set the men to do as she had asked, but he felt doubtful. "But will he dare come back? He must know we are on to him now."

Ottilia's hand reached towards the package he held. "If he does not, he will have done it all for nothing."

"And he is now a fugitive. Yes, in his place, I think I would dare all."

He spied a gleam in Ottilia's eye and looked a question. She smiled.

"Now you are thinking like me, Fan."

Francis quirked an eyebrow. "It must be catching."

She laughed and a glow of warmth lit his chest. But a moment later she became serious again.

"Once they have done, you must go directly to Bow Street. Tell them everything."

He nodded, the exigencies of the situation crowding his mind once more. "I had best set Stibbs and Turville to watch until Ingham can post his men."

She nodded, and it pleased him that she did not attempt to tell him how to do his business. Yet he felt humbled to have been in this predicament almost wholly reliant on her wits and ingenuity.

"And then, Ottilia?"

She looked up, the clear gaze darkening.

"We wait."

Ottilia could not be still. With Francis's departure, the lightness he invoked in her had vanished. The dark thoughts that had been revolving at the back of her mind came tumbling to the fore.

A modicum of relief had been obtained while she watched the dowager, together with an eager Mary Huntshaw, checking through the marchioness's jewels. Mrs. Thriplow, grim-faced and with set jaw, had remained in attendance, crossing items off the crudely made up list.

It had scarcely been necessary. Mary knew by heart what items should be among the gems. She detected instantly the missing necklace, which Ottilia had been able to reassure her was safely in the jewel box.

"Was it paste?" Ottilia asked her.

Huntshaw shook her head. "No, miss, it was real, all right. It's the one on the portrait."

"Ah, I remember," said the dowager. She glanced at Ottilia. "Too well-known."

"He'd have been fly to that, my lady," put in the housekeeper.

Her utterances were uniformly dour and Ottilia thought it would be long before Mrs. Thriplow could ease her conscience. She could not blame the woman, for her own was sorely beset.

"There's three rings missing, my lady."

"Are you certain, Huntshaw?"

"Oh yes, my lady. I know every one like they were my own. There's an emerald, and the small diamond. The other is only glass, though it looks like a diamond."

"Abel wouldn't know that," Sybilla said. "But it matters little. An emerald will have sufficed, assuming he sold them for ready money."

Once the inventory was satisfactorily concluded, the jewels were left in the dowager's charge while Mrs. Thriplow went away to "see if she couldn't get some sense out of her girls," as she put it. The discovery of Abel's perfidy had jolted the domestics even more, the housekeeper claimed, than had the murder of the mistress. She had sailed out, but Mary had hovered.

"What is it, Huntshaw?"

The lady's maid bobbed a curtsy. "If you please, my lady, it's the French madame."

"Well?"

"She's taken bad, my lady. I can't rightly understand what she says, but I think as it's because the master has been got by the justices. She's been crying herself into hysterics, my lady, and I don't know how to do."

This speech ended in a rising tone that showed the woman to be on the verge of hysteria herself. Ottilia looked a trifle apprehensively at Sybilla, recalling last night's altercation in the library with her elder son.

There was a shadow in the dowager's eyes, but she rose, straight-backed as ever. "Very well, I will go to her directly. You run along, Huntshaw."

Mary curtsied and went out, and Sybilla looked at Ottilia.

"I had best do what I may. I had hoped to avoid giving her an account of the happenings here, but it can't be helped."

Ottilia had been at first glad to be left alone with her unquiet thoughts. But they became rapidly too oppressive to be borne. She got up, pacing the room, only half conscious that she did so.

She could no longer take the slightest delight in the game she had undertaken. She yearned for that objectivity, which at the outset had served her so well. Francis had been right when he said that time had overtaken them. She could not even work out for how many days they had all been thus engaged upon what had begun for her as an adventure. A stark and horrid one, but an adventure nonetheless.

How had she become so deeply involved that every new development, every fresh occurrence, had all too much meaning? By degrees at first, and then in leaps and bounds. She was now so thoroughly enmeshed that she felt it as if these were her people, her very family. Their misfortunes, their distresses, had insensibly become hers.

Would that she had been able to remain aloof! Her vaunted common sense would have remained in play, and she would not have neglected to take those ordinary precautions she had criminally missed.

"Ottilia?"

She blinked out of her reverie and found the dowager had come back into the room.

"What is the matter, child? You look utterly riven."

Blindly, Ottilia gazed at her. Without will, she spoke the churning riot of her mind. "It is of no use. I cannot absolve myself. I am palpably to blame for that young man's death."

For a moment Sybilla stared uncomprehendingly. Then light entered her face. "Bowerchalke? But, my dear Ottilia, how so? You did not kill him."

Ottilia had neither power nor will to prevent the tears that trickled down her cheeks. "I might as well have done. I never thought — I kept it back when I knew —"

"No, you did not know." Sybilla came to her and seized her hands. "I will not allow you to do this, Ottilia. You are in no way to

508

blame for Abel's deeds."

"But don't you see? I did not look for him. Despite having my suspicions of him. But I became so engaged with the puzzles presented to me, I forgot the most elementary precautions. I know, we all know, how servants listen at keyholes. I knew at once it was how Mary heard what she did."

"I remember." The dowager's grip was hard and comforting. "But you are not thinking, my dear, and that is so unlike you."

"I am thinking too much, and I cannot bear my thoughts."

"Come, come sit."

She found herself pushed and ushered, thrust into the sofa, with Sybilla beside her, still holding her hands.

"My dear child, one does not notice footmen. Even had you done so, had any of us, we would not have 'seen' him, do you see? He had only to stand or walk away, and one would think nothing of it. Abel had business in every part of the house. That is the nature of a footman's work."

Ottilia's overcharged nerves began to settle a little. "You are right in that, of course. But last night, when we were discussing matters of such import? I had seen him open the front door!"

"Yes, but the news Colonel Tretower

brought was enough to distract anyone. Ottilia, you may charge yourself with neglect if you so wish, but it is absurd. What, were we to spend every moment looking out for spies? Even had we done so, only look at this house. There are a thousand places to hide. It would take an army to cover every avenue."

Obliged to see the sense in this, Ottilia's heart lightened a little. "Yes, I see that."

"But you are yet in the dumps." The dowager loosened her grip and began an absent stroking of the hands she held. "I think you are overwrought, my child, which is hardly surprising. You have taken the troubles of this whole family upon your shoulders and it has grown too burdensome."

A shaky sigh was drawn from deep within Ottilia's chest. "Perhaps. But I would not have had it otherwise."

"Nor I, believe you me. How we would have done without you, I cannot endure to contemplate."

At this, Ottilia let out a laugh. "That I cannot allow. I have only done as my mind dictated."

"As your heart dictated, Ottilia. I am not blind, my child."

Startled, Ottilia whipped round to stare at

her. Had Sybilla divined it all? She felt the warmth rush to her cheeks and struggled to avert the shame of giving herself away.

"It is true, I have grown fond — of all of you."

"And we of you, be sure."

The dowager fell silent and Ottilia willed her to remain so. Her hopes were not in any shape to be thrown beneath the light of exposure. Indeed, within the last four and twenty hours they had fluctuated so crazily that she had begun to doubt her ability to maintain composure in the presence of their object. So far she had held herself well in hand. Helped, it was true, by the undoubted bond of friendship and a shared sense of merriment. But to look beyond, into the veil of an unpredicted future? No, she could not. The whole was dependent not upon her, but upon Francis. And she could not answer for his affections being engaged.

As if the thought of him had the power to bring him to her, the door opened and she heard his voice.

"In here, if you will, Sir Thomas."

Confusion sent Ottilia shooting to her feet. She shifted out into the room and turned in time to see Francis usher in a gentleman of scholarly aspect.

"Sir Thomas Ingham, ma'am. My mother,

the Dowager Marchioness of Polbrook, sir."

The Bow Street justice! Neither Ottilia nor Sybilla had been present when he had arrested the marquis earlier. Ottilia had opportunity to observe him as he bowed over Sybilla's hand. He was of middle years, bewigged and soberly dressed, with a pair of spectacles on his nose.

"And this is Mrs. Draycott."

"Ah, the very lady I am anxious to meet."

Ottilia liked the firmness of his handshake and was immediately struck by his air of calm assurance.

"Sir Thomas has questions, Mrs. Draycott, that I am not equipped to answer."

The resumption of formal address hurt her, although she knew Francis held to it merely because of the presence of a public official. She tried for her habitual composure and was relieved when it came quite easily.

"Indeed, sir? I shall be happy to tell you anything you wish to know. Although I trust Lord Francis has told you enough to set you on the path of the right man."

He nodded, rubbing his palms together in a curiously unbusinesslike way. "Yes, yes, you need have no fears on that score. My men have been despatched."

"And Colonel Tretower has sent his own

troop scouring the town," Francis added. And, with a look at Ingham, "Not that I suppose they will be needed, but George was very willing and I wished to leave no stone unturned."

"My lord, indeed we are very glad of the help. Our men are first rate, but we lack manpower. Funds, sir, always the question of government funds."

"Was it Abel who laid an information?" asked the dowager.

"He gave no name, my lady," disclosed Sir Thomas, "but Grice, in whom he confided, was satisfied from his lordship's description that it is the same man. He brought something by way of evidence."

Reaching into a capacious pocket in his coat, Justice Ingham brought out a small object and held it up. Ottilia stared at the oval frame in which a woman's face was depicted.

"Lord Polbrook's miniature?"

Francis started forward, seizing the little portrait. "It is the image of Madame Guizot. Evidence, you say? Confound his impudence!"

Sybilla was looking from the item in her son's hand to Ottilia. "Is that the one you found under Randal's pillow? Do you say the villain had the temerity to purloin that as well as everything else?"

"And dared to present it to Bow Street to strengthen the case against Polbrook," said Francis, his tone savage with fury.

Justice Ingham held out his hand. "If you will be so kind, my lord, I cannot yet allow it to be returned."

Ottilia watched Francis hand the frame back as, with an obvious effort, he overcame his ire and gestured the visitor to a chair.

"Will you sit, sir?"

Sir Thomas politely indicated that Ottilia should first seat herself, and then took the chair opposite, in the dowager's usual place. Francis joined his mother on the sofa.

"Now, Mrs. Draycott, I will be much obliged if you will tell me the whole."

Ottilia gave a mirthless laugh. "The whole? I don't know where to begin, there is so much."

To her relief, Francis came to her rescue. "I have already related most of what we found and what you told us earlier. But I was unable to give Sir Thomas a precise account of what happened that night."

"Well, neither can I," Ottilia pointed out. "I was relying on poor Mr. Bowerchalke for that."

Sir Thomas coughed, drawing everyone's attention. "Naturally none but the participants can know just what occurred. What I am after, Mrs. Draycott, is an account of your suspicions. You see, until we have this footman apprehended, I have nothing at my disposal which may justify allowing the marquis to go free."

Ottilia nodded. It was just as she had foreseen. "It is supposition, of course."

"So much I had understood."

"But I think there is sufficient to show that it must have been Abel who murdered Lady Polbrook."

Sir Thomas gave her a prim smile. "I am open to persuasion."

"You will find her a remarkably acute woman, sir," cut in the dowager.

A gentle laugh was cast in her direction. "Ah, feminine intuition."

"Nothing of the sort," snapped Sybilla. "Ottilia would scorn to stoop to anything so paltry. She has a fiendishly clever mind."

Justice Ingham was not noticeably abashed, but he put out a deprecating hand. "Assure you I intended no offence, my lady."

"Shall we allow Mrs. Draycott to tell it as she will?"

Ottilia threw Francis a grateful glance, and though the dowager grunted, Sir Thomas inclined his head in her direction.

"Mrs. Draycott?"

She gathered her thoughts for a moment. Then she looked up towards Justice Ingham.

"This is what I think happened. Bowerchalke accompanied the marchioness home from the ball that night. They did not leave together, but he was seen to enter her coach. When they arrived, Emily — the marchioness —"

"Emily will do, ma'am," said Sir Thomas. "You need not interrupt your narrative for trifles."

Ottilia smiled and thanked him. "Emily sent him round the back armed with the key and instructed him to wait for her signal."

Sybilla was regarding her intently. "The candle in the window?"

"Just so. It had been, sir, an established pattern with the marchioness, as I found out from her former lady's maid."

Sir Thomas rubbed his hands. "We will take your sources as read for the moment, ma'am. Pray continue."

Ottilia retraced her thoughts in her mind. "Was this his first visit? Again, we cannot know. But I suspect it was."

"What makes you think so?" asked Francis.

516

"Remember that Emily applied fresh paint and powder to her face, and she wore a silken dressing robe. I think she had seduction in her mind."

Francis was frowning. "But when? And how signal the fellow when Randal was there?"

"I think the boy was in the chamber throughout. Emily had told her maid not to wait up, but Mary disregarded this. She had fallen asleep in the chair in the dressing room. I suspect Emily gave her signal before ever she knew Mary was there."

He sat back. "Yes, I see. Go on."

"While Emily was being undressed, Lord Polbrook came in. Bowerchalke hid himself behind the bed-curtains. He heard the row. When the marquis slammed out of the room, perhaps Emily went to get rid of Mary. Bowerchalke may or may not have come out of his refuge, but then Lord Polbrook returned and he necessarily hid again."

The dowager let out a snort. "It sounds like one of these absurd French farces."

"I was thinking just that, Mama."

"Yes," Ottilia agreed, "it would be funny if it were not so tragic."

"Go on, Mrs. Draycott."

There was sharpness in Justice Ingham's

tone. Ottilia wondered if he was impatient of these divagations.

"At last they found themselves alone. Emily ensured Mary had gone, and hastily rid herself of the encumbrance of extra clothing and applied rapid aids to beauty. By this time, Bowerchalke must have returned the fan, for her throwing it carelessly down shows her impatience."

"And then she proceeded to seduction," Francis said.

"One assumes so. She may even have taken the precaution of locking the door. Evidently they sat together on the chaise longue, where Emily perhaps removed her garters and divested herself of her dressing robe."

"At which point," put in Sir Thomas with a preliminary cough, "they — er — indulged in criminal conversation, I take it?"

"No."

"But surely —"

"They may have got as far as the bed. Indeed, I am certain they must have done. Emily was likely on the bed when Bowerchalke was encouraged to unroll the stockings from her legs, for he was in possession of them when they were interrupted. But no act of intimacy took place."

Sybilla reared up in her seat. "Ottilia, what

518

in the world can you mean? At the outset you made it plain Emily had so indulged."

"Yes, but not with Bowerchalke. Pardon my plain speaking, Sir Thomas, but her thighs were bruised. As I understand it, the boy was slight. He could not have inflicted such damage."

Francis was looking appalled. "Then you imply it was Abel who — ? But if she had given him up, and with her new lover just a hairsbreadth away —"

Ottilia clasped her hands tightly together and looked down at them. "I think Abel forced himself upon her."

"Dear Lord!"

"She is right," uttered the dowager in accents of suppressed agitation. "She is right, as always."

Ottilia looked up, facing them now that the worst was said. "When Abel came in —"

"How, if she had locked the doors?" demanded Sir Thomas.

Francis took that one. "He had a key to the dressing room. It is how he managed the theft."

"Almost certainly through the dressing room," said Ottilia, "because he may then have taken note of the fan. But I doubt Emily thought of locking that door once Mary had left the place. It was likely habitual for Abel to enter by that way. However that may be, when he came in, he was heard. The door opening, or perhaps he called out. Bowerchalke, already in a highly nervous condition, naturally assumed it was Polbrook back once more and hastily concealed himself again."

"Then he must have heard it all?" Justice Ingham was beginning to look a trifle grim.

She nodded. "Which is why Abel killed him. There will have been some sort of argument between Emily and him. She had given him up and I daresay had reneged on her promises to him. Abel was in an excitable state; perhaps he had been drinking while he took the porter's chair in the hall. He was certainly a good deal the worse for wear in the morning, but that is hardly surprising in the circumstances. He had seen the marquis leave the house and thought himself safe to take his chance and make his protestations. Emily repudiated him, as she must do with Bowerchalke in the wings. Abel lost control and forced her to coitus. She fought him, but was overcome. Maddened, fearful perhaps of the consequences of what he had done — she may have threatened him — he strangled her."

"And then walked away," Francis said.

"Ran away, more like," suggested Sir Thomas.

"I suspect he wasted some time in panic and remorse. Not knowing what else to do in the middle of the night, he went to his chamber, there to think desperately how he might avoid retribution."

"And Bowerchalke?"

"One can only imagine his repugnance and dismay, Sybilla. When at last he dared to emerge, what did he see? How dreadful was his situation. Emily brutally murdered, he a witness throughout. Who would believe him? He could not even identify the perpetrator, for he did not know him. All he had was a voice. The poor boy must have been terrified. What would you? He fled."

Ottilia sat back, as exhausted by the telling as if she had participated in these events herself. Her auditors were silent. She stole a glance at Francis and found him regarding her with a distant look. Was his imagination playing over the scene for him? Sybilla's disgust was patent. Ottilia allowed her gaze to shift to the magistrate from Bow Street.

Sir Thomas's eyes crinkled at the corners and his lips lifted a fraction. "I am inclined to side with her ladyship, ma'am, in reference to your powers of observation and deduction. A pretty tale! If true."

Ottilia shrugged. "It is as near as I can judge it, sir. Sadly, the witness upon whom I had relied is unable to assist us."

He nodded. "But the principal is still alive."

"And at large," Francis pointed out.

"Not for long, I hope. Once we have him, we will endeavour to unravel this history."

The dowager let out one of her characteristic snorts. "What need, when Ottilia has done it all for you?"

"Ah, my lady, but hearsay is not evidence. A conviction rests upon testimony or a confession."

A horrid premonition seized Ottilia. She sat up. "You will not torture him to get it?"

Sir Thomas's brows shot up. "My dear lady, we are not in Spain. I trust we have more civilisation than to conduct ourselves in the manner of our forefathers."

"But why, Ottilia, does it concern you?" Sybilla demanded. "Don't you think the fellow deserves punishment?"

"Due justice, yes. But responsibility does not rest with Abel alone. We are not always master of our fates."

"You mean he was led astray by Emily," said Francis.

"Partly. And the inequities of our society."

She brushed off an unaccustomed feeling of depression. "But this is hardly the moment to indulge in political debate."

Sir Thomas Ingham rose. "Quite right." He dropped his head a little and looked quizzically at her over the top of his spectacles. "A pity you cannot run for Parliament, ma'am. I should certainly support your candidature."

Ottilia was obliged to join in the general laughter, although Sybilla was looking thoughtful, as if she seriously considered the possibility. Sir Thomas bowed in her direction.

"I will take my leave of you now, my lady." And to Ottilia, "There are one or two points upon which I may need clarification, for I have not all the background to your reasoning. But that can wait until we have the suspect apprehended."

His departure signalled the breakup of the circle, the dowager declaring she was famished and it was high time a repast was served. Francis elected to go back to Bow Street with Sir Thomas to find out, if he could, what progress had been made and to confer with Colonel Tretower, with whom he would take refreshment at a convenient inn.

Ottilia found the day dragging. She ate

with Sybilla, and then there was nothing to do.

"It seems excessively odd not to be pursuing our investigations," remarked the dowager presently.

Ottilia sighed. "I was thinking the same thing, ma'am. I cannot imagine how we are to fill our days."

Sybilla threw up her hands. "For my part, I can think of nothing I would welcome more than the tedium of my former life."

Ottilia was aware of her employer's eyes following her around the room. At length the dowager broke into testy speech.

"Sit down, child. You are fidgeting me to death."

Ottilia threw herself into her accustomed chair. "I beg your pardon, ma'am. It is this waiting I cannot endure."

"That is it exactly. Have no fear. When the matter is settled once and for all, there will be all manner of problems besetting us."

Ottilia thought of the complications arising from the marquis's actions, not to mention the ensuing scandals gathering about the family's head, and was silenced.

But her eyes crept obstinately time and again to the case clock on the mantel as the hours crawled by.

CHAPTER 20

The only sound was the scratching of his pen. On George's advice, they had closed both blinds and shutters and doused all the candles bar the single one by the light of which Francis was writing a letter to his sister. That it was merely to provide himself with an occupation he did not deny. It seemed preferable to fretting the hours away.

His mother had refused to go to bed and was asleep on the sofa next the wall. Ottilia was, he hoped, dosing in one of the chairs. She had been fretful and uneasy. So unlike herself. She had told Francis it was the inactivity she could not endure. Once she had begun, inexplicably, upon some foolishness of being in some way to blame for Bowerchalke's death. Francis had scotched that without compunction.

"That is absurd, Tillie. How could it be your fault?"

She had clenched her hands into fists. "If I had spoken last night of my convictions of Abel's guilt, we might have acted sooner."

Francis had taken her fisted hands and held them. "It would have made no difference. According to the doctor, Bowerchalke had been dead for hours when he was found."

She had regarded him with painful anxiety. "You mean Abel went there directly? It was done at night?"

"Did you think he had gone in broad daylight for such a purpose?"

"I don't know. I had not thought. I only know he did it."

Francis had tightened his hold. "This is not like you, Tillie. Think it through. He had to take time to realise his position, to decide to act. I imagine he knew where Bowerchalke lived, for the boy had been known to Emily some weeks. It is likely Abel was sent with notes for the fellow."

"Doubly galling to him," Ottilia had said, and he'd known from her expression that her quick wits were in play, following his reasoning.

"Indeed. He goes to the house, but he is precipitate. That is probably why he neglected to take his booty with him. There are too many comings and goings. Perhaps

526

Bowerchalke is not yet home. He must wait for the place to quieten, and perform the deed under cover of deepest night."

"How did he get in?"

"Bowerchalke's chamber was on the first floor. An easy climb for a man of Abel's size and agility. The window must have been open, for it had not been broken. He slipped in and murdered the poor fellow while he slept."

To his satisfaction, Ottilia looked immeasurably relieved. She did not refer to it again, and he hoped the matter was closed in her own mind. Nevertheless, he was increasingly anxious about her. She seemed distrait, and once or twice he caught a glance from her of something unfathomable, but acutely disturbing. What could have distressed her? Unless she was at the point of exhaustion, as his mother had earlier suggested.

He resumed the account of events he had started. After all, Harriet would wish to know, and it might as well be written now as later.

It was eerily silent. The servants had long gone to bed, but he wondered how many of them were able to sleep in this house of unrest. Outside he knew there were men on the qui vive. It was uncannily like camp in wartime, with soldiers snatching those few precious hours while others stood guard.

When the watch had last called, it was two o'clock. Francis sighed. God send they would not all of them sit 'til dawn, and then in vain!

As if in answer, muffled sounds without the house came to his ears. He could not make them out beyond a grunt and a terse command.

Francis pushed back his chair and got up, shifting to the window and listening intently. Nothing. Of course he was on the wrong side of the house. All the action, if there was any, must occur in the back.

Somewhere a door slammed. Francis crossed quickly to the parlour door and opened it. Now he could hear something. Men's voices coming from without, low with an occasional louder warning. Francis toyed with the notion of heading for the domestic stairs, but he had not been a soldier for nothing. One did not butt into an action in which one had no part. Thus were errors made.

Straining to hear, Francis thought he made out the sound of several pairs of feet deep in the recesses of the domestic quarters below, accompanied by indistinct mumbling and the stamp and grunt of effort.

"He came back."

Francis turned quickly. Ottilia was standing in the open doorway. An outline only. He moved to her.

"It seems so from the commotion yonder. I daresay it will take some moments before all is settled."

He saw the shadow that was Ottilia clasping and unclasping restless hands, her attention held upon the darkness in the vestibule. Francis was scarcely less in suspense and could think of nothing to offer in the way of comfort. He wanted to draw her to him and enfold her in the warmth of his embrace, but the very intensity of this desire withheld him. He had not yet won the right to cherish and protect.

His startled mind threw the thought back at him, and he almost laughed aloud. What a moment to choose to recognise the state of his heart! Or would Ottilia say that it needed just such a moment of tension to jolt a man into knowledge?

"Someone is coming."

At once alert, Francis turned his attention to the matter at hand. Footsteps were coming up the stairs. As one, Francis and Ottilia moved towards the vestibule. Seconds later, a man swiftly rounded the landing. Francis started forward, Ottilia at his heels.

"George?"

Tretower was a mere shadow in the darkness, but Francis could almost see the triumph in his face.

"We have him!"

"Oh, thank God!"

Ottilia sank back, holding on to the newel post at the top of the stairs. Francis moved quickly to her, putting a supporting arm about her back.

"Into the parlour with you. Come, George."

He guided Ottilia back through the vestibule and into the parlour, obliging her to sit. In the dim light thrown by the candle, Francis saw that his mother was sitting bolt upright.

"What's to do?"

Tretower crossed the room towards her. "He has been taken, ma'am. He fell straight into the trap."

"Oh, bravo, Ottilia! Clever girl."

Francis echoed the words in his head and watched his friend move to where Ottilia sat, looking dazed.

"You were right, ma'am. He came back for the jewels. Ingham's fellows know their business, I'll say that for them. They let him scrabble for them and the moment the package was in his hands, they pounced."

His mother was all approbation, but Francis had his eyes on Ottilia. She yet wore that strangely distant air, as if she were not truly there.

"Where is he now?" she asked.

"Ah, there's a tale," said George. "There was something of a scuffle, for the man fought like a madman."

"Is he much hurt?" Francis asked.

"He has taken a little punishment."

"Was the fan in his possession?" Ottilia asked.

Francis had forgot the fan. Without doubt, she had the wit. He looked expectantly at his friend.

"I don't know, ma'am. To my knowledge they have not searched him."

"Lord above, they don't know!"

"Or it did not occur to Sir Thomas to advise them to look for it," Ottilia suggested.

"It must be found!"

"In due time, Mama," said Francis, putting out a hand to stay his mother's wrath. "Yes, yes, I know it is an heirloom, but first things first."

"Perhaps, Mrs. Draycott," George cut in, "you may discover where Abel has secreted it."

"I? How, pray?"

Francis glanced swiftly at his friend. Tretower's manner was diffident, a sure sign he had something distasteful to impart. "Out with it, man."

George threw him an apologetic glance and turned back to Ottilia. "The fact is, ma'am, that Abel made no real resistance until they tried to take him off to Bow Street. Grice had his orders, but in view of the man's attitude, the Runners chose instead to keep him here. One of them has gone to Ingham for orders, and a couple of my men are assisting the other to guard the prisoner. He has been put in the butler's pantry."

"But why in the world should he wish to remain here?"

Francis was glad his mother had voiced the question, but Tretower's silence troubled him. "George?"

His friend let out a sigh. "The thing is, Mrs. Draycott, the man insists he will speak to none but you."

"The devil he does!" Infuriated, Francis watched Ottilia shrink back. "Tell the fellow to go hang."

At that, she looked up at him. "No, Francis. They need a confession."

He cursed under his breath. "I was forgetting that. Very well, if it must be. But you are not going alone."

"Gracious, I should hope not! You must go with her, Francis."

"Try if you can stop me." He looked down at Ottilia, whose face was still upturned. He could not read her expression in the uncertain light. "You are not going to try, are you?"

There was no mistaking the warm smile. "No, indeed, Fan. I need you too much."

She held out her hand as she spoke, and Francis, a glow racing through his body, took hold of it and drew her to her feet. But he did not release her hand as he turned with her to follow George from the room.

The footman was seated, tied to the back of a chair with his hands behind him. Several candles had been lighted, and Ottilia saw the dark splotches on his face where bruises were beginning to show. He was unshaven, and the once smart crop was lank with sweat. Unsurprisingly, he was not wearing his livery, but a somewhat battered greatcoat over a greasy frock and waistcoat. A disguise? Or had his recent activities reduced him in this way?

His eyes held all the old insolence, and something more. Defiance? There was fierceness there, Ottilia thought. She took the chair opposite that Francis pulled out for her and saw Abel cast a resentful glance at him.

Francis had obviously not missed it. "You need not attempt to have me depart, Abel. If you want Mrs. Draycott, you get me as well."

The footman did not answer, instead transferring his gaze to Ottilia's face. She summoned all her habitual calm and faced him as coolly as she could.

"What do you want with me, Abel?"

He let out a harsh laugh. "That's rich, that is, madam, coming from you. It's your doing I'm here."

Ottilia felt Francis's motion and threw up a hand without looking at him. "No, it is your own doing, Abel."

"You set them onto me," he growled.

Ottilia nodded. "That is true. But I could not have done so had you stayed your hand."

For a moment he shrunk into himself, his eyes going dim. But then he rallied, and in his look Ottilia thought there was an echo of the passion that must have held Emily in thrall for so long.

"She deserved it, she-devil as she was!"

A satisfied sigh drew her attention to the Runner Grice, who was standing out of Abel's sight line. He produced a stubby

534

pencil and began to write into a grubby notebook.

Ottilia felt a surge of anger. "And what of young Jeremy Bowerchalke? Did he deserve it?"

Abel's gaze shifted, and he looked this way and that, biting his lip. "Silly young chub." It was a mutter only, but Ottilia caught the words. "He'd took my place, hadn't he? That was reason enough."

"But that was not your reason," she said, and his head came up. Did he think she had not heard him? "You killed him because he could bear witness against you."

"Didn't even know he was there. I knew him. Knew all her pretty gentlemen. Pah! Gentlemen!"

Ottilia's innate curiosity got the better of her. "What did she promise you, Abel? What was it she did not perform?"

He threw up his head, his mouth contorting in a species of agony as he groaned. "She said she'd see me right. She meant money. I thought she did. But it never come. I thought to set myself up in the world. You can't be a footman forever."

"Is that why you went in to her that night?"

He meant to lean forward, she thought, but his bonds prevented him. He shoved his

535

face towards her, a snarl in his voice.

"It was the last chance. I knew his lordship were going to France, and I knew his purpose."

Francis, who had been standing back a little, slammed forward, his fists landing on the table. Abel jerked back.

"How did you know? How the devil could you know what his family did not?"

"Servants talk, my lord," came the sullen reply. "I'll not say who or how, but I knew."

With an oath, Francis flung up and away. Ottilia could not blame him, but there was a task still to do here.

"You knew about Madame Guizot?"

"Aye, and that he meant to bring her to England. I knew there'd be the devil to pay. I knew my lady would have no time for me after."

My lady. An intimacy that was no real intimacy. Ottilia was conscious of a pull of sympathy for the man — a toy to gratify an idle fancy.

"So you demanded money?"

"I asked for what she'd promised." A glare came into his eyes. "She denied she said it. She made me wild." He shuddered then. "I don't know what happened. I was overtook by rage, I know that. When I came to myself . . . there she was."

The image in his mind was etched in his face. A pathetic end to a sordid tale.

Ottilia stood up. "I am sorry for you, Abel."

He did not answer. Francis went to the door and held it for her, but Ottilia did not move. She held out her hand.

"Give me the fan, if you please, Abel."

For a moment the footman stared with eyes sunken as if in pain. Ottilia wondered if he failed to understand her, or if he sought a last futile rebellion. Then a fierce anger overlaid his features and he jerked his chin towards his bonds.

"I can't, madam, thanks to these. But you may take it from me if you like. If you care to search me."

And he threw his head back and let out a roughened guffaw. Ottilia flinched, but she held her ground. With a few swift steps Francis was back at her side, his furious glare fixed upon the footman.

"She will not touch your vile carcass!"

Ottilia feared he might lay violent hands upon the man, but Grice the Runner was before him, raising a threatening fist.

"You keep your tongue sheathed, unless you want another dose of home-brewed." He glanced at Ottilia. "I'll find it, miss."

"The rings, too, if he has not sold them.

There are three rings missing."

It did not take the Runner above a moment to extract a long object from an inner recess in Abel's coat. It was wrapped in a pocket-handkerchief. The Runner held it out to Ottilia.

"Me hands ain't none too clean, miss. Obliged if you'll take a looksee and identify the object inside."

Ottilia took it automatically. "But I cannot. I have never seen it."

But she knew her reluctance to handle the thing stemmed rather from revulsion. She was not ordinarily squeamish, but the thought of the part the fan had played in the drama was one she found singularly distressing. Wordlessly, she passed it to Francis and watched him unravel its covering. He spread the fan and Ottilia saw it glitter in the gloom. Francis looked up.

"Yes, this is it."

Benjamin Grice gave a grunt of satisfaction. "Stolen goods an' all. You've a mighty long indictment coming to you, my lad."

Francis wrapped the fan up again and looked at Ottilia. "Are you ready?"

But the Runner stayed him. "Here, that's evidence that is, me lord."

"Then, should he wish for it, I will hand it to Sir Thomas Ingham. Content you with the rings, if you find them."

Ottilia felt him take her arm and went with him to the door. From there she took a last look at Abel. His head was down, his chin sunk into his chest, defeated. She turned from the sight and left the room.

The dining parlour had become the scene of vociferous argument interspersed with wild expressions of relief and joy. The marquis had returned from Bow Street shortly after the unexpected reunion of the dowager and Lord Francis with the son of the house. Giles, Earl of Bennifield, having travelled day or night without pause, so he said, and arriving just in time for breakfast, had been welcomed back from Italy with tears and laughter.

Barely had he been regaled with a brief version of events than a hackney deposited his father on the doorstep. As Madame Guizot and her children came down at the same time, pandemonium reigned for several moments.

Ottilia had borne little part in the excitement, although she had watched from the sidelines, enjoying the exuberance brought by release from tension. She had been introduced briefly, but effaced herself as quickly as she could, reluctant to detract from the family's happiest moment since the start of the afflictions that had befallen them.

Presently, when Madame Guizot, having satisfied herself of the safety of Lord Polbrook, had retired with her children, the talk turned upon the public face that must be decided. There was no avoiding scandal, the dowager held, but they must stand firm together against the world and their tales must be the same.

Breakfast was long over, but the party had lingered in the dining parlour, Giles full of question, and with the zeal of the very young, hot against the world for daring to criticise his mother.

These were matters in which Ottilia felt she had no part to play. Choosing a moment when everyone's attention was engaged, she slipped out of the room and into the vestibule. She had it in mind to go to her chamber, but she had barely reached the top of the first flight of stairs when lethargy overcame her. Turning, she sank down upon the step and rested her head against a convenient baluster.

She was weary and heartsore, and the end of the adventure left her utterly deflated. Her mind felt woolly and she could not think. Involuntarily, she closed her eyes.

"Tillie?"

Her eyelids fluttered up. Francis was standing in the vestibule, regarding her. Ottilia made to rise and could not. She sank back.

A frown in his eyes, Francis came quickly up the steps, halting just below her. "What is amiss?"

She put out a staying hand. "Nothing at all."

"I don't believe you."

She tried to smile, and felt pricking at her eyes. No, she must not weep. Swallowing upon a thickened throat, she did her best to make light of it.

"I felt de trop. What is being discussed in there is hardly my concern."

He was regarding her keenly. "Nor was it your concern to discover Emily's murderer, but that did not stop you."

The urge to cry was smothering her breath. "That was — different."

For a moment he did not speak, for which Ottilia was both grateful and disappointed. Then he caught her hand and tugged.

"Come with me."

Ottilia held back, a riffle disturbing her heartbeat. "Why?"

"That you shall know presently." An eyebrow quirked. "Tillie, if you don't come,

I give you fair warning I shall pick you up and carry you."

Despite herself, a tiny spurt of laughter escaped her. He grinned. "That's better."

Before she well knew what had happened, she had been drawn to her feet, led down the stairs, dragged willy-nilly through the little lobby where they had so lately eavesdropped upon Sybilla and Lord Polbrook, and was thrust without ceremony into the library.

Francis released her and closed the door. Ottilia's heart began to pound. All desire to weep had left her. Her throat was dry, but she managed to speak, albeit in what sounded to her own ears like a croak.

"What did you bring me here for?"

His gaze met hers and what she saw there drove the breath from her lungs. "Did you think I was going to kiss you in full view of the world?"

Ottilia could only stare, utterly taken aback, as yet unable to take in the implication of his words.

He uttered a laugh that broke in the middle. Next instant she felt herself gathered into a stifling embrace.

"Oh, Tillie," he breathed.

His face came down and Ottilia automatically closed her eyes. The warmth of his lips made her knees weak and her head dizzied. An uncountable time later, his hold slackened and he released her mouth, leaning back to look into her eyes.

"I've been wanting to do that for days."

Ottilia's hands came up without will and she set them against his chest. Her head was whirling and she could only say exactly what came into it.

"Why did you not?"

Francis smiled and her heart melted. "I did not dare. I would not have dared yet, if Mama had not this morning told me to stop being a prevaricating fool."

"Sybilla?" Ottilia was so surprised, she broke away. "She said that?"

"And more." He captured one of her hands, brought it to his mouth, and kissed her fingers.

"What more?" But her attention was wandering to the tingling sensation his lips produced in her hand.

Francis's eyes were alight. "She said that if I was by chance wondering why you had turned into a watering pot, I had only to look in a mirror."

Ottilia let out a gurgle. "Oh no. Does she think I have fallen in love with a handsome face?"

The hand holding hers stilled. "Have you?

Fallen in love, I mean."

All at once Ottilia was weeping. "Oh yes, Fan. Oh, so very much."

He cradled her, placing his cheek to hers and stroking her back. "And here I had thought you invincible, my dearest dear."

"Invincible?"

He drew back and wiped away her tears with his fingers. "Always so assured, so capable. Ready with a quip or a word of comfort at every hand. How was I to find the chink?"

Ottilia gave a watery chuckle. "You had no need to search. It cracked open at the first and widened thereafter in despite of all I could do."

"I am glad." He took her hands in his. "I love you very dearly. Will you marry me?"

"Yes," she said simply.

Francis kissed her again, a strong, persuasive kiss that went on for some little time and left her breathless and weak. He seemed to realise this, for he drew her to sit beside him on a cushioned bench between the windows. Here he indulged in a good deal of gratifying, if sentimental, conversation, in which Ottilia readily encouraged him.

At length, it occurred to her that things were more complicated than she had foreseen. "Francis, we cannot possibly be married — not yet."

He was playing with her fingers, but he looked up at that. "I am aware. But don't imagine I intend to wait upon a year's mourning, for I don't."

"And let us not forget I am still Sybilla's companion."

"By the time we are wed, I daresay Teresa's leg will have mended. But you will ever be my mother's companion. She is almost as enamoured of you as am I."

"Well, I am already very fond of her. But does she mean to take up her residence here?"

"Lord, no! She would be horrified at such a thought."

"But the house needs a mistress, and much as I love you, Fan, I cannot take upon myself such a role. I would be bored to death."

He laughed. "No, it is far too mundane a life to satisfy that superior intellect of yours, my dearest. But we are not going to live here."

Ottilia blinked at him. "No?"

"No." Francis slipped his arm about her. "You have not so far asked about my circumstances, but I am not obliged to live upon my brother's bounty."

Ottilia nestled into him. "I am not marrying your circumstances."

"I am gratified to hear it," he returned, dropping a light kiss on her hair, "but one must be practical. I have an estate. It is only in London that I choose to live here."

"A younger son, and you have an estate? How so?"

Francis hesitated. "It is not generally known, but it was willed to me by my wife."

Mischief rippled through Ottilia. "So having found your heiress, you lost no time in disposing of her so that you might live on the proceeds."

She heard the echo of her own voice with dismay, and felt the arm about her stiffen. Quickly she turned to him. "No, I did not mean it! It was a jest."

"In exceedingly poor taste, under the circumstances."

His tone was rough and Ottilia detected the hurt beneath it. She seized his hand. "Pardon me, pray. You must by this have recognised my besetting sin — I cannot stop my tongue running away with me. Francis!"

He turned pained eyes towards her. "If I can't forgive you for that, I have no business declaring my affection for you."

"No, I was wrong. So horribly wrong."

His smile was a trifle crooked. "My darling, don't take on so. Your besetting sin has been the making of this family. But for your unruly tongue at the outset, my brother would at this moment be languishing in gaol."

"Yes, but I —"

He put a finger to her lips. "Hush! Let there be no dissension between us."

Ottilia sighed. "I fear that is too much to ask."

"Well, if it comes, at least let us pledge ourselves to wash it away as swiftly as we can."

She let out a contented sigh. "You are unbelievably forbearing, Francis."

"No, why? We are setting out upon an adventure of discovery. After all is said and done, we have known each other but a few short days."

Ottilia spread his hand and slid her fingers between his, caressing his palm with her own. "I feel as if I have known you forever, but that is a trick of these especial circumstances. I daresay there are all manner of habits to disgust you of which you as yet know nothing."

"I know enough of you, my darling, to be sure you could never disgust me." But a gleam came into his eye. "You will undoubtedly madden and frustrate me and drive me to tearing my hair, but disgust? Never.

Especially if you will persist in chortling in that unscrupulous way to get under my guard and disarm me."

At this, her merriment bubbled over the more and all Ottilia's doubts and uncertainties melted away.

"Oh, Fan, I adore you."

A sudden grin lightened his features and he turned her face towards him, lifting up her chin. "A sentiment I wholly reciprocate, my infinitely adorable Tillie."

His kiss enchanted her. But when he drew away a little, she sighed. A faint crease appeared between his brows.

"That sounded less than contented."

She gripped his hand, beset by an inevitable reflection. "I cannot help but feel the poignancy of snatching happiness out of tragedy."

Francis pulled her hand open and set a kiss in her palm. "For my part, I am thanking heaven for the blessing of a silver lining in a cloud uniformly grey."

Ottilia gave a little shiver. "And I started out with hopes of entertainment."

"No you did not, my dear one. You began in compassion, and if you found a way to be merry on occasion, you lightened my heart in so doing. I will not allow you to belittle your motives."

"What, will you make of me a saint?" Her eyes pricked and filled. "Alas, I must ever fall short."

"No saint ever giggled the way you do, Tillie."

Ottilia did just that even as the tears spilled over. She dashed them away. "Your mama was right. I have turned into a watering pot."

Francis smiled into her eyes. "I have a reliable cure for that."

After which Ottilia was unable to utter a word for some little time, much less weep. When Francis at last released her mouth, Ottilia saw his eyebrow quirk and was swept with suspicion. She leaned back a little, the better to regard him.

"I mistrust that look. What now, pray?"

"It has just occurred to me. If we should ever find ourselves in need of funds — not that I anticipate such a contingency, but it is well to be prepared —"

"Fan . . ."

"— I will hire out my Lady Fan to untangle the difficulties of our neighbours."

She preserved her countenance, but her lips twitched. "Indeed? Well, to tell you the truth, I was thinking of asking Sir Thomas Ingham if he would care to employ your Lady Fan for a Runner."

"Oh, not a Runner, Tillie," said Francis, mock serious. "You are far too good for that. Let Ingham retire and we will ask the home secretary to set you in his place."

Ottilia could not hold back a laugh, but she leaned into him and curled her fingers around his. "I thank you, dearest Fan, but to be Lady Francis Fanshawe is ambition enough. This one brush with murder will content me."

ABOUT THE AUTHOR

An avid reader from an early age, **Elizabeth Bailey** grew up in colonial Africa under unconventional parentage and with theatre in the blood. Back in England, she trod the boards until discovering her true métier as a writer, when she fulfilled an early addiction to Heyer by launching into historical romance with Harlequin Mills & Boon, and fuelling her writing with a secondary career teaching and directing drama. Now retired from teaching, and with eighteen romances published, she has switched to crime. Elizabeth still directs plays for a local group where she lives in West Sussex, England. She also finds time to assess novels and run a blog with tips to help new writers improve. For more information, go to elizabethbailey.co.uk.